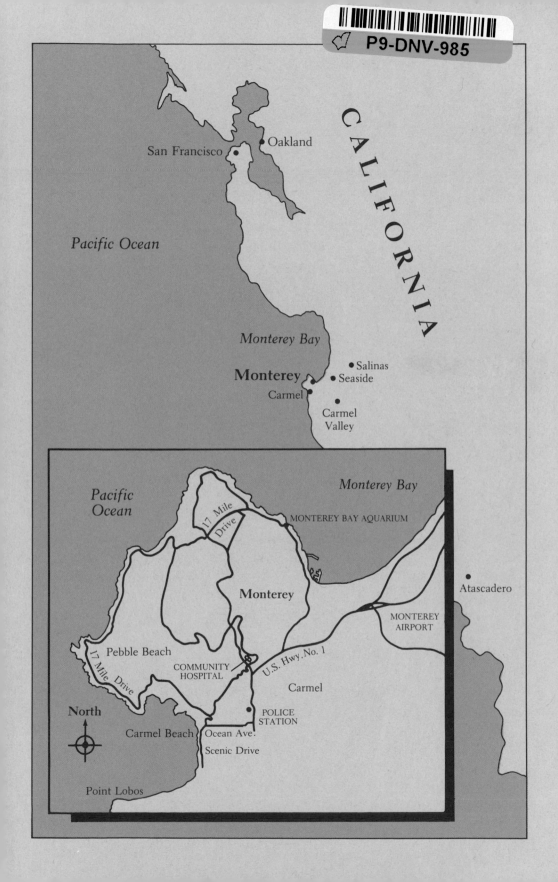

PROBABLE
CAUSE

ALSO BY RIDLEY PEARSON

PROBABLE CAUSE

Ridley Pearson

ST. MARTIN'S PRESS

New York

Probable Cause is a work of fiction. Although based on interviews with law-enforcement officials and specialists, any character resemblance to persons, living or dead, is coincidental and unintended. The story is entirely born of the author's imagination.

The author accepts responsibility—and offers apology—for any technical or logistical oversights, exaggerations, or errors in police or legal procedures and/or setting and locale.

Design by Richard Oriolo

Library of Congress Cataloging-in-Publication Data

Pearson, Ridley,
    Probable cause / Ridley Pearson.
        p.   cm.
    ISBN 0-312-03914-X
    I.   Title.
PS3566.E234P76   1990
813'.54—dc20   89-24127

First Edition

10 9 8 7 6 5 4 3 2 1

There are those people in our lives who miraculously appear and affect us in ways for which we are ever grateful. They bestow upon us their knowledge and experience and send us on our way. One such man came into my life five years ago in the form of my literary agent. He nurtured and encouraged, criticized and comforted. He has now "sent me on my way"—on to new representation. There has been, and will always be, a piece of him in every book I write. I owe my career to Franklin Heller. I will miss working with him very much.

ACKNOWLEDGMENTS

I owe a debt of gratitude to Detective Sergeant "Pete" Poitras of the Carmel-by-the-Sea Police Department for the many hours he gave to this book; Captain Rick Buvia, Monterey Police Department; Ray Jensen, Salinas Criminalistics Laboratory; Phil Soto, California Department of Justice Latent Fingerprint Lab; Dr. Christian Harris, forensic psychiatrist, Seattle, Washington; Dr. Donald Reay, chief medical examiner, King County, Washington; The Honorable Daniel Alban, magistrate judge of Blaine County, Idaho; Terry Hogue, attorney-at-law; Maida Spaulding, manuscript preparation; Mary Peterson, office manager; Ollie Cosman, reader; Tom McCormack, editor; Peter Ginna, editorial assistance.

Thanks also to Clare, Clarence, Briar and Tona. And, as always, Colleen for living through it.

Beware the fury of a patient man.
Law they require, let Law then show her face.

—John Dryden, *Absalom and Achitophel*

PROBABLE
CAUSE

PROLOGUE

James Dewitt approached his family at the rear of the courtroom, where they stood by the doors. He carried a keen intensity, an overt intelligence, in his eyes. The straight slash of a mouth and small cleft in his chin were reminiscent of a midwestern farmer. The thinning rust brown hair, the somewhat pointed ears, and the perennially irreverent, almost irksome expression that seemed indelibly stamped into his features invited curiosity but warned of the unpredictable.

You couldn't eat Italian and make a seven o'clock movie unless you got an early start, and so here they were in the Monterey County

Courthouse—all of his girls: his wife, Julia, and their two daughters, Emmy and Anna. With their shoulder-length blond hair and azure eyes, they looked so much alike, so beautiful, it was disarming—like an advertisement for Ivory soap.

Just seeing Julia made him stronger. Even after two children, she maintained the body of a twenty-year-old: fluid lines, firm chest, tapered waist, and a smooth-complexioned face that appeared both innocent and wise. His queen! In their fifteen years of marriage, she had yet to miss greeting him following a court appearance. Always there to ask how it went. Always there to support him. Always understanding and comforting. Where she found her strength, he had no idea—certainly not from him, regardless of what she claimed. She was an iron woman, seldom complaining, inexhaustible, forgiving, and kind. He felt like an imposter being her husband. Who could honestly deserve her?

Julia seldom brought the girls with her because preliminary hearings were often rough on the forensic investigator, and this one had been hell on Dewitt. He realized now that he never should have suggested the movie. This was a night for a few cocktails and a long sensual back rub. This was a night for forgetting.

Dewitt seethed with anger, a rare emotion for him, and Julia could clearly sense it as he approached. Centered between them, she tugged the girls closer to her for security. Her girls were her world—moons to her planet.

"James?"

"Lumbrowski screwed me." His voice was intense but discreetly low. Though behind him the judge had adjourned for the day, the principals were still milling around in front of the bench.

"James!" she chided, cupping her hands over the outside ear of each of her girls. They had this rule about language around the children.

Emmy, at thirteen, was the older of the two, was the independent, rebellious child. She was a social butterfly, filled with boundless energy and given to spontaneous declarations of her opinion and taste. Julia battled with her to keep her well mannered, for these vocal eruptions could occur in any given social situation. She had entered her boy stage recently and considered Julia's protectionism undeserved and misplaced. Mother and daughter had been at odds lately.

Emmy pulled the hand away, her expression betraying her excitement. Emmy loved controversy. Anna, five years younger, didn't seem to care.

"First he fabricates evidence I can't support. And then on cross, under oath, he claims I broke the chain of custody several times." Federal and state laws required a "chain of custody" be maintained for all evidence. It amounted to a well-documented paper trail that helped ensure evidence could not be tampered with between crime scene, laboratory, evidence rooms, and a court of law. To his wife, Dewitt said, "He pissed the whole case away, Jules. What it comes down to is that he arrested the kid on a hunch—old-school police work—and then got too drunk to support it with any hard evidence. So he creates the evidence he needs. Left me in one hell of a spot, I'll tell you that. It's bullshit." Emmy liked the swearing. She suppressed her grin.

"James!"

"Complete B.S. I warned Saffeleti right from the start we didn't have a case against this kid. So I suppose I should be happy, right? But all that it means is that we refile and try again in a couple weeks. This was nothing but a waste of time. I can't believe this sh— This kind of circus is bad for everyone involved. Lumbrowski's high on something, I swear. He ends up just now shouting at this kid that he's going to get the death penalty. The kid's scared out of his mind."

Anna's eyes looked beyond her father. She was their thoughtful child. The contemplator. Patient beyond reason. She was the amateur scientist who shared her father's fascination with marine wildlife. The reader. She had an unusual preoccupation with classical music—Bach especially—and was content to sit alone in her room for hours on end with her books and Walkman, content in a private world into which she rarely offered any glimpse. Ironically, she was the child about whom her mother was most concerned, ironic because Dewitt knew Anna was fine. Anna reminded him of himself at the same age. Anna was going places. She was simply taking the time to prepare herself properly.

Light seemed to flash inside Anna's eyes as a commotion erupted at the front of the courtroom. The courtroom doors were open, a single film crew in waiting. The powerful camera light switched on, blinding Dewitt. Dewitt turned to see Detective Howard Lumbrowski, a big bear of a man, lunging across the defense table at young Steven Miller, the accused. Two bailiffs attempted unsuccessfully to intervene. Within seconds, it was an out-and-out brawl. Like a football player emerging from an attempted team tackle, the defendant squirted out of the pack and raced down the aisle toward Dewitt and his mesmerized family beyond.

It wasn't until the kid raised his hand threateningly that Dewitt saw the bloodied drinking glass. Its jagged mouth swept out at him as Miller charged. Dewitt ducked to avoid the swipe. He looked up to see Steven Miller straight-arm a stunned Anna, palm to her forehead, lifting her off her feet, her unprotected skull connecting sharply with the stone floor and cracking as it struck. Her blood ran immediately. Dewitt knelt over his daughter, his stomach hollow, his legs weak.

Emmy, who had dived out of the way, crawled toward her father.

At the sight of her fallen daughter, Julia screamed and flailed at Steven Miller. He cut her arm with the glass, pulled her into a headlock, and dragged her backward into the corridor. Howard Lumbrowski, his revolver brandished awkwardly before him, rushed past Dewitt. "Let her go," Lumbrowski bellowed. Miller had cut him; there was an angry red gash below Lumbrowski's eye.

"Back off!" Dewitt called out, his fallen daughter's situation worsening by the second, his wife bloody and caught by the throat. "Shut that off!" he hollered at the TV news pair. They went right on shooting. Where was everybody? This was happening much too fast despite the visual slow motion that seemed to draw out all movement. He glanced once again at Emmy, who was now standing terrified with her back against the cinder-block wall, eyes on her sister. Dewitt raised his hand like a traffic cop: Don't move, it said.

Julia looked at her husband, and then at Anna. He had never witnessed such fear in his wife.

Lumbrowski shouted more demands at Miller, waving his gun like a careless conductor's uncontrolled baton. Miller screamed back at him, his words indistinguishable. Dewitt was a forensic criminalist, not a cop, but he was familiar enough with police procedure to know that Lumbrowski was handling this wrong.

"Lumbrowski, back off," Dewitt said in as even a tone as he could muster. "Give him some room."

"Drop it!" Miller concurred. He muscled Julia Dewitt into the hallway corner. Behind him was an enlarged photograph of a picture of Monterey in the late 1800s. He leaned against it.

Where the hell were the other guards? The bright TV light cast harsh shadows. It made it feel as if the floor were moving under him.

Lumbrowski threw the handgun to the floor. "Okay," he conceded, "cool out!" It slid to within inches of Dewitt's feet. Lumbrowski circled to his left now, forcing Miller to rotate to his right. With the movement, Miller exposed his body to Dewitt as he maintained his fixed attention on the cut detective, who continued his reckless advance.

Lumbrowski glanced hotly at Dewitt: *Shoot the bastard!* his expression said. His toss of the gun had been deliberate. Dewitt looked down at it.

"Stop!" Miller hollered at the detective, but Lumbrowski marched forward ominously.

"Brow! Don't crowd him!"

Miller tugged Julia's head back by the hair, stretching her throat, and placed the glass there in a final threat. Julia exploded into a frenzy—that was his Julia, ever the fighter. Dewitt heard a sickening, gut-wrenching gasp for air as the glass tore into her. Miller threw his hands into the air, a combined expression of surrender and satisfaction. The glass shattered on the stone floor, pieces showering out from where it fell. "I'm unarmed," he announced proudly.

Julia's perfect body slumped forward and folded into a bloody heap at Miller's feet, her throat deeply slashed.

Dewitt dove for Lumbrowski's weapon. In what seemed to him like one slow, smooth movement, he rose and fired at Miller, pulling the trigger repeatedly until the clap of gunfire ceased, the bittersweet smell of cordite enveloping him. Tears blurred his vision. Four rounds missed completely, but the remaining two drove Miller back against the wall. He was dead before he sagged to a sitting position on the floor.

Julia died in the ambulance, her husband at her side.

Anna, unresponsive, was rushed inside the hospital.

1

TUESDAY, JANUARY 10

1

"**D**BF at Scenic and Eighth," announced the warm-toned voice of Virginia Fraizer, who acted as both receptionist and radio dispatcher. Dead body found. Down by the beach. They used telephones where dead bodies were concerned. Too many blood-and-guts freaks monitoring police bands to use the radios for something like this. Thank God for Ginny. She seemed to hold the department together.

"I'm on my way," Detective Sergeant James Dewitt replied, returning the receiver to the cradle of the bedside phone. *DBF!* Not a one-eighty-seven, thank God. That would be a homicide. Not after just two months on the force. Had to hurry. Outdoor crime scenes deteriorated quickly, and to make matters worse, it had been raining when he had awakened at 5:30. He knew the location: a turnout in the blacktop in the otherwise impossibly narrow scenic road that fronted Carmel's beach. Enough room for three parked cars. A hit-and-run, maybe.

Dead body found. One thing was certain: He was wide awake now.

He was in his boxer underwear. He was waiting for the coffee to finish brewing, waiting to wake up Emmy and get her ready for school. He looked in the mirror. He was anything but on his way.

The body lay spread out on the pavement, posed inhumanly like a malfunctioning mannequin discarded on the showroom floor. Suicide, by the look of the car. A hose taped from the exhaust to the passenger window. Dewitt approached the body and stopped. Given the remarkable gift of life, he wondered how someone could *choose* death. Sight of the suicide made him angry and a thought flashed through his mind: If only this man's unwanted life could be traded for Julia's.

It was a chilly January morning. Dewitt wore his brown wool sport coat—his *only* wool sport coat—a garment that begged for replacement. Its two black buttons drooped like the sad eyes of a basset hound. His identifying trademark remained his bow ties, a holdover from his fifteen years in forensics: In the lab, a bow tie stays out of your way. He wore green paisley today, a gift from Emmy. He removed his glasses, exhaled onto their lenses, and afforded them a long methodical polish. He returned them to the bridge of his nose, seating them in a permanently pink dent there. He stepped over the body and squatted by the man's feet, taking one general all-encompassing look first, then focusing detail by detail, head to toe. James Dewitt still existed in the world of the microscopic particle. His eyes missed very little.

He was unaccustomed to victims—especially dead ones. Having served as a man of evidence for so many years, he tended toward the material evidence first, which justified, at least in his mind, disregarding the body at present, turning away and focusing his attention on the vehicle. Technically, he was *Detective* Dewitt now. Detective Sergeant. But at a crime scene such as this, he instinctively reverted to his former self, a forensic investigator, a specialist dealing in the invisible world of trace evidence. His colleagues derisively referred to forensic criminalists as "nitpickers." What did they know? Would your standard off-the-shelf detective have already noticed that there was no sand on the bottom of the decedent's shoes, this despite a sugarlike coating covering the entire parking lot? And if no sand on the bottom of the shoes, then how had the decedent placed that hose in the passenger window?

That was the beauty of hard evidence: It could either be explained or it couldn't. Witnesses might offer a dozen different accounts of the same incident, but the hard evidence eventually told one, and only one, story.

The car and the dead body would have to tell this story. Unlikely to have witnesses at this early hour. Dewitt carried surgical gloves and a Swiss Army knife in the right pocket of his sports coat; forceps, Baggies, small magnifying glass, and a Mag-Lite in his other. He snapped the pair of gloves on and called out to Patrolman Anderson, who was stringing the bright plastic POLICE LINE tape around the perimeter of the parking area. DO NOT CROSS, it warned. The wind changed and Dewitt could hear the comforting concussion of nearby surf more clearly, could smell the salt and the sap. The struggling Monterey pines with their wind-torn limbs and awkward weather-sculpted shapes leaned painfully toward shore.

Anderson ashamedly confirmed that he had dragged the body from the car. Dewitt was going to have to call a meeting of Carmel's twenty patrolmen and remind them of the responsibilities of the first officer, the first cop to arrive at a crime scene. The problem was not stupidity as much as unfamiliarity. Carmel saw few dead bodies in any given year. However, procedures were what kept investigations consistent, and the courts required consistency.

Dewitt fished out the dead man's wallet. California driver's license. Name: John Galbraith Osbourne. Sacramento. The detective experi-

9

enced a short flutter in his heart, like sudden indigestion. Third card down was the organ-donor card. Another flutter, this time more painful. The card contained an entry for the next of kin to be notified upon death: Jessica Joyce Osbourne. Everyone knew Jessie Osbourne, the fiercely outspoken Republican state representative. "Jammin' Jessie" they had called her last year because she had played basketball with the statehouse boys for a charity function and had come out of the game at halftime with two points, two assists, and a bloody nose. At fifty-five, Osbourne still had the spunk of a young woman.

Dewitt slipped the wallet into a Baggie and then removed his glasses again, polishing them slowly and then hooking them back around his ears, establishing them on his nose.

He circled the Tercel once, eyes alert. Osbourne had done a neat job of it—but why here? The location of the crime scene itself was as much a piece of evidence as anything. Did he want to die with a nice view? Had there been any view an hour earlier, or had it been too dark? Why here?

Rusty, his shepherd collie mutt, barked from the back of Dewitt's unmarked police car, a Mercury Zephyr. Dewitt shouted a reprimand and the dog went silent.

Dewitt knelt by the body again. Decent-looking guy except for his bluish gray skin. The headlights of the arriving coroner's wagon swept the pavement as it descended the hill of Eighth. Three jewels sparkled in the light, drawing Dewitt's attention. He duck-walked the short distance. *Fresh* motor oil by the look of it. It had been raining heavily when Dewitt had awakened at 5:30, yet this oil had not washed away. Was that possible in that strong a rain? Using his Swiss Army knife, he took a sample of some of the oil, sealed it in a Baggie, and then labeled it.

"Was your radio car parked over here at any time?" he shouted over to Anderson.

"No, sir," Anderson replied as he finished with the crime-scene ribbon by tying it off to the bumper of his radio car.

Dewitt carried what amounted to a portable crime lab in the trunk of the Zephyr. Besides the spare tire, the bulletproof police vest, and the first-aid kit, he kept two large black salesman bags back there. Between them, they carried every conceivable investigator's tool. He retrieved his camera and photographed the oil and its relationship to the crime scene. Rusty protested from the backseat and had to be silenced again.

"What's up?" Anderson asked, joining him a moment later.

Looking the young patrolman in the eye, Dewitt pointed his gloved finger at the dead man, John Osbourne. "He had a visitor," he said.

2

Police Chief Clarence Hindeman's office, the biggest in the building, was by no means large. The clock on the wall read 3:30. Dewitt had yet to eat lunch. Commander Karl Capp and James Dewitt sat in gunmetal gray steel chairs facing their superior, who presided from behind a large but nondescript matching steel desk, the window behind him looking out on Carmel's picturesque storefronts.

Karl Capp, who had been born perspiring, chewed vigorously on a Mongol number-two pencil. His soft round belly protruded over his tight belt, and he sat with his feet spread to accommodate its sag. He had a pale rubbery face and bright red cheeks. He lived under the conspiracy of angry eyes. Even when smiling, Capp had a bully image to overcome. Flecks of yellow pencil paint clung like canker sores to his lower lip.

Capp was clearly uncomfortable. A veteran Monterey Peninsula cop and a man who ran his own show—with Hindeman more as a figurehead, by his way of thinking—the commander didn't like being on this side of a desk. He made a point of establishing and maintaining the pecking order. Capp had yet to speak business in Dewitt's office. Instead, the detective sergeant was always summoned to the commander's office, where Capp apparently found security in his leather throne of an office chair.

Clarence Hindeman, a physical man, rock solid in his early fifties, sported an ash-gray trimmed beard that hid his lack of chin. He preferred an open-neck shirt and a Western bolo to a conventional tie. He used his hands when he spoke, hard calloused hands that reflected his hobbies of carpentry and river rafting. He spoke in a forced, hoarse voice through a constricted throat. "So what we've got here is the apparent suicide of Jessie Osbourne's boy."

Capp said boldly, "Apparent? We put this sucker to bed just as quickly as we can."

"*Apparent* suicide," Dewitt reminded. "There are some inconsistencies."

"What the hell does that mean?" Capp complained.

"I'd like to keep this open for a couple of days," Dewitt explained. "Wait for the various reports before we issue any statement. His clothes have been sent to the lab. Jessie Osbourne's people gave us the name of a cousin, Priscilla Laughton, to I.D. him. Wanted to speak with Jessie, but she hasn't returned my call. Autopsy is tentatively scheduled for tomorrow, though Thursday seems more likely. The thing of it is, Commander," he said, addressing Capp, "if we go making a statement that we then have to correct, we're a lot worse off. This'll take a day or two at the most. A couple of tests and we're a hell of a lot more certain what we have here."

"You have Jessie's permission for the autopsy?" Capp asked. "That surprises me."

"Don't need it," Dewitt said, looking to Clarence for support.

"Officially, Karl, we have to go with *suspicious causes* for the time being. That's why I thought we should talk. You've read Dewitt's notes I take it?"

"Manny Roth's not going to like this, Chief," Capp said. His tongue found a flake of yellow paint he had missed on his lip. He spit it out. "He and Jessie are tight. She's the one sponsoring his fund raiser, don't forget."

"Our distinguished Mayor is a former golf pro, Commander," Dewitt reminded, "not a policeman. There are certain procedures—"

"And our detective's a former nitpicker," Capp interrupted. "If you were a *policeman* with a little more *experience*, you might understand the difference in approach between the Salinas lab and a cop shop."

To Hindeman he said, "In my opinion we ought to rethink this assignment, Chief. I realize I'm supposed to be the desk cop, but Dewitt's only been with us two months. You couldn't have foreseen something like this when you brought him on."

For Dewitt, the five months since the death of Steven Miller had been hell. He had been arrested on a charge of voluntary manslaughter for the shooting of Miller, and had endured a three-week trial that carried with it the pain of front-page publicity. His acquittal by jury was covered by CNN's "Prime Time News" and picked up the following day by all three networks.

He had been rescued by his friend of several years, Clarence Hindeman, now Carmel's Chief of Police, who had called with a job offer of Detective Sergeant, a newly created position on the Carmel force, designed specifically for a man of Dewitt's talents and experience. He had hoped, by accepting Hindeman's offer, to settle into a quiet existence of tracing down bad checks and stolen bicycles in a small resort community. With the discovery of Osbourne's body, he sensed they had a major case on their hands. It would be a simple matter to accede to Capp's wishes, and forfeit the case. Instead, however, Dewitt, catching Hindeman's eye, shook his head no. He wouldn't give in that easily.

Hindeman said sharply, "It's Dewitt's case, Karl. He reports to you, same as every investigation. This *is* why I brought him on: He has fifteen years of forensics behind him. Eight of those as an investigator. We're set up just fine to handle this—"

"He's never handled a one-eighty-seven—"

"One-eighty-seven?" asked Hindeman. "Who said anything about a homicide? We're talking suicide here."

"He's talking one-eighty-seven," Capp contradicted, pointing at Dewitt. "He's *implying* a one-eighty-seven."

"I'm asking for some reports," Dewitt complained, "nothing more. Besides which, I've handled plenty of one-eighty-sevens as an FI. That's not an issue here."

All three launched into a brief shouting match, which was only silenced by Rusty barking from the corner. Hindeman allowed Dewitt

13

the luxury of having the dog in the station house. Rusty was technically considered a mascot. Hindeman gained control again. Dewitt snapped his fingers twice; Rusty lay down.

"I've handled dozens of one-eighty-sevens," Dewitt resumed. "There's very little difference—"

"There's a fuckin' *huge* difference," Capp disagreed.

"The point is moot," Hindeman roared. "Have you or haven't you read Dewitt's crime-scene notes?"

"So there's no sand on the bottom of the guy's shoes. So there's some motor oil nearby. It's a parking lot for Christ's sake. That's enough for suspicious causes, Chief? Gimme a break! We're talking about Jessie Osbourne's son, unless I missed something."

"Dewitt? You want to respond to that?" By nature of his rank and position, Hindeman tried to remain as neutral as possible, this despite their friendship, despite the fact their daughters were best friends. Although he slipped from time to time, Clarence Hindeman made a point of calling Dewitt by his last name when around the station house. He couldn't afford to play favorites.

"I'm simply pursuing a variety of possibilities," Dewitt explained. "One thing you learn as a 'nitpicker,' " he said with a glance at Capp, "the evidence will tell one and only one story. Anderson compromised the site. That's an added headache. If you read my report, then you're familiar with the fact that Osbourne's luggage was jammed into the back of the trunk. Why? Can you explain that easily?"

"Who cares?"

"I care! I have evidence that isn't adding up."

"Completely circumstantial," Capp sneered.

"Agreed. I won't argue that. The evidence *is* circumstantial, and it may be nothing. But we won't know that until all the evidence is in, right? Why are we making such a big deal out of this?" he asked Hindeman. "All I'm asking is we run a few tests and eliminate any surprises."

"You're asking to delay a statement to the press. This is Jessie Osbourne's son, Dewitt. This is an election year. You need it spelled out?"

"Since there are those in this department who do not hold my *opinion* in very high regard," he said, directing his comment at his commander, "I thought it only appropriate to solicit outside help. You *will* accept an opinion from the Salinas lab, I take it?"

"Don't start with me, Dewitt."

"Is that a yes or a no?"

Capp's face turned scarlet and he adjusted his weight in the chair. "I think this is a mistake. My vote is to clean it up, make a statement to the press, and get this behind us as quickly as we can. Drawing it out with a bunch of circumstantial evidence isn't going to help anyone, least of all Jessie Osbourne. And if Jessie's unhappy, then Manny's unhappy, and that's bad for business."

"Karl," Hindeman said, disappointed. "I'm not looking for votes, I'm looking for input. Are you saying that the John Osbourne death is clearly a suicide? This in light of what Dewitt has turned up?"

"I'm saying he hasn't turned up squat." He considered this for a moment. "You talk to Bill Saffeleti about some oil drops and the way this guy packed his trunk. You tell me how the DA's office feels about it. Save ya the trouble. They'll laugh you outta town."

Dewitt told Hindeman, "I think I'm being misunderstood here. We're a small outfit. We don't want to look like one by making a statement prematurely. A suicide note would help. A despondent phone call made to a close friend. Something along those lines. There again: We have to do the legwork if we're going to explain this thing. I want to know where Osbourne was coming from, where he was headed, what he was up to. I want to be able to sit Jessie Osbourne down and tell her exactly what her son did from say six last night to six this morning. The media, if no one else, will put his last twenty-four hours together. Do we risk playing catch-up with the media?"

"Karl?"

"I don't like it. The guy sucked fumes, Chief. Let's bury him, not slice him open."

Rusty growled and rolled onto his back, awaiting affection. "We'll wait for all the evidence to come in," declared Hindeman, eyeing the dog. "For now, it's an apparent suicide, investigation pending."

Capp pushed himself up from the uncomfortable chair and stormed out of the office.

"There goes trouble," said Dewitt.

"If that dog farts in my office, you'll know the meaning of trouble."

Dewitt and Rusty were gone in seconds.

3

The strip was held in a gloomy darkness, refreshed only by the occasional colorful glow of street signs and window advertisements. An eighteen-wheeler streamed past, its grinding whir caught in the Doppler effect, subsiding in the distance with a painful scream. The man paced in front of the pay telephone, toying with the quarters in his pants pocket. The air smelled of diesel. Across the way, through the dirty window of a bar, a pink neon palm tree pulsed intermittently, advertising a wine cooler. When the door to the bar was in use, the impatient man at the phone could hear the cheers from the Lakers game on the TV. He stopped his pacing and stared at the phone, his profile a craggy silhouette in the limited light. Would Lumbrowski even answer? They had to talk.

He slipped the quarter into the slot and listened as it descended, clanking into the guts of the phone. By now, the number was memorized.

One ring . . . He tapped his foot anxiously. "Come on," he said.

Two rings . . . "Bastard, answer the phone!"

"Yeah?" spoke the wet husky voice.

The sound of a voice took him so totally by surprise that he hesitated momentarily.

"Yeah?" Lumbrowski repeated.

"I've been trying to reach you all day," he said.

"Been busy. *Real busy*. Who the hell is this?"

"You should stay closer to your phone."

"You should mind your own fuckin' business." The phone went dead.

The man squinted, attempting to control his temper. He reeled his head back and exhaled indignantly. Calling to help, and he dares to hang up. "Mind your own business," indeed.

He stuffed another quarter into the phone and punched out the seven numbers.

"Yeah?"

"I saw what you did this morning," he told Lumbrowski.

Silence. The man's heavy alcoholic breathing could be heard clearly.

"I thought you might be interested in that."

"What do you know about it?" Lumbrowski asked.

"I have certain needs."

"Money?"

"That would help."

"Have we done business before?"

"No."

"I'm busy right now. I got my own agenda."

"I'm sure you do. But I *saw* you."

Silence again.

"You want what I have?"

"You want what I have," the man insisted.

"I don't think so." He hung up. Again.

The man pounded his fist against the phone and then tugged ferociously on the receiver. With both hands around the gooseneck sheath that housed the wire, he leaned his weight against the receiver and jerked on it repeatedly until it finally broke loose.

He studied the phone's receiver in his hand, its gooseneck casing and stripped wires dangling like a tail. He slammed it into its cradle and hurried across the street to the bar. He took a seat in a corner booth where the light didn't hurt his eyes.

After the game, a late-night "News Update" came onto the TV. He was on his third beer, and feeling better now. The anchorwoman wore a lot of makeup and smiled falsely, like a nurse. She said in a strident voice, "The body of the son of Sacramento County Representative Jessica Osbourne, John Galbraith Osbourne, was found by Carmel

17

authorities in what has been described by a police spokesman as an apparent suicide. No details have been released and an investigation is pending, but sources at 'News One' have been told by persons close to the investigation that murder has not been ruled out. Detective James Dewitt, who is handling the investigation, refused comment. More on the intriguing investigation on tomorrow's 'Wake Up News Hour.' "

The man drinking the beer set it down.

"Murder has not been ruled out." The words echoed in his brain.

"You want another?" It was the waitress.

"That changes everything," said the man with the beer.

2
WEDNESDAY

ewitt showed his badge at the Carmel gate entrance to Pebble Beach in order to avoid paying the five-dollar fee charged tourists to drive the seventeen-mile scenic loop around the peninsula. He knew his way around the labyrinth of twisting roads that wound past the showcase homes. The compound was a mixture of nature preserve and housing development—million-dollar homes hidden in cedar forests, wild grasses and shrubs, green velvet golf courses, the dazzling irregular rocky shoreline at the foot of the ever-restless Pacific Ocean. He couldn't help but wonder where all the money came from. This opulent display of wealth and privilege bordered on embarrassing.

Even with the help of the union, he was at his limit. Anna's head injury left her withering away in a fetal position in the Community Hospital and that, in turn, left Dewitt's savings withering, as well.

He had been advised to move her to a less-expensive public institution, and had weighed the decision carefully several times. With the closest available facility a two-hour drive away, however, James Dewitt rejected the idea, considering daily contact with family far more important for his daughter, despite her apparent physical detachment. They could try all they wanted—the doctors, accountants, even clergy—to convince him, but Dewitt would not abandon hope. Hope had proven a potent fuel these last five months.

Just the thought of money played these same tapes inside his head repeatedly—a downward, depressing spiral he did not enjoy. The key to overcoming the loneliness—to survival—was optimism, an attitude of gratitude. A dozen such clichés bounced around inside his head and it seemed appropriate that he should be driving inside a forest yet unable to see it. As if to snap him out of his momentary doldrums, Rusty lurched forward from the backseat and laid his pink tongue from collar to ear. Dewitt reached back and scratched him. Spotting a beagle on a wire run, Rusty leaped to the side window and barked ferociously—always one for a helpless opponent. Dewitt was still shouting through the cacophony as he pulled to a stop in front of Priscilla Laughton's ocean-view home.

The entranceway's redwood overhang was supported by nut-stained square pillars that stood twenty feet tall. Towering glass panels allowed Dewitt an unobstructed view through the house to the churning ocean beyond. Always changing colors—slate blue now. In front of twin doors of carved oak, an enormous tarnished brass bell hung inside an elaborate oriental frame. He rocked the hinged arm and the bell pealed sonorously, its haunting sound lost to the woods. Only then did he spot the lighted doorbell to his left. This bell was some kind of snappy uptown wind chime, he realized too late—probably from Neiman-Marcus.

Laughton was in her early thirties, dolled up, as this set tended to do so well. A two-hour face on a Jane Fonda body. A forearm laden with silver bangles. A two-hundred-watt tan, given the recent weather. A lioness hairdo. A small provocative gap between her bleached front teeth. Pink lip gloss, pale gray eyes, cosmetic cheekbones, dangling patinated earrings still swinging as she said, "You must be Detective Dewitt."

"Miss Laughton?"

"Priscilla." She showed him in. He looked around in awe, feeling unsure of himself, as he often did in museums. Where indeed did this kind of money come from? Gray granite foyer leading to a sunken living room with overstuffed furniture in designer fabrics. Fresh flowers everywhere, their pungent perfumes and vibrant colors intoxicating. Split-level and sprawling out toward an enormous lawn, manicured beyond reason, curling down to the doormat of the Pacific. The salmon couch swallowed him. He toyed nervously with a plaid bag tied with a red bow, which smelled like a pine forest in springtime.

"I spoke with your aunt's people," he began.

"Yes. I identified John late yesterday." She paused. "I had never been inside a mortuary."

"It's a terrible experience. I'm sorry you had to go through that." He paused until she looked at him. "Ms. Laughton, I hope you can appreciate that an investigation such as this can be extremely frustrating. Having never met the victim personally—"

"Victim?"

"Decedent," Dewitt corrected. She looked at him skeptically. "Any evidence we turn up tells the investigator much more when framed within a personality, within a structure of behavior. Death should be a personal thing. Unfortunately, suicide, untimely death of a suspicious nature, is not. We investigators go around with plastic bags and Magic Markers, digging into people's privacy. I've been through it from both sides, so I know how uncomfortable it can be. But we're in the information business: The more information we have, the faster we're through with the case. I mention this to you because Mrs. Osbourne's aides seem very protective. They seem more interested in distancing her from the investigation than anything else. I can tell you from firsthand experience—and I'm hoping you'll pass this along to her—that the more cooperative the family is, the sooner the investigation is wrapped up and put to bed."

"You don't want the runaround." She toyed with the bangles. "I'll help where I can."

Dewitt opened a stenographer's notebook and scanned a list he had prepared. He added, "People are tempted—family especially—to color the past of those who've died. That doesn't help anyone. It's too late to invent John Osbourne's reality."

She crossed her legs, maintaining her excellent posture. "I will do my best, Detective."

"I guess the best place to start is to ask if you know why John Osbourne was in this area."

She considered this, and it disappointed Dewitt, because when people thought too long, they generally edited their comments. "I could say he was passing through, which makes sense, doesn't it? But you asked for honesty, and quite frankly, I have no idea."

"You were close to John?"

"Closer than the rest of the family, which is to say we were on limited speaking terms. He was the black sheep, Detective. He communicated with his mother through me. They were estranged. They haven't spoken directly in . . . it must be several years now."

"No idea at all?"

She shook her head.

"Any guesses?"

"He loved the area. My *guess* would be a stopover either on his way to or from Orange County."

"We understand he was a lobbyist. That means someone paid his travel expenses, and yet we found no receipts on him or in his belongings. Does that surprise you?"

"I wouldn't know about his accounting practices. I'm sorry."

"But he was a lobbyist? Is that right?"

"Only in the loosest sense of the word. He represented entertainment interests in Sacramento. Composers of rock music mostly. Tax reform, accounting practices, copyright law. He worked extensively with insurance interests because, as I understand it, liability insurance has gotten out of hand for the big concerts and it's hurting the live-music industry."

"But he wasn't too serious about it?"

"That is my opinion. John was a frustrated musician himself. He enjoyed the Los Angeles side of the business, the Hollywood side, better than the Sacramento end. He liked to be seen with the big names in the business, sit in on recording sessions, be backstage at the concerts. A groupie, I guess would be the term. A grown-up groupie."

"That can mean drugs, can't it?"

The blush began at her collarbone and crept lusciously up the sides of her neck. A blush is an invaluable investigative tool. Dewitt didn't place much confidence in a lie-detector test, but a blush seldom failed. "I think a lot of that has changed," she said, cleverly avoiding an answer.

"I made a phone call to the LAPD. Would it surprise you that your cousin's name shows up on some Narco lists? Narcotics, Ms. Laughton. No charges filed. No arrests. But he's on their lists. You understand the implication." He waited. The color of the sea changed slowly like the skin of a chameleon; if he blurred his vision, it appeared as if he was looking out across the treetops of an endless forest.

She refused comment, seated firmly like a model posing for her portrait.

"One of Jessie Osbourne's campaign planks this year is a strong antidrug bill, isn't it?"

"Jessie's always been a leader against street drugs, yes."

She said it as if she was addressing a news conference.

"Was John suicidal?"

"No. My first reaction to that is, no, he was not. But who is suicidal? We often don't know until they've done it, isn't that right? He lived in an artificial world. The music business is . . . different. In some ways, he was manic-depressive. These last few years, no one could get close to him. Not even me, and well, we were close once, brother and sister close."

"Money?"

"His nemesis, I'm afraid. Initially, the source of his estrangement from Jessie."

"A family like the Osbournes . . . I mean, they're part of California history . . . there's family money, isn't there?" he asked, looking around the room.

She laughed in a contrived, predictable confidence. "There is, certainly. This, however, is the result of the work of a wonderful divorce attorney." The Priscilla Laughtons of this world never called them lawyers. "My husband was in the market." She pronounced it as a woman from Boston would: without the *r*. "He still is, actually." She grinned, loving every minute of it, every cent.

"Had John been cut off?"

"John was no longer supported by the trust."

She was getting on his nerves. Too much of this seemed prepared text, as if she was reading a TelePrompTer mounted just behind his head.

"We didn't find a suicide note," Dewitt said. "That bothers me. Any idea where he stayed when he was in the area? Did he ever stay here with you?"

"No, not here. He phoned me not long ago. From Seaside. Asked to see me. I drove all the way over there, but you should have seen the place where he wanted to meet! Believe me, I didn't even get out of the car."

"A bar?"

"A *dive*, is more like it. Just awful! Ick. Motorcycle types."

"Do you remember the name of the place?"

"The name?" she cackled. "You must be kidding!"

"And that was?"

"You mean when exactly? Oh, God, a year or so ago."

"Friends in the area?"

"Not whom I'm aware of."

"But he did stay in the area occasionally?"

"I assume so. And if his choice in motels was anything like his choice of bars, I wouldn't choose to know where." She studied him. "You appear disappointed, Detective."

"This area is a little long on motels, Miss Laughton. If we knew where he had stayed, we could look for a note. We might turn something up." Dewitt studied his pad, wondering whether there was anything to get out of Priscilla Laughton other than the traces of sweet perfume and alluring sideways glances.

"I wouldn't know," she told him.

"May I speak openly?" he asked.

"Please." She leaned forward, suddenly more interested.

"Sooner or later, I'm going to have to speak with Jessie Osbourne. The more involved making those arrangements becomes, the longer the case drags out and the more likely the press will stay with it.

"We would like to wrap this up," he continued, "as I've said. Quite frankly, her avoidance is somewhat curious at this point. As a parent, I would want to speak with whoever was in charge of my child's investigation."

"Avoidance is a strong word, Detective. Jessie and John had gone their separate ways long ago."

"One I chose carefully," he said. Didn't this kind ever offer you something to drink? "Well, I guess that about does it."

"May I ask you something?" she inquired. Dewitt cocked his head as if to say he didn't care.

"A name of a policeman, a detective, came up . . . last weekend at a party I was at. I'm not sure he's still a policeman . . . actually . . . but he was once, and he is evidently in consideration for a job to help my friends . . . well kind of a security consultant, really. You know, decide what their place needs in terms of a security system, do a little research for them. Not private detective work, but kind of a consultant. And I wondered, since you're in the same fraternity, if you might know him and be able to give me a reference."

"I might, if he's from around here," he said, sensing in her for the first time an insecurity. She was improvising. "What's his name . . . or *her* name," he added quickly.

"His name is Howard Lumbrowski."

Dewitt exhaled in disgust and glanced out the windows. Gray green waves undulated in slow motion. A tiny ship of unrecognizable purpose slipped slowly along the horizon.

"You *do* know him," she stated.

"Someone put you up to this?" he asked, his voice acerbic and clipped.

"No. I take it that means you would not recommend him?"

"I'm the wrong person to ask," he said.

"No. Please. I'm interested. I don't want her, my friend, making a mistake. She seems to think him quite capable."

"It's personal. I'm the wrong guy to ask, that's all."

"Anything you could tell—"

"It's *personal!*" he repeated harshly, struggling forward to be free of the plush couch, frustrated by the way it seemed to hold on to him. "What do you feed this thing?" he asked her.

"Are you seeing other people yet?" she asked somberly, standing.

"What?" Incredulous. His own words came back to haunt him: *Death should be a personal thing.* His name—his life's story—had been in the papers for months. Laughton was clearly up on her current events. For a few weeks back in late September, he had probably been the topic of cocktail-party conversation; the thought revolted him.

"Would you call me sometime? I mean for something other than an interview?"

If he had been anywhere but California, Dewitt might have been surprised. He had lived in the state for nearly fifteen years now, and he still wasn't used to this kind of aggressive sexuality, this open-book philosophy of "hang it all out there and go with your feelings." The avocado toothpaste and open-collar crowd still rubbed him wrong. "You know what we cops call Carmel, Miss Laughton?" She stared. "Disneyland without the rides."

"I see. And Pebble Beach?"

"I can find my own way out," he said, adding after walking a few feet toward the huge front door, "I think."

"Call me if I can be of *any* help, Detective."

*   *   *

26

That evening, with Emmy at home attempting to complete her schoolwork during marathon phone conversations, Dewitt reached the Community Hospital after visiting hours. It didn't bother him. He had a system all worked out. He drove around back, following signs for deliveries, and entered through the loading bay by the kitchen, where the door was left unlocked to facilitate the dumping of trash. He hurried down a back hallway, passing storage rooms, an employee lounge—empty at this hour—and the housekeeping department. He allowed himself to believe that none of the nurses, none of the security guards were aware he sneaked in after hours, this despite the fact he had been busted on numerous occasions—found asleep in a chair by his daughter's bedside.

He cracked open the fire door, peered into the patient-room hall-way, and made a dash for Room 114, two doors down. Once inside, he was illuminated by the eerie glowing and flashing from the myriad of life-support machinery. He located a towel and blocked the gap at the bottom of the door before switching on the overhead room lights.

The enormous stainless-steel bed resembled a Ferris wheel, rotating clockwise ever so slowly. It's purpose, ostensibly, was to reduce bed sores, though it did much more than that: It dehumanized her entirely. His younger daughter lay strapped in its netted grasp, her body curled like a wilting leaf, bone thin, her skin ash gray. Emmy called the contraption a gerbil cage.

This room, humming with a mechanical dissonance, felt more like a futuristic research laboratory than a place to heal his little girl. Mustn't dwell on it, he reminded himself. Acceptance was his watch-word.

Anna's was borrowed time. At first, the advice had been to transfer her. Now it included what to James Dewitt was an unthinkable option: Pull the plug.

Using the controls, he brought the bed around so Anna lay horizon-tally. He unfastened the restraining net and touched her cool face gently. Sliding open the bedside drawer, he removed the pink plastic hairbrush, lowered the stainless-steel restraining bar, and sat close to his daughter. He brushed what had once been a full head of hair, now

27

a few wispy patches that pulled loose with his efforts. He leaned closely to her and spoke softly to her. He knew for a fact that recovered coma patients reported having been able to hear and understand conversations that had taken place while people presumed them unconscious. He considered these one-way conversations therapy.

"I missed you last night, honey. Sorry about that. There's a case, an investigation that I'm in charge of, and it has got me pretty well booked up. You'd like this one, I think. It's different. I actually feel like a cop. I went to a beautiful house in Pebble Beach today. You would have loved it. View of the ocean and everything. Thing was so big, it had its own ZIP code. When you move from one room to the next, you change time zones." He looked for even a twitch to her lips. Nothing. "I didn't see any whales, but I saw a ship and it reminded me of all those times we went whale watching. You wake up and we'll do that again, honey. It's a promise." He brushed her hair some more, his face and throat tight with memories. "Not much news since Monday," he added. "Rusty got a bird, or at least he left part of one on the back door. Your sister misses you, sends you her love. She spends any more time on that phone, it's going to have to be surgically removed." He leaned back and studied her gaunt features, absent-mindedly tugging the fine hair from the brush, which he returned to the drawer. He polished his glasses and took the paperwork into his lap.

There would be no tears tonight; he was all but through with tears. He liked doing his paperwork here, enjoyed the company of his daughter, regardless of her condition, her reliance on this machinery. The paperwork seemed endless. This one was for the California Department of Justice—the DOJ. Male, Caucasian: He penciled in the two little boxes. Only 138 questions to go.

3
THURSDAY

1

Early Thursday morning, in the middle of a shave, James Dewitt was startled by the corrosive ringing of the phone. A sense of dread struck him, and he thought that physicians must suffer this same anxiety over unexpected phone calls. A vision of Osbourne spread out on the pavement floated before his eyes—the skin gray and pasty.

Another ring or two and Emmy would answer it. She slept more heavily than any human on earth—something akin to bears in hibernation—but with the extension only inches from her head, even Emmy awakened after five or six rings.

It had been a rough night for Emmy, her recurring nightmare

waking her in screams and tears. He had spent most of the night with her, sitting on the edge of the bed, holding her hand, staring at her with a father's concern. Had the nightmare been fiction, it would have been easier, but of course it wasn't. She had relived that moment in the courthouse a hundred times, probably had another hundred to go for all he knew. He took comfort in the thought that she had made it through what the experts deemed her most difficult months. There were several major leaps yet to make, perhaps the largest of which was convincing Emmy to do away with her mother's ashes. That ceramic urn on Emmy's bureau had come to symbolize her dependence on the past. Her father still prayed for her future.

The disposable razor slipped into the sink and floated amid the icebergs of shaving cream. As he lifted the receiver, he noticed that the bedside clock read 6:30.

"DBF at Del Mar," Ginny said solemnly, her tone cautious, almost apologetic. "James?" she asked when he failed to respond.

"Who's on it?"

"Nelson. Says he hasn't touched a thing. Looks like your little lecture got through." That was Ginny: Build you up when you needed it. Dewitt had used Wednesday's roll calls to conduct refresher courses on the duties of the first officer. She was exaggerating his effectiveness: Nelson was the best uniform on the force.

"A suicide?"

"That's right, sweetie. I wish I was callin' to tell you you won the lotto, but I ain't."

"Who's been notified?"

"You're first, James. I got the list right here. You want me to wake up the commander?"

"Capp? I guess you had better. And call Hindy, Ginny. Fill him in. Tell him I'm on my way over there." That would ensure someone would look after Em this morning. "Call Zorro—Dr. Emmanuel—I want him there; and wake up Brian Marney and have him send an FI over. I want this handled as a proper crime scene this time. Better call the DA's office; they may want to send someone down. We'll need more radio cars today. See who's on-call. Use the phones. I don't want anyone using the radios; we don't need a zoo scene down there. Let's detour Ocean up top. Same with Scenic."

"The wooden barricades?"

"Please."

"Done."

They hung up. Dewitt turned and watched Rusty stretch by the door; he was oblivious to any of this. A dog's life.

Only half-shaved, Dewitt hurried into yesterday's clothes, convinced that the dead body in the parking lot was no suicide; it was a one-eighty-seven—a homicide.

2

Upon his arrival at the Carmel Beach parking lot, which the patrolmen referred to as Del Mar, Dewitt said to the beefy Patrolman Buford Nelson, "Brutus, kill the lights on the radio car. No sense in attracting any more attention." Nelson had the roof lights going. A small gathering of onlookers huddled by the parking-lot entrance. The roped-off lot contained the lone Chevy Luv truck, off-white with a battered camper shell. Its engine was running and blue-gray fumes escaped the cab. The two men stood inside the police tape and glo-cones.

"Checked his neck for a pulse," Nelson explained. "Nothing doing. Skin was cool. Didn't touch anything but the driver's door."

"We'll get him out in a minute," Dewitt said. "I'd like to wait a minute, get some photographs."

"Was careful where I walked, like you asked. Oh, yeah, and I found that same oil again. I drew a chalk mark around it." He pointed out the circled area of pavement not five feet from the small pickup truck.

"A triangle?"

"Looked like the same thing you described to us yesterday at roll call."

Dewitt approached the chalk mark slowly and cautiously, eyes trained on the pavement immediately in front of the toes of his shoes.

His chest filled with the familiar pounding of too much coffee; he hadn't taken any coffee yet this morning. There it was: a similar triangle of motor oil circled at his feet.

Surprisingly, his reaction was not that of a forensic investigator—he didn't need chromatographies and comparison photographs to tell him this oil was from the same vehicle that had been at the Osbourne site. His reaction instead was a detective's cold panic from groin to throat. The uncomfortable acceptance of responsibility for another life being lost. A *victim*. The very word conjured up an urgency. From this moment forward, it was up to James Dewitt to stop this from happening again.

The responsibility bore down on him. Somewhere nearby was a killer—a premeditative killer attempting to disguise his acts. A man? A woman? Black, Caucasian, Asian, Hispanic? What age? In what mental condition? Two victims in three days. It was a strange inexplicable feeling for James Dewitt, an intense fear mixed with the exhilaration of the challenge before him. He had been thrown into a race in which other people lost with their lives if he didn't win.

He had heard the stories, knew of the investigations. The names were on the tip of his tongue: Ted Bundy, Green River . . . . This couldn't be *that* he told himself, still staring at the oil. Too carefully planned. Too visible. God, the attention it would receive. He glanced back at Nelson, who was watching him and awaiting instruction. He reached up and tugged on his bow tie. It was red today. It felt tight. "Check with the neighbors," he ordered.

Rusty yipped from the backseat. His nose had drawn snail lines on the glass. Low fog crept into the parking lot from the beach, like smoke from an unseen fire. The skies threatened rain. Dewitt removed his glasses and polished the lenses while in contemplation. With the fog, the parking lot grew colder. He hooked his glasses behind his ears and then headed to his unmarked car to get his gear.

She was a lovely complexioned woman of about thirty, a Sigourney Weaver in librarian mode. Dewitt appreciated beautiful hands like hers; she should have been a piano player. She wore Perry Ellis glasses and just enough lipstick. Her blue rain jacket zipped up the front, trapping a wool scarf at her neck. The blue jeans stretched her already long legs. She had that welcome look about her: bright, athletic, yet coyly unsure of herself. He had noticed her around the lab; she wasn't one to miss. It wasn't until he saw her expression that he realized she had noticed him, as well.

They introduced themselves with a firm handshake. Clare O'Daly, forensic investigator with the Salinas Criminalistics Laboratory. He saw confidence and he liked that.

She asked him, "So why does a former FI call in an FI?"

"I suppose I could have done some of this myself," he admitted, hoisting one of her heavy black bags from the trunk, sensing she would rather do this herself. "I do carry some gear in my trunk."

"I hear it's more like a lab truck," she interrupted.

"The smaller cases I do my own work; that was part of the idea of making me the detective over here. But I know from experience that Bill Saffeleti, our diligent District Attorney, likes separation of power on the bigger cases. He would rather the lab work come out of the lab, would rather not explain an elaborate chain of possession to a jury."

"Jury?" she asked, slinging an automatic Fuji over her head. "This was called in as a DBF."

"We're investigating it as a possible one-eighty-seven," he corrected.

"Not a suicide?"

"Right," he said, the force of his voice intimidating. "That's as much as I want to say right now. I don't want to influence your investigation. That could come back at me later."

"Saffeleti," she stated. "You're already thinking ahead to a trial."

"My forensic background, I'm afraid. Always protecting the evidence. They steal it away from you so easily, the lawyers, the courts. You learn to think of everything in terms of the trial, whether or not a case ever reaches the courts."

"Don't proselytize, Detective."

Their eyes met. "No," he said, then apologizing.

"You want to quiz me, I understand. That might even help me: I'm new at fieldwork, but I won't be lectured."

"I only meant to say that if it appears I've led you on, that I aimed you at certain evidence, it hurts everyone concerned. Better if you tell me, than if I tell you. It's your investigation, forensically speaking."

She liked that. She said, "Give me a minute alone before this place turns into a zoo."

"Take as long as you need," he said, stepping back. Watching her begin the forensic work proved more difficult than he had imagined. The feeling was not dissimilar to that of watching Emmy board the school bus for the first time.

He moved well away, beyond the bright orange police tape that Nelson had strung. She spent several minutes circling the vehicle and taking photographs.

Rusty barked and James turned around in time for the arrival of the coroner's wagon, and right behind it, Dr. Emmanuel's silver seven-hundred-series BMW.

Dr. Ricardo Emmanuel wore trifocals with thick black frames, the lenses enlarging his eyes. "James," he said, the two then shaking hands. Zorro, as he was called, planted a Sherman nonfilter between his lips and dented his cheeks as he inhaled. He wore black polyester slacks, black loafers with shaggy leather tassels, and his raven hair was combed straight back in a wet look that seemed prepared for gale-force winds. He carried a cup of coffee in a 7-Eleven driver's mug; the brown-wrapped cigarette was pinched deeply between his fingers. Slate gray smoke escaped his nostrils. He sported a pencil-thin mustache that contributed greatly to his nickname, and, like so many surgeons, he kept his hands spotlessly clean and his nails permanently manicured. When he smiled, he showed off a set of bright white teeth, marred only by a diamond-shaped brown stain dead center, a by-product of his nonfilters. Although Zorro's English was impeccable, he retained a thick accent. "You believe in coincidence, James?" he asked, the thick smoke escaping both nose and mouth.

"No," Dewitt replied.

"Me, neither."

Although paid modestly to conduct autopsies and occasional fieldwork, the three local surgeons who rotated in the job of medical examiner did the work mostly out of a sense of public service. Zorro rattled off something in Spanish. Dewitt didn't speak the language. "The devil makes an odd bedfellow," he said in English. "I wish there was someone else whom you could call upon, James. I'm hardly qualified for crime-scene work."

"You fit right in, Zorro. We have a lab tech turned FI," he said, pointing to Clare, "an FI turned detective, and a surgeon turned medical examiner. Welcome aboard."

"What exactly is it you want me to do? You've done many more of these than I, James."

"In a case like this—*apparent* asphyxiation—the medical data becomes all the more important."

"I hate the paperwork. It's the worst part of the job." Emmanuel dropped the Sherman and extinguished it with the toe of his brightly polished loafer.

"Two bodies in three days. But who's counting?" Dewitt said.

"No one has touched the body?"

"One of my uniforms checked for a neck pulse. That's all."

"Good."

"I need to know when he died, how he died, and where he died, if at all possible."

"How?"

"Osbourne showed no contusions, right? No sign of violence. Blood chem showed no drugs and only minor intoxication. So if it's a one-eighty-seven, what does this guy do, ask his victims to sit still while he gasses them?"

"Interesting. How indeed? I hadn't thought of that."

"Maybe he charms them to death. Like you and the women," Dewitt added. Zorro enjoyed the much-exaggerated reputation of a ladies' man.

With the help of the two firemen who manned the county coroner's wagon, the corpse was removed from the cab of the pickup truck. Zorro retrieved his doctor's bag, snapped on a pair of gloves, and began his examination, while a similarly gloved James Dewitt examined the contents of the man's wallet. Clare O'Daly was busy photographing the pavement behind the truck. This raised Dewitt's curiosity, but he suppressed it.

"Asphyxiation, by the look of it, James," the doctor said. "Again, no apparent contusions." He checked the dead man's eyes and then ran a gentle hand down the arms, squeezing occasionally to check the bones. Reaching the hands, he said, "Some bruising here," which drew Dewitt to his side.

"Meet Malcolm McDuff," Dewitt said, reading the driver's license.

Zorro nodded to the man's bluish face.

"Lives up in Santa Rosa."

"*Lived,*" Emmanuel corrected. "Look here," he added, pointing to the outside of the man's right hand. "Light bruising, and by the coloring, I would suggest just prior to death."

Dewitt hurried to his Zephyr, opened the trunk, and came out a few seconds later with a pair of white paper bags and a roll of masking tape. He returned to the corpse and helped Emmanuel seal both hands in the bags, a necessary precaution to retain any possible trace evidence. This dehumanizing the corpse reminded him of the other crime scenes. Collectively, they were treating McDuff as a lump of potential evidence.

The doctor lifted an arm and let it back down gently. He then touched the man's neck. "Dead two hours at least."

"No receipts," Dewitt said, checking the wallet, "but there's cash."

"I won't know more until I have his clothes off."

"I won't quote you on that," Dewitt said, bagging the wallet, sealing and labeling the bag with the case number and date.

"You do, and you'll be finding yourself another medical examiner."

At that moment, exactly 7:30 A.M., the dead man's wristwatch began emitting a high-pitched electronic alarm. Dewitt and Emmanuel each reached for a different wrist. Dewitt tore at the mouth of the paper bag to get at the watch. The alarm stopped of its own accord. Dewitt said, "Wait." He reached across the body and pointed to the band of pale skin on the decedent's right wrist. "See that?" Dewitt questioned.

"A tan line," Emmanuel said, "caused by his—"

"Wristwatch," Dewitt finished, holding up the left wrist. "So what's it doing over here?"

"I switch my watch when I operate."

Dewitt looked at McDuff a moment. Overweight, middle forties, graying hair. "When you're going over him, Zorro, not only bag all his clothing but let's run the laser over him and check for prints."

"In case someone else dressed him."

"Exactly. This someone else may have left a fingerprint behind on McDuff's skin, not realizing we have the technology to see it."

"The laser is your department. That's crime-lab stuff."

"Agreed."

"You have to be at the Osbourne autopsy today, anyway. We get the paperwork handled on this guy, we'll do two in one day."

"I can't wait," Dewitt quipped. "No lunch today."

"You've been through autopsies before," Emmanuel insisted, as if he knew.

"A very long time ago. One of the joys of forensics is that they place the corpse in a body bag and take it away."

"Which is exactly what I'm about to do," Emmanuel explained, signaling the two men from the coroner's wagon that he was ready. "See you for lunch," he said.

Clare photographed the truck from a variety of angles. Reconstruct the crimes, she reminded herself, well aware of his eyes on her.

If murder, as he had suggested, then the killer had left the body here, had rigged the truck, had fled the scene. She dropped to hands and knees, looking for footprints, gaining a fresh perspective from only inches above the pavement. She spotted bubble gum, pebbles, a Popsicle stick, cigarette butts, the crushed cap of a beer bottle. She adjusted her angle, and suddenly the patterns in the sand jumped out at her. She could clearly make out the truck's tire tracks leading into the lot. What intrigued her more, however, was a thin waving tread pattern that weaved its way back toward the Day-Glo cones Nelson had set out. A bicycle-tire track!

Maintaining a similar angle, and using a tape measure for scale, she took several close-ups of the tread pattern, realizing their potential significance to the investigation. A gust of wind blew beach grass across the parking lot, constantly contaminating her crime scene. She worked more quickly. Reconstruct the crime. The killer had fled the scene by bicycle. The bicycle had been stored in the back of the truck. The killer had driven the truck to the site. God, she could see him doing all of this, as if a movie were playing in her head. So *this* was the thrill of fieldwork! He parks the truck, rigs the hose . . . She was reenacting it now, step by step, following his imagined work.

Reconstruct the crime.

He tapes up the passenger window, checks his work. It must be pitch-black or close to it. He's wearing gloves to avoid leaving prints. He approaches the back of the truck, lifts the gate to the fiberglass shell, opens the tailgate, and pulls out the bike. Three requirements for a forensic investigator: good eyes, innate curiosity, patience.

She began a thorough investigation of the bed of the truck, starting with the tailgate, mentally dividing the area in front of her into quadrants, eyes carefully scanning each quadrant, alert for the slightest inconsistency. Midway across the rounded lip of the tailgate, she zeroed in on a fresh scratch mark that led directly to a distinct discoloring. Paint! The top of her kit held an abundance of tools: a variety of forceps, scissors, a scalpel, wire cutters, a small saw, measuring tape, and a large-field magnifying glass. She studied this paint first through the magnifying glass, then photographed it, then scraped it loose with the scalpel into a petri dish, which she labeled with the location of the evidence and her name. After several more minutes, climbing inside, she located a smear of lightweight oil and followed the same textbook procedures of photography, sampling, and labeling.

He avoided the Day-Glo surveyor's tape she had placed on the pavement. "How are you coming?" he asked Clare O'Daly from behind, his mind immediately turning it into a sexual pun. She was kneeling on all fours in the truck bed, her movement limited by the overhead fiberglass shell. There was something about that pose: For an instant, he remembered Julia in this same position.

"Nicely," she replied to his inquiry. "A forensics feast," she said, working her way out of the truck. Pointing to the area between the surveyor's tape, she explained, "A bicycle track leading directly to or directly away from the truck. I photographed it to scale. We should get a very good tread pattern, and if we're lucky, be able to tell what make of bike and quite possibly the weight of the rider. This," she said, displaying the petri dish, "may tell us what kind of bike."

He noticed the dark-colored flakes then, and recognized them as paint.

"Found it on the tailgate," she said proudly. "Also some oil, chain oil if I'm not mistaken. I'll have to run chromatographies on both of these. I want to hold off on the cab's interior, no reason to do the detail work here, but I take it you noticed the gaping hole in the dash? By the look of those wires, that stereo was—"

"Stolen?"

"We'll check the cab for prints back at the lab. Have the tow truck take it out there," she said authoritatively. Repacking her kit, she said, "It's your call, Detective, but from a forensic point of view, a suicide is more difficult to explain than a one-eighty-seven. Unless," she conditioned, "he carried a bicycle in the back of the truck. If that happens to be the case, you can reconstruct a theft following suicide: Steal the stereo, steal the bike, and take off. That remains a possibility."

"One-eighty-seven?" he asked. "My words, or your words?"

"Why did Brian Marney happen to assign *me* this case?"

"Who's quizzing whom?" he asked. When she didn't reply, he answered, "You must be handling the lab work on the Osbourne case."

"Bravo! Who better to send than the person familiar with the evidence of the first case? That garden hose and PVC fitting look awfully similar, don't they? And the duct tape on the window? We're trained to distrust coincidence, aren't we, Detective?"

"James," Dewitt corrected.

"Sir!" Nelson approached at a run. "We've got a possible witness," he announced in a winded voice.

3

His name was Anthony De Sica, and in body type, he reminded Dewitt of his commander, Karl Capp: round, soft, and built low to the ground. He had almost no hair, carried bags of coffee grounds below his eyes, and his lips were shiny from saliva. De Sica churned with high-strung energy, manifest in the shifting of his substantial weight from one foot to the other.

Dewitt introduced himself and shook the man's stubby calloused hand. "You saw a car, Mr. De Sica?" Dewitt asked.

"Right down there," De Sica replied. "You see there? Right through the trees."

Dewitt turned and followed the line of sight. He could make out the rear of McDuff's pickup truck. He instructed Nelson to return to the Zephyr's trunk and collect his camera gear; he wanted a shot from here, showing the perspective. Nelson took off at a clip. "What time would that have been?" Dewitt asked.

"I told the kid," the man explained, "that I make the coffee right at five, every morning. Ten minutes for the thing to make the stuff. I was just getting my second cup. Must'a been right around half past the hour."

"And someone pulled up?"

"I didn't see no one pull up, no. I heard this loud bang, like a gun going off." Dewitt's heart sank. They occasionally ran into "creative witnesses" who would fabricate a story in order to be part of the investigation. Perhaps De Sica had heard there was a dead body down there; he had jumped to the conclusion it involved a gun and was now making up a story. Dewitt tried to keep an open mind, though his brief flirtation with enthusiasm had been muted.

De Sica continued, "That's when I seen the cars."

"It would have been dark at five-thirty," Dewitt suggested.

"Lighter than you might think. I seen two cars." He corrected himself, "One car and that truck."

"Did you see either of the vehicles arrive?"

"No."

"Did you happen to see either driver?"

"Sure did. Sort of. Like I told the kid . . . a big guy. He came around to the door of the truck when I seen him. Switched on a flashlight . . . but I couldn't see nothing. Then he got back in his car and took off. Door made that same noise. A real loud *pop*."

"Do you know what kind of car it was?"

"Two tone, I can tell you that. Maybe a convertible, with a white roof."

Nelson arrived with the camera bag in hand.

"You gonna take my picture?" De Sica asked.

"No, sir," Dewitt said, looking back down at the parking lot. How much could this man have actually seen at that hour?

On his note pad it read, "Two-tone convertible? Loud bang? Big man."

"I'd like to change my shirt if you're going to take my picture," said Anthony De Sica.

4

Shortly thereafter, the perimeter of the crime scene filled with reporters and authorities of varying importance. Dewitt briefed Commander Karl Capp, as well as an investigator from the District Attorney's office, and a lieutenant from the Monterey County Sheriff's Office.

Capp issued a brief and carefully worded statement that essentially paved the way for a later press conference. He refused to give a specific time for the press conference and refused comment on cause of death, warning that "undue speculation on the part of the media could place unnecessary burden on the citizens of Carmel." His facial expressions belied his confidence. He slipped away unnoticed a few minutes later.

Dewitt arrived at the office at eleven o'clock, weeded through a stack of pink memo slips, and then shared his suspicions with the ever-supportive Clarence Hindeman. By noon, he had phoned the records department at the Department of Justice in Sacramento, requesting the case files of all deaths by asphyxiation in the last five years.

Ginny miraculously located an FBI Violent Criminal Apprehension Program report for him. VICAP, a division of the FBI's Behavioral Science Unit had been established in the early eighties to keep track of all violent crimes. If any crimes similar to these had been committed in California, then the information from Sacramento would help him. If murders such as these had been committed out of state, then the FBI would know about it. He thought it ironic that the information he sought was the last information he wanted: If either of these agencies confirmed his suspicions, then chances were he was in pursuit of a serial killer. Even the most veteran of cops feared those two words put together.

Dewitt arrived at the Community Hospital early afternoon and peeked in on Anna, but only briefly because two nurses were in the process of cleaning her.

He drove on to Pacific Grove, to Maratia's Funeral Parlor; its architecture was a throwback to the late-eighteenth-century Spanish influence—stucco and red-tile roof—when Catholic missionaries had first settled the area. The wrought-iron gate clicked shut musically behind him. Even in January various shrubs declared themselves in spectacular bloom. Windham Hill music played from ceiling speakers in the reception area. The room deodorizer smelled like raspberry jam, attempting to mask the chemical odors that worked their way insidiously from the windowless back room. The butcher shop, he had heard the room called.

That's where he found Dr. Emmanuel perched on a stool, his glasses dramatically enlarging his eyes as he looked up. "You've spoken to McDuff's wife about I.D.ing the body?" the doctor asked.

"Yes, and I'm going to see her tonight. She won't make it down here until early evening."

"We can't cut him until we have a positive I.D.," Emmanuel informed him.

"What a shame," cracked Dewitt. "You mean we only get to do one of these today?"

Dewitt delayed the autopsy by first checking Osbourne's body with the portable laser. The laser light, viewed through special goggles, turned hairs and fibers a fluorescent green against the backdrop of the corpse's skin. The technology, which had come into use in the early eighties, allowed much greater scrutiny than previous high-power-magnification examination. The resulting detection of trace evidence at crime scenes and in the lab had improved considerably as a result.

Emmanuel switched off the lights. As Dewitt waved the small wand over Osbourne's leg, Emmanuel looking on, he related a story of how the laser had solved a rape/murder two years earlier when a latent fingerprint's natural oil had been found on the victim's thigh. As with hairs and fibers, a fingerprint became visible under the laser light as well, showing bright green and giving the device a nickname within law enforcement of the "magic wand." It was just such advances in technology that made forensics fascinating for Dewitt, and at moments like these, he felt completely himself, secure in the comfort of his expertise, surefooted and confident. He was soon picking hairs and fibers from Osbourne's limbs and torso, depositing them in vials that Emmanuel then labeled. Discouraged by a lack of any fingerprints, he made up for it by discovering an abundance of cotton pills on Osbourne's calves, buttocks, and shoulder blades. Natural fibers such as cotton were often dismissed because they were so common to any crime scene. As a criminalist, however, James Dewitt dismissed nothing: All evidence was meant to be collected, whether or not it ever became relevant to the investigation.

At long last, Dewitt reached John Osbourne's head, and a half-dozen smudged fingerprints where the victim had groomed himself. Dewitt was working the spray of the light across Osbourne's hair when he asked without looking up, "You sent his clothes to the lab?"

"Yes, each bagged separately as you requested. Why, what have you found?"

Dewitt worked the forceps carefully into the hair and pinched a fiber. Like any professional, Dewitt had become familiar with the elements of his trade. Where a carpenter could pick a tenpenny nail out of a pile of nails, or a surgeon such as Emmanuel could identify an organ, Dewitt knew hairs and fibers. "These are all through his hair on this side," he said, casting the light on the synthetic squiggle held by the jaws of his forceps. The fiber appeared electrified as it caught the light.

"What is it?" the doctor asked.

"If I'm not mistaken," said James Dewitt, "I would say they're synthetic carpet fibers." He placed the wand down, walked over and switched on the room lights, able for the first time to see the true color of the fiber. He held it up to the light. He recognized that color. "Osbourne's luggage was found shoved to the back of the trunk. That puzzled me at first. I think we now know why."

"And why's that?"

"The trunk was too small for the bicycle," he said, confusing the doctor, who didn't know the details of the case, "so he put the body there instead."

4

Having failed to find a replacement, Dewitt arrived for his volunteer work at the Monterey Aquarium at ten minutes before seven. He had been a marine-science major in college, until the criminalistics bug had bitten him. Like so many in law enforcement, he wasn't exactly sure how he had gotten there. These evenings at the aquarium brought him back to his old love, however; they served the purpose of a welcome diversion.

The aquarium, a U-shaped renovated cannery facing the ocean, was relatively empty tonight, a relief to Dewitt, because the tour-bus nights proved draining and anxiety-ridden. He entered, as always, via the members' side entrance, passing beneath a sixty-foot life-sized replica of a gray whale and calf. The overhead ventilation system kicked on much too loudly, and Dewitt bristled that it still had not been repaired. He headed directly for the information booth, straight ahead. Above him, a pod of plaster orca whales swam toward the picture windows. A dozen curious visitors were split between the raised-deck and floor-level viewing areas for the sea otters.

Dewitt stopped at Information to speak for a minute with Cynthia Chatterman, an extremely active board member, a try-too-hard divorcée with costly clothes and a raspy voice. Dewitt took his station at The Kelp Forest. At thirty-one feet deep, sixty-one feet long, this, the largest tank in the aquarium, held 335,000 gallons of seawater and a good many of the aquarium's five thousand species of aquatic life. Dewitt knew the English and Latin names for each species in this tank, had nicknamed a few of the more distinctive inhabitants; his favorite was Wax the turtle. His job was to be the walking encyclopedia, the Mister Know It All for the curious, and he had taken the responsibility to heart.

The thirty-foot trees of deep green kelp swayed with the artificially controlled movement of the water; sharks, salmon, and needlefish nosed the viewing windows. Dewitt explained to a young couple how the nutrient-rich ocean water was pumped into the tank at a rate of two thousand gallons per minute during off-hours in order to keep the inhabitants fed. Filtered at a similar rate in the early morning, the seawater was then cleared of the cloudy nutrients for another day of viewing.

With the light crowd, his work was steady but not frantic. At 7:30, he headed around the U to the public cafeteria. Beatrice McDuff sat alone at a table. He recognized her by the black dress and the sadness in her eyes. He checked to make sure, "Mrs. McDuff?"

She bit her lower lip and nodded.

"Detective Dewitt," he said. "James."

She nodded.

He sat down facing her and waited a few long minutes until she looked up. A couple at the next table was complaining to some friends about people smoking on the tour bus. A six-year-old was standing at one of the picture windows, gazing outside at the lighted rock pools, saying "Whales, Mommy. Whales." He was watching a frolicking pair of sea otters, one of them pregnant.

"I appreciate your taking the time to come over here," he began. "I couldn't find a substitute." In fact, he knew she was staying at a hotel less than a mile away.

She drew a fingernail along the imitation grain in the tabletop's plastic veneer. "It's a long drive down," she said. "Tell me something," she said bitterly. "I have to *identify* him, but I can't take him home, can't have him back yet. Is that your doing?"

"As much as anyone's, I suppose," he admitted.

Her face tightened. She waved her hand at him and looked up with lifeless eyes.

Dewitt said, "There's a reason for the delay: We believe your husband may have been murdered. As evidence—"

"Oh, thank God," she said, interrupting him. "Not suicide?" she added. He realized then that she had been living with the unacceptable thought that she had failed her husband, had driven him to suicide. "I *knew* it wasn't suicide," she said clearly, suddenly animated.

"I need to ask some questions," he said.

She agreed with a nod of her head.

"There appears to have once been a tape player in the truck. Can you tell me when it was stolen?"

"Stolen? That's impossible." Dewitt waited. If you wait long enough, the other person invariably starts talking again to fill the void. She said, "When I spoke to him yesterday noon, he didn't mention it. Impossible. My Mac, he loved his C & W. He would have been furious. Stolen?"

"You spoke to him yesterday at noon?"

"Tried to call me twice a day if he could manage."

"He didn't mention the tape machine?"

"No, sir, he did not."

Dewitt took notes. "And he didn't call you a second time?"

"Can't say for sure. I was over to a neighbor who's not well. Mac might have called. But if his stereo had been stolen, I can tell you one thing: He would have called you people right away. You gotta have a police report for the insurance. We learned that last year when his decoys were stolen."

"He was in this area on business?" Dewitt asked.

A private, reflective voice attempting to sound strong: "Yes. Repaired microwave relays."

"And he dealt in home satellite dishes as well, isn't that right?"

"Yes, that's right."

"We found related equipment in the back of his truck," he explained. "And this trip?"

"Microwave problems out at Fort Ord. Seems he's down to Fort Ord once or twice a month. They have their own people, but Mac could fix most anything. Was Army once himself."

"Fort Ord," Dewitt repeated.

"That's right."

"So he was staying in the area?"

"Depends how his schedule was working out. Had other work down south of here at Big Sur. If he got through early enough, he wouldn't have stayed, no."

"If he had stayed, any place in particular he might have been? Favorite eating spots, motels, anything like that?" Notebook out. Pen ready.

"Not my Mac. No, sir. Mac was always trying someplace new. That's just the way he was. Oh, I'm not saying he wouldn't go back to the same place now and again, but not as a rule, you know. *Variety is the spice of life,*" she reflected. "That's my Mac."

"I see."

"That's bad?"

Dewitt shrugged. Doesn't make things any easier for me, he felt like saying. Instead, he asked, "Did your husband keep receipts, a logbook, anything like that?"

"Sure he did."

"Which?"

"A notebook. A smaller notebook than the one you've got there."

"We didn't find anything like that on him, or in his possessions."

"No notebook? That's not right. You must have missed it. Mac carried that thing around right here," she said, lifting a hand to an imaginary breast pocket, "like a preacher with his Bible. He was real good about keeping track."

"He didn't leave it at home, something like that?"

"No, sir. And even if he had, he woulda just bought another."

"And the receipts?"

"Kept 'em in his billfold. Right rear pocket," she said fondly, lowering her eyes again. She rubbed her fingers together absentmind-edly, and Dewitt could picture her having removed that wallet at the washing machine.

"We found no receipts in the wallet," he said.

"No, sir. That's not right," she objected. "That *can't be*, Detective. He empties that billfold last day of the month. Rubber-bands and files the receipts. I oughta know; I do the bookkeeping for him. Should be at least two weeks of gas receipts and whatnot in there. He's been on the road an awful lot this month. Has to be lots of receipts in there."

Dewitt scribbled a note.

"Someone took them?" she asked.

"Could be," Dewitt admitted. They had found no receipts on Osbourne, either. "Did your husband ever mention the name John Osbourne?"

"The one in the papers? Are you telling me the same man who killed my Mac killed that boy, too? Is that what you're saying?"

"If there was a connection between your husband and John Os-bourne."

She shook her head. "That's a name I wouldn't forget."

Both victims had jobs that carried them up and down the coast and its communities. Was McDuff a drug dealer, as well? He said, "Is there any way their businesses might have overlapped? John Osbourne was a lobbyist for the entertainment industry. Was your husband active in the organizational end of the satellite industry, anything like that?"

"All the dealers are active, what with the scrambling and the government poking its nose into it. 'Specially free-lancers like Mac. I see what you're saying. I suppose they might have known each other, but I don't think so. I would remember that name."

He ran a dozen more questions past her, trying to nail down specifics of her husband's schedule and habits, frustrated by the fact that "Mac" McDuff ran his own one-man shop and varied his habits to keep road life tolerable.

He returned to the question of receipts. "From the look of his truck, your husband wasn't exactly obsessed with order. Is that a fair statement?"

"You're saying he was a slob. He mighta been messy, but he knew where everything was. He had one of those kinda minds. If there was a clean pair of socks in his suitcase, he knew exactly where it was. Did you check his suitcase for his receipts?" she asked, the thought just occurring to her. "If he got too many, he would rubber-band them and put them in his suitcase. Like I said, it's been a busy month. Might be one bunch of them in his suitcase."

"I'll check," Dewitt said, thanking her. "None of the lab work is in yet."

"Check his suitcase," she repeated softly.

Beatrice McDuff grew distant, perhaps recalling packing that suitcase. Dewitt reached across and took the woman's hand gently. She didn't seem to notice. It may not matter to you right now, Mrs. McDuff, he wanted to say, but we're doing everything in our power to catch the person responsible. He tended to think in clichés when he felt uncomfortable. Instead, he said, "I lost my wife a few months ago. You're a very strong woman, if that's any consolation."

She nodded politely as her tears began to run.

5

Howard Lumbrowski felt ill. Following the Steven Miller incident, he had failed a blood test and had been placed on psychological disability—suspended with pay. He was supposed to be in treatment. Instead, he had been in the bars. Now he was trying something new: not exactly cold turkey, more like lukewarm. He had cut back to four drinks a day—just enough to keep the shakes from rattling him apart.

His stomach burned. He broke into sweats unexpectedly and his heart took off like he was mainlining adrenaline. Dizzy spells, nausea.

It all started with John Osbourne and the coke he had been carrying in the glove compartment. What a shock that had been! It complicated everything. He had begun making phone calls immediately, had started the ball rolling: There was someone out there missing a few thousand worth of soda, and *he* had it. Not the kind of situation to handle drunk, no sir. He had to get this thing worked out.

That phone call from the snitch further added to his problems. It had followed a drink, and he had screwed up. Snitches were as unpredictable as women. The guy had seen him, that much was clear. He should have arranged a meeting and reminded him who was in charge. Handle him. But was he a snitch, or was he the one missing a heavy bag of soda?

The thing about it was, he had to keep himself straight. There was opportunity here. Just like the old days.

He did, however, owe himself a deep one. It was 10:30 P.M., but it felt like 3 A.M. He'd been up over eighteen hours. He tipped the bottle slightly and let the vodka run sensuously into the glass. He had poured it a little short the night before, had been unable to keep it down, and had slept restlessly through hellish nightmares of the swirling fumes . . . the blue-gray skin . . . .

He wanted to drink it slowly, but he didn't. The moment that taste touched his tongue, he opened his throat and poured it down luxuriously.

Five minutes later when the phone rang, he was praying to the porcelain god on hands and knees, wishing to hell the drink had stayed down and done its job. He felt betrayed by his best friend. Nothing remained loyal forever, not even vodka.

He rose up painfully, wiped his mouth on his shirt sleeve, and answered the phone. "Yeah?"

"I saw you again this morning." The same voice. "I can help you, you know?"

"How?" Lumbrowski asked.

"We can help each other."

"How?"

"You're not hanging up this time, are you? That's good."

"You want what I have?"

"I told you last time," the other man said. "*You* want what *I* have."

"You're pissing me off. I'm gonna hang up on you again if you don't stop pissing me off."

"*Don't* hang up! You'll be sorry. I saw you, don't forget."

"Yeah? You saw me doing what, buddy?"

"I love the beach in the morning, don't you?"

Lumbrowski felt it coming up again, boiling like fire. He slammed the receiver down and ran to the toilet. Some blood this time. Hell of a world. No loyalty whatsoever.

6

Dewitt stood at the doorway to Anna's hospital room. Like returning to a childhood home so many years later, he saw the room through the eyes of a stranger—in this case, Clare O'Daly. He had been thinking of Clare much of the evening. I'd like to introduce my daughter, he could hear himself saying. Would another person recognize that fetal-poised body with its wafer-thin arms and cotton-candy hair as his daughter? It was a body, and barely that, its spiritual inhabitant long since vacated. *Its!* He realized that he no longer thought of *it* as *her*, Anna, his daughter. This body was a stranger. A revelation: His daughter was gone.

He stepped closer to *the body*, impressed by the effect a single day had had upon him. She looked more like one of the victims than his daughter. He knew there existed a specific temperature where ice turned back to water, a day on the calendar when winter ceased to exist, an exact minute that marked the passage of night into day. The ice was no longer ice; the wind no longer cold; the sky no longer dark; the body no longer his daughter. So radical was this thought, so apparently sudden his acceptance of it, that he first began to laugh and then to cry. He squeezed his daughter's frail hand, as fearful of the future as he was of the killer who still eluded him.

7

District Attorney Bill Saffeleti didn't like to kowtow to anyone, much less a golf pro in psychedelic plaids. He had kowtowed for too many years, earning the confidence of the voters, pressing the flesh, wooing the judges, winning the cases. He didn't need to be told how to do his job—not by anyone. He picked at a piece of stray lint on the sleeve of his dark gray wool suit, finally pinching and extricating it. The suit cost $780, the wing tips—a pair of goddamned shoes!—$233. Then today, he's in a hurry, and he's feeling both generous and guilty, and he lets some homeless guy shine his shoes and the guy uses some kind of oil by mistake and leaves this permanent blotch dead center on the toe of the left shoe. Ruined. They looked like some cat had pissed on them.

Mayor Manny Roth paced by the windows of his lavish Carmel-by-the-Sea home. Roth was a former PGA golfer who had gained more fame for his TV commercials than for his tournament wins; his trademark was nauseating color combinations. Today, he wore plaid in Sanibel lime and Nantucket pink, with yellow socks and red leather shoes. He was a bald, ferret-faced man with moon eyes and Dumbo ears. A comic! Saffeleti considered the man part fool, part genius. With an iron, he was deadly; a wood, unparalleled. At a city-council meeting, he was less than convincing. But the voters loved him for his ribald humor and willingness to depart from prepared text. After Clint Eastwood's departure, Roth had easily parlayed his celebrity into the Carmel mayoral office.

His recently redecorated home reflected his seven-figure earnings for the past several years. If he kept his approach shots in control, he had a chance at the hall of fame. The one thing Manny Roth lacked was a wife. He had tried five—used them up like wooden tees—the most recent having left him only two months earlier for, it was rumored, a sports promoter out of L.A. As a result, Roth, who had this pent-up-energy syndrome, was pacing the floor like an expectant father. What he needed was a night in the sack with a paid professional. There were rumors circulating about that, as well.

"I'm meeting with them in the morning, Bill. I'd like to know the do's and don'ts," Roth said.

"I wouldn't meet with them directly, Manny. Use Tad, for Christ's sake. The city administrator can stick his nose into this kind of thing."

"I want to handle this myself."

"This is an active police investigation. Guys like Clarence Hindeman and Dewitt take that very seriously. A person like Capp, that's a different story. He's old school. You've got to watch yourself, Manny. You can tell them how this case effects your side of things, but you can't tell them how to run their show."

"But the *evidence?*"

"The evidence is weak so far. But there's a lot of work yet to be done."

"Enough to call it murder? That word scares the hell out of me. You know what it could do to this town?"

"From what you've shown me here—and I won't ask how you got these files, Manny—it's circumstantial. There's no real case here, not yet, although the implications are obvious. Dewitt is probably the best forensics man I've ever met. If he gets a bug up his ass . . . I know this guy. I trust his instincts. On paper, we've got a couple of suicides with some coincidental evidence. Have you ever seen the inside of the Salinas lab, Manny? You ought to pay them a visit sometime. One case we had, Dewitt finds traces of pollen in a victim's *earwax*, for Christ's sake. No shit. It proved enough to swing the jury and win a conviction. A triangle of motor oil may look like nothing to you and me—"

"You're saying you *do* or you *don't* have a case, based on what you've read here?"

"Manny, it's not that simple—"

"Do, or don't?"

"Don't."

"Ah! So it would be premature to call it murder at this point, Mr. Prosecutor?"

"Homicide."

"Whatever."

"No way to call it suicide unless you know it's suicide," Saffeleti reminded.

"Damn it all, Bill! It's suicide until we can prove it's murder."

"Not technically, no, it's not. Technically, Dewitt has ruled that circumstantial evidence suggests *suspicious causes*—"

"I hate that term—"

". . . which puts the case into a middle ground of indecision until all evidence can be judged for its probative weight."

"As long as we take this 'no comment' approach, we're sitting ducks. The press is free to speculate."

"You asked for my opinion, so here it is. Dewitt is handling this well. He's being patient, despite Jessie Osbourne's involvement."

"Who said anything about her?" Roth asked indignantly.

"No one has to," Saffeleti responded. "One thing I should tell you, Manny, as a friend." He hated to kowtow, yes, but Bill Saffeleti knew how to use the ropes as well as the next guy. If the Republicans swept the area, then Saffeleti might win another term on Roth's coattails alone. Teamwork was the key. "These copies," he said, referring to the Osbourne file in front of him. "Cops follow strict procedures for copying active files. This copy is undocumented and therefore illegal to have in your possession. What I'm saying, Manny; I wouldn't go pulling this out of my briefcase if I were you. And just so you and I have things straight," he said, standing and locating another piece of stray lint, "you want to play these kind of games, that's your business. But I never saw this file."

"Agreed." Roth began to pace again. "I didn't know how it worked. Thank you, Bill."

"One other thing to consider, Manny. Whoever copied these files for you had to have access, which means he or she *did* know how the system works. If that person didn't tell you, well, the motivation behind such an omission is something worth considering. We're elected officials, Manny. We're vulnerable."

"Understood."

"Let me know how it turns out tomorrow."

"Will do."

They shook hands. Maybe the guy was color-blind. Maybe that explained it.

4
FRIDAY

1

When the phone rang at 7:30 Friday morning, Dewitt wasn't too concerned because it was a fairly common time of day to hear from his mother, or even Clarence Hindeman.

"It's me. Clare," she began, voicing immediate concern over calling too early, fears that he assuaged. "I stayed late last night, and I have some good stuff, and since I live in the valley, too, I thought it would be better to deliver it in person rather than explain it over the phone." She sounded nervous.

"Coffee's on," he said. He offered her directions, hung up, and conducted a speed clean of the living room, an activity that caught the sleepy-eyed attention of daughter Emmy, who observed him from the adjoining kitchen. She held a glass of orange juice in hand. "Get dressed," he told her. "Someone from work's coming over." Seeing her in a tight skimpy T-shirt reminded him his daughter was no longer a little girl but a young woman. The physical changes that had begun two years earlier were manifest now in a swelling of bust, a lengthening of leg, and widening of hips. What made the transition eerie was Emmy's resemblance to her mother. He was living with a miniature Julia, and he found the experience both disconcerting and welcome.

He was cleaning the bathroom—while Emmy attempted to use the sink—when Clare knocked on the front door. He tangled up with Emmy while trying to rinse his hands, and it was during this confusion at the sink that she said, "It's a *woman*, isn't it?" She was finding reason for his frantic actions. He couldn't reach a towel. Refusing an answer, he grabbed her T-shirt and dried his hands on its back. "Get dressed," he repeated.

"It *is* a woman," she proclaimed.

Dewitt glared, but his glares hadn't been very effective in the last few months. Emmy had his number, and it worried him.

Disobeying, Emmy watched from the hallway as he answered the door. Introductions were made at a distance and he led Clare to the sofa. She carried a briefcase, which she placed beside herself and opened.

Rusty, wagging full force, approached Clare. She showered him in affection and then he retreated to the kitchen and began eating noisily.

"Several things here of importance, I think," she began, "all of which require your immediate attention. With the weekend coming up, I wanted to get as much of this handled as we could. First is that both motor oils match: It's a ten-forty Pennzoil with identical percentages of ferrous aluminum, indicating engine wear. The same car was parked alongside both victims' vehicles. It's as good as a fingerprint. Second, we turned up animal hairs on the inside door panels of both vehicles. Dog hairs . . . a collie mutt," she said, eyeing Rusty. "By all available tests—medulla, cortex, cuticle, scales, length, and coloring—they are from the same dog." She eyed Rusty again.

"It's not from Rusty," he said.

"I'd like to check that out if I may," she said.

"I told you," he said defensively, "I didn't touch McDuff's truck. There's no way—"

"Even so, I'd like to eliminate that as a possibility."

"So do it!" He threw his hands up. "Who cares? But you're wasting lab time."

She bristled, fished out a folder, and handed him a loose stack of black-and-white photographs. "This is where we go beyond circumstantial," she explained as he leafed through the pile. "Each photograph shows magnified enlargements of the torn ends of the duct tape used to seal the car windows. In the bottom margins, you'll see a numbering system and case information. We can connect each piece of tape to the piece from which it was torn. Three pieces of tape used on each window . . . economical and distinctive. First piece is wrapped around the hose left to right, second and third seal the remaining space in the window. Both McDuff's and Osbourne's vehicles were sealed in a similar way." *Identical* was a word any criminalist avoided because it had no place in court, no place in the physical universe. No two anythings were truly identical.

"A behavior pattern."

"Third photo," she advised, "is what hangs him. We can match piece three from the Osbourne site to piece one at McDuff."

"Same roll of tape."

"There's your hard evidence, James. They've got to be one-eighty-sevens. Same guy taped both windows from the same roll of tape. He also used a *similar* make and age of garden hose . . . two different sections cut from the same hose, although we don't have tool markings to confirm that." She checked his list. "We're lacking reference material on that bike tire, but we think Sacramento has it. We're working on it. You asked about those fibers found during yesterday's autopsy. We haven't run all the tests, but visually that synthetic found in Osbourne's hair matches in both color and length the fibers discovered on his clothing, which, as you guessed, are actually fibers from the carpeting in the car."

"And in the trunk," he added.

Emmy interrupted, wondering whether she was supposed to take the bus or whether he would drive her. He said he would drive her. Clare seemed anxious to leave. Dewitt kept her for a moment longer, and Emmy wandered back to her room.

"Fingerprints?" he asked.

"None on the tape. None on either hose. We developed dozens inside the cab using the vapor technique. I sent them up to DOJ Sacramento for analysis. They run ALPS seven days a week. They get a hit, they'll pass it on to you."

The California Department of Justice's Automated Latent Prints System—ALPS—contains over six million electronically filed fingerprints. The computer data base is subdivided into felons, state employees, and a third section that contains the prints of all day-care center workers, hospital employees, private investigators, and similar personnel that the DOJ is now required by state law to keep on file. A sophisticated artificial intelligence software identifies a print's individual characteristics—whorls, loops, and ridges—and then searches the data base at thousands of prints per second, attempting to match the prints. The computer often "kicks" a dozen or more possible prints, and then a human fingerprint expert narrows the field to a single "hit" by manually comparing the prints.

Dewitt asked, "Will they be willing to run our case?"

"I may be able to help there. Why don't you leave that one to me?"

"You know Ramirez?"

"No."

"I do. He was a narco detective when I was working as an FI up in the city. It's been a couple of years."

"You want to chase after him, or you want me to?" she asked.

"You sure you don't mind?"

"I wouldn't offer if I didn't want to do it," she said, settling back confidently into the couch.

Dewitt picked up the photographs of the matching ends of tape. "This is exactly what I needed. It's good work, and about five times faster than I thought we would get it."

"Now that the one-eighty-sevens are confirmed, Brian will put more people on it, make it the priority case. We should get through the rest of this fairly quickly. Chances are he'll approve some weekend overtime."

"Obviously," Dewitt said, "from my end . . . I need all of it just as soon as you have it. Fiber analysis, the bike tread, the organics from the autopsy. Don't hesitate to call me here if I've left the office. This is a seven-day week for me."

She stood and collected the photographs. "What's it like being on the other end . . . as a detective, I mean?"

He considered this and spoke the only word that came to mind. "Overwhelming," he said.

2

It sounded like a gun being shot. Dewitt spun in his office chair, split the venetian blinds, and peered out into the back parking area that both the unmarked and radio cars shared. There was no smoking gun; it was a smoking car and Dewitt recognized it immediately by the bumper sticker: I BRAKE FOR NOTHING. Howard Lumbrowski's profile filled the car window as the Mustang turned left. The Mustang was powder blue with a white convertible top, and Dewitt recalled his interview with Anthony De Sica the day before when the man had described just such a car, right down to the loud *thunk* of the door closing. He flipped through his notebook anxiously, nearly tearing loose several pages. His note read, "Two-tone convertible? Loud bang? Big man." "Howard Lumbrowski?" he wrote on a fresh piece of notepaper.

He had no time to dwell on it. The meeting was in three minutes.

Mayor Manny Roth's presence affected both Capp and Hindeman. Capp was wearing his sport coat and Clarence had abandoned his authoritative position behind his desk for the more congenial approach. He arranged the gunmetal gray chairs as if the four were in a bridge tournament, without the card table. Roth wormed his hands nervously in his lap. Capp drummed his well-chewed Mongol number two on his thigh.

"Was that Lumbrowski I just saw?" Dewitt asked. Capp pretended he didn't hear.

To Dewitt, Hindeman said, "We filled Mr. Roth in on this new evidence, James, the tape, the hose, and he asked to speak with us. His concern, if I'm not mistaken, is how much we tell the press."

Roth began harshly, "Listen, I'm not trying to tell you guys your business." He stood and walked behind Hindeman's desk to the window. He pulled on the cord and lifted the dusty Levolor blinds. Dewitt didn't know him well, but it seemed he must have had some drama coaching at some point in his life. He pointed out the window theatrically and said, "But that out there is *my* business. Those streets, shops, galleries, restaurants, you name it. If we go saying that there's a killer loose in this town, those sidewalks are going to dry up overnight. And those tourists are what keep us going, gentlemen. No tourists, no business, no taxes, no salaries—"

"No votes," Dewitt said under his breath.

"What's that, Detective?" Roth exclaimed in a quick pivot.

Dewitt said, "I appreciate your concerns, Mayor Roth. But we need to use whatever means available to stop this guy. The press is a very effective tool. Not only do we alert the public, and therefore gain thousands of eyes and ears, but we may scare this guy off, make him think twice. The press has already been speculating about the possibil-ity—"

"Speculation, yes," Roth said, interrupting Dewitt. "But no one with authority has actually come out and said it is murder. See the difference? How can there possibly be harm in issuing a statement that the deaths are of a suspicious nature and that the investigation is ongoing? That avoids the word *murder* but keeps us honest with the public."

Capp growled, "Besides, Dewitt, we sure as hell don't want to give them the evidence. If you tell them *how* we know it's homicide, then the perp knows what to avoid next time. Even by issuing a statement, we clue this A-hole into the fact that we're on to him. It may be better for everyone if we just lay low for a while."

Hindeman said, "That kind of approach can come back to haunt us, Manny. Eventually, what we knew and when we knew it will become public, and unless we've been up front about this, there are those who will inevitably claim that had we been more forthcoming, lives might have been saved."

"What we're saying," Dewitt explained, drawing the lines—he and Hindeman on one side, Capp and Roth on the other—"is that this guy is unlikely to just stop doing this. Cases like this . . . there will be more killings. We may be able to scare this guy into giving it up. I propose we release a statement that we *know* they're homicides, that we have the cooperation of both the District Attorney's office and the Monterey County Sheriff's Office, and that a major manhunt is being mounted."

Roth paced by the window, his profile unflattering. Dewitt couldn't believe the way the guy dressed; he wouldn't be caught dead in one of those plaids, much less all of them at once.

"Let me ask you this, Detective Dewitt. If someone came through that door in the next five minutes and confessed to the crimes, but you had no more evidence than you currently have, would Bill Saffeleti have a case?"

Dewitt looked over to Hindeman. It was a rigged question. *No more evidence than you currently have.* "If we had a confession, then we would have a search warrant and we'd likely turn up more evidence, so that's kind of a tricky question to answer."

"But if you didn't turn up more evidence? What I'm asking . . . does any of the evidence hold any promise of linking a particular individual to either of the crimes?"

Attempting to dodge the question, Dewitt said, "We might find the car that left behind that motor oil."

Capp said stridently, "That motor oil doesn't do you no good 'cause all it does is suggest someone was *nearby* the kills. That doesn't give you probable cause. And you sure as hell aren't going to convict a guy with *dog hairs*," he mocked.

62

"We've got fingerprints we're processing," Hindeman reminded.

"Fingerprints?" Roth said in surprise.

Capp countered, "There's no saying the guy who lifted the tape player is the perp. We've been over that. Why weren't there prints, other than McDuff's, found somewhere else in that truck cab?"

Dewitt could feel it slipping away. When someone pulled on the rope really hard, you could often knock them off their feet by just letting go. He said, "Listen, it is circumstantial evidence. I know that." He witnessed the shock register on Hindeman's face. "Enough for probable cause? Doubtful, right now. But like any investigation, one piece of evidence often leads to two or three more. The question we're throwing around is whether or not we inform the public. I, for one, don't want another victim on my conscience. You want to play this differently," he said directly to Manny Roth, "then that's *your* decision. You live with the next kill, not me. Remember, our first responsibility isn't to catch him." Roth viewed Dewitt skeptically. Dewitt affirmed, "It's to *stop* him. I want this guy knowing we're on to him. I want him looking over his shoulder."

"I'll handle the press conference," Hindeman said, his decision obvious.

"Jesus," Roth exclaimed, "this thing's getting out of hand."

Dewitt said, "Getting?" He excused himself and left the room in a hurry.

3

Howard Lumbrowski arrived back at his apartment at a few minutes past four, frustrated by what he considered a wasted day. The place smelled worse than the vacant lot next door. The worn couch and beat-up desk were all that remained of his furniture, excepting the milk crate that held the black-and-white television with a screen the size of a toaster. He'd had a canvas-backed chair at the desk for a while, but the back had blown out and Lumbrowski had tossed the whole thing out the window onto the fire escape, where it still remained.

Things were not going well. He had to find out who belonged to that coke, before it became a major liability. It was either his meal ticket or his death warrant.

There was something about the phone ringing at that exact moment that triggered his cop's distrust of coincidence. You don't serve on the force for seventeen years without gaining certain instincts. He was being watched. Perhaps followed.

He could have allowed it to ring, not answer it, but why? You used people in this business, used whomever you had to use to get the job done. He had tried it the other way for a while—a couple months was all—way back there as a rookie patrolman. However, then he had learned an easier way to get the job done. If you busted a hooker for the fourth time, when both of you knew she was going to do time if she was booked, you offered her a choice: drop to her knees and do you service or drive her downtown and take cutesy photographs with numbers as a necklace. If you had to hit a guy a few times to get the correct story out of him, hit him where he wouldn't bruise. Tricks. Little ways to lubricate a constipated system that reeked of shitass laws meant to protect the very assholes committing the crimes. Why did Lady Justice wear a blindfold? So she couldn't see who was screwing her.

"Yeah?" he answered, checking his watch and wondering whether it was too early to drink a stabilizer.

"It's time we do business," said that same voice. "You must be tired of running around."

"I'm listening."

"For a change."

"Don't push me, pal." Lumbrowski's eyes found the third drawer down in the kitchen. It was in there, lying on its side. Waiting.

"We need to talk. Person to person. Not over the phone. I have photos I think you'll be interested in."

"Photos?" Lumbrowski asked, trying to remember how much available light there had been those mornings. Could someone have actually taken photos?

"That's right. I think you'll be *very* interested in seeing them."

"How much?"

"It's negotiable," said the voice. "Nothing tonight. This is a get-acquainted meeting."

Lumbrowski said, "Talk to me."

"I name the place. You'll be searched by someone. He'll set up the meet. I get any indication you're trying to burn me, you'll never see me again. You waste me, you won't be able to stop those photos. You won't like where they end up. For now, you go back to The Horseshoe. I'll call you there."

The line clicked dead.

"Wrong guy, pal," Howard Lumbrowski said aloud as he entered the kitchen and pulled open the third drawer. He hesitated before reaching inside. It wouldn't be smart to be drunk. This guy wasn't stupid: He had thought it through carefully. He would obviously be watching his every move for the next few hours. He was a professional.

So what the hell had he been doing down at those parking lots at five in the morning?

4

At a few minutes past four, following the autopsy of Malcolm McDuff, which had left his stomach queasy but had yielded some interesting evidence, Dewitt decided to follow up on Lumbrowski's Mustang, his curiosity aroused by that loud door pop earlier in the day. He looked in on Anna—no improvement—and then drove to Lumbrowski's Seaside apartment complex. A few minutes later, he found the powder blue Mustang. It was parked in the apartment building's carport.

Dewitt let Rusty out to roam the adjacent vacant lot and find a place to relieve himself. Rusty tried to initiate a game of chase, then gave up and followed his nose into the lot.

The carport parking spaces were numbered, which meant they were more than likely assigned. Dewitt checked beneath the vehicle, removing a hand covered with motor oil. A triangle of motor oil? he had to wonder. No way to know without running a more objective test—papering a clean floor and parking the car above it—and that kind of test would require a proper warrant. The presence of the oil, combined with De Sica's description of the car, might prove enough to convince Saffeleti to petition a judge for a search warrant, but he doubted it.

The man's voice had the distinct quality of a slowed-down recording. "Defective Dimwit," Lumbrowski said from the stairway entrance, "to what do I owe this displeasure?"

Dewitt came to his feet, removing his handkerchief and cleaning his oily hand. Lumbrowski, a grotesquely huge man, carried a distended gut that stretched his wrinkled shirt at the buttons. His pallid face and flushed neck looked as though they were filled with compressed air. His shoulders hunched forward, the small scars in his face and the permanently swollen knuckles and crooked fingers belonged to a boxer.

"Curiosity," he said, explaining. "We have a witness who I.D.'d a blue and white car at our second kill."

"You know what they say about curiosity and the cat, Defective."

"Yes, the cat gets killed." Rusty barked, rushed up, and greeted Lumbrowski like a long-lost friend.

Lumbrowski petted the dog. "See? *He* likes me, Dimwit."

"I wouldn't take it to heart, Lumbrowski. Rusty once tried to get a mannequin to pet him." He slapped his leg and Rusty heeled at his side. "Tell me something. You ever spend any time down by the Carmel beach?"

Lumbrowski smiled. "I don't have to answer that, Detective." He took a step forward and deliberately crushed Rusty's paw with the toe of his shoe. As the dog yipped in pain, Lumbrowski used the situation to fall forward and throw his weight against Dewitt, slamming him against the Mustang strongly enough to knock the wind from him. "I'm sorry," he said, grabbing Dewitt by the lapels and crushing him against the car again. "Jesus, but I'm clumsy," he said, abruptly dropping both arms.

Dewitt felt like saying something macho: Next time, I won't be wearing the badge—something like that. But the god-awful truth was that Lumbrowski was the wrong guy to pick a fight with. He weighed an easy 240 and was renowned as a former Golden Gloves boxer. So instead, Dewitt tried intimidation. "You might want to get a lawyer, Howie."

"Dream on, Dimwit. You ain't got nothing. You got a plate number? No, I don't think you do, or it wouldn't have taken even you this long. I don't want a lawyer, Dimwit. I want a drink. Now pardon fuckin' me. And watch out for your dog. I don't look too careful when I back up." He opened the door to the Mustang. The hinge cried and let out that painfully loud *thunk* as he jerked it open, and again as he closed it.

Dewitt called Rusty to his side with a single slap and watched as Lumbrowski nearly hit the Zephyr on his way out the drive.

5

Dewitt found District Attorney Bill Saffeleti in the reception area of his Monterey offices preparing to leave for the weekend. Saffeleti didn't offer him a seat. Instead, he said curtly, "I've got drinks with the AG in about thirty minutes. He's down here for Manny's tourney. What's up? Where's the fire?"

"I have a witness from the McDuff crime scene who offered a fairly good description of an aging blue and white sports car. Driver was a big guy." He explained overhearing Lumbrowski's car door and that he had checked the car out, and that it was leaking oil. "I know it's a Friday . . . but this is a homicide, a double homicide, and I'd like to impound Lumbrowski's Mustang and check the pattern of oil." Noting Saffeleti's skeptical expression, he added, "We all get hunches, Bill. If that car *is* leaking a triangle of oil, then I want to impound it and run it by the lab for comparison."

"Oh, Christ, Dewitt," Saffeleti said, turning away, walking a few feet and looking back. "Based on?"

"The eyewitness."

Saffeleti shook his head. "Your *dislike* of Lumbrowski is widely known in the judicial branch. Would you concede that?"

"It's no secret."

"So how do you think this is going to look? The first warrant we pursue is aimed at your archenemy. You're setting yourself up, James."

"Would I be violating his rights by slipping a piece of newspaper under his car?"

Saffeleti said, "You're still collecting evidence." He thought a moment. "Maybe we don't need a warrant just yet. You have a fairly good case for suspicion based on your witness. That may allow you some headroom on collection of evidence." He led Dewitt into his office, located a leather-bound volume on the bookshelf, and leafed through it. He paused twice to read and finally looked up. "That oil could be considered discarded evidence, as when a suspect throws an object from a moving vehicle, and the discarding of the object is observed by law-enforcement officers. That's valid evidence, as long as the object was observed being thrown."

"You're saying that if I actually see a drip of oil fall from the undercarriage of Lumbrowski's Mustang, that slipping a newspaper beneath the car to catch that oil is like retrieving discarded evidence?"

Saffeleti cautioned, "No arrest, no seizure without an exact match, James. An exact match gives you probable cause to suspect Lumbrowski directly. Once the car's impounded, it's up to the lab. If the lab comes back positive, then you can bring him in for questioning . . . *but only questioning*," he reminded.

"Understood."

"If you plan on impounding, make sure you have a one-eighty with you. If it's not on your turf, we'd have a stronger case if a uniform handled it. And make sure you run the license plate through C.L.E.T.S. *after* you check that oil pattern, *before* you impound. With your track record with Lumbrowski, you do this in the wrong order and it will look like entrapment."

6

Dewitt returned to the office to pick up a CHP 180 Impound Form that all the police departments used because it was a good form, and good forms were hard to come by. Ginny, at reception, stopped him with a conspiratorial look and hushed voice. Her skin was very black, her eye shadow a disturbing lime green. She was one of his favorite people here. "James. You have a job like this, you see things now and then that catch your attention because they're out of the ordinary, you know?" She smiled. She was up to something. Purple lipstick today, some of it stuck to her front teeth. "Thing of it is, I *never* see *him* in the records room. Capp," she added, as if he didn't know to whom she was referring. "The man don't know which button to push, for heaven's sake. So maybe I just happen to catch a glimpse of what's in his hand when he comes out, and maybe I happen to see it's one of your reports. Now, James, you know damn well that we gals got to keep strict records of any copies of investigative reports. That's a P.O.S.T. requirement. So maybe I check your master on file in there, and come to find out, there's no record of *his* copies. Now that ain't right, James! If we got to do it right, then so does he."

"When, Ginny?"

"Thing is, James, it didn't click until the second time. I didn't even check until after the second time."

"Second time?"

"McDuff. First time was Osbourne. Didn't record either of them as far as I can tell."

Dewitt thanked her.

"Why's he doing that, James?"

Dewitt shrugged.

"How come the commander don't follow procedures, when the rest of us get screamed at if we don't?"

"That's something I intend to ask him," Dewitt said.

"Oh, by the way," she added, "you've got a visitor."

Dewitt headed to his office, Rusty close on his heels.

"Sam?" he said, catching the man "reading" the *Sports Illustrated* swimsuit edition.

Rusty shoved his nose deeply into the man's crotch and wagged his whole body enthusiastically. The man tried to force Rusty's mug out of his groin, but the dog was too strong. Short but stocky, Hector Ramirez, whom everyone called Sam, carried hard, inquisitive brown eyes beneath a long black unibrow. His face was slightly acne-scarred, his nose oversized and red at the nostrils from a constant battle with allergies. A middle-aged man, he now headed the Department of Justice's fingerprint department in Sacramento. "Only been here a couple minutes. Clarence said he expected you back. Said you wouldn't mind—"

"Not at all."

He wore a dark houndstooth sport coat, blue-and-white-striped shirt, and black knit tie. In the breast pocket of the sport coat was an incongruous pink handkerchief. Rusty shifted his attention and nosed at the trash can. Dewitt sent him packing to his place in front of the file cabinet. The dog collapsed into a heap and sighed.

Dewitt took the visitor's chair. It wasn't terribly comfortable.

"I never wrote about Julia. I should have," Ramirez apologized. "Damn shame."

Dewitt shrugged. "This isn't a social call. You only wear a tie when you're on business."

"Always the observant one."

"The Manny Roth golf tourney and fund raiser? I thought you were a Democrat."

"Not that thing. A quick errand is all. Got to be back in Sacramento by nine tonight."

"It must be something good, or you wouldn't drag it out this long, would you, Sam?"

"I had to speak with Saffeleti about the Sanchez case. Goes to trial Monday morning. Both of us are putting assistants on it and we wanted to iron out some details. I'm also playing delivery boy. These are the records you requested . . . all vehicular asphyxiations over the last five years that resulted in criminal charges. Everything from baby brothers trapping their sister inside the family car, to raging lunatics. It's all yours." The pile was thick and Dewitt realized immediately that he would have to pass along the task of searching these files for similarities to their two homicides. Someone like Nelson could handle it. "But this," Ramirez said, hoisting a manila envelope, "is the real prize."

He tossed the folder across Dewitt's desk to him. "You can thank O'Daly over at the Salinas lab. Some A-hole poured coffee all over an original document that's needed on the Sanchez case: test results of the quarter ton of coke they pulled from the hull of that trawler. You shoulda heard Parker. Christ, he was squirting Hersheys over this thing. Seems no one had thought to make a copy of the test results, no one in the Monterey office, that is. So, for some reason, it was channeled through us . . . through Sacramento DOJ. And, of course, we didn't have the damn thing, so we passed the request on to Salinas, who had done the initial testing. So, this afternoon, a couple hours before I'm scheduled to fly down here, I get a phone call from that hairpie in Salinas saying that if I give you the ALPS runs on the prints from McDuff's truck, she thought she might be able to locate the document we're looking for. Get a load of that, will ya? Some freshman split-tail turning the screws on yours truly! I nearly popped a hemi."

Dewitt opened the envelope and withdrew the many pages of the computer printout. "What do we have here, Sam?"

"Like I said, a gift."

Dewitt looked up. "You're going to make me read through all this?"

"This O'Daly had sent us thirty-five separate latents, including fourteen partials from wires beneath the dash. Tricky partials, I might add. Very few whorls and loops. Photos show 'em one through fourteen," he explained. "You know how the ALPS works: Computer searches the data base for similar patterns to the prints we scan in. Partials like this means we tie the sucker up forever; computer has to work its brains out. The one you're interested in is labeled number seven." Dewitt sorted through and found it. "All the others proved a wash. No hits. A couple proved to be McDuff's."

"Number seven has priors?"

Ramirez directed Dewitt to a photocopy of an arrest record near the bottom of the pile. "Marvin Wood is your man. Presently living in Seaside. Out on probation on grand theft. A sheet of priors a mile long. Seems he likes to lift car stereos. Sound familiar?"

Dewitt eagerly fumbled through the pile of papers and finally located Wood's paper-clipped file. His mug shots showed a black man with wide-set eyes, a gentle face, and a flat profile. He was listed as six-foot-one, 210. Single. Arrested nine times. Convicted twice. Probation both times. He had been on probation for most of the last three years. Probation report listed current employment at the Shell station in Carmel.

"We can *prove* Wood was inside McDuff's car," Ramirez explained. "We can *prove* he handled the wires that led to the car stereo. You read up on him, you get the idea Wood's not exactly Fulbright material."

"Any of the other prints his?"

"No, not a one."

"So you're on the stand. How do you explain prints on the wires but none anywhere else in the cab?" Dewitt asked. It was his responsibility to troubleshoot, to think three steps ahead.

"Hey, you got some smudges, don't forget. Those could be his. Or he coulda remembered to wipe down the hardware but forgotten about the wires. Or he coulda slipped out of his gloves to feel for the wires. That's fairly common."

"I'd buy that."

"Thank you, Mr. Prosecutor. Listen, I can put Wood inside that car. The rest is up to you and yours."

"No prior assaults," Dewitt noticed, reading Wood's arrest sheet. "Nothing violent in his past at all. That doesn't fit very well with a killer."

"I noticed that, too," Ramirez admitted. "So people change. How's your daughter?"

"Emmy?"

"The one who was hurt."

"That's Anna. Not doing well. Still in a coma."

"If I had a smaller shoe, I could just carry it around in my mouth, Dewitt. It would save me sticking it there. Sorry for asking."

"No sweat. Emmy's doing great. Fourteen years old going on forty. She's been great."

"I hear ya."

"Your family?"

"Rosita and I divorced about two years ago now. I live alone with a cat named Beans and a color TV named Sony. You still got your exotic fish? You had the goddamned Sea World in your place, didn't you?"

"Good memory, Sam. No. Sold them off. Place we're in now is too small. Too many memories. You know."

"Yeah. Me, I sold our bed in a garage sale. Every time I climbed in the damn thing . . . I don't know. I had to sell it. You understand?"

Dewitt nodded. When Ramirez left the room, he reached for the phone.

The first call was to Buford Nelson, the second to Marvin Wood's probation officer, the third to the Seaside Police Department.

7

Clare O'Daly hurt because the chair was cheap and uncomfortable. They conserved on the chairs, the tables, the salaries, even the building itself, electing instead to spend the public's money on chromatograph computers, electron microscopes, and portable lasers. It struck her as odd that the tax-paying public would allow the incidence and severity of crime to exist at present rates, when all it required was money to bring it under control. Law-enforcement agencies suffered from being understaffed, often undertrained, and appallingly underfunded. Clare O'Daly was no politician; she shied away from politics; but she lived in constant amazement that *the people* would choose to live with crime.

The box sat in front of her. It contained all nonorganic evidence collected during McDuff's autopsy. Organic evidence—tissue and blood samples—was sent over on packed ice in red Igloo coolers. Clare nurdled her way around the contents of the box, searching for something interesting with which to begin her work. *Nurdled* was her mother's term for nosing around, and she thought of her mother now, because her mother did not approve of her current lifestyle. Her mother was a Georgia girl, a Georgia *lady* through and through, and though Clare had managed to shake the slight accent, she would never shake off the stigma of having pursued *man's work*. If her mother had had her way, by now Clare would be pregnant, sitting uncomfortably at the kitchen table, probably a soap opera on the tube while something overcooked in the Crockpot. Her mother called every morning asking about men in her life. For the past few months, they had had little to talk about.

The notes concerning the small vial before her read, "Found beneath index and middle fingernails, right hand." She unscrewed the top and peered inside at the pale substance. The thing about a homicide investigation, she realized, was that a dozen or so people contributed equally, most of them in a thankless fashion and unseen. The exciting element of any investigation was the teamwork. They were a small chamber orchestra—the medical examiner, the forensic investigator, the lab technicians, the latent-fingerprint experts, the various cops and patrolmen—autonomous, anonymous, and yet under the confident direction of the investigator who served as conductor. She liked their conductor a lot. They toiled individually, as she did now, taking a sample of the flaky white substance from the vial and preparing it for the chromatograph, a supermachine that overheated a substance to vapor and then computer-analyzed the gasses to determine chemical composition. The resulting graphs, when compared to those in three-ring reference binders, could reveal not only the identity of a substance but often the manufacturer, as well. This graph led her to the area in the notebook labeled SYNTHETIC RESINS. She moved more slowly through these because the graphs were very similar, finally reaching a page that showed an identical graph to the one on the screen. The substance found beneath McDuff's fingernails was a low-grade Plexiglas manufactured by Phillips Petroleum.

She filed it all according to the strict procedures required by a court of law. One of the first things a criminalist learned was that, far too often, damning evidence was collected and examined, only to be thrown out by the courts because of some clerical oversight.

Similarities, she had been taught, are an investigator's signposts. Coincidence did not exist. Because of this, when she came across another vial marked FIBERS COLLECTED FROM EPIDERMIS, she set it aside and began work immediately. From the evidence room down the hall, she removed a sealed petri dish containing the cotton pills found during the autopsy of John Osbourne. Using a comparison microscope that allowed simultaneous viewing of two different items— one dedicated to each eye—she then examined these fibers side by side with those found on Malcolm McDuff. Discovering them to be *similar*, she decided to run chromatographies on both these samples, as well. Minutes later, she was thumbing through the loose-leaf binders, her heart beating quickly, for this was the true stuff of forensics that often catapulted an investigation from the puzzling to the solvable. To be part of that process . . .

She abandoned this reference book and sought another, turning quickly through the pages. Slowing now. Nodding. Eyes jerking between the graphs on the screen and those bound in the notebook. None of the pages offered an exact match, but two-thirds of the screen matched perfectly. Dewitt would certainly be interested in this. He would beg for it! At the top of the page it read:

PERMANENT-PRESS BLENDS
COTTON / POLYESTER % = (60/40)

The rest of the graph remained a mystery to her. A familiar chemical compound of some sort, which she couldn't place. She located yet another reference book of graphs and began turning the pages.

8

"I don't get it," Emmy said from the other side of the dinner table. Lean Cuisine lasagna tonight. "Why don't you just pick this guy up? You've got his prints."

"Legal stuff. I called his PO, his probation officer, and had him call Wood so I would know if he was home or not. He's home. That's a problem for me. California's got this law called *People* vs. *Ramey*. It says you can't arrest a guy in his own home without an arrest warrant having been issued. Normally, all we need to arrest a guy is a good-enough reason . . . probable cause it's called. It's Friday. A big political weekend here. To get an arrest warrant, I would have to get a complaint signed by the DA and walk the complaint through the system; get a judge to sign it. Next to impossible tonight. Tomorrow's a different story, though it may be easier just to wait for the guy to leave his trailer."

"That doesn't seem fair."

"If the law is fair to one side, it rarely is to the other."

"And you *have* to have a warrant?"

"I could arrest him on probable cause, but because of *Ramey*, I'd probably lose him in court."

"You want a bagel?"

Dewitt ate. "Seaside's got the guy's trailer under surveillance. If Wood steps foot outside that trailer, he'll be arrested."

Rusty, sniffing around with his nose to the ground, discovered some fallen crumbs, lapped them up, and then looked to Emmy for more. "Don't beg," she told him.

"You look pretty tonight. What are you up to?"

"Spending the night at Briar's," she reminded.

"I mean where are you going?"

"The mall. Clarence'll drive us over and pick us up."

"Mr. Hindeman. I don't want you calling him Clarence."

"He doesn't care. Why should you?"

"Em, we've been over this."

"*Em, we've been over this,*" she said, imitating him. "Jeez, Dad, what a lame excuse. Just because we've been over something—"

"We've been over that, too!" he interrupted. "Sorry," he added.

"You're uptight because of this case," she said. "Chill out. You're going to get this guy.

"You should leave Rusty tonight. He's looking a little neurotic. Too much time in the back of your car," she added, petting the dog. "You're looking a little stressed-out yourself, Dad," she said, standing and running her hand gently across his temple and pushing his hair behind his ear.

9

Cops are like game on the Serengeti in September: They return to the same water holes. A veteran like Lumbrowski was likely to be found at one of only four or five places.

At eight o'clock, Dewitt spotted Lumbrowski's Mustang at The Horseshoe, a Seaside watering hole whose flashing sign could be seen for blocks. Dewitt took a piece of butcher paper from the trunk. Usually used to wrap evidence, it would make a good surface for the oil to hit. He slid it under the Mustang's engine, anchoring it with stones. How long before a drip pattern would be visible?

He returned to the Zephyr and waited, missing Rusty's company.

Dewitt tried to envision the kills. Did the killer hide inside the victims' automobiles, lying in wait in a beach parking lot or restaurant? Did he sweet-talk his victims—as many psychopaths did—and manage somehow to gain control over them with little or no violence? Did he rig their cars to break down and then arrive in a tow truck, seemingly to provide assistance, but actually to kill them?

Evidence remained the key. The evidence should, if properly arranged, tell him exactly how these murders had been committed.

Ten minutes. Long enough? He fished the Mag-Lite out of his coat pocket and returned to the Mustang, shining the light beneath the car and seeing two large drops had fallen onto the paper. *Similar*, he thought, to the ones found at the crime scenes. One drop to go.

Worried that Lumbrowski might stumble on to him for the second time in one night, he checked through a side window. Lumbrowski was sitting at the bar, drinking. Good.

He kept an eye on the big man, checking the butcher paper periodically. After five minutes, Lumbrowski set the glass down heavily and checked the wall clock. Or was it the pay phone? Nervous. Dewitt could *feel* the man's anxiety. Dewitt decided Lumbrowski was about to leave. Why else was he so restless? When Lumbrowski rose from the bar stool, Dewitt made his move for the front door.

By the time Dewitt was inside, Lumbrowski was back on the stool and Dewitt realized he'd only gotten up to tug on his pants. Lumbrowski's bloodshot eyes rolled slowly in his head as he caught Dewitt in the mirror. "Defective Dimwit," he called out. "Again? Business or displeasure?" Same smoker's voice, like truck tires on pea gravel.

Dewitt nodded hello to a couple Seaside cops he recognized in a booth. They were camped around a half-empty pitcher of beer.

"How's your memory?" Dewitt asked.

"Crystal fucking *Absolut*-ly clear," Lumbrowski responded, hoisting his iceless vodka. He didn't sound a bit drunk, but his slow, protracted breathing gave him away.

Dewitt remained standing, just off to Lumbrowski's right. Bartender asked whether he could get anything for him. Dewitt declined.

"Not even a milk?" Lumbrowski asked. "How about a chocolate milk for you, Dimwit?"

Dewitt glanced absentmindedly at his watch. How the hell was he going to buy himself five to ten minutes? Keep the man thinking. He said softly, "Brow"—an affectionate term others of Lumbrowski's friends used; this caught the man's attention—"as one cop to another, I think I owe you this."

"You're no cop, Dimwit. You're a nitpicker. Always will be. You don't know shit."

"The way it is," Dewitt continued, "I'm going to take you in for questioning on these homicides." He thought it noteworthy that Lumbrowski didn't seem surprised at the use of *homicide* in place of suicide.

Lumbrowski returned his attention to his glass and brought it to his lips. "You weren't on duty, I'd knock your fucking teeth out," the big man said. "What the fuck do you know about investigating a homicide?"

"You want to talk to me now, then we can play this entirely

differently. A person volunteering information is a whole other matter."

"Don't know what you're talking about." He signaled the bartender with a twitch of his index finger. As with a farmer at a livestock auction cuing the auctioneer, the movement would have been lost on anyone other than the bartender. A vodka was delivered. Again the man checked with Dewitt. Again, he declined.

"You know how this works, Howie—"

"Which is more than I can say for you, Dimwit. Get lost." He checked his watch and began tapping his foot impatiently.

Dewitt continued, "I make the offer this once. Next time, it gets ugly. Of course, you're used to ugly, I suppose."

Lumbrowski came off the stool like a bantamweight, lowered his shoulder, and drove at Dewitt like a bull. Dewitt lifted off his feet and landed back first against a table. The four cops came out of their booth in seconds. They hit Lumbrowski in a team tackle. Even so, the former detective dragged them ahead with him as he closed in on Dewitt. Being on duty, Dewitt was forced to either arrest the man on assault charges or get the hell out of there. With a man like Lumbrowski, fighting back was not a smart option. With Lumbrowski still restrained, Dewitt left.

The flashlight confirmed he had stalled long enough: an isosceles triangle of motor oil patterned the white paper. Euphoric, he slipped the sheet of paper out from beneath the car and carried it carefully to the Zephyr. Locating a tape measure in the trunk and exposing a few feet of it alongside the drops of oil, he photographed the triangle to scale for future enlargement, the camera's flashes punctuating the darkness. He placed a sample of the oil into a small vial and labeled it. This done, he sealed the butcher paper in a large plastic bag. He picked up the radio's hand grip microphone, but then rethinking, decided against it. It would be too risky to mention over the radio the link between the impounding of the Mustang and the murder investigations. If the press picked up on it, he'd have himself a scene. As a precaution, he blocked the Mustang with the Zephyr and then searched for a pay phone.

A check of the C.L.E.T.S. computer system revealed registration to Lumbrowski. A uniformed patrol would be dispatched from Seaside immediately, a tow truck to follow.

Dewitt returned directly to the Mustang to inventory the car prior to its being impounded, the CHP 180 form in hand. Excited, he forgot about the loud pop the door would make. He froze momentarily at the sound of it.

The interior light came on, illuminating the well-worn bucket seats in a yellow pallor. Dewitt reached toward the glove compartment.

Without a warning, a hairy claw took him from behind and a monstrous weight crushed down on him. He was jerked backward by the hair. "Get outta my fuckin' car," Lumbrowski's voice rasped in his ear. Dewitt smelled the hot acrid odor of a man who hadn't showered in days. His neck jerked backward and a ten-pound ball of knuckles, skin, and hair split his lip. Dewitt reared backward. Lumbrowski's head smacked the convertible's frame. He stumbled away from the car. Dewitt scrambled out of the car, ready for the fight, but Lumbrowski stopped abruptly and brushed himself off. He finger-combed his hair and nodded at Dewitt. His hand came out bloody. "Okay," he said. "Truce."

Dewitt didn't understand the change in attitude until he saw a Seaside radio car approaching. It pulled to a stop. The driver, in no hurry, had obviously not witnessed their struggle. He said hello to Lumbrowski by name, nodded at Dewitt, saying, "You must be Dewitt."

Smart kid.

To Lumbrowski, Dewitt said, "We're impounding your car as possible evidence in a homicide investigation."

"What?" Lumbrowski whined, realizing if his car was towed, he would not only risk missing the phone call from the snitch but wouldn't have a car in which to get anywhere. "This is bullshit, Dimwit."

"Do it," Dewitt told the uniform, touching his raw lip and coming away with blood on it.

"You all right, sir?" the uniform asked, suddenly realizing both men looked disheveled and were breathing hard.

Dewitt glanced at Lumbrowski, knowing he had the opportunity to file assault charges but realizing how it could bias the entire investigation by making it appear that the attention on Lumbrowski was motivated by personal reasons, not professional ones. Better to pretend nothing had happened. "Fell down," he said unconvincingly.

"This is a stupid thing to do, Dimwit," Lumbrowski warned. "It'll never hold."

"It'll hold, Lumbrowski. I'm not worried about that. I'd get a lawyer if I were you."

"Meaning?"

"That requires translation?" Dewitt asked. And as long as I have a witness standing right here," he said, referring to the cop, "you are hereby requested not to leave town."

"Leave town?" Lumbrowski griped. "In what?"

Dewitt waited for the tow truck, and then left the Mustang in the care of the uniform, as Saffeleti had advised. He had turned up nothing of use in his initial inventory. He needed a warrant to dig any deeper and still protect the evidence. He planned to head home and complete the 180, fully aware he faced an uphill battle of obtaining a warrant on a Saturday, even with all the paperwork properly handled. His temptation was to rush everything: get the vial of oil to the lab tonight, compare the triangle of oil on his butcher paper to the scaled photos from the crime scenes. The lab had been closed for hours, however. To convince Brian Marney, the director, to open the lab on a Saturday would be quite the accomplishment, but he just might win that one— homicide investigations had a way of creating exceptions. Friday night? No way.

At nine, he stopped by Clarence's to discuss Lumbrowski.

When Tona Backman opened the door, Dewitt felt an immediate sense of unease, because Clarence wouldn't invite Tona over when

Emmy was spending the night. Their time together limited, these two tended to make the most of it. It was on these nights that Dewitt took Briar, not the other way around. Tona, a runner and a horsewoman, carried a casual elegance in her slim and well-toned body. She wore a brilliant blue dress and was barefoot. On the table behind her, Dewitt saw the remains of their dinner still on the plates.

"It's James," she said enthusiastically, as if he hadn't interrupted.

Hindeman rounded the corner.

"Surprise," Dewitt said, not entering. "What time were you going to get the girls?"

"Me?"

"I dropped Em over here."

"Right, and I drove them to the mall, and you're supposed to pick them up and take them home."

"I thought they were staying here."

"You guys are thick, especially for cops," Tona interrupted. "Em says she's staying here. Briar says she's staying there. Oldest trick in the book."

"Talbot," Dewitt said. "The guy has been sniffing around the bushes in the past few weeks. Has his own car. Shows up at odd hours. Gives me the creeps. I checked him out with Tammy Cary, the attendance supervisor at the high school. He's a complete JD. I warned Em off him. That was brilliant thinking, huh?"

"A Conquistador?" Hindeman asked.

"A what?" Tona questioned, signaling Dewitt, who again refused to go inside.

"Conquistadors," Hindeman told her. "There's been a string of well-hushed-up pregnancies in the past two months. One of the boys held responsible was being charged with statutory and he plea-bargained information on a teen gang calling themselves the Conquistadors."

"The object," Dewitt said, "is to 'have' the most virgins by year's end."

"That's *disgusting*."

To Clarence, he said, "From what Tammy's told me, it wouldn't surprise me one bit. He views himself as a Ferris Bueller type."

"I'm coming with you," Hindeman said, turning toward the hall.

"Let me have a look around first. See if they're at the mall. See if there is a party. I'll give you a call."

10

He spent thirty minutes at the Monterey Mall, a favorite teen hangout, and then checked the phone book for the address.

Several cars crowded the driveway of the Pebble Beach home. Rock music pounded loudly. He blocked the driveway with the Zephyr, radioed in that he was going off duty, and locked his gun inside the glove compartment. A civilian father, he marched angrily to the front door and opened it without knocking.

The rooms were dark, the music unbearably loud. He smelled the heavy stench of pot smoke.

Switching on the lights got their attention. Kids wrapped in pairs. He began moving frantically room to room. He broke in on one teen couple in the throes of lovemaking, switched on the light and told them to get dressed. He found Briar, Emmy, Billy Talbot, and another boy in the hot tub out back, all of them naked. Emmy kept herself together quite well. Briar came undone. "I'll be in the living room," Dewitt said.

A few of the kids escaped. Dewitt ordered anyone who had driven to phone their parents. He found an empty paper bindle, a mirror, and a razor blade on the coffee table.

Talbot approached from Dewitt's left in a terry-cloth robe. He was a good-looking athletic kid.

"Parents home, Billy?"

"You didn't knock."

The gall, he thought, the *audacity*.

"Are they due home?"

"You're here uninvited, Mr. Dewitt. You have not shown me any kind of warrant. You are trespassing."

The boy's stoned expression was almost frightening in its coldness. When Dewitt had been a kid, the word had been *warped*. Billy Talbot was warped: the embryo of intellect developing improperly. "So call the police."

"We might have worked this out," said Billy Talbot in an improbable monotone as his friends continued to use the phone. "There was no need for this."

"These girls are underage, Billy. That can mean serious charges. Very serious."

Talbot smirked, cocky and insolent. "I thought you're supposed to be catching this murderer. Or are high school parties more your speed?"

Dewitt turned abruptly and took a step toward the boy, his intention obvious.

"Try it," the kid challenged, drawing him on with an inviting wave of his fingers. Big, tough Billy Talbot. Dewitt stopped. The investigation was wearing on him: Threatening a kid was something Howard Lumbrowski would do.

"Or maybe you guys are too busy down at the station snorting the dead dude's soda to actually look for the guy who killed him."

"What are you talking about?" Dewitt was genuinely puzzled for a moment.

"From what I hear, the dead guy was carrying some coke that never got delivered. I hear you guys found it and haven't said anything about it." Talbot was showing off now, growing even cockier. Seeing Dewitt's surprised expression, Talbot said, "Shit, you *didn't* know, did you? You cops are too fuckin' stupid for words. Don't you know *anything*?"

"How could *you* know, Billy? Was he *your* connection?"

"I just told you: You hear things."

Had Dewitt told Emmy that they suspected Osbourne of dealing? Had he mentioned it around Emmy? Had Emmy violated one of their most sacred agreements, to *never* discuss police business with anyone but himself? He looked over at her now, searching those young eyes that reminded him of his wife, but he came up blank. "Amelia, wait with Briar in the car, please," he said curtly. Emmy backed out, leaving Dewitt alone with Talbot in the living room.

He took a couple of steps toward the boy, then a deep breath to settle himself. "Where was this coke supposed to be delivered, Billy?" Behind his anger, Dewitt felt a sense of urgency, too. There might be a lead here. "You heard a shipment never arrived," Dewitt guessed, making it a statement. Talbot did not reply. "Listen, boy, this may be your way out of one hell of a lot of trouble. You want to think about that, or you want to try your luck at a charge of contributing to the delinquency of a minor? I can make that stick, Billy."

Talbot stared blankly at Dewitt.

"Do you understand this is a murder investigation? *I'm not fucking around here!*"

Talbot blinked; the intensity in Dewitt's voice had startled him. He looked away, then back at Dewitt. He said, "There's coke in the school, right? Weekends come along and demand goes up. You hear things, that's all."

"Go on."

"I *heard* that if you wanted anything for the weekend, then you had to buy early Thursday, and you had to pay a few bucks more. Supply was down, so the price went up."

"What else did you *hear?*" Dewitt prompted. "If you don't give me specifics, Billy, you're sizing yourself up for a pair of bracelets."

"I *heard*, you know, from no one in particular, that the guy who bit it was carrying, that someone might have been expecting a delivery that never happened. The way I heard it, you guys lifted the soda and then decided to keep it out of the news. It caused a few impromptu vacations from the area, if you understand me." This kid seemed to get all his lines from "Miami Vice."

"A name would help your situation a lot, Billy."

Talbot grinned. It was a practiced expression, intended to imply a knowing slyness. He looked stupid. "These kinds of people don't have names, Mr. Dewitt. Trust me, the guy was carrying an ounce of coke, whether you guys found it or not."

*   *   *

The first parent arrived then and spoke with Dewitt privately, concerned, it seemed, more with the legal ramifications for himself than with how sex, drugs, and alcohol might affect his son. This first experience stunned Dewitt, but it prepared him for the parents who followed. Most had the same legal concerns.

Talbot grew impatient, and was less able to hide his intoxication as the hour wore on. He protested loudly on several occasions, from his confident repose in an overstuffed chair. Each of his complaints came closer to a direct threat. Did Dewitt realize what he was doing? Did Dewitt know that crashing parties brought people bad luck? The threats began to wear on Dewitt, but he refused to show it, refused Talbot any success.

When the last of the kids was gone, Dewitt walked over to Talbot and, looking down at the boy, said, "What you're going to learn someday, Billy, is that playing it tough is risky because there's always someone tougher than you."

"My sentiments exactly," agreed Talbot, deliberately misconstruing Dewitt's warning.

"I'll be checking in with the narco boys. Your name comes up in the future and you're dead meat. This time, we'll let it slide."

"You wouldn't want to drag Emmy into this, would you?" Talbot asked.

"As for having sex with fourteen-year-old girls . . . you can be put away for *years*. Put away in places where guys tape your ankles to broomsticks and take turns checking your oil. Loads of fun."

"I'm trembling all over. Can't you see?"

"You think I'm joking? I'll arrange a little tour for you and your pals."

"Me? I think you're a hypocritical asshole, Mr. Dewitt. I think if Emmy hadn't been at this party, you would have driven right by tonight. Or is this some sort of teen crusade you're on? Am I missing something here?"

"What you need, Billy, is some physical education."

"Ready when you are," the boy said.

11

Dewitt reached home in a foul mood, Emmy silent in the backseat. As he turned the car off, he said, "This is life without parole, young lady. You're grounded forever. No phone privileges. No arguments. When you're ready, I'd like a full explanation and an apology. No bullshit, Amelia. I won't tolerate any more bullshit. Now go to your room and stay there."

She ran from the car in tears, fished in her purse for keys, and let herself inside. Dewitt remained behind the wheel, hating himself, wishing Julia were around to balance him out, wishing this case was solved and that life could get back to normal—whatever that was.

Clare's note was taped to the door. "Have some interesting stuff. Call."

She dropped off her notes a few minutes later. He invited her in for a drink, but his invitation was less than enthusiastic, and she declined.

Interesting stuff, indeed, he thought as, drink in hand, he reviewed her lab report. Plexiglas under McDuff's nails. From his work, or had he been scratching at Plexiglas immediately prior to his death? The cotton/polyester pills found on the skin of both men seemed to be "identical" and had been treated with the same commercial bleach, though Clare had yet to identify the manufacturer. The tread of the bicycle tire indicated a Korean brand manufactured exclusively for Schwinn. Clare was in the process of getting paint samples from the company to compare with the flakes of paint found in McDuff's truck.

As a former criminalist, Dewitt knew the feeling: The evidence was building, the investigation gaining momentum. It took him two Scotches and an hour and a half to fall asleep.

He came awake with a start at 3 A.M. "Dad, Dad." Emmy leaned over, shaking him, her breath still tainted with the beer of the party. Emmy, who lived with nightmares of her mother's death. Despite all his anger, he immediately felt sorry for her. He prepared himself to talk her through it as he had dozens of times. Blue light from a street lamp colored the walls of the room. Slanted shadows formed patterns like prison bars. "Someone's out there," she whispered. "Out back. Dad, Dad."

He pulled himself out of bed and tried to clear his head.

"I heard someone out there."

"Rusty," he explained, coming to his feet sleepily.

"No. Rusty hasn't even barked."

"It's raining," he said, reaching the window. "That's all you heard." Then, spotting the open gate, he exclaimed, "Damn! The gate's open. It *was* Rusty."

"I suppose Rusty opened the gate? I heard the shed door *twice*. I'm sure I did." She handed him his holster and gun. "Please."

This was something she never did. Dewitt looked at her curiously and accepted the weapon. "Stay here," he said.

Dewitt pulled on a pair of pants and, gun in hand, walked through the kitchen, unlocked and headed out the kitchen door. A warm rain fell on his shoulders. Silver drops slipped in single file from the back-porch light like teardrop diamonds. He called for Rusty, whistling the three-note tune that was theirs and theirs alone. The young stud was probably out terrorizing the bitches of the neighborhood. Six months ago, he had broken through a garage window to get to a Labrador in heat. Dewitt put the gun in his pocket and inched his way down the back steps in the dark, the vines to his left extinguishing the porch light. He smacked his shins against the wheelbarrow and cursed. It wasn't in the shed as it belonged. Tempted to return inside and get his flashlight, he turned and saw a worried Emmy in the doorway. She got the flashlight for him. Dewitt kept hoping to hear the familiar rattle of Rusty's collar. Instead, he heard the roar of the rain striking the vegetation.

With the fog-clouded illumination of the flashlight leading him, James pushed past a stubborn branch, soaking his trousers, and broke into the shrub-choked driveway, less than half its functional width. The weather-beaten wood of the dilapidated toolshed held oddly shaped patches of shifting shadows on the twin barnlike doors. The bolted piece of two-by-four that served to hold the doors shut was rotated out of its opposing block, leaving the doors hanging open a crack. Dewitt stepped closer, thinking, Something's wrong. He spread the light around him, suddenly uneasy. Perhaps Emmy had heard someone. His hand touched the butt of the gun.

Something moved inside. He turned violently and shined the light into the black void of falling rain.

Just as quickly, he reversed his position, for a gust of wind tore open the shed doors in a rusty-hinge scream. Instinctively, he raised the gun and trained it on the shape looming before him. He called out a warning, his words clipped as his slower left hand leveled the light on that shape in the shed.

There, not ten feet away, was this man's best friend, Rusty.

Hanging by the neck.

5
SATURDAY

1

Grief had earned its place as an uncomfortable bedfellow for James Dewitt, a luxury he could not afford given the emotional hair trigger that had been forced upon him by recent events. For Emmy's sake, he had been living in a delicately dangerous no-man's-land, preserving what remained of himself after that day in the courthouse. Rusty's murder nearly threw him over the edge. He spent hours in the rain searching the small property for any sign of an intruder, any evidence, his only discovery a small piece of ground beef—tainted, by the smell of it.

He had two prime suspects, Howard Lumbrowski and Billy Talbot.

He had aggravated both the day before, either could have sought to punish him. What toyed annoyingly in the back of his head was the realization he had put hundreds of men and women in jail with his testimony as a forensic investigator. Any one of these persons could have caught up with him. Such a consideration was so enormous in scope, he held it back with leather reins prohibiting its advance.

The pink iridescence of morning found him exhausted and slightly drunk, a rosy blur flooding the broken sky, a similar blur of memory and Scotch flooding his thoughts. He drank in silence as Emmy nibbled at a bagel, her appetite gone, her smooth-skinned brow furrowed into a knot of worry, glancing over at him occasionally as if she didn't know him.

"Could we do it today?" she asked. He knew to what she was referring; her tone of voice told him that. "I'd like to get it over with. It would be better for *both* of us, I think."

"I suppose we could—" he began, but his words slurred and he stopped in embarrassment. He slid the glass beyond his immediate reach.

"I think we should get it over with right away. We could ask Clarence and Briar to come."

"Mr. Hindeman," he corrected.

She didn't like it. She pushed away from the table in disgust and glared defiantly at him. "This afternoon would work for me," she said, as if her life were tightly scheduled. "Get your act together, Dad."

"My act," he repeated softly, stretching to retrieve the glass.

"Can we get him cremated on such short notice?"

He nodded slowly, his head heavy. Emmanuel could arrange it for him.

"Am I still grounded?" she questioned from the hallway.

Dewitt shook his head, though she couldn't be sure he had heard her.

"Can I help, Dad?" she asked in a voice trembling with concern.

"You do help," he said with a lump in his throat. "More than you could possibly know, Em. Without you . . ." He hung his head.

That brought her to tears and to his side, into his arms in an embrace of desperate worry. "I'm right here, Dad," she said.

Dewitt nodded, a headache thumping around in his skull like something was loose. When the phone rang, he checked the clock in panic: 8:30. "Thank God," he said.

2

The gray fabric walls of Peter Tilly's office cubbyhole at the Seaside Police Department were covered in posters and cutouts from calendars of bronzed, sinewy divers, male and female—mostly female. Outrageous bodies in high-cut spandex, hard nipples and firm buttocks. The picture of Tilly blended in well.

Tilly appeared as fit today as he was in the photo, a Southern California boy all the way—beach-blond hair, baggy clothes, a gold I.D. bracelet, blue eyes, and a hard jaw. He wore contact lenses and squinted continually. When the man moved and his coat opened, Dewitt spotted the nickel-plated .38. Flashy. Dick Tracy gone Yuppie. He spoke in a smooth high tenor, an unusual voice. Tilly, who kept a pair of Heavyhands on the edge of his desk, was working a springed hand exerciser in his right hand.

"I talked to Saffeleti just now," Tilly said. "The deputy DA on-call wanted me to check with the boss. It's been cleared for us to search the trailer. Paperwork's on its way over. He's all pissed off 'cause it's the weekend. You want to talk to Wood first, or check the trailer out?"

"We didn't violate the *Ramey*?" Dewitt asked. He thought it only polite to say *we*.

"Hell no. That's why we had the place staked out all night, isn't it? Wood came pimp-rolling out of his place this morning, and our boys picked him up. Piece of cake. We didn't screw with *Ramey*. We're not dumb over here you know . . . just overworked." He smiled. He had perfect teeth and thin bloodless lips. "You don't look so good, Dewitt. That your Don Johnson look, or what?"

Dewitt felt as if he was walking on eggshells, because technically this was Tilly's arrest. He ignored the man's comments and recommended they search the trailer first.

"Just so we understand each other," the young detective said, "I've been working for a couple weeks on a thing. Some stores here sell legitimate car stereos up front of the store, but install hot stereos of the same models into the cars. Guys like Wood feed them their hot stereos, which is to say I have an ongoing interest in your perp. I got no quibbles with you; your homicides obviously take priority here. But if you could toss me some scraps . . . you know, if I could get a couple of minutes with him . . . I'd really appreciate it. I could use an insider on this thing. We know what's going down, but we're having one hell of a time proving it."

"Fine by me."

"Good. Thanks."

"We'll need a uniform with us when we search."

Sensing Dewitt's impatience, Tilly stood. "Got one ready and waiting. Let's go."

A set of rotted wooden steps led up to the lime green mobile home. The windows were clouded with brown soot. A regiment of black sugar ants streamed along a piece of corrugated siding, disappearing into an unfilled drill hole where a rivet had rusted out. A bed of yellowed litter had been pressed into the mud—a newsprint lawn. No more than ten feet separated one trailer from the next; Dewitt could hear a Neil Diamond song playing inside the adjacent, decaying Airstream.

Dewitt handed Tilly a pair or surgical gloves. "Put these on, please."

"You got to be kidding me." He put on the latex gloves then, as Dewitt had already done.

"Top to bottom," Dewitt explained. "Systematically and thoroughly. I'll take the back. Any questions, any problems, I want to hear them now, not next week at this guy's prelim."

"Fuckin' pigsty," said Tilly, fanning the air.

With the curtains drawn, the interior of the small trailer felt even more confining. A car seat was propped up on several milk crates facing a banded-up black-and-white television that utilized a bent coat hanger as an antenna.

Dewitt searched the kitchen first. The refrigerator held four cans of beer, ketchup, mustard, eggs, and a half quart of whole milk. The frost-encrusted freezer compartment contained several frozen dinners stacked next to half-empty ice trays. A Baggie partially filled with pot had been pushed to the back. This tiny quantity wouldn't even be discussed by Saffeleti. Strictly misdemeanor.

He continued down the confining passageway into the back, encountering foul odors in the phone–booth-sized bathroom, green-black mold having taken over every crack in the cheap pink tile, the surface of the plastic shower curtain, and the base of the toilet. Dewitt used his pen to move things around.

The bedroom was no more than an oversized vertical coffin with a closet wide enough for six hangers. It smelled like a very old sneaker. The sheets might have been washed several months earlier—anybody's guess. Stack of dog-eared *Playboy*s by the lamp and a near-empty bottle of Vaseline Hand Care. Clothes in piles on the floor: dirty, dirtier, dirtiest. Dewitt discovered a small removable panel that lead to the hot-water heater, and alongside it, a cardboard box containing a variety of impressive electronic gear.

"Got something," he called out, carrying the box out into the cramped kitchen.

Tilly joined him and looked over his shoulder. The cardboard box contained several cannibalized car tape decks and a Panasonic cellular phone. Dewitt moved the decks around with his pen as Tilly steadied the box.

"The way it works," Tilly explained, to hear himself speak, "a guy hits a car tonight, he puts his take away, puts it in inventory for a few weeks so it can cool down. Tomorrow, he fences something he ripped off a couple weeks ago. All of 'em got inventories like this. What exactly are we looking for, Dewitt?"

"This baby," Dewitt said, reaching the deck on the bottom of the pile. "Pioneer car stereo, model KP–fifty-five-fifty." He handed the machine carefully to Tilly, who took it by the edges in his gloved hands. Dewitt stepped toward a window for light, flipping through the well-used pages of his notebook. After a moment, he said, "Serial number: HF twenty-one-seven—"

"No good," interrupted Tilly. "He's scratched up the numbers. No good."

Dewitt told him, "Doesn't matter. We have McDuff's car. We have confirmation of Wood's prints on wires beneath the dash." Dewitt pointed to the clipped wires leading to the back of the stolen car stereo. "If this is the fifty-five-fifty taken from McDuff's truck, then we should be able to show tool markings and match up all the wires. I'd like to find a toolbox. That would help with the tool markings. But chances are, we've got him with this alone. Let's write it up and rush it over to the Salinas lab."

"On a Saturday?"

"There's someone over there by now. Some other evidence—" he said, catching himself. Lumbrowski had been a Seaside detective, and loyalties ran high among departments.

"Has he invoked?" Dewitt stared through the two-way mirror at the big black man sitting restlessly at the interrogation table. Standard procedure was to let some time pass between the reading of the Miranda and the interrogation. If the perp invoked the Miranda, you had to leave him alone until the hearing. Some invoked. The seasoned ones knew that a good deal of the bargaining took place before any official filing. The only chance to walk away clean from an arrest was to cooperate fully, and always in the presence of an attorney.

"No," replied Tilly. "Arresting officer thought he might be high," he said, reading the sheet. "He looks kinda high," he added. "He requested a PD be assigned to him."

"Experienced. Who's on-call?"

"Mahoney's on her way. You know her?"

"No."

"Too bad for you."

"How long 'til she gets here?"

"Not long. If I know this one, she was out sucking off the deputy

AG all night. She's a comer, Dewitt . . . in more ways than one, if you follow. Has her sights set on the Attorney General's office. We call her 'Lay-ya Moaning' around here. A real Crusader Rabbit, she can be a real bitch. A regular nympho from what I hear. Jumps everything in sight, uniforms, brass, other PDs, DA's office. Anything she can find."

"You have any coffee?"

"If you can call it that."

Five minutes later, Dewitt entered the room with a cup of burned coffee. The interrogation room smelled like cigarette smoke and armpits. One sip of the coffee and it suddenly tasted the same. He placed it out of reach.

Wood didn't look up. He knew Dewitt wasn't his PD. Probably knew them all by name. "What we've got here, Marvin, is a big problem," Dewitt said.

No reaction.

"Big, as in capital *B*, capital offense." Dewitt waited. "You think I'd be here at ten on Saturday morning if this thing was about stealing a car stereo? Think about *that*, Marvin," he said, circling him now, talking behind the man's head. "You know the system. Why the hell would a Carmel detective be talking to a pink-sheeter like you on a Saturday morning?"

"We wait, whitebread. And the name ain't Marvin, it's Wood, man. We wait for my main man, then we talk."

"When was the last time a lawyer helped you, Wood*man*? I mean actually helped? *I* can help you, Woodman. This is *my* case. It isn't Detective Tilly's, it isn't even Seaside's. This is *my* case. You do any trading, any negotiating, it's going to be with me. You wait for your PD, you get a lawyer all involved, and this thing is going to get real messy. Bad. You follow? You want to know why? Because I'm investigating two *homicides*, Marvin. And guess who my prime suspect is?" He was across the table from him now, staring into stoned eyes. "You hear me, Woodman?"

Wood leaned up on one cheek and broke an enormously loud

amount of wind and smiled slightly. "I hear ya, whitebread. Still, I best wait for my man."

The smell was horrible. Dewitt fanned the air. "It isn't whitebread, Woodman, it's Detective Dewitt. Kiss your foul ass goodbye, *dude*. I'm talking two counts of murder one." He paused by the door, hoping the man might change his mind.

The door banged open and she stormed in. "As I understand it, Detective," Mahoney began before offering an introduction, "my client requested representation *prior* to counsel. The door's behind me. I'll call you when, and *if*, we're ready." Mahoney took off her jacket, read from a folder, and then looked up at Wood. She stood with a broomstick posture, breasts thrust out, nipples denting the sheer fabric. Not much of a face, stretched skin on a frame of sharp bones, a pointed chin and matching hook nose. Cats' eyes. Wood stared straight at her breasts. She seemed accustomed to it. She perched her sumptuous butt on the edge of the table, her skirt hiked up to mid thigh, her legs long, slender, and muscular. Two different women: awkward, birdlike, and self-conscious behind the face; bold, beastly, and well-provided from the neck down. "We're waiting, Detective."

Dewitt left the small room and closed the door. "She's a hardass," he said to Tilly.

"Depends on who you talk to," Tilly said. "Like I say, that ass gets around. Rumor is that those lips of hers can suck a cork out of a wine bottle." He added, "And I'm not talkin' about her mouth."

When she finally called him in, Leala Mahoney studied Dewitt, regarding him, it seemed, as a butcher might regard a side of beef. In his case, disheveled, exhausted beef. She was staring. She squirmed and shifted restlessly in her chair, the tip of her tongue moistening her already-glossy lips, which she had set in a beguiling smile. She preened herself, continually tucking this into there and smoothing this flat and tugging on that. Her voice was naturally creamy, her hair had been weaved in streaks of blond, and he was guessing she was somewhere in her early thirties and that she wore pigmented contact lenses. No one could possibly have eyes that green. He nearly asked her to stop doing that with her tongue.

"I can only assume, Mr. Dewitt, that your presence here at Seaside indicates—what would I call it?—an *interest* in my client that perhaps supercedes the present charges."

"That's true, Counselor. I explained that to Woodman, here. He didn't seem too interested."

"I be interested, whitebread. I just got to wait for my—"

"Main *man*," Dewitt interrupted, hoping to irritate Mahoney. She struck Dewitt as a woman proud of her accomplishments in what had once been a predominantly male profession—criminal law. It would be to his benefit to drive a wedge between Mahoney and Wood if he could.

"Am I correctly informed, Detective Dewitt, that you are heading up the current homicide investigations and that Mr. Wood's detention is somehow related to this investigation?"

"I don't want nothing to do with no murders," said Marvin Wood in a low guttural growl.

Some PDs insisted on interrupting every other sentence and breaking your train of thought. Dewitt tested the waters. "That may depend on your willingness to cooperate, Woodman. What I'm telling you, Woodman, and you, Counselor, is that we—I—can make this just as hard on both of you as I want. Okay? What I have here," he said, waving the folder at them, "is hard evidence connecting you, Woodman, to a pickup truck in which a murdered man was found." He watched for Wood's reaction and actually felt disappointment when the man looked so genuinely surprised. "Cooperation is the name. Besides me, on the other side of that mirror are a couple of cops who are just dying to bust you on grand larceny—"

"Ain't no *grand* larceny, man. Alls I done is lifted a car stereo."

"You've lifted at least a half-dozen car stereos, Woodman. We did a little work on your water heater, if you understand what I'm saying."

"Shit. Man, I got me a job at stake here!"

"Mr. Wood is concerned that violation of his probation and the present charges may restrict his ability to retain his current employment," the woman said, brushing off something from her padded shoulder.

"If you like the job," Dewitt said, "then start talking."

Reading, Mahoney informed Dewitt, "The terms of Mr. Wood's most recent probation dictate he maintain steady employment for a period of no less than eight months, and that should he be charged with a criminal offense, he will be resentenced, with a possible jail term of four years without parole."

"Four years, eh, Woodman? That's a long time to spend *bent over* with your legs spread," Dewitt emphasized, "isn't it? But four years is nothing compared with *life*."

"Fuck you," Wood said.

"You got that wrong. It isn't *me* they'll be fucking. Excuse me," he said to Mahoney, catching amusement in her eyes. "You might keep that in mind . . . a life sentence, Woodman. Maybe we can work with this. Perhaps there's a solution here we're overlooking."

"Fuck you, whitebread. My ass is fried."

Dewitt checked with counsel, who, reading from Wood's folder, nodded at him. Wood knew the boundaries of his probation better than Dewitt. He was obviously a veteran.

"You haven't been charged yet, Woodman. We're just having a talk. You were arrested on *suspicion*."

Wood viewed Dewitt skeptically. "Cut the shit, man. What you trying to say?"

"Yes, what exactly are you saying, Detective?" Mahoney asked, stirring again.

"I would welcome Mr. Wood's cooperation. If I gain the information I need, and if further investigation suggests Mr. Wood was not directly involved in the homicides—"

"Don't want *nothin'* to do with no murders."

"I see little reason why Mr. Wood couldn't walk on the present charges. We might want him later as a witness. Tilly might want his help on another matter. But this is all negotiable, Counselor."

The attorney checked that her client understood Dewitt, which he did. Wood said, "I help you out man."

"Mr. Wood, I'm going to show you a couple of photographs. One of a cream-colored Chevy Luv pickup truck, the other of a Pioneer KP fifty-five-fifty car stereo. According to a statement made by the man's wife, the stereo must have been stolen the day or evening of January eleventh. Possibly the early-morning hours of the twelfth." He handed a Polaroid to Wood, who examined it indifferently. "That particular car stereo was found in your possession. I would like to know how that came about. I need to know exactly *where* that truck was parked. That's my sole interest in this."

"Shit, man, you kiddin' me? When's this again?"

Dewitt repeated, "Wednesday, Woodman. Maybe very early Thursday morning. We're talking two, three days ago."

Wood scratched his head. "You think I keep a diary or something, whitebread? How the fuck, you know, am I supposed to remember that?" He mocked, "A Pioneer fi'ty-fi fi'ty. What the fuck, man?"

"Where do you steal the stereos from?"

"Who says, you know, I stold *any* stereos, man?" He looked to his attorney.

She frowned at him. "Mr. Wood, I would think carefully if I were you. The detective is offering you a trade. You can skate on this charge if you use your head."

"I mean, you know, I hear what you sayin', whitebread, but sheeit, you know, I don't know shit about no fi'ty-fi fi'ty."

"What I'm talking about," Dewitt said harshly, leaning forward, "is this pickup truck. How many pickup trucks did you hit this week, for Christ's sake? You left your prints in the truck. The man was dead. You see how it works? Your prints, a dead body. You need it any more clear than that? What I'm *offering*, what I'm *suggesting*, is that you think real hard before you screw this thing up for yourself. Okay? You stole those stereos, didn't you, Marvin?"

"Yes, sir. That's right. You *know*, that's right," he said, nervously looking between the two. "I stole it, that's right."

"From where?"

He ran his big hand over his mouth and shook his head. "I just cruise around, you know. I see a good hit, I make it. I'm outta there. Where? Shit, man, I don't know where."

"Apparently, I'm not getting through," he said to counsel.

"Mr. Wood," she said in that warm molasses voice of hers, "Detective Dewitt would appreciate it if you would detail for him the locations a person might steal a stereo from, places a person might feel safest. If you can't remember this particular truck, that's fine. This week, what *types* of places did you hit?"

Wood nodded somewhat apprehensively to himself, as if answering some internal question. He clearly didn't trust either of them. "You're askin' me cause I'm like an expert or somet'in," he said to Dewitt. "Is that what this bitch is saying?"

Mahoney delivered a wicked backhand across Wood's cheek. She took him by the chin then, as Dewitt used to take Rusty by the chin, and she said venomously, "I am not a *bitch*, Mr. Wood. I am not a *cunt*. I am not a *broad*. I am not a *split-tail*. I am your attorney. I have a name and you'll address me correctly, or you'll have yourself another public defender, one whom you will find much less tolerant than me. Is that clear?"

Wood's nostrils flared.

Dewitt had never seen a public defender strike a suspect. Marvin Wood seemed less shocked than Dewitt. His nostrils flared, but he said nothing.

"Clear?"

"I gotcha," Wood said.

"From where, Mr. Wood, might you have lifted that stereo?" Dewitt asked.

"The whole deal is to find a car that you *know* ain't gonna get no traffic. Can't be no traffic in the lot, neither. You catch that?"

"Where, for instance?" Dewitt asked.

"Movie theaters, motels is good, city park maybe, you know, during a ball game or somet'in. A couple 'a smaller bars. An office building, you know, the underground garage, you know, at night. You know. Anyplace the man ain't gonna come up and surprise you. Listen up, there are dudes who hit cars in the middle of the day, you know, we're

101

talking about one minute of work. Crack mostly . . . you know, they gotta get their next hit. But not the smart dude. Smart dude wait for dark and pick a spot he know he cool. Hit one car, maybe a couple, and lie low for a few days." He waved his hand and said proudly, "Never hit the same kind of place more than once a month."

Mahoney looked over at Dewitt. Dewitt had caught it, too. "So you *do* keep track of the places you've hit," he said. "You must keep track or you'd repeat."

"The *kind* of place. Sure. But not no Pioneer fi'ty-fi fi'ty. Not no Chevy Luv truck."

"What *kind* of places did you hit this week? What *kind* of places are off your list right now?"

"Right now? No more motels right now." He looked to the ceiling. "Hey, that's it, right, whitebread? I probably hit it at a motel, 'cause I'm staying away from motels right now." Wood looked first to Dewitt and then to Mahoney.

Dewitt nodded at him and said, "What we're going to do, Wood, is run some lab work on your car, its contents, and your trailer. If you weren't involved in the actual murders, then more than likely, we can prove your innocence—"

"That'll be a first," he grumbled sarcastically.

Dewitt continued, "I don't believe you killed McDuff, Wood, and I think we can prove it. But you've got to help us. Talk to me about the stuff in that box we found."

"I'm careful, man. That's all. I cut way back on my lifting. I got me a job, I got me probation. Things okay right now. So I'm careful. I happen to lift somet'in', then I sit on the shit at least three weeks, sometimes longer before I fence it, you hear? Word on the street is that Seaside real pissed off about all the car stereo shit going down, so I back way off, right dude? At least three weeks, and then I fence it maybe San Jose or Santa Cruz. I ain't no amateur, man."

"No, you're no amateur," Dewitt agreed. "No one would argue that." He paused. "Which motels are off your list, Wood?" Dewitt asked, thinking that the killer might have cleaned out all receipts in an attempt to hide a particular motel or lounge where the victims had been spotted. For an instant, he could actually see the killer lurking in the shadows, stalking his victims. He felt his blood pressure rise. Was he stalking someone at this very moment?

"I don't *know*, man," Wood moaned. "Shit. Seems to me it was at a motel, man. Okay?" Wood said. Dewitt couldn't tell whether he was simply providing him with what he wanted to hear or telling the truth.

"In Seaside? A motel here in Seaside? Or was it Monterey, or Carmel?" If he couldn't narrow it down, the information might prove useless—the Monterey area had more motels, it seemed, than gas stations.

Wood scrunched his eyes tightly. "Shit, man. Too many fucking questions."

"Think," Mahoney encouraged. "He's willing to make a deal with us, Marvin. You understand? A deal. No charges."

Tilly broke through the door, disturbing the moment and drawing their attention. "You can't go offering that, Dewitt," he said.

"Peter!" Dewitt chided.

"Detective?" Mahoney asked Dewitt.

Tilly added, "You want to trade away the homicide, that's your stupidity, but you sure as hell can't promise 'no charges.' Not without consulting Saffeleti. Not without some discussion."

"You been bullshitting me?" asked a horrified Marvin Wood. Mahoney and Dewitt looked over at him. "Fuck! You *bullshitting* me?"

"Get out of here, Tilly!" Dewitt shouted.

"You can't make that promise," the detective repeated. "That's not right," he told Mahoney.

"Out!" Dewitt took a step toward him. "Shut the door, Tilly!"

Tilly backed off.

"What the fuck?" Wood asked. "You *bullshitting* me?"

"Detective?" Mahoney inquired.

Dewitt looked toward the mirror and glared at Tilly, who he knew was on the other side, ear to speaker box. "Detective Tilly will want some questions answered, as well. I explained that up front. But if you're willing to cooperate, cooperate fully, there's no reason to think you will face charges."

"You're bullshitting me, aren't you, man? What the fuck? Same fucking shit, whitebread. I was *lying* about all of it, man. Okay? Don't know nothin' 'bout no Chevy. Don't know *nothin'*!"

"Marvin," Mahoney pleaded, "don't do this. Trust me."

Wood stared at her. "I want me another PD. I want me a *man*, not some cunt," he said.

Mahoney began packing her briefcase immediately, her motions hard and jerky. Dewitt slumped in fatigue. "Fool," he said to Wood. He waited for her. They left the interrogation room together.

As he pulled the door shut, she said, "I'd like to talk with you in private, Detective, when you have a moment." She didn't wait for a reply; she walked down the narrow hall, hips pumping like pistons, and rounded the corner.

He followed her into the officer's lounge, a room with two worn couches, some folding chairs, a partially melted Mr. Coffee and two concession machines, soda and munchies. Her skirt was hiked up high, her shoes off, and she was rubbing her feet. When she bent over to work on her toes, she offered Dewitt a view of tan full breasts. He wondered whether she was aware of that, deciding, Of course she is. "What a business," she commented.

"I thought we had something going," he said, realizing too late that she might take it as a pass.

"Me, too," she replied in a warmer tone of voice, aiming her green eyes at him.

"You've dealt with Tilly before?"

"Detective Tilly thinks from the waist down," she said, bending over and offering him that view again.

"You gonna call another PD?" he asked.

"To hell with him," she said. "Let Tilly do it. I'm done with this case."

"What do you think?"

"About what he said?"

"Yes. Was he just handing me what I wanted to hear, or was he telling the truth?"

"My opinion?" she asked. "It's not everyone who asks for my opinion."

"I'm asking." His fatigue made him intolerant of her games.

She fiddled with her hair. "He hit that truck, and I think he hit it at a motel and doesn't remember much more than that. From his sheet, I'm guessing Seaside."

Dewitt nodded in agreement. "That's what I thought, too. From his sheet, I'd guess Seaside, but—"

Mahoney cut him off. "Why don't we talk about this later?"

"Later?" Dewitt was surprised, and a little annoyed at the way she interrupted him. Mahoney leaned over to slip her shoes back on. "You look a little tired. Stressed-out. I make a mean cup of espresso, have a hot tub with an outrageous view, and give a hell of a back rub. It is a Saturday, after all."

There it was: the invitation. Dewitt didn't know what to say.

"A massage always helps me to unwind," she said, running her hand through her hair, closing her eyes, and heaving a sigh of exhaustion, with emphasis on the inhale and its effect on her chest.

Escalation. She'd gone from a back rub to a full massage.

"Are you interested?" she said in a lascivious voice.

"What *is* it with you?" Dewitt asked. He was too tired: He knew he should stop himself, but his mouth ran on without him. "Why the show-girl act? You flaunt yourself like there's only one thing on your mind. I don't buy it. You're brighter than that. You have guys like Tilly hard at a hundred yards. Is that the challenge for you? Is that the thrill?" He stood up. "Christ Almighty! Are we doing business here or are you running a singles spa? Espresso and a massage? I'm trying to stop a goddamned killer, in case you missed the headlines. Your client has information I need. That's what *I'm* after. What the hell are *you* after?"

She stood. "Forget it, Dewitt! Fuck you and your white horse."

Her face bunched up like a crushed paper bag. They *were* contact lenses. One of them was coming out. There were tears in her eyes. She stalked toward the door.

"Leala!" Dewitt tried in an apologetic tone, realizing he had gone too far. A lot of good that did.

She paused just long enough to say, "See you in court, sometime, *Detective*. Good luck if I do. We'll see what we see."

Her forced smile was anything but reassuring.

3

Back in his office in Carmel, Dewitt glanced into the corner by the file cabinet, hoping beyond reason Rusty might be there.

"You okay?" Nelson asked, the DOJ files stacked on Dewitt's desk in front of him.

"Wish everyone would stop asking that." He took his seat behind the desk. "So," he said, "you think you've got something."

Nelson set the folder down, as if precious and fragile. "They gave us the stack in alphabetical order," he explained. "It's top-heavy. It took a while to get to the C's. How could there be so many asphyxiations in just five years?"

Dewitt opened the file. On the tab was printed the name Harvey Collette. Inside, the face was thin, gaunt, the expression placid, the skin lactic. Bug eyes and a bottle-cap mouth, remorseless and distant. "Talk to me," he said to Nelson.

"Sacramento area nearly five years ago. Fuckin' file doesn't tell us much except that he staged the asphyxiation to cover rapes. The thing that caught my eye was the use of a PVC fitting and garden hose. It's damn close, Sergeant. I got through all of these," he said, touching the pile.

"If this guy wasn't already in the nuthouse, I'd say he did Osbourne and McDuff."

"PVC?"

"And garden hose."

"Staging the asphyxiation?"

"Made them look like suicides to cover the fact he had actually suffocated them. Trick was, he suffocated them into unconsciousness, raped them, and then got 'em sucking fumes before they came to. Looked a lot like suicide. Nakimita was the one who caught it," he said, referring to the legendary medical examiner. "Found cotton fibers on the tongues of all five victims. From the pillowcases. Guy copped an insanity plea and has been locked up in Atascadero ever since."

"It's good work, Nelson. I'll follow up. You feel like taking on something else? I know you're supposed to be off this weekend. I can pass it along to M.C.S.O. if need be."

"I'm game."

Dewitt dug out Clare's lab report. "It's a Plexiglas made by Phillips Petroleum. I need to know common usage, availability, and dealers in the area. Understand?"

"How it's used and who can get it."

"That's it."

"On a Saturday, I don't know."

"Refineries run twenty-four hours a day. Someone, somewhere knows something. Right?" Dewitt asked.

"That's what we're taught. *If* you believe everything you're taught."

"If you get that handled, then check with M.C.S.O. They have some informants inside the high school. There's a rumor John Osbourne was carrying an ounce of coke. It apparently was never delivered. We sure as hell didn't find it on him. A name or two would help our cause. See what they have."

"You think the kills are drug-related?"

Dewitt shook his head. "With this link to Harvey Collette? No, I don't. I think we're dealing with a copycat psycho. But what the fuck do I know?"

4

Commander Karl Capp lived in a housing development on the north edge of Seaside. Dewitt felt awkward interrupting Capp on the weekend, even having phoned ahead. Capp was a nine-to-five cop.

Charlotte Capp looked like Mrs. Santa Claus, a portly woman with pale skin, Irish cheeks, and legs mapped with varicose veins. "He's in there," she said curtly after opening the door.

Dewitt wiped his feet on a rubber mat that read, HOME SWEET HOME, and found Capp standing in the small living room. It occurred to him that most of the time he saw Capp, the man was sitting down. A toy poodle, wearing a pink collar and a coat of white fluffy fur shot out from behind a forest-green vinyl recliner and wagged its stubby tail vigorously. James didn't touch it.

Capp wore his game face. "This won't take long, I hope."

"Shouldn't."

"Good."

Dewitt reviewed Clare's most recent evidence for the man, the discovery of Harvey Collette, and then said tentatively, "Since I report to you, I wanted to get your agreement that we should put a BOL out on Lumbrowski and bring him in for questioning as soon as possible. I also—"

"Based on?" the commander interrupted.

"The motor oil," Dewitt said. "We've got him dead to rights. He was at both crime scenes."

The commander paced his small living room, his poodle following behind loyally, stub wagging. Dewitt's heart panged for Rusty; he was briefly caught up in memories.

He reminded, "And an eyewitness."

Capp said, "Forget the eyewitness, Dewitt. Too far away to do you any good. And as for that oil . . . you know he beat the impoundment, don't you?"

"What?"

Capp seemed to stumble over his words. "I heard you tried to have the car impounded . . . but that he beat it on a technicality. Thing about the Brow, Dewitt, is you gotta know what you're up against, who you're up against. As I understand it, it was a question of procedure. He's been a cop longer than you. You could bring him in for questioning, but you can only impound the car following specific charges, or if it's in violation of a traffic code. At any rate, he burned it. Deputy DA on-call couldn't reach Saffeleti and wanted no part of it himself. So what I'm saying is, I don't think that oil will do you any good until your ducks are in a row."

Dewitt thought it strange that Capp should know so much detail on a Saturday concerning a Friday-night incident. It was entirely out of character and Capp had that look about him, like a person who had improperly revealed a secret.

"He was at both crime scenes, regardless."

"He was in those parking lots, you mean? Whether or not he was at the *crime scenes* remains to be seen. Let me tell you something about the Brow that may surprise you, Dewitt. The man walks the beaches every morning, real early. Goes back to him and his old lady. It was something they used to do together, and after she . . . died, he kept up the tradition."

"So he just happened to be there? Is that what you're telling me? You sound like a defense attorney."

"Come on, Dewitt, admit it: You're frustrated by this case. You're chasing straws in the wind. Let me tell you something: You got to shift down a gear here, pal. Two kills in three days . . . four days now . . . that's got you all in a snit. Take a long look around you, Dewitt. These cases can go on for *years*. We're talking serial killer here, right? Hindeman says this is your baby, fine. But you're *my* detective. Experience says you downshift a gear and get ready for the long climb. You keep going like this, you'll burn out by the end of next week."

Dewitt nodded, too tired for this kind of lecture. He had such a different relationship with Hindeman. He had to remind himself of Capp's rank. As a subordinate, he was required to follow unspoken as well as written rules. He hesitated before asking, "You wouldn't know anything about a few extra copies of my reports circulating around, would you?"

The commander's face turned scarlet. His piggish eyes focused on Dewitt and seemed to cut right through him. The poodle was down there shaking its stump and attempting to hump Capp's leg, the dog license chiming like a bell. Capp kicked it away and it scurried to a hiding position in the kitchen. "Don't know what you're talking about," he tried.

"Undocumented photocopies of active reports," Dewitt said, attempting to make it sound as if he was quoting regulations. He knew that P.O.S.T. issued guidelines for such things, though he doubted they took the form of regulations.

"Are you accusing me of something, *Sergeant?*" He asked.

"I'm suggesting," Dewitt said cautiously, "that there is a possibility you may have copied one or more of the investigative reports and forgotten to record such a copy."

"I'll look at any damn file I please, Dewitt. Where the hell—" Capp began to nod then, stiff little marionette-like jerks to his stumpy neck and dimpled chin. Begrudged acceptance slowly replaced the anger on his face. Capp knew when to modify his position.

"Just so I can keep the records straight," Dewitt added, giving Capp some room to maneuver. "Tons of paperwork on these cases. If we go to court, then we'll need to have all our paperwork in order. That's all I'm talking about."

"Yeah, sure. Yeah, right."

"Exactly what is your interest in those files, sir? Perhaps I can help."

"Interest? This case falls under my command, *Sergeant.* That's my interest! Quite frankly, I wonder about your competence, your experience." Capp glared at him viciously then, his jaw muscles flexing as he ground his teeth. "We'll get this all straightened out on Monday." He moved slowly. Dewitt could feel the man's every joint ache under the excess weight.

Dewitt swallowed away his frustration. It would be improper—and a mistake—for him to pursue this further. Ginny may have been mistaken. The resulting silence grew from awkward to claustrophobic. Only the poodle remained oblivious to the tension in the air, scratching once again at the calf of his master. To Dewitt, the dog looked more like an albino rat with a permanent.

Capp had the door open. The poodle streaked outside in a flash of white fur. Capp called it back in a growling, angry voice. With Dewitt outside and the dog inside, Capp shut the door.

Dewitt walked down the short stone path to the driveway and the waiting Zephyr. He was walking with his head cocked down in deep thought, sorting through their discussion. He stopped short of his car, staring at the driveway's yellowed concrete. Just beyond the toes of his scuffed shoes, a few feet ahead of the Zephyr, he spotted that same triangle of motor oil.

Howard Lumbrowski.

Dewitt glanced back toward the house. Karl Capp, poodle cradled in his arms, was watching him through a window. Capp petted the poodle once, his eyes still on Dewitt, then turned and disappeared into the interior of the house.

5

The man crouched next to the fence that ran behind the car wash. It was cluttered with bleached, rain-wrinkled trash, road litter mostly. Some plastic bottles and many pale pop cans lay crushed and pressed into the mud, although most of the aluminum ones had been salvaged by winos for their refund value. It was a terrific place for cats. Cats loved the fence. Loved to rummage around in the piles of litter. They made noise out there at all hours, screamed murder during intercourse, scratched and clawed out a meager existence. They were a nuisance and the man appreciated them where few others would. He had use for them. Purpose.

He reached into the bag of Kitti-Bitties and distributed a trail carefully. He was careful about every facet of his life, had been for years, and he wasn't about to change now. He counted the Kitti-Bitties as he scattered the line, counted them like a poker player and his chips. An effective trap required specific bait. Kitti-Bitties were just the thing. They were shaped like wagon wheels, the Kitti-Bitties. Eight, nine . . . he popped the tenth into his mouth and chewed it up. Chew your food a hundred times, his mother had always said. He smiled at the thought, pieces of Kitti-Bitties stuck between his teeth.

They weren't that bad—tasted a little bit like liver. He loved liver and bacon.

The trail led around the corner of his building, where he left a very small bowl of milk mixed with codeine cough syrup. He placed his worn-out lawn chair not five feet from the bowl and sat down, waiting. Patience was something he had learned a long time ago. Patience was what made careful planning pay off.

It took a little longer than usual. About forty-five minutes. A mangy tom, a cat he had seen for several days now, came around the corner looking like it had six fathers and poor eyesight. It was steering by its nose, chewing up the Kitti-Bitties as it went along. Wiry. Wild as all hell. The man sat unnaturally still, his breathing contained—one of his well-developed talents. A useful talent at that. The tom planted his greedy face into the bowl and just about inhaled the milk.

Curiosity didn't kill the cat. Nor did greed. The man did.

He let the cat walk away when it finished. Part of the fun was following; watching. Same with people. Part of the fun was the knowledge it was all over before it began. They never made it far. None of them had. This one did better than average. A little farther. Thirty or forty yards maybe. He could always tell by the tail. When the codeine hit, they couldn't hold their tails up. They became tail-heavy. He could approach them then, as he approached this tom now. The tom glanced over his shoulder, a glazed look in his multicolored eyes, like a skid-row bum who hears you coming up behind him, unable to negotiate out of your way but eager to do so. The man slipped on the pair of thick leather gloves and scooped up the cat. "Good kitty," he said softly into its ear. Goodbye kitty, was more like it.

Inside the room, the man wrapped duct tape around each paw, nullifying the claws. When he was done, the tom looked confused, puzzled. In his dazed stupor, he bit at one of the taped mitts. "No, no," said the man, placing the Baggie over the cat's head and fastening it there with a thick rubber band doubled to hold it tightly. He released the tom then, allowing it to wander the room.

It only took a few seconds for the plastic bag to fog. Then the body had no head, no eyes. The cat pawed at the bag but to no avail. In the process, it used up more of its precious air. It began to move quickly then. It ran full speed into the opposing wall, blinded by the fogged bag. It bounced off the wall, staggered, and started running in circles. The man laughed at the sight. Stupid cat.

This one took eleven minutes. It banged its way around the room comically, shook its head violently, cried out in its ugliest back-alley voice—but to no avail. The man kept right on laughing, grinning, enjoying it, until the tom keeled over and lay panting frantically. Briefly. Then it was still. The man applauded. On a scale of one to ten, this was a definite six or seven.

Better than average.

He gave the carcass to his dog to play with, and enjoyed this nearly as much. The dog nosed it around in the dirt briefly, just as he did with the man's socks, then bit down and tore off a leg.

That was enough for the man.

He hated the sight of blood.

6

Clarence Hindeman showed up for Rusty's Point Lobos ceremony in khaki shorts and a jungle jacket from Banana Republic. Point Lobos, the spectacular coastal state reserve, had played a major role in Dewitt's marriage, grief, and recovery. Forested with Monterey pines, its jagged shoreline weathers the interminable pounding of turbulent breakers boiling white in emerald waters. It is a magical place where sea lions languish indolently, soaking up intermittent sunshine on mossy islands of rock outcroppings, and malformed overhead limbs twist and recoil in stark protest to the brutal tenacity of offshore winds.

This afternoon, the breeze, heavy with salt spray and pine sap, carried with it a physical weight as it barreled inland. Brown grasses and naked shrubs rustled stubbornly, whispering, hissing at them like bums from the shadows.

Hindeman carried a cold beer in hand as he led them onto the

Cypress Grove trail. They walked out to The Pinnacle lookout, passing beneath a tree curling painfully away from the sea, hunched like a businessman holding his hat against a wintry gust. The insistent surf exploded far below them, tossing plumes of white foam twenty feet high and sounding like muffled explosions. They huddled together then, pulling in close and taking the wind to their backs. Dewitt was thankful for friends like Clarence and Briar. They were family, these two.

Emmy opened the lid to the urn. Some of the ashes lifted in the wind. She slapped her small hand over the top and sealed them inside.

"Looks like he's dying to get out." Hindeman tried a joke on the other three, only winning with Dewitt, who grinned. Briar looked at her father with acute disapproval.

Emmy had memories here—memories of her mother, of their family on weekend outings—and although it was her choice to be here, she faltered briefly and looked to Dewitt for comfort. He wrapped an arm around her and squeezed. "We don't need to do this, Em," he whispered.

"Are *you* going to say something?" she asked her father.

He said somberly, "Rusty and I have never needed words to understand one another. He knows how I feel. He'll always be with me, Em. Always. In that way, he's immortal." He reached over and touched the ceramic urn.

Emmy, staring down into the container, eyes brimming with tears, then looked up at her father. "We've been here before, Dad, haven't we?" she asked.

"Yes, we have, Em," he answered, consumed then by his own memories.

She was weeping now, teeth biting her lower lip, eyes squinting. Dewitt felt tears slip from his own eyes. Nothing hurt as much as watching Emmy cry. She said, "So, I guess all I can really say is that I loved Rusty a whole lot. We *all* loved Rusty a whole lot and now . . . now he gets to be with Mom forever. Lucky him."

Dewitt hugged his daughter from behind. He could see Rusty running, could hear him barking, could feel his hot sour breath on his neck, his tongue on his cheek. Nothing so sweet. He placed his chin on his daughter's head and his tears ran into her hair.

"Lucky Rusty," Emmy repeated. She threw the urn from the cliff, ashes spraying out a fantail of gray. She pivoted and buried her face deeply in Dewitt's chest. "It's not fair," she complained.

He watched over her shoulder as the urn descended. "I'll miss you, boy," Dewitt whispered privately.

Emmy laced her fingers in her father's and they headed back to the car, embraced in a deep and painful isolation.

7

Howard Lumbrowski was taking no chances. He'd had the car in the shop most of the day while they replaced seals, tightened bolts, and changed the oil. Let Dewitt impound it now; he'd end up with mud on his face. No oil leaking now. He ordered his second Absolut, a double this time, proud he had limited himself to what he considered two drinks. Just enough to keep the heart pounding and ears from ringing. The genius move, he decided, was drinking at the Boar, because Dewitt would never, ever look for him here; he would be looking over at the dives in Seaside. And even if he did look here, he would have to look carefully: The Mustang was parked around back, behind the dumpster, completely out of sight. No cops ever came in this place, and Pete, behind the bar, was a close friend. He'd given this number to Bret at The Horseshoe, warning him that Dewitt might be on the warpath. Certain that Bret would never betray his confidence, he knew if the phone behind the bar rang, and it was for him, that it could only be one person: *Him*.

"It's for you," Pete said, handing him the receiver as if hearing his thoughts.

Lumbrowski, feeling warm in the face, said into the receiver, "I had a little trouble last night. Couldn't keep our date, sweetie."

The now familiar voice responded, "Yes."

"So?"

115

"You remember what I said last time?"

"You gonna get on with it?"

The man named a motel. Seaside. "You're expected. I'll be along when I'm convinced it's safe."

Lumbrowski handed the phone back to Pete. "Another D-cup starlet wants some aerobic instruction. Gotta run."

The motel was a T-shaped single-story structure with about a dozen units. The sign read, NO VACANCY, in a broken neon script. There wasn't a single car in sight, only a mangy dog wandering around the front of the office. A hand-scrawled note in the office window read, TEMPORARILY CLOSED FOR REPAIRS, PLEASE TRY US AGAIN. Lumbrowski knocked and waited for the door to open. It was dark inside the office, the only light from the glow of another neon sign advertising cable TV. The guy was big, and Lumbrowski felt uncomfortable. He hesitated for a moment in the doorway.

"In," said the other in a way that disguised his voice.

Lumbrowski ventured inside. The guy pushed the door closed, slapped a key into his hand, and spun him around. The fingers wormed over him carefully. The guy knew what he was doing, and wasn't afraid to check the groin, which told Lumbrowski something about him immediately: professional. It was a good sign. The snitch was probably worth something.

"Which room?" he asked, feeling the cold key in his hand.

"Twelve." Low, unremarkable voice. Also professional.

6

SUNDAY

1

The patrolman said, "There's another one, Sergeant." Dewitt didn't need to ask another what. "But this time it isn't on our turf," Nelson continued. "I've got a Bearcat scanner at home. Monitor it most of the time. They slipped up when they called it in. Used the radio. I had to check it out. I'm here now."

"Where?"

"At a pay phone. You know the Seaside public baseball diamond?"

"Seaside? Brutus, protect that crime scene. If they used the radio, it's going to be a zoo."

"Already is."

Dewitt groaned. "Whatever you do, keep your eye out for Lumbrowski. He beat us to the first two crime scenes. He's wanted for questioning."

"He beat us to this one, too," Nelson informed him.

"The oil again?"

"No, not the oil. The stiff in the car, Sergeant? The one sucking fumes? It's Howard Lumbrowski."

The crime scene infuriated Dewitt as he drove up: too small. Unacceptable. Two Seaside uniforms were *inside* the sectioned-off area, thereby negating the very purpose of the police tape.

He was grateful, however, not to see any detectives. He had phoned Tilly to request an invitation to the crime scene—a necessary technicality. In another department's jurisdiction, Dewitt was a guest, the investigation out of his hands. What he now hoped was that whoever headed this investigation would extend Tilly's "invitation." That was anybody's guess. He identified himself to the patrolman in charge and went to work immediately, acutely aware that his authority might be usurped at any moment. Nelson was dispatched to reestablish the crime scene in a scope and purpose more to Dewitt's liking. He was then to have Ginny alert Clare O'Daly and Dr. Emmanuel.

It began to rain heavily. Dewitt donned his rain jacket and headed directly to the Mustang before he lost any exterior evidence, camera at his ready. On hands and knees, he studied the cracked pavement from a variety of angles, drawing mocking, skeptical looks from the Seaside patrolmen. He spotted a sandy tread pattern by the passenger door—a bike?—but the rain washed it away before he had time to get a photograph. He handed the camera then to one of the uniformed onlookers and had him record Dewitt's opening of the driver's door and initial inspection of the corpse. The uniform did so reluctantly. Frame after frame recorded Dewitt's every move.

Lumbrowski had been in a fight—a much worse fight than the two of them had had. His knuckles were cut, his lip split; there were several ugly red spots on his neck. Dewitt hadn't seen sores like that before.

He leaned over the body in an attempt to grab hold of a roll of masking tape when he heard from behind, "That'll be all, thank you." A deep voice. He turned to see Lieutenant Rick Morn, a man in his late fifties, a poor dresser, losing hair, a cop's intensity in his eyes. They knew of each other through prior investigations.

"We'll include you, Dewitt. More than likely we'll share with you at some point, but we've got to do this our way for the time being. This is our turf. You can appreciate that." Dewitt signaled for the uniform to stop taking photographs. "Investigator from the DA's office is on the way down. Too many cooks, you know?"

"It's part of my investigation," Dewitt protested.

"We'll see," replied Morn. "What'd you find there?" he asked.

Dewitt was anxious to be kept informed about the Lumbrowski investigation because of its obvious connection to the suicide murders that he was already working on. But a veteran like Morn had his own way of doing things. Dewitt dared not challenge that. The best he could hope for was an occasional phone call.

"A roll of tape. He used masking tape this time, not duct tape." Dewitt pointed to the sealed window. He felt emasculated, the child sent to his corner. How could they simply take the investigation away from him—these churls who knew next to nothing about evidence collection? Most of the old-timers like Morn lacked faith in trace evidence, misunderstood its importance, believing it instead to be *circumstantial*, a word any FI abhorred. Dewitt walked away dejectedly from the crime scene. Nelson followed a few feet behind like an obedient attendant.

"Sorry, Sergeant," Nelson said. "You deserve the case, not these guys."

"We'll see who gets this case," Dewitt replied, returning his gear to the trunk of the car. "Leave it to Lumbroswki," he added. "He can piss me off, even in death."

2

Dewitt was amazed that once in a great while the system actually worked. Following his discouragement at the Lumbrowski crime scene, he returned to the office, to discover a message from the director of the Atascadero State Mental Hospital. A phone call later, based on the urgency of the case, he had arranged an afternoon interview with convicted murderer Harvey Collette.

Despite the fact that Collette had been interned at the time of both kills, the modus operandi between these murders and the Collette kills was too similar to be considered coincidence. Someone knew the details of Collette's methods, which made it worth talking to Collette.

He used the nearly two-hour drive to review the evidence and dictate his recollection of the investigation to date. He ate a Quarter Pounder for lunch and arrived at the institution at ten minutes past one.

The director's office reeked of that same pungent medicinal odor that plagued all doctors' offices. The refurbished utilitarian furniture implied a budget stretched by demand and limited by legislature. The older man behind the desk, Dr. Bradford Shilstein, was pale-faced and sad-looking. He wore smudged glasses with heavy frames and had an oblong gravy stain on his tie. A folder lay open in front of him.

"Mr. Collette is one of our permanent patients," he began, "a *resident*. You asked for anything I can tell you about him that might help your investigation. Some background is in order before your interview."

"Please."

"You won't find this in any police file." He eased back comfortably, a man prepared, perhaps even desperate, to talk. "Harvey Collette's *fascination* with death and asphyxiation seems to have begun during adolescence, and developed rapidly into a preoccupation. One common trait among homicidal psychotics is an initial experimentation with house pets. It's not fully explained, but we see it repeatedly. It may have to do with a form of conditioning . . . preparing one's self for taking a human life by first starting with a less challenging prey. Collette is a good example. The first life he ever took was that of his mother's cat. He asphyxiated it by trapping and containing it inside a piece of Tupperware. By the age of twenty-one, he was working as an animal-control officer, terminating strays at the pound. He was later transferred to the actual collection of the animals; he became a dogcatcher, Detective. Only he wasn't bringing all the strays back to the pound with him." He read from the folder in front of him. "He killed fifty-seven strays on his own. All by asphyxiation. He was caught and arrested. And this is where the system first failed us: He was fined three hundred dollars, given a preliminary and cursory psychiatric evaluation, was found 'competent' "—he glanced up—"whatever *that* means, and was released. Within a year he had found employment at a muffler repair shop. His preoccupation with asphyxiation continued. By the time authorities caught up to him, he was suspected of having killed two people, both by rigging their exhaust to 'leak' into their vehicles. Substantial proof was not forthcoming, or if it was, it was not properly handled. The case was dismissed before going to trial."

"Will he cooperate with me?"

"You can try. We place Collette in restrictive wear when his area is being cleaned, when his medication is administered. In the past year, he's grown quite violent. Nearly killed an orderly. Very unusual for a trapper."

"A what?" Dewitt asked. Shilstein's buzzer rang.

The doctor said, "That'll be Collette. We can talk more afterward." He glanced up. "Did you bring the movies as I suggested?

Dewitt tapped his briefcase. "The tapes," Dewitt corrected. "I could only find a couple new releases."

"Then by all means barter with him. He's on medication, but don't let him fool you: He knows exactly what he's doing. He'll control you if you allow him to. Look him in the eye. Do your best to imitate his tone of voice, his words. Meet him on his terms. Establish a rapport. If you befriend him, he'll open up to you."

The drab tile hallway and acoustic ceiling were reminiscent of the schools of his youth. Smoke detectors had been added recently; a galvanized conduit ran the length of the corridor, connecting the sensors. A linebacker of a male nurse took Dewitt's briefcase away from him, made him empty his pockets and remove his belt and both shoelaces. Shilstein had mentioned none of these precautions, and

Dewitt found the routine unsettling. Finally, the door marked VISI-TORS A was unlocked and Dewitt was admitted.

The room had survived the years poorly. The table, bolted to the vinyl floor, was badly chipped along its edges. Four metal chairs surrounding the table were also bolted to the floor. Collette's shoulder-length hair and thin but shaggy beard did nothing to enhance the appearance of sanity. A different man than the one in the mug shots taken five years earlier. Wet red lips, bloodshot eyes, flat nose with enough hair escaping each nostril to make a paintbrush. This was how the movies portrayed insanity. Guys like this. What went on behind those eyes? The straitjacket showed faded bloodstains that someone had endeavored to bleach. He sat there with his bound arms folded defiantly across his chest, his skin as pale as the straitjacket, his eyes in a drug-induced half-mast. He looked as if someone had stabbed him in the eyes.

Dewitt felt fear creep up his spine and tighten his throat. A hideous odor filled the small room, a smell completely foreign to Dewitt, a smell that had not been there just moments before. It terrified him, this odor. As a result, they sat in an uncomfortable silence for several minutes. Dewitt rubbed his hands in an attempt to warm them, finally lifting them unconsciously to his mouth and blowing into them.

Collette saw this and grinned. "My name's Harvey," he said.

"Yes, I know. I'm James Dewitt."

"Another doctor?"

"No, a cop." He added, "I'm Detective Dewitt. I need to ask you some questions."

"Federal?"

"No," Dewitt said.

"Married?"

"No."

"Did Shilstein tell you the reason I killed them?" He answered himself: "Because the dead make such quiet lovers." He rolled his eyes and his thick pink tongue moistened his lips. "You get tired of the animals. I hear sheep are nice"—he grinned—"but there weren't any sheep in my neighborhood."

Dewitt attempted to collect his thoughts. "I have questions."

"Let me out of this and we'll talk."

Dewitt ignored it. Recalling what Shilstein had told him, Dewitt said, "Your crimes were very difficult to solve."

The man nodded.

"You fooled the police by making it appear the victim had committed suicide."

"They *did* commit suicide. They died of asphyxiation."

"How would you feel if someone were copying you?"

"Imitation is the most sincere form of flattery."

"Is someone imitating you?" Dewitt asked.

"Are they?"

Dewit described the two crime scenes—Osbourne and McDuff—and then asked, "What do you think?"

"It's not what we think, it's what we *know*," said Collette, rolling his eyes.

"And what do you know?"

"More than you," the man said. "At least you think I do or you wouldn't be here."

"I'm here to try and learn from you," Dewitt said. "Someone is imitating you, but unlike your case, we've found no indication of suffocation prior to the staged suicides. How do you suppose a person could pull this off, Harvey?"

"The killing is nothing. It isn't even particularly fun. It's being with them afterward that's amazing. The body cools quite quickly. Did you know that?"

The bitter odor filled the room again. Dewitt pulled at his collar and unfastened the top button of his shirt.

"You look stupid in that tie. Has anyone ever told you that?"

"Everyone tells me that," Dewitt said, still trying to maintain the recommended rapport. He pulled off his glasses and polished them.

"I'm an original, Dewitt. I'm a genius. Did Shilstein tell you I'm a genius? Did you talk about my tests?"

"A genius could figure out how this is being done."

"I've seen it on the news. I know *all about* your cases. More than you think. *Much* more. But you'll walk out of here. I won't. That requires a little motivation."

"Now I think you're lying. Don't lie to me, Harvey. I brought movies with me—new movies—but you won't get them if you lie."

"Let me see them."

"They wouldn't let me bring them in. They think you're dangerous, Harvey."

He began to wrestle inside the straitjacket. "I *hate* this thing!" He fell off the chair. Dewitt stood and moved toward him. A guard burst through the door, confirming they were being watched. He held a stun stick in his right hand—a souped-up version of a cattle prod, brother to the more advanced Taser. Dewitt knew about them from a seminar in special weapons.

"Stand back!" the guard demanded. "It's a ploy. He wants to bite you." The guard waved the stick threateningly at Collette. "Back into the chair, pal, or this here hard-on is going to bite *you*."

Collette was back into the chair immediately, eyes on the stun stick. With the guard standing by, Dewitt spent the next five minutes attempting to make contact with Collette.

"Get me out of this," is all the man would say.

Shilstein entered the room and stared at Collette. "Okay, Harvey, you win. We'll transfer you to tennis court. But if you don't help the detective here, no television—none—for a week. That's what your little charade just bought you. Come with me," he said to Dewitt. "It'll take a few minutes."

They were walking down the hall, Dewitt's unlaced shoes giving him trouble. "That smell," he said.

"Strange, isn't it? But not uncommon. Quite a few of our residents in this wing display this same behavior. Potential victims, those who have escaped harm, say the odor is even stronger just before the kill. One woman claimed it was paralyzing. You all right?" he asked.

"When you don't see this side of things . . ." Dewitt began. He wasn't sure how to finish.

"Unsettling," the doctor replied. They reached the office. Dewitt took the same chair, Shilstein his place behind the desk. "It should only be a few minutes until they're ready for you."

"The stun sticks?"

"We used to use medication in emergency situations. On low-voltage settings, the sticks are far more practical. No risk of improper medication, no preparation time. To our surprise, the presence of the sticks—just the threat of their use—has reduced violent outbursts by over fifty percent."

"And on higher settings?"

"The guards are discouraged from using the higher settings," Shilstein said, adding, "You did pretty well in there. Very important to establish the rapport early. Perhaps you noticed the effectiveness of negotiation. Especially true of Collette. You need to use those tapes more effectively. He wants them. You understand?"

"The guard claimed he would have bitten me. True?"

"As I said earlier, he's broken out of the trapper mentality. It's not entirely understood why. People like Collette, they're continually making us rethink ourselves. We should always remember there are no rules, there are only patterns." He wrote something down and then tapped the two files in front of himself. "You asked me to review these."

"As a forensic psychiatrist, I thought you might offer some insight into the character of the killer I'm after. A psychological profile."

Shilstein smiled. "Former forensic psychiatrist. I'm out of that business. I'm an administrator now. Oh, I still keep up on it. I dabble. Have you asked the FBI for a profile?"

"This has all happened so quickly. I thought I'd call them tomorrow."

"Those fellows at Quantico are amazing. You're familiar with the cases of Dr. James A. Brussel?" He didn't wait for Dewitt's acknowledgment, assuming all in law enforcement were at least aware of the father of forensic psychiatry, a man who could, by simply visiting a crime scene, predict the age, behavior, habits, and clothing of the at-large suspect. "There are people at Quantico as good as Brussel. I am not one of them," he said. "Forensic psychiatry is a tricky field. The psychiatrist walks a delicate line between his own thoughts and those of the psychotic he's after. Even for the most stable of minds, it can end up a Dr. Jekyll, Mr. Hyde existence." A wry smile then of a man afraid of himself. "It was Brussel who said it's amazing the human mind works at all, even more amazing that most of us manage to keep it under some sort of control. *Some sort of control*, Detective. You see the wisdom of that statement?"

Dewitt waited out Shilstein's contemplation. The doctor said, "I did look these over briefly, and of course I've followed the cases on the news. For what it's worth, I do have an opinion. Mind you, as I said, this is no longer my field."

"Please."

"You asked about trappers. I'll come to that. First, we need to discuss *bloodless crimes*. Are you familiar with the work of Dr. Ogden Spires?" Dewitt shook his head. Shilstein shrugged. "It doesn't matter." He checked his watch—a man waiting for a train. "There are those—women, most often—who, despite their perceived need to kill, abhor bloodshed. Not murder, but the spilling of blood. What we see in these cases are poisonings, drownings, arsons, electrocutions, and suffocations. Harvey Collette is—was—one of these killers. Clearly your killer seems to be one of these. Or, I should clarify: He wants you to believe he is one of these. That is a more complex concept, and we will come back to that, perhaps, but I believe our first assumption is that he is a bloodless killer. None of his victims had been physically abused in any way, correct?" he asked rhetorically. "And that is significant." He tapped the files again. "I believe you are correct in your assessment that our friend is not a serial killer, or even a sensational killer, but instead, wants you to believe that is what he is. This we can assume from the similarity to Collette's murders. This modus operandi is merely a convenience . . . something he has convinced himself will mislead authorities. However, we mustn't overlook the possibility that this manner of killing is not only of convenience but necessity. That is to say, the work of a bloodless killer who lacks originality and quite possibly is working from a different agenda. It would be premature to speculate what that agenda is. But this bloodless trait leads us directly into Spire's term *the trapper syndrome.*"

He toyed with his watchband. "We divide sport hunting into four broad categories: those who hunt for pleasure; those who hunt for profit; those who hunt aggressively; those who hunt passively. A guide hunts for profit; your weekend Joe, for pleasure. Most buy a shotgun or a high-powered rifle and kill their game. But a subset individual hunts passively . . . *bloodlessly*, trapping his prey in snares, nets, or pits, or poisoning a food or water supply. The vast majority of homicidal personalities we see are aggressive killers, but certainly not all. A small percentage—homicidal arsonists, et cetera—kill their prey through the method of trapping. Incapable of bloodletting, they must find a way to perform the act in what they deem a clean manner.

"An example: Harvey Collette. A rapist, unlike other rapists, he did not brandish a knife or a handgun; he suffocated his prey . . . and his prey were trapped inside the confines of their own houses. Collette was driven by sexual fantasy, encouraged by pornography," he said confidently. "Collette can recall his kills in remarkable detail. He will describe to you the way her skin felt, the way her hair smelled, exactly how he performed the murders and especially the sex act. Others, with less vivid a fantasy, are incapable of such details.

"I believe your killer," Shilstein continued, "to be incapable of a blood-related crime. This, I believe, he or she shares with Collette, which is why he chose Collette to imitate. He is a trapper, adept at luring his victims into his trap—in whatever form that takes—and subsequently killing, presumably through asphyxiation. But a serial killer like Collette? No. Highly unlikely." Shilstein closed his eyes tightly. He reviewed the files for several minutes and then looked Dewitt in the eye.

"Your killer is single, living alone. He is employed in a managerial position. His forte is organization. He is in his middle forties. He drinks lightly before his crimes. What he lacks in creativity, he makes up for in meticulous execution. He is a careful planner. He fantasizes about his kills. He follows the investigation in the papers. He had no interest in his first two kills. His target all along was Howard Lumbrowski. He could be a cop, though I think that unlikely. He dresses casually, has no trouble in social situations. Blends right in. And, of course, the obvious . . . I assume that's why you're here, and you're to be complimented for your insight. He has had contact with Harvey Collette. Intimate contact."

Dewitt shook his head—that wasn't why he was here. Or was it? The buzzer sounded and Shilstein checked his watch and smiled, proud of his timing. How could one trust such a profile? Dewitt had read about the accuracy of such things but had never experienced this directly. The doctor's certainty in his tone of voice, his relentless eye contact, disturbed Dewitt. His palms were sticky. His scalp itched. This world of stun sticks and straitjackets upset him. How many like Collette? he kept thinking.

"I can see the doubt in your face, Detective. This is an inexact science." He tapped the folders and then handed them back to Dewitt. "Your collection of evidence is to be commended. It's the evidence that tells me about your killer. I've interviewed over six hundred convicted murderers. Each one is uniquely different . . . and yet such profiles are possible through their similarities. Try the FBI. See what they say. I could be way off. Now," he said, standing, "Collette is waiting."

The tennis court was nearly twice the size of the other interrogation room. Across it's center was an open wire net of foot-square sections, the ends of the cables U-bolted to dozens of thick steel eyelets fixed to the floor, walls, and ceiling. A Mack truck couldn't break through that. Beyond this, on the inmate side, set three feet farther back, was a second net, hemp this time, and of similar foot-square grids. The hemp ropes were spliced one through the next in an elaborate braided method sailors use. A two-inch-wide red line had been painted on the floor at the barrier, three feet from the steel net. In both English and Spanish were the scuffed words DO NOT CROSS in stenciled red paint. On the observation side, four chairs were bolted to the floor immediately behind a similarly secured table. Dewitt took a seat in one of the chairs. An unrestricted Collette paced the inmate side behind the hemp. Five minutes of silence passed. Collette said, "Much better, don't you think?"

"Much."

"This is where the state board of review occasionally interviews inmates. Did you know that?"

"No," answered Dewitt.

"They call it the tennis court because of the nets."

"Yes."

He went back to his pacing, continuing another five minutes before speaking again. Dewitt found this practice annoying. He began to fidget, picking at his fingernails. It reminded him of Emmy. Emmy had a thing about her nails.

Dewitt reminded, "I brought you tapes. Recent releases."

Collette replied angrily, "I need more than that! For what I've got to tell you, I need much more."

Dewitt waited, heart pounding. There was something about Collette's delivery: firm, confident, intelligent—a different man than in their first confrontation.

"You're the expert. You know much more about this than I do. I think I can stop whoever is copying you, but not without your help."

"You stop him if you want. I don't care. That's your thing, man. I got other concerns. In a place like this, you got certain needs."

"What can I do for you?" Dewitt asked. "If I can help, I'll help."

Collette approached the hemp net and hung his head through one of the frames. He widened his eyes and stared at Dewitt and began to nod. Dewitt felt his heart begin to pump strongly. Collette said, "Yeah . . . there we go, now you're listening."

The man began to pace again. "The thing is, what a guy would like here, what a guy *needs*, is a remote-control Mitsubishi twenty-seven inch, full cable, I mean *full* cable, and one of them Panasonic fully remote VCRs. All for himself. That and maybe a mail-order arrangement with one of them tape stores down in the city. You know, like ten tapes a week for as long as they hold me here. That's the kind of thing makes a joint like this tolerable. We're talking needs. They dope you up. No problem there. Ride's nice and easy, but your mind's got nowhere to go. Nothin' to focus on. Know what I mean?"

Dewitt hesitated. "That's a tall order. I'd need more than I've got if I'm going to dig up that kind of thing."

"Come on, Dewitt." He was hanging from the net again, apelike. "Don't fuck around with me. You get me the gear, we'll talk."

"I can't *do* that, Collette. Use your head. I need *something* to prove it's worth the cost. You're talking a couple thousand bucks. The state isn't going to put up that kind of money on a hunch."

"You're not listening. You cops never listen. That's your problem."

"I *am* listening."

"No you're not." He paced. "I'm telling you, I know *all about* your case. Let me ask you this, *Detective*, has anyone determined if they actually died inside their cars? They didn't, you know. So if they didn't, then where did they die? How did he kill them?" His words echoed inside the hard-walled room. With Collette pacing, and himself sitting, Dewitt felt it was he was being interrogated.

"That's why I'm here, Harvey."

"You're here because he's imitating *me*."

"He traps his victims," Dewitt tried.

"Of course."

"In a public place?"

"There are two kinds of traps. Baited and unbaited. Baited, you lure them in. Unbaited, they simply stumble into the trap. You want a specific animal, you bait the trap. You don't care what you get; you simply put a snare on a trail and you wait. Are you learning anything?"

"Yes."

"Of course you are. That's because I'm teaching you." He laughed. "But teachers get *paid*, Dewitt."

"I brought five tapes with me. They're yours."

"More. I want my own system."

"I told you I'd try." His words echoed hauntingly. "I'll need specifics."

"I've got news for you, Dewitt. He's improvising. His plan went south on him. This isn't how he planned it. Imitation is the most

130

sincere form of flattery," he repeated. "You think I'll give that up for five movies? He's made me immortal, Dewitt. My genius lives again through his actions. Would you give that up for five tapes? Would you? You know how I got women, cop? I hung out in a supermarket. The housewives shop for food, I shopped for housewives. Someone baited my trap for me, you see? The divorced ones were the safest. And the most stupid. You know how you tell the divorced ones? They have kids but no wedding ring. Simple. Follow them home or maybe get in line behind them and take their name and address off their checks. Little tricks. Watch their place. Make sure you're right."

"I don't care about you!" Dewitt shouted, unable to sit through this.

"I think you do," said Harvey Collette. "Guard!" he called out. "Get me my system, cop."

The guards entered.

Dewitt shouted, "I need specifics."

"You? You need an undertaker."

"Lie flat and spread 'em," the guard with the stun stick said. The other held the straitjacket. "Facedown. One twitch and I'll fry your asshole shut for a week."

"Twenty-seven inch. *With* remote control," said Harvey Collette, grinning from the far side of the nets.

3

At Clarence Hindeman's insistence, Dewitt was to make himself ready to escort Clare O'Daly to the Manny Roth fund-raising dinner. The mayor had passed the word to Hindeman: Jessie Osbourne would make herself available. Dewitt barely had time to drop Emmy at Hindeman's and change clothes. Exhausted, he answered the door promptly at seven o'clock. He appreciated a woman who was punctual.

Clare wore coffee-colored cashmere slacks, a mohair hand-spun wool sweater with a scoop neck, and a gold necklace holding a setting with a single pearl at its center. She carried a perfect posture. He kissed her on the cheek. They took her Saab.

They were soon passing through Pebble Beach's Carmel gate and winding along the scenic roadway that snaked through the compound. Dewitt directed her through the series of turns and stop signs.

"Let me catch you up on the latest," she said, Dewitt pointing out a turn.

"Please."

"We didn't get anywhere identifying the bleach in those cotton pills found on the bodies. Same with the paint chip from the bike. Can't reach the right people on a Sunday. Tomorrow should be another story. But the Lumbrowski evidence is what's of interest. A couple of things: One is that it was masking tape this time, and as you saw, we have the roll of tape. What you didn't see was that there's a latent print on the inside hub of the tape. We developed it with vapors, and it's being rushed up to Ramirez and his ALPS computer because we compared it to prints on file and it doesn't belong to Lumbrowski. There are several of us on the case, so I'm not seeing all of the evidence by any means . . . in fact, Morn seems to think that because of my association with the first two cases, I shouldn't be on Lumbrowski at all. Thankfully, Brian doesn't see it that way, and Brian's my boss, not Rick Morn. Another difference: The hose is not the same. From what I hear, Morn thinks Lumbrowski committed suicide."

"No way."

"He's going to rule copycat suicide; that's what Brian tells me. There's another rumor says Morn wants to put the first two kills on Lumbrowski."

"Impossible. Something's going on here that we're not hearing about. There are two kinds of rumors, you know: those you're not supposed to hear, and those people *want* you to hear."

"Morn and Lumbrowski were rivals on homicide. He's not worried about tarnishing the man's record."

"It's a smoke screen. Don't believe it. Someone wants these put to bed. That's got to be what's going on here," he said. He pointed left. The road was clogged with parked Mercedes, Lincolns, and BMWs.

She pulled over and said, "The bad news is that we checked

Lumbrowski's Mustang. It no longer leaks oil. He must have had it repaired and had the oil changed; it doesn't match."

He nodded. He had worried about this since hearing from Capp that Lumbrowski had beat the impoundment. He said, "That also creates a technical problem: I never had the right to impound it. At least I can't prove I did. That could be questioned now, made to look bad. I didn't tell you this, but we fought outside the bar, his car, actually. There could be evidence . . . I didn't report it. If I report it now, there's no way I'll get this investigation back."

"Evidence?"

"It got pretty rough. I was trying to inventory the car. He didn't like it. But it all depended on that oil. Maybe there's oil on the undercarriage—"

"Steam cleaned, top to bottom."

"So we can't prove the car was at either site. Terrific!" he quipped sarcastically. He sat there contemplating where this left him. He had no witness to his discovery of the matching oil pattern gleaned outside The Horseshoe; it would be his word only—and his personal dislike for Lumbrowski was a well-known fact. "That all, I hope?"

She nodded.

As they approached Priscilla Laughton's home, they heard the live jazz. Clare gripped his arm firmly then and pulled tightly against him.

An attractive woman in a maid's outfit answered the door. Dewitt sensed their problem immediately as he caught a glimpse of a man wearing a tux, the woman on his arm in a full-length evening gown and high heels.

"Oh, no, James," Clare said, tugging on his elbow. "This isn't casual! The Laughton woman told me casual," she complained.

The man of the hour, bald Manny Roth, neared, his politician's grin contorting his otherwise worried face, hand outstretched, wearing an eye-damaging lime green plaid tuxedo, peach bow tie and cummerbund.

"We can't stay, James," she hissed at Dewitt.

He dragged her inside by the elbow. The mayor reached them.

"James, James, good to see you. I know Jessie is eager to talk with you. I don't believe we've met," he said to Clare. Dewitt introduced them. Clare blushed and mumbled an apology for her appearance.

Dewitt said, "Seems we misunderstood the dress code."

"Don't be silly," said Manny Roth. To Clare, he said, "You look stunning. Come in. Come in."

She flashed Dewitt a helpless expression as the mayor pushed the door closed behind them.

The living room stretched before them, packed with elegant, tanned people milling and chatting. They formed clusters, like a dozen football huddles, the din of laughter and conversation deafening. Waiters and waitresses serviced them. The jazz came from another large room off the front foyer. Dewitt and Clare were steered toward a spiral stairway that led to the bottom floor, where a huge room had been converted to seat the dinner guests. It was the size of a banquet room, the far wall glass. Dewitt saw the twinkling lights of Carmel and the darkness of Point Lobos beyond. There was yet another room off of this, a room busy with a bevy of the heavy drinkers and two bars, each manned with a bartender. More huddles in this room, a quarter-back in each group receiving the attention of the others, calling the plays.

When drinks were in hand, Roth led the two of them aside and said, "You know that everyone here is talking about the murders, don't you? It's good of you to come. *Both* of you. From what I understand, you're part of the team," he said to Clare.

"Sort of," Clare allowed.

"Well, bad news about Lumbrowski." He stared directly at Dewitt. "But at least this may be the end of it."

"If you're suggesting Lumbrowski was responsible for the other two kills—"

"You're the one who placed him at both the crime scenes, as I understand it."

"Even so—"

"And now he commits suicide in the *exact* same manner." To Clare, Roth said confidently, "I'd say the road ends here. And that's exactly what I expect to say tonight. We could all use some good news for a change."

Dewitt said, "Lumbrowski was involved, certainly, but that's as far as it goes."

"As far as *you* go, from what I hear. Isn't that right, Detective?" This was the Manny Roth who meant business. Clare flushed and sucked down a third of her drink, as if she hadn't heard.

"Are *you* the reason Morn hasn't invited me on to the Lumbrowski case?"

"Oh, no. You did that all by yourself. Seems a few Seaside detectives had to hold Lumbrowski off you at a local tavern. You were seen arguing with him. You think you should run the investigation? With the history you two had? Not the best thing for public relations. There's no room for soloists in my band, Detective. We play from the same charts and we play in harmony. Let me make something perfectly clear," he said, stepping a few inches closer. "Lieutenant Morn is convinced that Lumbrowski committed suicide and is connected to the other murders. They're processing some evidence," he said to Clare, "but from what I hear, it's a formality."

Dewitt said, "So I'm supposed to step back and watch you guys make complete assholes of yourselves?" Clare tugged on his arm. "You're playing the wrong tune, Manny. The longer you continue, the more noticeable it is."

"If you'll excuse us," Clare said.

Dewitt placed his drink down, waited for Clare to do the same, took her around the waist, and started dancing with her even though the music was coming from somewhere upstairs.

"James," she pleaded as they became the focus of attention.

He drew her closer, pressing his cheek against hers. "You don't want me to hit the guest of honor, do you?" She giggled into his ear. "Then hold me close and dance." He spun with her, passing a number of huddles, interrupting them.

"We're making a scene," she said.

"Yes. How 'bout that?" A second later, he said, "Look!" and spun so she could see over his shoulder. Two other couples were dancing. "We're trend setters," he said. She held him more tightly, pressing her body strongly against his. Softly. Her leg slipped between his, and they spun around again. It was more than a dancing pose; she was telling him something. It had been so long, some of it was lost in translation.

Upstairs, the song stopped, but they didn't. When the next piece started, they adjusted their rhythm. It was a slow, slow piece that featured a plaintive tenor sax. The horn carried downstairs in a wailing, lonely, breathy whisper. He was overcome by the sweet-sour smell of her, the touch of her hands, the softness of her body. He felt her warm damp breath on his neck. He blindly kissed her ear, and she nibbled on his neck. "This is getting out of hand," she said.

"Mmm," he replied, nibbling again.

They danced past the banquet tables, along the floor-to-ceiling windows overlooking the Pacific. The clouds had broken. Stars escaped through.

"There you are," said Priscilla Laughton, nudging Clare rudely aside and facing Dewitt. She wore a pale teal skirt with a madras sash, her hair up high on her head, and silver and turquoise earrings. To James Dewitt, she said, "Catching up on business, are we?" She called coarsely across the room to the mayor, drawing everyone's attention: "Manny, introduce Miss O'Daly to some of our guests, would you please? I'm going to steal Mr. Dewitt away and sweep him off his feet."

Clare stiffened. Dewitt felt Priscilla's hand take his, and then found himself being dragged through the crowd.

Dewitt was led upstairs, where he literally bumped into a woman from behind, a woman wearing a tight blue velvet dress revealing an acre of skin and backbone, scooped down to the very cleft of her buttocks. When this woman turned around angrily, he saw it was Leala Mahoney, drink spilled across her hand. Priscilla Laughton introduced Dewitt to Mahoney, who bristled and said in a nasty voice, "Yes. We've met." The public defender had worked her hair into a complex French braid. She had rigidly square shoulders. The velvet dipped alarmingly low in the front as well, cut wide across her shoulders and tapering between her breasts to a knife blade that ended just above her navel. Even with that lopsided face, she was ravishing. Dewitt mumbled an apology, Mahoney glaring at him angrily. Laughton finally had the good sense to pilot him away.

"One of your fans, I see," she said when they were well enough away. "What did you do to her to deserve that?" She added, "They tell me *Lay-ya* gets around."

"Why am I here?" Dewitt asked bluntly.

"I misspoke when we last met, and I wish to correct that situation." She looked away from him. "Better late than never," she tried demurely.

"Misspoke?" he asked.

"I inquired about Mr. Lumbrowski."

"Yes, I remember."

"He wasn't in line for a job with a friend; he had been making calls to me. Soliciting me, as it were."

"For?"

"I wouldn't want you thinking that I deliberately withheld information from the police."

"I'll play along, Miss Laughton, if you insist. But I'm growing tired of Jessica Osbourne's chess games. Lumbrowski wouldn't have called you. He would have called your aunt. I need to speak with your aunt."

"It's been arranged. Consider this a briefing, if you don't find that term offensive. Background. It will save you both time."

"She hired him," he stated.

"She listened, that's all."

"That's not all, or I wouldn't be here."

"With his death . . . There's some concern the investigation into Mr. Lumbrowski's death may indirectly involve her somehow. You understand?"

"I'm beginning to, yes."

"Jessie's role in all of this was purely advisory, I assure you. She put Mr. Lumbrowski in touch with me. I handled him following that."

"Handled him for her," he corrected. "You were what we call the go-between."

She explained curtly, attempting to clarify, "My role was simply this: I contacted Mr. Lumbrowski and questioned what information he might possess that might interest us."

"When was this?"

"Thursday, the afternoon of the second murder. He was quite evasive, I assure you, and yet convinced me that it would be worth my while to 'support his efforts,' as he put it. There was no mention of actually hiring him. I was to provide an expense account."

"He convinced you? How did he manage that? Did he offer you evidence?"

"He aroused my sense of curiosity. This morning, after reading about his death, I got cold feet. Our relationship was only days old. Whether my participation was right or wrong, I came to believe that this was the kind of information you, the police, must have if you're to conduct a proper investigation. Have I broken the law?"

"Listen, Miss Laughton, you're the go-between again. Nice try. You're supposed to feel me out, to see how I'll respond, to see if I'll play along with your aunt."

"And will you?" came the familiar voice from behind him. He knew that voice from television. Dewitt hadn't expected Jessie Osbourne to be so tall and elegant. She had one of those anchorwoman faces: the girl next door with a dash of "wouldn't you love it"; camera-ready but aging quickly. She wore a basic black tea-length dress, a black sapphire and gold necklace, and matching sapphire earrings. Her hair had been highlighted, curled, and glued to stay there. Her huge mouth was her trademark: Area cartoonists depicted her with a severely pointed chin and oversized teeth like something from a jack-o'-lantern. "So *you're* James Dewitt," she said, offering him her firm hand.

"I'll leave you two," Priscilla said, backing away and taking over a huddle.

"Shall we find someplace quiet?" Jessie asked, though it was a statement, not a question.

Above the din of guests and music, he said, "I didn't know such a place existed."

"I know *all* the secrets," she said, waving a finger at him to follow her.

I don't doubt it, he thought.

She led him down a hall, removing a purple ribbon gate that blocked off a hall. "You see," she said, "all the tricks."

The library study was teak paneled, with two teak inlaid tables holding brass banker lamps with emerald shades. Three of the four walls held books, floor to ceiling. The fourth, all glass and post like the banquet room, faced the ocean. One wall of fiction, one of reference, the largest, facing the ocean, nonfiction. Jessie wandered in front of the titles for a moment, the only light in the room coming from one of the desk lamps. A teak ladder on a track system accessed the reference wall.

"Your department handled my son's tragedy very well. I wanted to thank you personally."

Dewitt knew the rules. "That would be my captain or chief who deserves that credit."

"No. It's you, Detective Dewitt. I have my sources, you know. As strange as it may sound, as a mother I was relieved to know my son did not take his own life."

"Mrs. Osbourne—"

"Jessie—"

"Then why have you been so carefully avoiding me? You could have helped this investigation. Instead, you've stalled it. That needs explaining." He offered a smile then that said, I won't play your stupid games.

"I beg your pardon?" She studied the titles for several long seconds, noisily clicking her painted fingernail across them. "I have advisors, you know, Detective. Horrid little men and women who spend hours trying to pamper and protect my image. Droll, in a bizarre sort of way. One gets used to it, even grows accustomed to it. I've been in this game for many, many years, as I'm sure you're well aware. When word of John's suicide hit us, my people put out a gag order. Horrible expression, all things considered. They have insisted I be extremely careful about my position in this. Election year and all. I apologize for the method of our meeting, if that is offensive to you. Some things are difficult for me to control."

I doubt that, Dewitt thought. He took a seat at one of the tables within the green wash of the banker's lamp. A moment later, Jessie Osbourne joined him. The direct light was unflattering. He said somewhat harshly, "What is it you want from me, Mrs. Osbourne?"

"There are two people at this table, Detective Dewitt. No one forced you to be here. Perhaps I should ask what you want from me, or is it merely curiosity that brings you here?"

"Me? Yes. Curiosity. *Honest* answers. I also need you to pick your pocket, or that of one of your guests," he said, cocking his head to indicate the party. "I need twenty-eight hundred dollars to pay an informant for information on the identity of your son's killer. I need it immediately. Carmel doesn't have anywhere near that kind of money for such things. And I doubt they would give it to me if they did."

"Mr. Collette," she said, shocking him.

"You *do* have your sources, I'll say that! You see how few secrets we police have?" he asked, "And what is it *you* want?"

"Your help," she said. "What I need is your *help*, Detective. I will attempt to give you what answers you seek, and I will also find you your twenty-eight hundred dollars."

"You must want a lot of help."

"I have chosen for my own reasons to deal with you directly. My advisors don't know about this meeting. If they did, I would be hung by my thumbs. I asked around about you, of course, and I've been told you are a man of your word, a man who can be trusted completely, and so before we go any further, I must ask for your promise that what we discuss here remain confidential—off the record—if that is within your power to control."

He considered this a moment. The implication was that he might not be able to control the confidentiality, which to him meant that whatever it was she wanted to share with him might come out in a court of law—the one place he would be *forced* to reveal it. He then thought this through aloud for her benefit.

"That's right," she said. "I don't expect you to lie for me, only to protect that which you are able to protect."

Dewitt agreed to go along on those conditions. "But if I sense you're withholding information from me, Mrs. Osbourne," he cautioned, "then the deal is off. I need *substance*, not prepared copy."

"I understand your reservations."

"Do you?"

"You think I'm a fast-talking politician about to hoodwink you."

"Yes, you do understand."

It provoked a wry smile from her. "I like you, Detective. Since you're the suspicious one, then why don't you ask first? Perhaps we can break the ice that way."

"Lumbrowski telephoned *you*, not Priscilla," he told her.

"Yes." She nodded.

"How many times?"

She considered this. "Five times. We actually spoke on three of those occasions."

"You installed Priscilla as your go-between. She was to handle Lumbrowski from then on out."

"Yes." She nodded.

He wanted to be taking notes but he knew it would interfere. His mind began to fill with the noise of excess information, bits and pieces nudging each other out of the way, like taxicabs in rush-hour traffic. "Lumbrowski went along with that because by this time the two of you had reached an agreement of some sort."

"Yes."

"And that agreement was?"

She looked past him for what felt like several minutes. At one point, her eyes brimmed with tears, but she maintained her self-control. She looked him in the eye and said, "Like so many things, dealing with the human condition, Detective"—the tears threatened once again—"this can be stripped down to the simplest of things. There are a

141

limited number of motivating factors when you strip away the clothing. No? For both Mr. Lumbrowski and myself, it was a matter of face. In the simplest of terms, we were after the same thing, and perhaps it is for this reason that I went along with him in the first place. Common ground. I *understood* him, Detective." Dewitt waited her out. "Detective Lumbrowski was due for review in less than eight weeks. The ruling of that review board would have governed the rest of his life, would have determined his eligibility for pension and benefits, would essentially have been judgment on his years of public service. He believed that with his former police experience, he might be able to contribute to the solution of the murders. You see, he convinced me from the very beginning that my son was *murdered*, that it wasn't suicide like the papers, and even the police, were reporting. As a parent, as a human being, I didn't want to believe my son had taken his own life. Thus, we struck up a bargain. If he could prove my son had been murdered, and eventually convince the police of this, I agreed to help him, where able, with knowledge of the active police investigation, and, if he were ultimately successful, I would testify on his behalf at his hearing."

"Insuring his reinstatement."

"He seemed to believe my testimony would contribute in a positive way."

"You said from the 'very beginning' he convinced you your son was murdered. How?"

"He told me to look at the first officer's report and at your report, Detective . . . the inventory of the crime scene. He told me a very simple thing had been overlooked."

"I'm listening," Dewitt said. In fact, he was on the edge of his seat with anticipation. Something definite that Lumbrowski had caught that he hadn't? A nightmare is what it was—a nightmare because he knew Lumbrowski's years of experience overshadowed his own, and he dreaded the thought of having missed something.

"The roll of tape, Detective. 'So simple,' he said, and it was. Nowhere, on any of the police or forensics reports, was there mention of the roll of tape. In fact, there was no roll of tape ever found at the crime scene, and without a roll of tape, how was John able to tape the window shut?"

The two stared eye to eye.

"Simple," she added.

He slowly nodded his agreement, the hot crimson rush filling his face. While he had been busy with sand on shoes and carpet fibers from the car, he had missed something. If Osbourne were committing suicide, there would be no reason for him to dispose of the tape he used. Lumbrowski had beaten Dewitt to a simple deduction: John Osbourne had been murdered.

"As I have said, that convinced me Mr. Lumbrowski was of value. We formed an uncomfortable alliance."

"Capp copied the reports for *you*, not Lumbrowski," Dewitt said in astonishment, thinking aloud.

Jessie Osbourne straightened her spine.

"You promised to give me the answers you could," he reminded. "Capp provided you with photocopies of the files. You passed these on, through Priscilla to Lumbrowski, as part of your deal."

She shook her head. "Not exactly. I made the request to Manny. He handled it for me. Whether or not Commander Capp was involved, I couldn't tell you."

"How many reports?"

"At first, just the crime-scene inventory and your report. Eventually, he got it all: coroner's protocols, forensics reports, first-officer reports, memos. All of it."

"You're leaving something out. You wouldn't condone that kind of behavior without substantial motivation."

"I have to trust you, I suppose." The two studied each other briefly. She said, "Lumbrowski discovered a substantial amount of cocaine in my son's car." She broke into tears. It was several minutes before she regained her composure. "Essentially, it was nothing more than poorly disguised blackmail, Detective. Lumbrowski would keep his discovery quiet if I would supply him with police records and make a statement

143

at his hearing. He also believed the murder was drug-related and said he intended to pursue that avenue. His point was that as a one-man effort, he needed all the intelligence he could come up with."

"We're looking into the drug connection," he informed her.

"You knew?"

"We had some sketchy information, is all. There was a source that implied an ounce of cocaine was missing. One of my men is looking into it. I can't say for sure, but at this point I don't think the deaths are drug-related. You were telling me about the arrangement?"

She nodded and continued: "After the second murder—Mr. Mc-Duff—Priscilla said that Detective Lumbrowski became somewhat paranoid." Dewitt absolutely hated the fact that everyone continued to refer to Lumbrowski as a detective. "I found out later, that the paranoia was justified. Both John's car and Mr. McDuff's had been parked alongside Detective Lumbrowski's while he was out walking on the beach. Lumbrowski evidently believed someone was trying to frame him for the murders."

It explained the discovery of the oil. He thought aloud: "Lumbrowski wasn't arriving at the crime scene *before* us, the crime scene was *coming* to him." He recalled his discussion of a trapper with Dr. Shilstein. Had the killer lured Lumbrowski by relying on a man's instincts as a cop?

"It apparently concerned Detective Lumbrowski that he might be implicated in the deaths."

"I *need* that twenty-eight hundred dollars, Mrs. Osbourne. Howard Lumbrowski is not the killer. But we have an informant who may know who the killer is."

"I'll write you the check myself."

Dewitt remained deep in thought while Jessie Osbourne left the room and returned with her purse. She picked through the purse and located a checkbook. As she began to scribble out the check, he said, "Better make it to cash and endorse the back." It was a month's pay to James Dewitt.

She handed him the check and looked up. "I abused my power,

Detective," she said. "I allowed my emotions as both a mother and a politician to dictate my actions. I involved myself in a criminal investigation; I obstructed justice; I solicited and received privileged information. And I was stupid. Those documents went through me . . . from Manny to me, to Priscilla, to Lumbrowski. Our fingerprints are all over those documents. I never considered that. I don't know where Detective Lumbrowski kept them, but if they're found . . . well, yours, mine, any public servant has his or her fingerprints on record with the Department of Justice. How long until I'm connected to the case?"

"*That's* why no one wants me on the Lumbrowski case."

She shrugged. "If those papers are found, we're all in trouble. My offer is this: I will try to see that you are asked to help out with the Lumbrowski case, in return for certain considerations should that evidence surface." She hesitated. "I will withdraw from my current political contest, I will slip quietly out of public office, if you can save me from the embarrassment that evidence would bring me. I am not without ego. I would just as soon be remembered favorably than driven out of office by a hostile campaign waged around my stupidity in this matter. Most importantly, I would like to avoid, for both Priscilla and myself, any criminal action that might result from the discovery of that evidence. I do not wish to be impeached by my colleagues."

"No one's after you, Mrs. Osbourne. At least I'm not. You're a living legend in this state. I'm not going to be the one to end that. What you did . . . Well, it just got out of hand, that's all."

"It certainly did."

"Lumbrowski had a way of making things get out of hand. One of his trademarks, I'm afraid."

"Then we have a deal?" She held out her hand.

"I'm new as a cop, Mrs. Osbourne. I told myself when I started up that I would avoid this kind of thing if at all possible. The back-room deals. The back scratching. But even then I knew there would be exceptions."

Dewitt continued: "I can forgive you your reasons. Not Commander

Capp, not Manny Roth. Their motivations are far less forgivable. They knew exactly what they were doing . . . misusing the system, back scratching. Copying a few files isn't enough to demand their stepping down; I don't mean that. But perhaps Capp could finish out his twenty years somewhere else, another department, and Manny Roth could be convinced to stop dividing his time between the links and town hall. He's away too often, Mrs. Osbourne. He doesn't understand this town well enough. We could use a mayor who is serious. Eastwood divided his time, but he took his job as mayor quite seriously. Did a fine job." He added, "If someone else finds those papers, then all this is moot. If not, then perhaps you use your persuasive powers. Either way, you better hope I'm put back on the Lumbrowski case."

"I'll see what I can do."

"We're out of here," he whispered into Clare's ear from behind. She was listening to a very tan gentleman in his early sixties as he explained to her the potential market for biodegradable plastics. Dewitt pulled on her elbow.

"Aren't we staying for dinner?" she asked.

He could tell that this was her third or fourth cocktail. He started to take the drink from her, but she slipped it away, upended it, and drained it down to ice. "There," she said. She kissed him on the lips. "Where to?"

Fifteen minutes later, they parked in the Ocean Avenue parking lot, placed Clare's dashboard notice out in full view—OFFICIAL POLICE BUSINESS—to avoid being towed, and, hand in hand, walked down toward the water. It was cold, though Clare didn't seem to notice, and they held each other tightly as they walked along the water's edge.

She said, "While you were with Jessie, Manny Roth tried his best to glean every little piece of evidence we have on the Lumbrowski case. Specifically, he kept inquiring about Lumbrowski's apartment. They invited me to try and pick my brain."

Dewitt detailed his meeting with Jessie Osbourne.

She asked, "James, why the different evidence on Lumbrowski? If it isn't suicide, which I agree, then why the changes?"

"There is another explanation," Dewitt admitted. "Someone killed Lumbrowski in a copycat kill to shut him up. Let's say Lumbrowski became demanding and threatened to expose where he had gotten those files from. How would Capp have responded? We know they met at least twice: once at the station house; once at Capp's. I can't believe Capp would have intentionally killed Lumbrowski. But if he had discovered that those files went from himself, to Roth, to Osbourne, and then to 'his buddy' Lumbrowski, he would have been furious. They might have had a fight. Something could have gone wrong. Then Capp would have plenty to hide, and the only person likely to connect him to all of it—"

"Is you," she interrupted, squeezing him more tightly.

"Is *us*," he edited. "I downplayed this to Jessie, but he could suffer badly for copying those files, for working with Manny behind my back."

It began to drizzle. He asked whether she wanted to return to the car and she told him no. She wanted to keep walking. He thought it might be so that she could sober up. She was loose: a good time to get her to open up. He said, "What about you, Clare?"

"Me?" she asked.

"How did you get into forensics?"

"A case. A case while I was in college. It wasn't any major news-breaker or anything. A coed was murdered. It happens. I followed the case."

"And?"

She walked farther before explaining, "The cops didn't have any leads, didn't seem too interested. I know better than that now, but at the time that's how it seemed. I went to the crime scene . . . an alley. Found a couple shoe prints down an adjacent alley. Wide steps, like someone running. I talked to a professor of criminology about it. He referred me to criminalistics. I didn't know what criminalistics was. One thing led to another . . . a professor spoke to the cops because they used our lab on occasion. Some forensic evidence was turned up.

The cops gained a renewed interest in the case. The medical examiner identified the murderer's hair color, red, and his blood type. We had what proved to be one of his shoe prints. Cops reinterviewed the boys she had been seeing. One on them was a redhead who wore Converse All Stars. They ran a blood chem: perfect match. He confessed when they presented him with the evidence. I was hooked." After a moment, she said, "You know I never tell that story. We all get into this for our own reasons—sure not the pay—and somehow when you explain them, they sound kind of stupid. I've heard a lot of stories how people get started in this business. Most of them are personal; you can't understand them unless you were there."

"Who was she?"

"Who?"

"The girl who was killed . . . who was she, to you, I mean?"

The question gave her a moment's pause. Waves rolled to shore, silver-edged stilettos cutting the silence. Dewitt placed his hand on her back. "She was my roommate," she said, "Nancy Gail Adams." She pawed the sand with her foot. "One night, she went out to have a beer. The next day, she was buried back on page seventeen, a statistic. I had lived a fairyland existence. People didn't get raped and stabbed in my world. That's what he had done to her. Nancy was as normal as they come. Could have been me that night; I didn't feel like going out."

They finished out the walk despite a brief but torrential downpour. They held to each other like a pair of ice dancers.

"I make a mean omelette," he said as he pulled her Saab into his drive.

"I'm drenched," she said.

"There's some stuff. You could change." He waited behind the wheel, hoping she might accept, then said, "Oh, well. Maybe another time."

"Her stuff?"

"No. I gave that away. I've got some sweats, you know, that kind of thing."

"What kind of omelette?" she asked, opening her door. They discussed available ingredients on the way inside.

"Will we wake Emmy?" she asked as they reached his front door. Testing.

So *that's* what she's worried about, he thought. "Staying with a friend," he informed her.

Closing the front door, he looked down the hall. It stretched endlessly to his room and offered a glimpse of the bed. "Third drawer down. Some shirts in the closet," he told her. "I'll cook."

He went about preparing the eggs, his ear cocked toward the bedroom. Out of nervousness, he started whistling. He was whipping the eggs into a yellow froth when he heard the pipes whine. She was taking a shower, a good idea considering how chilled they both were. However, the image of her in there did nothing to help his concentration. Still whipping the eggs, he lost hold of the bowl's edge and the motion of the whisk sent the bowl, eggs and all, careening across the countertop like a flying saucer. He dove to save it, but futilely. It spun off, flying briefly through the air and plummeting to the floor, miraculously sparing the bowl but leaving a spreading gooey yellow puddle. He hastily effected a cleanup, only to realize those were his last eggs. He was standing there with an egg-soaked towel in hand when she appeared in the living room, barefooted in his terry-cloth robe. He had washed it in a load of blue jeans a few months back, so it was now what Emmy called "bachelor blue." Her damp hair was combed straight back, her face plain but attractive without makeup. The open neck of the robe reached between her breasts. "*That* was incredible," she said. "I hope you don't mind. I was headed for a cold without that."

"Don't mind at all."

She tugged the robe closed. "I've never looked very good in sweats. Your turn," she instructed, pinching his damp shirt between her fingers. "Out of these things. I'll finish up here."

"I ah . . . We're out of eggs."

"Go," she said. "I'll think of something."

The bathroom held her slacks, blouse, bra, and panties, all hung neatly on hangers, hung to dry above the forced air vent. The bathroom mirror was fogged except for a polished oval where she had checked her face. The comb lay on the counter with a few of her long hairs caught in its teeth.

He slopped his clothes in a heap on the floor and ran the shower water until steam climbed and curled over the frosted glass door. The hot water melted his uneasiness.

He was soaping up when, above the sound of the running water, he heard the bathroom's clock radio switch on. Classical music filled the tiny room. He leaned back against the cold tile wall knowing she was coming to him. The automatic night-light came on as she turned off the bathroom light. When she opened the shower door, the pale bulb cast a candlelight glow behind her, capturing her naked form in an alluring silhouette.

She came to him as a mistress might come to a man, sensually and thoughtfully, with a deliberate slowness that stimulated him. In the darkness, he could not make out any expression on her face. Was she smiling as he was? "Clare," he said, but she placed her finger to his lips to silence him and pressed herself firmly against him. She ran her nails delicately down his back, pulling them more tightly together, folding her head tenderly into his chest.

She was careful with him; he tentative with her. They echoed each other's explorations. Steam swirled. The bar of soap was down there somewhere, down where he had dropped it, squirting beneath his feet as he stepped on it, shooting around the shower like a hockey puck.

They held each other closely, the water running warmly. She looked up at him. His eyes had adjusted to the dim light and he saw that unmistakable expression on her face: desire, wonder, intrigue. Their lips met—an amazing and welcome sensation.

His knees felt weak. Her hands fluttered over him, the skittish wings of a bird.

"I want you, James," she whispered above the rushing water. "I know it's awfully quick," she added, "but I know who I am. I know what I want."

There was something in that hungry tone of voice that reminded him so much of Julia that it was no longer Clare in the shower with him but his late wife. Stunned, Dewitt stepped back, separating himself from her.

"James?" Clare asked in a frantic, anxious voice that feared rejection.

He heard Julia's voice. He sank slowly to the tile, dropped to a sitting position. Defeat.

"James?" She tried once more. "Say *something*. Don't do this to me."

He shook his head, unable to look up at her.

She left the shower quickly, tripping, nearly falling.

He heard her fumbling with her clothes, heard a hanger bang on the counter.

"Clare?" he called out.

"Don't, James. I *don't* want to hear it."

He made it out of the shower. "I didn't mean—"

"Don't!" She had her bra and underwear on. She was struggling comically with the slacks. He stepped up from behind her and wrapped his arms around her. She slapped the slacks down and pulled on his hands to release her.

"I freaked out, that's all," he said.

"You made me feel cheap. *That's* all!" she replied. "Me and my big mouth," she added.

"Please," he said.

She was struggling with the slacks again. "Goddamnitall!" she thundered, bending with the slacks over her arm to grab her shoes. Crying. She pushed him away and ran from the bedroom, out toward the front door, where she hesitated only briefly before charging into the darkness in her underwear.

Dewitt snagged the robe from the bed and tried to fish his arms into it as he followed her, the whole time calling out her name and apologizing. He followed her outside, a fraction late as she slammed down the car's door lock. "Clare," he pleaded through the window, finally tying the robe shut. She reached for the ignition and then slammed her fist on the steering wheel and leaned forward in tears.

Dewitt walked around the car and opened the passenger door, which she had neglected to lock. "I've got the keys inside," he informed her. "It was Julia, Clare," he explained. "I think that was my final farewell to Julia. I *know* it was. There's someone more important now. I'm not going to fall into the same trap that holds Emmy. I want out, Clare. I *need* you."

"James," she pleaded, shaking her head in confusion.

"Please," he begged.

She had deciphered the inverted leg of the slacks and was pulling them on, arching her back and tugging.

Dewitt climbed into the car, took her by the shoulders, and kissed her. She released the pants and tentatively reached for his face, returning his affection. He was trying to explain between kisses, and she to him, but neither understood the other's words, the touching more important. Her hands slipped inside the robe, and then just as quickly, she opened her door, took him by the hand, and dragged him through the car and out the other side. He wouldn't allow her to simply walk away. He swallowed her in his arms, she laughing now, trying to delay him, trying to keep hold of her unfastened slacks, which impeded her movement.

"The door," she said.

Dewitt let go and returned to kick the passenger door closed. The interior light went off. She hopped toward the front door then, struggling with the slacks, looking like a young girl in a potato-sack race. She fell through the front door, laughing hysterically, sensing Dewitt's pursuit. She limped down the hallway, glancing several times over her shoulder. Dewitt had decided on an imitation of Franken-stein, marching forward, the robe hanging open. He heard wet slacks hit the floor, heard her dive onto the bed, still bawling out her nervous laughter, heard her clawing toward the headboard, where, as he reached the bedroom door, he found her waiting for him, naked, her skin fleeced with gooseflesh, arms open, eyes sparkling with excitement. Anticipation.

He pushed the door shut behind him and shed the robe. As he reached for the wall switch, she said in a husky and sensual voice, "Leave the light on. Please. I want to see you smile, James. I want to make you smile."

7
MONDAY

1

Monday morning presented Dewitt with a stark reality: He was living again. Had he been more aware, perhaps he would have looked back on himself as having been something of an automaton over the last five months—getting through the daily grind but seldom rising above it. In front of him lay three stacked manila folders, names of the dead scribbled on the tabs. He wanted no part of the dead. Intoxicated by a magical fatigue that soaked clear through him, he felt rebellious, confident, composed. In one night—a few short hours—she had made him feel appreciated. Loved, again—if only for an evening. And though guilt briefly attempted to steal his pleasure, he would not allow it to do so. Julia, of all people, would want him to feel love again, in whatever form it manifested itself. There was no greater feeling. That two people could physically connect so perfectly amazed him. Clare's unbridled passion, her ability to prolong, to massage the two of them to such an explosive climax, left him steeping in the deep ache of bliss.

The first unavoidable event of the day was a phone call from Leala Mahoney. She was short with him, her sentences clipped, her mood strictly professional. Peter Tilly, he was told, was willing to drop all charges if Marvin Wood would wear a wire for his theft investigation. "That leaves you, Dewitt," she concluded rudely. "You either have to charge him or let him go. You offered my client a deal. I believe he cooperated as fully as he was able. Is your offer still good, or do we do the dance?"

He needed to stall her. His voice was sure as he said, "No charges on this end, Counselor, but I may need to talk with him, and I don't want to have to call out the National Guard to do so. Clear?"

"You're keeping some rather chichi company, Dewitt. Since when does a Carmel detective get a private audience with Jessie Osbourne?" She sounded jealous. "And then to skip the banquet. You had to catch up on your *lab work*, Dewitt, was that it?"

Hoping to break the ice, he offered, "It was good seeing you last night, Leala. That dress is very becoming on you."

"Go to hell, Dewitt," she said. The dial tone hummed in his ear.

"Dewitt?" Commander Karl Capp, his protruding belly hunching his shoulders forward, stood at the door. "You mind?" He jerked his head toward the chair in front of Dewitt's desk. Dewitt nodded his approval, doing his best to conceal his surprise that Capp was entering his territory. Was he supposed to stand? He began to get out of the chair and Capp said, "I got it," and closed the door. Sitting, the fat man said, "So, you're trying to bust my stones," an icy stare biting into Dewitt. "Let me tell you something about life, kid. You never play a hand too early, you always keep your cards facedown, and you never sit in front of a window or a mirror. You go sucking up to a political animal like Jessie Osbourne, you better know what the fuck you're doing. She'll chew you up and spit you out faster than you can think." He smiled then, a grotesque confidence that on any previous day would have disturbed Dewitt. "You've been invited back on to the Lumbrowski case as of now. I don't know exactly what was said, but this kind of a move attracts attention, buys you enemies. What I hear: Morn has been suspicious of your involvement in all of this because of your little spat at The Horseshoe. You have *motive*, Dewitt. Your and Brow's relationship was not exactly a secret. *That's* why you were kept off the case. Now you've gone and stolen it back. You see? That's okay. That takes some serious stones—"

"Me? Morn was trying to call it suicide, blame it all on Lumbrowski, make him look bad. And what motive? I'm Lumbrowski's *defender* now!"

"You're in the big leagues, Dewitt, and I'm not sure you're ready. Guys who move to the bigs in their rookie year, they either become stars or they disappear. The reason I bring all this up," he continued, "is that with your getting this invitation back onto the Lumbrowski case, then this case is sort of under me . . . because *you* are under me," he emphasized. Remember, your performance reflects on all of us. You brief me *every step of the way* on Lumbrowski, Dewitt. You withhold even one of your fuckin' little fibers . . . And as for these copies of your reports . . . you think you aren't a suspect here? Guess again. You think I'm worried about these *alleged* copies you keep referring to? Can you produce these copies?" He waited for an answer. "Well?"

"No."

"No, you can't. Can you even say for sure that such copies exist?"

"No."

"No, you can't, can you?" He snickered and then jeered. "Okay, then hear this, Dewitt, Mr. King of Evidence: Until you can produce them, they *don't* exist. Am I right? Damn right, I'm right. So if you think I'm losing sleep over your damned copies, you've got another think coming."

Dewitt felt his blood pressure rising, the heat of rage in his cheeks.

He assumed this meant Capp had found the Lumbrowski papers and done away with them. He wondered about the missing ounce of coke. "I think you had better leave, Commander. It's beginning to stink in here. You forget to brush your teeth, or are you just breathing out your asshole?"

Capp turned crimson. "The thing is, Dewitt, a person's got to pick his fights carefully. You pick the wrong fight . . ."

"Maybe you can answer me this, Commander," Dewitt said, standing and walking to the door. "What exactly did you and Lumbrowski discuss when he came over to your house on Saturday morning?"

Capp stood. From his expression, the question had caught him by surprise. "What?"

"Yes, Commander, what? *What* did you discuss?"

Capp marched to the door, opened it, and turned at the last minute. "The Brow was right: You're a stupid fuck, Dimwit. You don't know when to quit."

Dewitt was so close, he could feel the man's breath. "I never quit," he said softly.

"We'll see," said Karl Capp, refusing to look at the man.

Dewitt returned to his desk, thoughts whirring. How involved was Capp? What, if anything, did the man plan next? He pulled Jessie Osbourne's check out of his wallet, delivered it to Ginny, and instructed her to find out how to process it into petty cash and arrange for Collette to get his personal entertainment center. "It's a hell of a system, Ginny. The convicted murderer ends up with a nicer TV than you or I will ever see."

"Maybe we're in the wrong business," Ginny said.

2

"Hi, Emmy," Billy Talbot said as he stepped out from the recess of a classroom door, startling her. He wore a dungaree jacket and a white T-shirt.

"Billy," she said, blushing. "I'm sorry about my father—"

"No sweat. You can make it up to me," he said, sliding his hand onto her behind and holding her there.

She wiggled away from him even though it felt good. He smiled confidently, as if he knew what she was thinking. "I don't think so."

"I heard about your dog," he said. "Real sorry to hear about that." He said it in a funny way.

"I've got a class," she tried.

"No you don't," he told her, returning his hand there. She didn't wiggle free this time because Liza Smart and Gennine Falk were approaching, and if she were seen talking to Billy, then maybe they would include her in a few more things. Billy squeezed her there as the two girls passed and Emmy felt an instant warmth all the way up into her breasts. She wondered whether he could see the flush below her neck. She fiddled with a button there, using her hand as a screen.

"You going to the mall tonight?" he asked.

"The aquarium. Monday. My dad's working at the aquarium."

"Not the mall?"

"I can't, Billy."

"What if I picked you up at the aquarium? Would you take a ride with me?" He squeezed her again. "A short ride?" She pulled away. Was Billy as bad as her father said, or was her father just being overprotective? No one at school thought he was bad—that was for sure.

"He'd see you," she said.

"No he won't," Talbot corrected. "I'll meet you at eight-thirty out front. We'll take a ride over to the mall."

"I don't think so, Billy. I don't think it's a very good idea."

"It's a great idea. Eight-thirty, Emmy. *Don't let me down.*"

He joined up with some friends and was lost in the jam of students.

Emmy stepped up to the safety glass of the classroom door and used it as a dim mirror. Her chest was as red as a robin's.

3

Nelson entered Dewitt's office without so much as a knock, waving a small piece of notepaper in his hand. "This shit's a lot more satisfying than traffic work," he said.

"What do you have, Brutus?" Dewitt asked. The nickname fit the broad-shouldered, dark-featured man. It struck him then that he really didn't know Nelson nor any of the uniforms well. Professionally, yes. He knew a man like Nelson was the brightest of the bunch; But how this man spent his free hours—*who* he was—remained a mystery.

"The Plexiglas," Nelson announced proudly. "Just got word back from a distribution-center manager. Had a list of all retail facilities that sell the Plexiglas. It's a lower grade, cheaper, and not that many places carry it. That's in our favor, 'cause the more industrial stuff is used a lot by custom-campertop makers, some home-security outfits, marinas and boat-makers, and all combined there are a shitload of those guys. So, what I got here, Sergeant, are the only three stores within a hundred miles that sell the shit we found under McDuff's fingernails."

"Seaside?"

"One store."

"Get over there. See if there's any way to determine how much Plexiglas they've sold over the last six months. That specific grade. Find out anything you can. Who buys this lower-grade stuff and what do they use it for? Information, Brutus. We want as much information as we can gather. Even if it seems insignificant, write it down."

"I'm supposed to pull a patrol this morning," the uniformed man complained.

"I'll square it, don't worry about it. You do this right, Brutus, you'll have that uniform in mothballs before long. You hear me?"

"Loud and clear."

After Nelson left the office, Dewitt returned to his premise that given enough of it, the evidence would tell the story. The investigation was stuck on a matter of sequence. In the terms of a mystery novel or a movie, he could not determine who done it until he understood how done it. He still lacked a plausible explanation of how the victims had been "convinced" to sit still while the killer gassed them. He took his folders, thick with crime scene and laboratory photographs, into the lunchroom and carefully laid out the evidence picture by picture on the larger tables: Osbourne lying where Anderson had dragged him to the pavement; the triangle of motor oil; a typed version of his notes on the Laughton interview; Clare's comparison photos of the ends of the tape; Osbourne's personal belongings, and his open suitcase with the clothes neatly folded; McDuff's truck; the gaping hole in the dashboard; the bike track and the lab enlargement of the paint chip; the cotton pills found on both victims; a transcript of his interview with Mrs. McDuff; the back of McDuff's truck filled with junk; McDuff's personal belongings, and his open suitcase with the clothes neatly folded. . . . He paused, his fingers still on the edge of this photo. He reached back up the line and pulled a similar picture of Osbourne's suitcase out of the group, placing it side by side with that of McDuff's. Next, he reached for the transcript of the Mrs. McDuff notes. Police work: papers and pictures, pictures and papers. He flipped through the pages.

McDuff a slob, but he knew where things were. Beneath that was written, *Receipts in suitcase?* He had checked that. There had been no receipts found, which implied the killer had taken them. That, in turn, meant the receipts somehow threatened the killer. But it wasn't the receipts that interested him. It was the photograph of the suitcase.

4

"What do you see?" he asked Clare.

"A suitcase," Clare said from the opposite side of a pink linoleum-topped table.

The café on the outreaches of Salinas was marked by a neon sign in the window that read, CHINESE FOOD. As best Dewitt could determine, that was the name of the place. They shared a booth on the far wall. The first half of the restaurant was dedicated to a genuine soda fountain, complete with swivel stools and bowling trophies over the glass-doored refrigerator.

The egg rolls were delivered first—greasy tubes with bean sprouts and Chinese cabbage, but good. Dewitt soiled his pants with a gob of juice and tried to rub it away. It looked as if he had pissed in his pants.

He untucked his shirt so that when he stood, the stain could be hidden.

"Tell me about the person who packed that suitcase," he said.

"Neat and organized, likes his clothes that way, too."

"That's McDuff's suitcase. By his wife's admission, he was a complete slob."

"So someone packed for him."

"My thinking exactly."

"I thought this meeting was to discuss what *I* have."

He bit into the greasy roll, ignoring her. "No receipts," he reminded.

"You're quizzing me!"

"Yes. I want to see if two of us can come up with the same explanation."

"You're forgiven. Go ahead."

"Cotton pills with the same bleach, but on two different bodies."

She summarized, "Someone packed for him. Stole his receipts. Cotton pills with the same bleach indicating the same place."

"Factor in Marvin Wood, and that McDuff would have reported that stolen tape player."

"The pills were on their skin. That means they were both naked and came in contact with the same material . . ."

"The suitcase," he reminded. "That's where the killer screwed up. He shouldn't have packed McDuff's suitcase so neatly."

"A motel," she said. "He stalks his victims at a motel. It backs up what Wood told you."

"It has to be," he agreed. "Yes, that's what I came away with. And if he follows Collette's method closely, which it sure looks like, then he suffocates them to unconsciousness, gets them out of the motel, and stages the suicides. They have the same cotton pills on their skin—"

"Because of towels or bedding," she concluded. "James, that's it. That's fantastic!"

"Only one small problem: There're more motels in this area than there are permanent residents. That's what held us up in the first place. We have to narrow down an area to search."

"It also suggests that Lumbrowski was either a suicide or done by someone else in a copycat crime. The first two were out-of-towners. They had reason to stop at a motel. Would Lumbrowski? We're still going through the Lumbrowski evidence, but we don't have a bike track, and no luggage, of course. Would this guy have hit a local at a motel? That's got to be unlikely."

"Depending how you look at it, that makes sense, I suppose," he said. "That's certainly what I thought at first."

"But now?" she asked.

He reminded her, "There was a bike track at the Lumbrowski kill, Clare. The rain stole it away from me, so it's useless information as far as the courts are concerned, but I *saw* it. Sure, it's possible a copy cat used a bicycle to maintain consistency, or that it was from some kid's bike and had nothing to do with the case, but we're trained away from coincidence. If it was a copycat kill, then it was a damn good one. And it was done by someone with inside information. Only a dozen of us know about the bicycle. There's a possibility, if you believe a guy like Dr. Shilstein, that the first two kills were bait for a trap intended to snare Lumbrowski. What Jessie told me about the crime scenes coming to Lumbrowski, not the other way around, backs that up."

"Bait?" she said with a puzzled expression.

"Osbourne and McDuff, yes. Selected at random from the same motel. The distribution pattern of the cotton fibers supports that. Both men had been lying down. I think this guy gets them in their sleep somehow—same as Collette. Maybe he got Lumbrowski in his sleep." He asked, "Why are you smiling?"

"Just because," she said, staring at him. "Besides, you haven't asked me yet why *I* wanted this meeting."

"And why did you want this meeting, Ms. O'Daly?"

"I thought you'd never ask." She opened her briefcase and handed him some papers.

Dewitt accepted the papers, saying, "If it wasn't for government, we would have a lot more forests." He read the piece of paper: "Suspect's weight = 155–165; height (if average) 5'8"–5'11"; bicycle = Schwinn 'Hillclimber' mountain bike."

She explained, "The paint chip. Schwinn came through with the reference information as promised. FAXed it this morning. The bicycle that was in Lumbrowski's trunk is a metallic black Schwinn 'Hillclimber.' If his tires are filled according to manufacturer's specs, then he weighs exactly one hundred sixty-two pounds. We know that from measuring the compression of the tread in the crime scene photographs. According to the chart, an average male weighing one-sixty is between five-nine and six feet. So if he is average, then we do have that much of a description of him, yes. And if you put me on the stand, Detective: The reason we believe he's average is because that particular bike model is mid-size."

"So I check for stores that sell 'Hillclimbers,' or stolen-property reports. Hope to narrow down an area. Nelson came up with a single store in Seaside that retails that Plexiglas. That may help us to narrow it down, as well."

She tried some of the fried rice. "You're making headway, James. You have a general description and a general area, even a general idea of how it's done."

"General Dewitt, at your service," he said.

She offered him a mocking salute. His pager sounded an obnoxious electronic pulsing at his waist. "Nice timing."

He excused himself and called the office. When he returned, he dropped fifteen dollars on the table.

"Where to?" she asked.

"Seems Collette likes his television. He wants to talk. Lucky me. I get to spend the afternoon driving to Atascadero and back. Would you do me a favor and call Zorro—Emmanuel—over at the hospital. Tell him I'll be late for the Lumbrowski autopsy but to go ahead and start without me."

"He'll never believe me," she said.

"No, he probably won't," admitted James Dewitt. "But give it a try. If he suggests you sit in for me—"

"Forget it!"

"Exactly."

5

The drawn and impossibly pale Collette paced the "tennis court" restlessly in long confident strides, like a military character in one of his afternoon matinees. He looked over his shoulders at Detective James Dewitt, without belt, without shoelaces, appearing as impatient as he felt.

"I kept my part of the bargain," Dewitt said loudly, too loudly for the room. The man's head bobbed in response. "I've checked with Shilstein. You're in permanent lockup here. If that's true, how could you possibly have a name for me?"

"It is true. It amounts to solitary confinement in a padded cell. This is a prison, after all. And who said I had a name?"

"You better have, or the equipment goes back."

"The equipment hasn't even been delivered. Shilstein tells me it will be if I cooperate, and I trust Dr. Shilstein to keep his word." He stopped abruptly and viewed Dewitt with disdain before returning to his anxious pacing. "People like you have no concept of this existence. None whatsoever. Unless I have the good fortune to escape, I will spend the remainder of my days here. Can you fathom that? The rest of my days. And that," he said, inserting an overly dramatic pause, "is what they mean by an eternity. If you think I would risk losing this system I have negotiated, you are a fool. I never promised you a name; I promised you information."

"It had better be good information," Dewitt cautioned.

"It's true I'm in lockup here. They give me magazines with staples removed. All my mail is read. I'm not permitted to shave myself. I'm groomed infrequently by a man who is blind in one eye and has a slight limp. This system I have negotiated will be mounted outside my reach and accessed by remote control . . . did you know that? They won't allow me access to any electronic wiring . . . this I suppose in case I should decide to do myself in. Ironic that they should insist on keeping me alive, isn't it? And after what I've done! And I'll do it again if I ever get out. Gladly. Enthusiastically." He looked at Dewitt again. "Know it's true, James. May I call you James? Know it's true."

Dewitt understood the importance of maintaining a rapport but felt his skin crawl. Collette had conceived an alarming arrogance, which he flaunted in a rigid carriage and a smooth, controlled voice. He had seized control—he had a captive audience—his intention clearly to make the most of it. "You're the expert, Collette," Dewitt said tautly.

"I'm in lockup here, yes. But did you know I've served time elsewhere? No, I can see by your face you did not. You needn't check the files, although it must be in there somewhere. I'm telling you the truth, James. Know it's true. Shilstein didn't mention the transfer? I'm surprised. Something to do with asbestos. Discovered it when they installed the smoke detectors. A few of my colleagues got hold of matches . . . very dangerous in the wrong hands, James. Nearly burned us all up. That caused some inspired thinking on the part of some governing agency and a smoke-detection system was installed at the taxpayers' expense. Know it's true. The discovery of asbestos created a mandatory leave of absence from this wing. We were transferred to Vacaville State Prison—the mental hospital there. How loose they are with terms like *hospital*, James. Know it's true. Is there any healing done there? Not your concern, I know. Not your concern." His pacing had become more frantic, and immediately reminded Dewitt of Manny Roth in Hindeman's office. So little separated the two of them, he thought: some netting and a few laws. That they were of the same species—related, as it were—disturbed Dewitt. He wanted no association with Harvey Collette whatsoever.

Collette explained in that same confident monotone: "It was during my brief but welcome stay at Vacaville that I encountered the individual in question. An aside, Detective: Do you know how wonderful, how tempting, how teasing that long bus ride was? The smell of the farmers' fields? People going about the chores of everyday life? The women in the cars that passed us, their skirts hiked up by the seat, their long elegant fingers twitching impatiently on the steering wheel?" He was stopped, eyes squinted shut, head tilting back in recollection. "There are no smells on television; you cannot taste the air. This . . . this is a *crime*. Know it's true." He began his pacing again, saying softly, "The individual in question."

Dewitt sat on his hands to keep them from shaking. A busload of Harvey Collettes out on the open road. So little separating them: some glass and steel and a few laws.

"We seldom use names in places like this. Did you know that? Quality conversations are limited, and well, quite honestly, the level of medication . . ." He faced Dewitt again. "Did you know Shilstein dried me out for this interview? I bet he didn't tell you that, did he? Can't have all the patients acting like zombies . . . someone might figure out what's going on here. You get out of hand here, the guards hold you down—naked, mind you—and put a stun stick to your balls. You report them and you get it worse the next time. Cozy little family here at the motel—"

Dewitt leaned forward, pulling out his notebook. "The what?"

"The motel. That's what we call it . . . the inmates. The Medication Motel . . . that's the full name. The rooms are cheap, the views limited."

Dewitt took down a note.

"That interests you, James?"

"Tell me about Vacaville. About this person."

"As I was explaining, we don't use names. But I can tell you all about the individual in question. We played chess together. Did I tell you I'm undefeated, James? Three years now, undefeated. Know it's true. He lost at chess—this individual in question—I won. But I always let it be close, to maintain his interest. I'm *that* good, James. I can control the game." He added with a perverse smile, "*Can't I?*"

Dewitt went about polishing his glasses.

Seeing this, Collette commented, "I'm nearsighted. Did you know that? Yet they don't allow me glasses. Not even plastic lenses. And they say we have rights. But not in here. Know it's true. Here, there are only wrongs." He chuckled. "Talk about nearsighted," he said, self-amused.

"Tell me about him," Dewitt said, hooking the glasses behind his ears.

"We shared common interests. He began by leaving pet food out, attracting a pair of noisy neighborhood dogs. He taped the dogs' jaws shut, placed plastic bags over their heads, and watched them run around the house until they dropped. That's how he felt: choked. I *know* that feeling. I *live* with that feeling, James. Know it's true. The streets are choked; the cities; all of us. Yes, we shared common interests. Escalation, James. The history of the world is told in terms of escalation. Dissatisfaction. The leaders, the workers, all the same. Dissatisfaction followed by escalation. It was in Sacramento, I think, though of this I am uncertain. They never caught him, James. You, the police. Whatever town it was, you will find a Girl Scout missing. She was the first for him. Came right to his door selling cookies. Last stop for her. Others followed. A woman taking some kind of poll, or was it the census? Yes, it might have been, that would be ironic . . . taking the census. You see? By the time she's through—*he's* through—there's one less in the population. Change in the census. Another woman, selling perfume, I think he said.

"If you learn one thing out there, it's that the law moves slowly. Know it's true. What did they get him on? Not the Girl Scout. Not any of the women. He was always careful to move the bodies late at night, a great distance. He distanced himself from the crimes, you understand?" A self-satisfied chuckle. "They didn't even get him on the arson. They got his nephew for that. No, what they got him on was the pets, you see? In practicing for the arson, he burned his own place down. Putting out the fire, they came across the skeletons . . . the pets! Over a dozen dogs by then, I believe is the number he said. All, in various degrees of decomposition, with their mouths taped. They sent him to the hospital at Vacaville for examination. Ninety days, because all they could prove was the pets. That's where we met, as I've said. We shared histories." He stopped and faced Dewitt, his thin body framed by the double set of netting. "He's the only one I have ever shared the details with. He was good enough to share his with me. I don't know his name, but he's your man. I sacrifice him only in self-preservation. Survival of the *quickest*, James. Seize every opportunity as if it's your last. Know that it's true."

"A description?"

"Angry eyes. I remember those eyes. An attractive man, I think you would say. Big. Indian blood in him. Apache? Blackfoot? Not much, but you could see it in his bones. He liked to brag about it."

"If I showed you photographs, could you pick out a face from a photograph?"

"Perhaps Shilstein didn't tell you: I'm a genius, James. Know that it's true. A photographic memory. What you ask is kid's stuff. Of course, it's up for negotiation. I'd like to see the system installed first. I'd like to see the rental agreement with that video store."

"There's no time for that."

"You're on the wrong side of the net, James. Ball's in this court. Over here, there's plenty of time. Nothing but time. I have to protect my assets. Be grateful I don't ask for a transfer. I'm not a greedy man, James. Simple needs. Really quite simple. Make a few phone calls, James. That must be something you're capable of. We'll talk. You know where to find me. Guard!" he shouted.

"His name, Collette. I know you know his name. You must have called him something."

He smiled widely. He was missing several teeth on his left side. "I called him Trapper John. He called me Hawkeye. That's because I'm the funnier of the two of us. Oh, and because he had been married. In the show, Trapper John's married, you know. Hawkeye's not."

Standing. "That's not right," Dewitt corrected. "A genius, Collette? I don't think so. It wasn't Trapper; it was B.J." Collette looked troubled, even puzzled by his error. "Know that it's true," Dewitt added, scrunching his toes so that his feet wouldn't fall out of his shoes as he walked.

6

Dewitt phoned Capp from Shilstein's office. With a two-hour drive ahead of him, he wanted to take advantage of the few remaining work hours in this day. He explained the session with Collette and suggested that because of the increasing evidence uncovered by Clare O'Daly, a task force be organized utilizing investigators from both the District Attorney's office and the Monterey County Sheriff's Office, both of whom had been consulted throughout the short investigation. The purpose of the task force would be to show photographs of Osbourne and McDuff to motel employees in an attempt to determine where each had stayed the night of their murders. A job of enormous scope in this tourist area; nonetheless, it was one that Dewitt felt must begin immediately.

Dr. Bradford Shilstein, emotionally charged by participating in an active investigation again, used his contact with authorities at Vacaville to have copies of all records of inmates discharged within the past six months sent both to Dewitt and himself. Further arrangements were made with a downtown electronics store to have Collette's entertainment system installed immediately. Dewitt left Atascadero feeling something like a conductor: He could wave the baton, but the performance depended on the players themselves.

7

"Do you believe in God?" asked the heavily accented voice of Dr. Ricardo Emmanuel. "Allow me to rephrase." Pause. "Do you believe in the Scriptures?"

"I plead the fifth," replied Dewitt. The back room of Maratea's Funeral Parlor smelled sour.

Zorro's Sherman nonfilter cigarette was pinched between his long fingers. He indulged in the flavor of the slate-gray smoke by passing it from his mouth and recycling it up into his nose. The room was also exceptionally cool. A pair of bloody latex gloves lay in the trash.

Lumbrowski's body lay covered by a sheet on an examination table.

"You remember the story of Jonah and the whale?"

"Yes."

"Are you a believer in ultimate irony?" The doctor pronounced it *ironing*.

169

Dewitt took a seat on an adjacent stool. Zorro and his drama, his smoldering cigarette, his fiery brown eyes and theatrical eyebrows. Get on with it, Dewitt wanted to say. He waited.

"Our swollen friend over there was your nemesis, would you not agree?"

"We didn't get along too well."

The comment elicited a coquettish grin from the doctor. "An understatement, indeed. He was your archenemy, this whale-livered dipsomaniac, was he not? And so who would believe it would be Howard Lumbrowski who ended up doing James Dewitt a favor?"

Dewitt adjusted himself on the uncomfortable stool. There was no rushing Zorro, just as there was no rushing anyone in this business. Each person had to be left to their own script, and Zorro seemed to be relishing the moment.

He slid a beaker of clear fluid before Dewitt. It smelled like alcohol. "Behold," Zorro said, waving the cigarette carelessly. Dewitt anticipated an explosion. "An olive branch. A final offering of peace from Howard Lumbrowski to James Dewitt. If it had your name on it, I could not read it more clearly."

Dewitt moved the glass. Lying on the bottom of the beaker was a key. "Jonah," he echoed.

"Yes, Detective," Zorro proclaimed proudly.

"You found this *inside* him?"

"Bravo."

"He swallowed a *key?*"

"Immediately prior to death," the doctor prompted. "I have no doubt that this was the last thing Howard Lumbrowski swallowed. Probably his last act."

Dewitt picked up the beaker then and studied the key more carefully. Stamped into the metal of the key was the number 12. It was clearly a commercial key. A *motel* key.

"It will require the diligence of a good detective to find what door that key fits, but on the other side of that door, I believe you may find the clue to Howard Lumbrowski's murder. A person must be fairly determined to swallow a key, after all. Not terribly palatable. I can only presume it is, for lack of a better expression"—he cast Dewitt a self-satisfied look—"a dying clue."

"It's a commercial key. The kind used by motels," Dewitt said.

"So it appears," the doctor agreed. "Did you see the face?"

"Yes."

"The hands?"

Dewitt nodded. "He got in a fight?"

"If he did, his opponent was a wall. I found splinters in his knuckles."

"What about those red marks?" Dewitt asked. "The ones on his neck?"

"No idea," said Zorro. "Some kind of abrasion. It's unfamiliar to me."

"He put his hand through a wall?"

"You're the detective."

"May I keep this?"

"To preserve the chain of custody, I would prefer it be delivered to the lab. There couldn't possibly be prints, of course, because of stomach acids, but rules are rules."

Dewitt checked his watch. "Ten minutes to five. What if I ran it over to the lab for you?"

"Won't they have closed?"

"Not if I make a phone call."

"So make a phone call. I have about twenty minutes more here."

<h1 style="text-align:center">8</h1>

Clare admitted him through the laboratory's back entrance, a double-door arrangement for added security. At any one time, the laboratory's evidence room contained hundreds of bags of various controlled substances and weapons of every kind, a potential target for looting. He delivered the box of vials and petri dishes containing various trace evidence from the Lumbrowski autopsy. In the cooler, he carried the organics. She explained that a coworker was out picking up some fast food. The two of them would tackle the Lumbrowski autopsy evidence tonight. She promised to have a copy of the key to him in the morning.

He caught her up on his interview with Collette. She leaned over and kissed him in the middle of his talking. It was a long sensuous kiss. "How fast is that fast food?" he asked, his implication obvious.

"It's pizza. She'll be at least twenty minutes." As she unbuttoned his shirt, she asked, "Have I shown you the evidence room lately? We really should put all this stuff away."

He mirrored her efforts, drawing her shirt open button by button.

"You smell wonderful," she said, burying her face in the crook of his neck.

"Are there still blankets in the evidence room?" he asked.

"You bet," she said, taking him by the hand.

They were back in the lab well before the pizza arrived. Clare handed him a piece of paper. "Today's major victory," she explained. "We identified the manufacturer of the bleach found on the cotton fibers."

Dewitt read from the page. This woman had a habit of saving the best for last—in and out of the office, he thought. The industrial quality bleach was manufactured by Pacific Rim Chemical Corporation. Also listed were the three commercial laundries between San Jose and Salinas that were clients of Pacific Rim. Brighton Laundry and Cleaning Service, the last on the list, was located in Seaside. "We're putting together a task force. We were prepared for a door-to-door of all motels, health clubs, and the like, to show photos of Osbourne and McDuff. This just saved us a few thousand man-hours. We'll run down Brighton's clients first. If Brighton can give us a list of motels—"

"Mind if I play devil's advocate for a minute?"

"Shoot."

"Why the emphasis on motels? As you've just said, it could be a health club, a massage parlor, a whorehouse . . . anyplace these men might have lain down on a sheet or towel. So what if Wood stole the stereo while McDuff was at a motel? McDuff could have gone on from there—" Dewitt shook his head, interrupting her.

He explained: "Wherever that stereo was stolen from was McDuff's last stop while alive. He would have reported the theft to his wife— and she insists he would have to us, as well—had it been stolen prior to their speaking early the evening of the eleventh. Next day, the twelfth, when we found him, it was missing from the truck. Therefore, it must have been lifted that evening. Had McDuff gotten back into that truck alive, say at a restaurant or a health club, he would have needed a police report for his insurance." He raised a finger. "I should condition that. He may have gotten into the truck alive, but in that case, he never came back out. Add to that Wood's statement that he had recently hit a motel parking lot—"

"But can you trust that?"

"Until this key showed up, I wasn't sure. Now I'm convinced to start with motels. If that key fits a door, we have probable cause to get ourselves a search warrant."

Clare speculated: "The killer locates his victims at a particular motel, stakes out their vehicles, and hides inside the car, waiting?"

"Collette killed his victims *while they were asleep*. This guy has imitated the rest of Collette's techniques. Why not that one, as well?"

"Inside the room?"

"It's possible. I need that key. I need to find this room. I think Lumbrowski was tortured, was beat up by somebody. He left this key to lead us back to the crime scene. This key is the best piece of hard evidence we have. We lead with our strength and hope Collette comes through with a name. I think he will. It's the *combination* of evidence that tells the story here. Let me call the aquarium. I'll try to stay and help you."

"No, you will not," she interrupted. "You're the detective on this, not the FI, and you admitted the aquarium is the one place that gets your mind off all this. You *need* that, James. Go. Maybe I'll stop by your place with some good news later on."

"Even without good news," he said.

"We'll see. I don't want to wear you out," she said with a smile.

"I wish you would," he said, taking her hand and stroking her fingers.

9

Emmy and Briar walked over to the aquarium following their Tae Kwan Do class. Dewitt realized that this meant being with Clare tonight was out. Briar said bluntly, "He's spending the night with Tona and thinks I don't know about it." Emmy seemed nervous. Dewitt asked her what was wrong and she mugged her way through a "Nothing. No problem." It didn't feel right, however.

The girls had showered and changed, their hair damp and faces still red.

"Break any bones?" Dewitt tried.

Emmy ignored him and said, "This is the busiest I've about ever seen it here."

"Tour buses were delayed," Dewitt explained. "It'll be this way 'til closing."

"Lucky you," Emmy said. Briar laughed. "We're going to wander around, okay?"

"Sure," agreed Dewitt. Briar blushed. "What's up?" he asked the girl.

She shrugged and glanced at Emmy.

Dewitt told them about a newborn pair of baby otters. "You might want to check it out," he told them.

"Sure thing," Emmy said, taking Briar by the arm and dragging her away.

"Emmy?" he called out.

The girls were quickly absorbed by the thick crowds of senior citizens and camera-clad tourists.

Dewitt fielded a variety of questions. Some evenings he felt like a human tape recorder, delivering his memorized information with all the enthusiasm of a directory-assistance operator. He found himself reciting the feeding procedure and why the tank's windows were seven inches thick. Slowly, he got back into it. Since he had sold off his own collection of nearly two hundred rare species, the fish in these tanks had become his hobby.

Cynthia Chatterman, the ever-present board member, came waltzing up to Dewitt from behind and said, "Phone call for you. I had it transferred to administration."

Dewitt hurried through the door marked EMPLOYEES ONLY and found his way to administration. If it had been business, his pager would have sounded. "Dewitt," he answered, punching the phone's only lit button. "Dewitt," he repeated. "Hello?" No one answered. He heard the annoying ventilation system kick on, looked to the ceiling, and then realized the sound was coming over the phone. A practical joke of some sort? He might have allowed himself to believe this on any other day, but with Rusty's recent murder, he felt he had to look. He started off at a walk, breaking quickly into a run. What if the intention was to get him away from his post temporarily? Away from Emmy?

He took a shortcut: out the building, around the side, and back in through the member's entrance.

The receiver of the third pay phone was off the hook, hanging by its wire. He glanced over at the nearby otter tank viewing balcony that he had recommended to the girls, and spotted them immediately in the crush of tourists.

Seeing the girls relieved some of his anxiety. Still, he didn't like the mysterious phone call. He decided to speak with them and ask them to stay by him over at the Kelp Forest until closing.

It was on his way over, as he looked up a second time, that he spotted a man standing in the crush of onlookers. As the girls moved, so did the stranger.

Dewitt began to walk slowly toward this display area to get a better look. Don't run, he chided himself. Don't attract attention. As he passed beneath the giant whales, he briefly lost sight of the crowded balcony. He picked up his pace, stitching his way through a sea of cotton-haired retirees shuffling and pointing their way from one exhibit to the next.

He didn't dare take the time to call Security. He broke into a run, rounded a cement pillar, and wormed his way rudely up the stairs. With the popularity of the baby otters, visitors swarmed around the huge viewing windows, packing the stairs, overloading the balcony. Dewitt shoved his way through the pack, leading with a strong shoulder, ascending the stairs at a frustrating pace. When he finally reached the upper platform, it was so mobbed that he lost sight. Too many heads, faces, cameras, images swirling: strobed, brilliant, spiked flash reflections sparking off the thick glass, drenching the horde in a sterile blue-white light; intrigued, childish, adoring smiles; the puckered, weathered faces of the seniors, confused, even frightened as Dewitt elbowed his way past them.

He finally fought his way to the very front of the group, turned and looked back at all the gleeful faces, their attention focused past him, through him. A strange feeling of invisibility overtook him.

Gone . . . No Emmy, no Briar, no mystery man.

More desperate now, Dewitt exploded to his right, wrestling his way to the far stairs and descending them hurriedly. There, in front of him, not twenty yards away, he spotted the man—and he *was* following the girls—who were now just below the pod of suspended orca whales in front of the information booth.

How could there be this many people? He was so accustomed to his somewhat protected position by the Kelp Forest, he rarely grasped the enormity of the crowds. That a majority of tonight's visitors were aged, frail, and slow only made matters worse.

As Dewitt rounded the corner by the aquarium's small theater, facing the stairs to the next level, his chest swelled with pain. Only yards ahead, on the incline of the stairs, he spotted the back of his daughter's head, Briar alongside of her. Five or six steps behind, followed *the man*. He caught himself about to shout but held off—to do so would only stop Emmy and cause her to turn, giving her pursuer a few more steps to reach her. The man suddenly paused and looked over his shoulder, directly into the eyes of James Dewitt. Shock, even fear, flooded his face. He panicked and started to run.

Dewitt moved to the rail, took hold, and lunged his way up the stairs, his right hand seeking out the knurled grip of the .38 at his side. Only once in his life had he fired a weapon at another individual. That had been Steven Miller. He wondered whether he could do it again. He gained precious little ground. The man bounded up the stairs and disappeared around the corner. An older man slipped and fell to his hands and knees just in front of Dewitt. People piled on in domino fashion, forming a wall of confusion and producing several cries for help as others went down.

Dewitt vaulted the dividing rail to avoid the knot of fallen people, and charged into the oncoming stream of descending visitors. By the time he crested the stairway, he faced a drove of visitors, an impenetrable wall of casual clothes and childlike faces. A boxlike structure ahead of him, an island of Sheetrock, housed the rest rooms. To his left was the second-story viewing area for the Kelp Forest, a display of anchovies, the Kelp Gallery, Kelp Lab, and back toward the center of the building, a display on tides and an overlook at the downstairs foyer.

No sign of Emmy or Briar. No sign of *him*. It was at that moment he spotted the youthful Billy Talbot just ascending the stairs to the third level.

Talbot? No time for Talbot, although it explained Briar's blush: The girls had arranged a rendezvous.

Dewitt searched the second level at a run. After several minutes, he rounded the corner and assaulted the stairway to the third-story level, an area that opened onto a balcony to the right, and to the left a restricted rooftop area. He came face to face with his daughter, Briar, Billy Talbot, and a boy he recognized from the party. They were laughing.

"Dad?" Emmy asked, seeing his flushed face, his frantic look.

He walked over to Talbot and took him by the front of his shirt. "Did you make that phone call, Talbot?" Talbot shook his head. Dewitt grabbed him more tightly. There was no mistaking his rage. "It's important! Did you?"

"Yeah."

"Dad!" Emmy beseeched.

Talbot explained in a troubled voice, "I didn't want you to see me. The only way to get upstairs was to walk right by you. What's the big deal?"

"Dad!"

Dewitt released Talbot and told him to leave. The boy ran down the stairs three at a time and disappeared.

"Dad!"

Dewitt unleashed a diatribe on honesty, deceit, and kids like Billy Talbot. Briar was crying. Again. The verbal abuse made him feel better. When he was through, he announced they were going home immediately and that he "didn't want to hear a word."

On the way, he wasn't thinking of Emmy or Talbot, or Cynthia Chatterman's disapproving glance as he left. He was thinking about a face in the crowd, and what it meant if that face belonged to whom he thought it did.

10

Trapper John's face caught the light briefly, though he shied from it instinctively. He preferred the privacy, the safety of darkness. His eyes, brown as wet earth, sparked with the light, an intensity in them like that of a caged animal. He knew all about cages. He would not be caged again. The bridge of his nose held a twenty-year reminder of a high school fistfight; he wore his thick dark hair slicked back. With a square chin and high cheekbones, he was proud of the ten percent Cherokee blood he carried in his veins. To see him, one would think him quite handsome, though on this night the steely defiance in his sharp movements and calculated efforts warned of his intent. Like a cat slinking close to the ground, there was no mistaking his purpose. If truth be known, purpose drove him on.

His finger found the light switch and pushed it down.

The agony hit him in waves, pain as he imagined a cancer victim must feel, a ripping at the fiber of his heart, a tearing away of his flesh;

the stinging grief of loss like a tumor. The same now for five long months. It seemed appropriate that this pain should find him as he entered the back-lot kitchen entrance to the Community Hospital. The aquarium had been a failure. This would not be.

He had followed Dewitt here on numerous occasions, knew to turn left down the service hallway, knew that at this time of night the only threat was from the surveillance cameras. That was why he had switched off the hallway lights. If, in fact, those cameras were monitored—which seemed unlikely—he would appear as a dark form, if he appeared at all. How long could it take to pull a couple of plugs? He would be in and out before anyone knew the difference.

The pain stung into his chest again. God, how he missed the boy. He held to his grief like a skid-row bum to his bottle. It fueled his imagination, quickened his heart, drove him like a jockey's crop.

That the plans could end up so much junk infuriated him. Ad-libbing now for the better part of the week, he was beginning to fray at the edges. He had not slept more than five hours in four days. This, in itself, was nothing new; insomnia was an accepted way of life. The problem was having to think clearly while so fatigued. It had all seemed so straightforward during the planning stages. Then Lumbrowski with his arrogance; Dewitt with his investigation.

He reached the hallway and peered through the crack at the camera that rotated left to right. He could see a single nurse at the nurses' station, head bent as she worked on paperwork. When the camera rocked right, its single eye looking away, Trapper John moved confidently across the hallway and into number 114. He could hear his own breathing above the hum of the life-support machinery. He did not deny himself the excitement of such moments. He felt no remorse over Anna's defenselessness. People got what they deserved. This wasn't about Anna Dewitt, it was about her father.

He moved directly to the far side of the huge bed, dropped to one knee, and pushed his way behind the blue enameled machine. He withdrew the paper clip from his pocket and then tugged the plug from the wall. Briefly, the machine switched to a warning tone. The change in sound charged adrenaline into his system, but his fingers did not pause. He slipped the unfolded paper clip between the tongs of the plug and forced it into the wall socket. A blue-white flash flared from the socket and all the room's machines went dark and silent. He yanked out the plug, removed to his pocket what was left of the charred paper clip, and looked up at her.

He would have liked to stay to watch. It wasn't so different from the others. Not really. However, he couldn't count on how, or even whether, the hospital monitored blown circuits. If this failed, he would be back.

He moved across the hallway, having waited for the camera's rotation, and was about to open the door to the back hall when he heard voices ahead of him. He glanced over his shoulder at the persistent camera, now returning its focus toward him.

Go away! he willed the people down the unseen hallway on the other side of the door. He glanced in panic once again at the camera, this time directly into the lens. The voices faded and died. He pushed open the door a crack to check. Clear.

He switched off the light and hurried down the hall toward his freedom.

One down. One to go.

11

. . . *an emergency*: Dewitt heard the words ringing in his ears as he drove at a breakneck pace along the twisting Highway 68. He had dropped off Emmy and Briar at Clare's. Following the trouble at the aquarium, he was taking no chances.

The hospital hallway suddenly seemed so long. He rounded a corner and found himself walking the corridor that held his daughter's room. The large clock on the wall read 2:20. A small group of nurses was gathered by Anna's door. Dewitt slowed, nearly unable to place one foot before the other. A pain stole into his chest. One of the nurses began to cry audibly as she spotted him. He forced himself on, the distance between himself and the room refusing to close.

When he entered Anna's room, the first thing that struck him was the silence. The absolute stillness. No beeping, no electronic humming. The rotating bed was empty, the sheets wrinkled. He spotted Anna then—all there was to see of her: a wisp of blond hair escaping from beneath a crisp white sheet on a gurney.

He walked over to her, pulled down the sheet, leaned over, and pressed his cheek to hers. He knew that temperature: His daughter was dead. Tears. He cupped her fragile head in his big hand and held her tightly, repeating her name quietly, hoping, miracle of miracles, she might yet come alive. "Anna . . . ," he gasped.

"I'm sorry, James," said the voice of Dr. Jerry Rosenberg from behind. A gentle hand touched Dewitt's shoulder. "A freak occurrence. Or perhaps, just perhaps, James, there's a higher power at work here. Her time had come."

Dewitt spun around with angry bloodshot eyes.

"The odds of this happening—" the doctor said.

"The odds?" Dewitt asked through tears.

"A power surge. Something like that," the doctor said, still groping. "We don't have any warning system for that, per se."

"Power surge?" Dewitt asked, motioning Rosenberg away and examining the area around the bed. His eyes—the eyes of a forensic investigator—roamed the wires, the dials, the enamel blue stands with their black rubber wheels. There, on the pristine white speckled flooring, he spotted a small amount of dirt—dried mud by the look of it. He studied the dirt more closely. It had been raining when they had left the aquarium. He jerked a monitor out of his way. By the base of the machine, he found more dirt. One thing about hospital rooms, they were kept clean. Why the dirt? He disconnected the cord. Melted metal studs had welded themselves to the plug's tines. "Not a higher power, Doctor," he said. "This was the work of a mere mortal. She had a visitor."

Dewitt brushed past the doctor, eyes to the floor. More dried mud by the room's door. Two smears of mud on a line from this door across the hall to the door Dewitt often used to sneak in here late at night. When he reached this other door, he looked back toward Anna's room. It was then he noticed, to his astonishment, the security camera. He had never bothered to look up, had never considered that his unauthorized visits had been witnessed.

Rosenberg stood across the hall studying Dewitt.

"How long has *that* been there?" he asked, pointing.

"A year now. A little more," answered the doctor.

"It works?"

"Of course."

"Runs all the time?"

"Yes."

"It's monitored?"

"Taped. For insurance purposes."

"I need to see those tapes," insisted Dewitt. "Now!"

"We'll call Hank," said the doctor.

Hank Johnson had dressed quickly. Director of hospital security, famous for his white cowboy hat, the black man wore his uniform shirt partially untucked.

On the way down in the elevator, Johnson explained: "We've got cameras in every hallway. Insurance company required it after some fool sued us, claiming he had slipped on a wet floor that never existed. Sued the *hell* out of us. Now the cameras cover our ass. We don't monitor them. They run on twenty-four-hour loops. If we have a problem that warrants it, we file a tape away and hold on to it."

The basement room was small and very hot. "Way it works," the man explained, "is we got fifteen recorders." He pointed to the bank of VCRs. "Hallways and stairways most important to the insurance company, so we got twelve machines dedicated." Johnson spent several minutes with the machines, Dewitt looking on. The numbers of a twenty-four-hour counter rolled at fast forward in the upper corner of the television screen he was monitoring. Nurses walked stiff-legged at exaggerated speeds, like characters from a silent movie.

Seven o'clock: The minutes in the lower-right-hand corner sped past. Because the camera rotated in the hallway, there were equal sections of time when Anna's door was out of view. Look right, look left . . . look right, look left . . . like a tennis match. Eight o'clock: visiting hours over, a parade of differing emotions read in the departing postures and embraces. A hospital is a place of great thanks or great despair.

Nine o'clock: Nurses on final rounds, checking on patients. Ten, eleven, midnight, one o'clock. Traffic in the corridor had quieted to none at all.

"Wait!" Dewitt said. "Back it up."

Johnson worked the machinery. The same time period ran at normal speed. "Again," Dewitt instructed.

Dewitt then asked for the same passage one more time, requesting the tape be slowed this time. Johnson noticed what had caught Dewitt's eye. "The hallway door," he said. "It closes shut." When the camera panned back to include the door to Anna's room, the large door thumped shut. "Shit," the security man said, "he's inside the room."

James Dewitt felt his tears threatening, his throat tighten. On the other side of that door, his daughter's killer. Two passes later, the camera looked back down the hall as Anna's door opened a crack. In darkness, a face could not be seen. Dewitt said, "He's waiting for the camera."

"Making sure the hall is clear," Johnson agreed.

The camera tracked away and, as it returned, it caught the man standing, his back to the camera. "He's frozen," Johnson observed. "Must be someone in the hall."

"Turn around!" Dewitt demanded, leaning his face to within inches of the screen. "Look at me, you bastard!" he insisted.

The man suddenly obeyed, glancing over his shoulder in a blurry panic.

"Freeze frame," Dewitt ordered. Although Johnson tried several times to get a single frame that showed definition onto the screen, the face came up a blur of features each and every time. "The tape gets recorded over too much; it loses its clarity," the security man explained.

After several more tries, Dewitt took the tape from Johnson. "That's all right," he said in a dull, stunned voice. "I know what he looks like. We met earlier tonight."

8
TUESDAY

1

"I thought we were a team?" Emmy pleaded from the Zephyr's passenger seat, the pale blush of dawn filling the sky, glowing on the roofs of the vehicles in the ever-moving chain of freeway traffic. She had taken the news of her sister well. Too well. Dewitt worried for her; she was stonewalling her emotions.

"Don't, Em. It's settled," Dewitt said.

"We need each other, Dad, don't we? A team?"

"I don't like this, either, Em, but—"

"I *hate* that line, you know that? If you *don't like it*, then why are we *doing* it?"

"It's not up for discussion."

"We're talking about *my life* here, Dad, and it's 'not up for discussion'? Gimme a break! You can put me on a plane to Gram's, but how long do you think I'll stay there? You want to spend the next week picturing me hitchhiking back to Carmel? A runaway?"

"Em . . ."

"Teammates don't abandon each other; they work together."

Dewitt glanced out his side window, cars streaming past heading south on the other side of the freeway's retaining fence, hundreds of expressionless faces in bright shiny vehicles too similar to differentiate. "I'd rather be safe than sorry. Give me some time, Em. I'll have you back just as soon as I can."

"You need me," she insisted.

"You're right, I do need you."

"We're teammates," she tried tentatively.

"We are." He couldn't explain it to her properly. There were ways around this: He could shuttle her between Clarence, other parents, and himself, making sure she was kept careful track of, but the easiest for everyone seemed to be a short vacation.

A long heavy silence passed. Looking out her window, Emmy shocked him, asking, "How do you do it, Dad?"

"Do what?"

"Act like she never existed. Never talk about her. I don't see how you can do it. I miss her so much."

"Nothing wrong with missing her, Em. I miss her, too. But we've got to let go. We've got to go on."

"That's what I mean. You're a lot better at that than I am."

"Am I? You sure about that?"

She studied him. "What do you mean?"

"Em, sometimes we act in order to impress other people. Other times, we act to preserve our own sanity." This is new ground, he thought. Was it wrong to show her this side of himself?

"You're *acting?*"

"Sometimes."

"How come?"

"Because there're two of me inside here, Em. One of me wants to die every day I wake up and realize your mother's gone. The other sits up in bed and rubs his eyes."

"Acting?"

"Sometimes, sure. Especially at first. I had to act it out until it felt familiar. You were counting on me, Em. Without that, I might never had made it. I owe my sanity to you. Your reliance on me forced me to be someone I wasn't."

"How come you never told me this?"

"You never asked," he said.

She considered what he had said. Dewitt turned on the radio and found an oldies rock station. Doobie Brothers. *Oldies?* he thought.

"I'm supposed to act?" she questioned.

"You're not *supposed* to do anything. I'm just telling you how it was for me."

"I'm supposed to act like everything's okay, is that it?"

"Don't act for me. I love you as you are, Em. I feel for you. I worry about you. You know that. I'm just telling you how it was for me. It was like I was in a movie and I had to remember my lines. Then one day I woke up, and things weren't perfect, but they were a lot better. I could handle it."

"I love you, Dad."

"Same here." He said tentatively, "I want you to think about something while you're away. Just think about it, that's all."

"Mom's ashes," Emmy said intuitively.

He reached over and they laced fingers and held each other's hand strongly. She had the hand of a young woman, not a girl, he thought. He didn't let go until he stretched for the automatic ticket at the airport's short-term parking nearly an hour later. His hand was sweaty then, and like a child, he thought, I won't wash it for a week.

She began to cry after check-in. "We *are* a team," he said, wrapping an arm around her, his throat tight.

They stopped before Security. Dewitt was wearing his gun; he wouldn't be allowed past without endless hassle. At that moment, exhausted, sick of the investigation, in grief over Anna, worried about

Emmy, that gun at his waist seemed to represent everything bad, everything wrong with his life. His daughter went through the area without incident, looked back at him once and, on the verge of tears, waved.

Dewitt watched her until she was no longer visible, consumed by the teeming hordes of travelers.

He found the men's room. Locked himself inside a toilet stall, sat down on the seat fully clothed, buried his face in his hands, and wept.

2

Dewitt spent the afternoon organizing a joint task force comprised of three detectives from M.C.S.O. and two investigators from the District Attorney's office, with himself as its head. Rivalries existed between all law-enforcement agencies, most of them of a personal, incestuous nature: people having worked closely together and later transferred apart, creating an atmosphere of competition, prejudices, and/or envy. When it came to a homicide investigation, however, there was an immediate sense of camaraderie, us against him.

They were gathered around one of the large tables in the lunch-room, Dewitt at its head. They all wore sport coats, button-down shirts, and ties. The two from the District Attorney's office were younger than the others. Only one of the five had facial hair, and he smoked. Dewitt directed their attention to the photocopy of a map of Seaside. "The two B's on the map are the only two bike shops that service mountain bikes. One is also a dealer, though we're assuming this guy stole the bike he uses for his escapes. The H is the only area hardware store that sells the Plexiglas we found on him. All six of us have different lists of clients of Brighton Laundry, motels at the top, and we all have copies of the key found in Lumbrowski. The hardware store and the bike shops aren't much. I realize that. But they're a starting point, and that's all we're using them as. The places on my list are inside the immediate triangle formed by the shops and the store. Each of you handles a quadrant, working out from that center.

"We try the key first. We don't talk to management; we don't announce ourselves. If the keys fits, we have enough probable cause to secure the area until a search warrant can be obtained and a search conducted. You don't go inside that room, understood?" he asked rhetorically.

"For the time being, we're referring to the suspect as Trapper John. That's how it'll be over the radio if you get a suspect. The face I've given you is a photocopy of an Identi-Kit face I put together. This may or may not be Trapper John, but anyone resembling this man should be detained for questioning. We estimate he's between one-fifty and one-sixty, just shy of six feet tall. He may or may not own a red-haired dog with collie or shepherd markings. Trapper John is to be considered dangerous, and although the experts tell me he's not likely to carry conventional weapons, treat him as if he does. One thing we do know about this man: He's incredibly cunning. More then likely, he trapped at least two of his victims, possibly all three. We don't know exactly what that means at this point, or how he might have accomplished this. So keep your eyes open. Any questions?"

The briefing continued for twenty more minutes, until just after the red winter sun extinguished itself in the ocean. Some days, Dewitt almost expected to see steam rising as it did so.

Clarence caught up to Dewitt just as he was leaving. "About Anna," he said, his eyes glassing up. He shook his head. Dewitt placed a hand on his shoulder.

"You want to help our cause," Dewitt said. "Keep riding Shilstein at Atascadero. We want Collette going over those files—those photographs—until he has something. Nelson has my notes. He's going over the same files, looking for background information that matches. You might also check why Ramirez hasn't gotten back to us on that roll of masking tape found in Lumbrowski's Mustang. He's supposed to be running a print through ALPS for Rick Morn." Dewitt heard the tension in his own voice. He never spoke quickly, but he had just talked a blue streak.

Hindeman asked, "Are you all right?"

"No," answered James Dewitt. He forced a confused grin and hurried down the hall.

Dewitt knew from his reading that when an FBI profile identified a specific search area—typically defined by the location of the bodies—it was best to start dead center and work your way out in a logical fashion. In this case, the targets were determined by the customer lists of the only local laundry that used the commercial bleach found on some cotton pills. Although it couldn't be considered hard evidence, it was all they had. No reason not to conduct the search in an organized and logical manner. Dewitt divided his mile-square territory into four separate grids. He had six motels to check, a massage parlor, and four restaurants.

The first two motels on his list failed to help: One, the Star-Lite, had only ten rooms; at the second, the Best-Vu, his key didn't fit. The third motel Dewitt parked near interested him immediately, for it not only fit the seamy description Priscilla Laughton had given John Osbourne's lifestyle but piles of dog excrement dotted the landscape.

Dewitt monitored the radio channel the task force was using as each of the five others regularly checked in with Ginny, announcing their locations, their departures from and their return to their automobiles. Ginny, along with Commander Karl Capp, mapped the progress, tracking the movement of each, using colored pushpins to indicate an investigator's status. Dewitt knew, as he now called in his arrival at the Just Rest'Inn, that a yellow pin would be placed at his location. When he checked back in, the pin would be switched to green.

He walked across the dirt parking lot, the night air cold, and could picture that this might be a place where Marvin Wood would rip off a car stereo; dark, isolated, foreboding. He could also picture a killer lurking in the abandoned adjacent car wash, sipping on some cheap wine, awaiting another victim, his eyes possibly trained on him at this very moment. Dewitt felt the muscles in his upper back stiffen with the thought. Darkness did this to him in general; James Dewitt was not a friend to darkness as some people were. He preferred open spaces and the company of sunlight—the bluffs of Point Lobos. Darkness stimulated his imagination. As it did so now, he could picture a man waiting, stalking, killing, and stealing the body from one of the rooms. Perhaps that helped to explain his trembling hand as he withdrew the key from his pocket, slipped it into the lock of the door to Room 12, and found it not only fit but it turned.

He knocked. No response.

Dewitt was well aware of the rules: This was where he returned to his vehicle and called in the troops. This was when he started the gears in motion to have a search warrant walked through and signed by a judge. Yet Dewitt could not turn away from the door. Inside this room might be the solution to the murders that had baffled and frustrated him for so many days now. His brain told him to back off and play it by the book. But something more powerful pushed him forward. He pulled out his weapon, twisted the knob, and stepped into the room.

He pushed the door gently shut. His penlight scattered ovals of light around the narrow walls, over the small bed. The room was tiny, its cinder-block walls painted a dull colorless wash. With no one inside, Dewitt returned the gun to its holster and snapped some surgical gloves onto his hands to avoid leaving his own prints. He elected not to switch on the lights, not to announce his presence in this way. He moved to the room's only window, a small horizontally mounted window at shoulder height. He was about to pull the brief curtains when headlights from the street caught the surface, illuminating four long yellow lines that were immediately apparent as scratch marks. It was then he realized the window was fixed and not glass, but *Plexiglas*. Synthetic resin: the same substance found beneath the nails of Malcolm McDuff. Suddenly the modus operandi became vivid in his mind. The victims were not stalked, abducted, and killed; they were gassed in a motel room. *This* motel room: a death chamber. A tiny room would require precious little time to fill with gas and asphyxiate the inhabitant. They had been gassed in their sleep, the cotton pills of the bedding clinging to their skin. McDuff must have awakened and clawed desperately at the window before the fumes overcame him. The killer then dressed his victims, packed their bags, and moved their bodies. Trapper John indeed.

Dewitt's forensic mind began to plot this possibility immediately as he moved from location to location: the vent above the bed, the bedding itself. *It's possible,* he thought, stepping into the tiny bathroom and casting his light about. No window. Another vent grate.

What he had not looked at carefully was the trim surrounding the motel room door, the trim that carried a single pair of bell wires leading to a small magnetic switch above the topmost hinge. This, had he spotted it, would have told him much more than the evidence he now sought.

The man who thought of himself as Trapper John rested peacefully in front of a "M*A*S*H" rerun, his favorite, laughing when the television laughed, still experiencing the resonant glow from his accomplishment at the hospital. Despite all the fuckups, the changes in plans, he was only one kill from the end. Satisfaction seeped down his throat in the form of a beer. He petted the dog, who rested his head on his thigh. The Valium warmed his brain. Life was good.

When the buzzer sounded, announcing Dewitt's entry into Room 12, Trapper John sat up in alarm. The buzzer was intended to monitor a potential victim's movement in and out of the room; he had only left it armed because he had been unable to find the key he had given Lumbrowski—and though he knew Lumbrowski didn't have it, from having searched him carefully, he was taking no chances. He jumped up from the bed in the small room off the motel office, reached into the closet, and threw the switch he had wired there. The wires from this switch ran in the crawl space for the distance of the motel: four dollars from Radio Shack. They tripped an electronic "night latch" that, when reversed as Trapper had reversed it, made the inside door knob useless, effectively sealing the inhabitant inside the room.

He kept the stun stick hidden inside the sleeve of a jacket he had hanging in the closet. He had ordered it mail order from the want ads in the back of *Armed and Dangerous*, his only magazine subscription. One hundred and fifty-six bucks. No tax because it came from Texas. There was sweet irony in using the same device the guards had used on him—and he knew damned well its effectiveness. Set to its maximum, it would knock a person unconscious for at least fifteen minutes, giving the exhaust plenty of time to hold the victim there. All in all, it was a perfect system, designed for the economy-minded killer. He took the stun stick in hand and hurried out the back door.

The sudden change of light caught Dewitt's attention. He hadn't heard a thing; he blamed that on his pounding blood. Something behind him! He spun around quickly, fear pumping adrenaline into him, arms swinging out at the dark. Light flashed briefly across a hairy face. The man lunged at him. Dewitt raised his hand to block the blow, knocking the arm aside. Another lunge, straight forward. Dewitt feared a knife, but as he blocked the attempt, it felt more like a nightstick. The next attempt caught him in the hand. The shock, so sudden, so severe, paralyzed him. He fell to the floor. Electrocution! None of his muscles obeyed him, limp and lifeless. Helpless.

That stick came at him again. A gooey blue substance seeped in from behind his ears, unconsciousness flirting with him. The last thing he saw was the back of a man's shoes as he hurried in retreat.

As he came awake, there was a bitter taste in his throat, though not really an odor. *Exhaust.* His right hand and arm were numb from the electrical shock. A blinding headache pounded from behind his eyes. He rubbed his right hand. It was hot. Perhaps the latex glove had provided a thin layer of insulation from the enormous power of the stun stick, reducing the delivered voltage and sparing Dewitt the normal period of unconsciousness. One thing he understood perfectly well: The man had fried his victims with a stun stick—something Emmanuel had missed—and was now waiting for the piped-in exhaust to kill him. A death chamber indeed.

Instinctively, Dewitt checked for his gun. Gone. His pants pockets had been emptied as well, but the man had missed the pockets to his sport coat. He still had his few tools and his penlight.

As he attempted to move, the headache slammed into his forehead. Carbon monoxide poisoning. He knew the symptoms: He would become drowsy next, heavy-limbed; his heart and lungs, starved for oxygen, would begin to work harder, which in turn would only hasten his suffocation, increase his light-headedness. Reaching the door, he fell to one knee, a sailor on land for the first time in months. A kind of giddy, euphoric drunkenness overtook him, almost dreamlike. He was tired—his body begged him for sleep; the nearby bed called out to him. He knew that asphyxiation, like drowning, produced euphoria— a blissful gliding toward death and, as he stumbled again, he knew if he did not escape quickly, if he did not find air, he would die here. He hurried to the door. Locked: The Plexiglas window was fixed and unbreakable. Piece by piece, the solution to the puzzle fell into place—only now he was trapped by the solution: No way out. Was this the same panic McDuff had felt?

He tried to suck air from the small gap at the bottom of the door, but it was sealed tightly and he feared he was simply recycling room exhaust, his lungs tightening. How long until he was checked on?

Think! How to find fresh air if the door is locked from the outside and the window can't be broken?

Back into the small bathroom, the filtered exhaust pouring through the overhead grate. He steadied himself at the sink, ran the water, and splashed cold water onto his face. If only he were a fish, he could suck the oxygen right out of the water.

Then it occurred to him.

He dropped to his knees, groping for the sink's drainpipe. He pulled on it, shook it, but it remained fast. He had done enough home repair to know that the purpose of a sink trap is not to catch a lost earring but to provide a water block from the horrible smell of the sewer. Overhead stacks vented the sewer pipe in order to prevent a vacuum effect and to allow the waste water to drain. On the other side of the sink trap, there was air.

Every effort he made only served to further tire him, to increase his headache, to choke his lungs and squeeze his heart. He braced himself against the toilet and kicked out at the pipe. It moved. He kicked it again, and again. The linkage of pipe began to bend away from him. He kicked harder. That blue gel worked him down like the fists of a determined boxer. The pipe bent toward the floor. He twisted and wrestled with it until the trap broke off completely. Dewitt wrapped his lips around it and inhaled as deeply as he could. It was foul, putrid air, but never a sweeter sensation to his lungs. The welcome influx of oxygen charged his system and he felt the flush of stability.

The problem quickly went from his lungs to his stomach. He backed off and vomited, only to glue his lips back there and drink in the precious oxygen despite the stench. His stomach turned again. He glued his mouth to the plumbing like an opium smoker to the end of his pipe.

With his murky head calming, he began to contemplate his escape. The man had sneaked up on him. There was no way he had entered by the front door; Dewitt would have heard it. There had to be another entrance to the room, a clandestine means of retrieving the bodies without the risk of being seen.

The ceiling seemed impractical. More likely, a trapdoor beneath the carpet. James hyperventilated the grotesque air, charging his system with oxygen, and checked the corners of the carpet, attempting to tug it from the floor. Firmly fixed. He returned to the pipe for more air and then headed back out into the room again, pulling on carpet corners. Nothing.

If not a trapdoor, then what, a hidden panel? He ferried back and forth to the pipe repeatedly, building his lungs back up, then returning to the room and conducting a thorough panel-by-panel inspection of the walls.

The back wall of the closet showed two open seams in the Sheetrock, which didn't make construction sense. The Sheetrock should have been taped, spackled, and painted. He checked the carpet, running his hand over it and finding it damp. The entrance. He pushed on the panel but it didn't move. Running his penlight beneath the shelf, he spotted the latch. It slid to the left. He pushed against the Sheetrock and it opened. He ducked, stepping through the hidden doorway and into a darkened shed. Tasting the fresh air felt as good as diving into a pool on a hot summer afternoon. He could feel his system purging the exhaust.

Dewitt turned and popped the panel back into place, then shined the light around. The shed was cluttered with broken lamps, televisions on their sides, windowpanes, and bits and pieces of furniture. At the opposite end, two mattresses leaning against it as a muffle, a rubber hose running from its oversized muffler, was a black Schwinn mountain bike retrofitted with a small engine like those used on mopeds. The rubber hose then ran through what appeared to be a homemade filter, plugged into the wall above the Sheetrock panel, no doubt directly entering the duct work to Room 12.

The addition of the moped motor to the bike would make light work of what otherwise would have been a long and at times difficult ride from Carmel to Seaside. The ruggedness of the mountain bike's frame and suspension would allow the killer to use off-road and back-road routes where, even at five in the morning, he would not be spotted. Here, then, Dewitt found himself standing in the midst of a forensic gold mine. Much, if not all, of the evidence necessary to convict the killer was in this room.

Without a weapon, and without backup, Dewitt was far too vulnerable. He picked his way past the bike and opened the shed door slowly, peering outside as he did so. He spotted a small doghouse at the far end of the string of rooms. The dog could bark and announce his escape. A single room window glowed a third of the way down the building.

His frustration built; he hated to leave all this evidence behind, even for a few minutes. If the man should discover his escape . . . However, at the moment, he was defenseless. He cut around the end of the building, holding close to the motel wall. The man's absence had confused him until he saw his Zephyr was gone. The routine obviously included outfitting the victim's car while the victim was being asphyxiated.

The thing to do now was reach a phone and call in for backup. He ran in shadow toward the abandoned car wash.

No pay phone.

A block later, he located a pay phone, but some fool had torn the receiver from it. Across the street was a bar—had to be a phone in the bar.

Ginny answered.

"The Just Rest'Inn," Dewitt said, out of breath, the patrons looking at him, listening in. "It's him! Need backup! Hurry!"

At that moment, through the soot-coated window, Dewitt saw the first in a series of brilliant yellow flashes erupt from Room 12. Sections of roof exploded skyward, the fire licking hungrily into the darkness and sweeping quickly along the roof, room to room. Dewitt dropped the receiver and ran outside. The entire motel was ablaze.

Dewitt sprinted toward the fire, sirens already sounding in the distance, a radio police car racing through an intersection and speeding toward the inferno.

He came to an abrupt stop then, stunned by the sight before him. A man—the same man from the aquarium, quite possibly the man who had killed Anna and had just tried to kill him—was standing across the street from the motel, a dog on a leash by his side, his face orange in the glow of the fire.

From this distance, the man's voice was lost to the roar of the fire, but Dewitt saw the man shout at the Seaside patrolman. A moment later, the cop's attention fully upon him, this man turned and pointed to Dewitt with an unmistakable intensity.

He pointed the finger of accusal.

9

WEDNESDAY

1

Seaside detective Peter Tilly, with his Wheaties body and surfer looks, came striding into his captain's office, where Hindeman and Dewitt awaited him.

"Talked to McNeary," Tilly informed them, "the arson investigator for the ladder boys. Says no question it was arson—"

"Brilliant," Dewitt said.

Tilly glanced at him oddly. "And that the far end of the motel is a complete meltdown. Says Marney's Salinas crew won't come up with nothing but ash in there." It was 2:30 in the morning. To Dewitt, the last few hours had gone by like minutes. "There's an interesting wrinkle here," he added, looking at Dewitt again and pulling a chair over to the two of them.

"We'd like to interrogate him," Hindeman interrupted.

"That's the wrinkle. Like I explained to Dewitt here, he says Dewitt broke into the motel, planted some shit, and lit the place off. Claims he nearly died in the fire."

"Well, he's a fast thinker," Dewitt said. "I'll give him that much."

"Not that easy, Dewitt," Tilly said confidently. "You said he moved your Zephyr, 'cause it wasn't where you parked it."

"So?"

"Our boys found the car parked behind the bowling alley."

"The Zephyr?"

"Not the end of it. Keys were above the flap. In the backseat of the car, they found some fusing and three five-gallon gas cans. Empty," he added with punctuation. "You got an explanation for that?"

Dewitt stared ahead blankly. He could feel Hindeman's eyes boring into him.

Tilly continued, "Man says he didn't have any reason to run from the cops because he's got nothing to run from."

"You haven't booked him?" Hindeman asked.

"Booked him? On what charges?"

"Try murder one," Dewitt said.

"Based on?"

"That key fit the room. By his own admission, he was managing that motel. He's got a dog that fits the description. *He* fits the description Clare gave us. He's the same guy I saw at the aquarium. What do we need here, a signed confession?"

"Something that will hold in court," Tilly said bluntly.

"This is *bullshit!*" Dewitt hollered.

"James," Hindeman reprimanded. "Who's questioning him?" he asked Tilly.

"Morn and me. Listen, we want him too, but he's playing it real cool. Claims Dewitt here rented a room from him on Saturday night and met a big heavy guy drove a Mustang. He remembers the car. Sound like anyone you know?"

199

"He's building himself a backstop," Dewitt said. "He knows we've got him."

"He's getting it all on the record, is what he's doing. At this point he's a witness, Dewitt, not a suspect. Now, if you had seen his face inside that motel room—"

"I told you: It was dark."

"You see my problem?" Tilly asked Hindeman. "We don't got squat."

"I'm not liking the sound of this one bit," Dewitt told no one in particular.

"Book him, Tilly," Clarence Hindeman said.

"On?"

"Suspicion of arson. Attempted murder. That should hold him a few days."

"You sure?"

"Positive. Mirandize him, fingerprint him, and get those prints up to Ramirez. I want to know who this guy really is."

"Says the name is Quill, Michael Quill. I ran the name," Tilly said. "No priors."

"That's exactly what I mean," Hindeman said.

"Save his clothing," Dewitt said, "in separate bags. Get him into a jump suit. Treat the clothes like a murder suspect's. Get them over to the lab following the proper chain of evidence procedures. And take a hair sample from the dog—"

"The dog?" Tilly questioned, glancing to Hindeman for support. His eyes said, Is this guy crazy?

Dewitt was nodding furiously, the fatigue taking its toll. "You want some irony?" he asked. "That guy hung my dog, but in the end, his dog is going to hang him."

2

At nine o'clock the next morning, following two hours of sleep and three cups of coffee, Dewitt sat at his office desk in a coma, missing

Emmy very much. The last seven days of his life felt more like a month; Clare seemed more like a dream. In his mind's eye, he saw the man who called himself Quill standing unperturbed in the glow of the motel fire, the leashed dog at his side.

Quill's arraignment had been set for early afternoon in hopes of giving the lab a chance to tie Quill to the murders. It was a pins-and-needles morning for Dewitt. Everyone seemed to have something important to do but him. He was attempting to write a report on the incident at the motel, on his third draft now because the first two had seemed so fantastic: Would anyone believe a drain pipe had saved his life? The men of the task force were busy showing Quill's photograph to the bike shops, hardware stores, and Anthony De Sica in hopes he might be identified. Nelson continued to pore over the Vacaville files.

Dewitt feared they might lose Quill to a justice system that favored the accused. He was convinced of the man's involvement. Those around him were not. He knew of too many Quills of this world who had walked out of a station house free men, never to be heard of again. Such thought proved considerably distracting. The work on the report went more slowly.

At 10:20, Shilstein called from the Atascadero State Mental Hospital. "Dewitt," he said, "according to Collette, the man you're after is named Michael Quinn, not Quill. His psychiatrist at Vacaville was Dr. Harold Christiansen. I've had a brief talk with Christiansen . . . an *illuminating* talk. I believe I've persuaded him to share with you. He practices in the city. I'd get my butt up there if I were you, ASAP." He provided him Christiansen's phone number and closed with, "That system of Collette's is awesome."

Dewitt placed an immediate call to Ramirez at the Sacramento DOJ, who, though initially hostile, warmed when Dewitt had a specific name against which to run "Quill's" prints. A direct comparison could be made by eye—by human!—and spare taxing an already overworked computer system. Ramirez promised to leave a message if he couldn't reach Dewitt directly.

Dewitt took a twelve-noon puddle jumper from Monterey to San Francisco International.

3

"So you're the infamous Detective Dewitt," Dr. Harold Christiansen said from behind his desk. Through the window behind him, Dewitt could see a piece of the Golden Gate Bridge—as well as several empty lots where houses had once stood before the October earthquake. Christiansen was a big man with a clipped gray beard, hard eyes, and a firm handshake. He dressed casually in a thousand dollars' worth of haberdashery. "Oddly enough, I might as well know you, Detective. I've known *of* you for quite some time." He motioned for Dewitt to sit.

"From Quinn?" Dewitt asked.

Christiansen nodded, concern stealing his welcome. "I contract out to the state for their more interesting cases. It allows me to maintain a substantial private practice while, at the same time, doing my bit." He smiled cordially.

"Quinn is in custody. We think he may be our 'suicide killer.' If you're able to share any pertinent information . . ."

"I won't stonewall you, Detective. Then again, I do have certain responsibilities to my clients. Confidentiality serves a useful purpose. Hopefully, it protects the client when he needs protecting. In this case, the public may need more protecting than the client. If Quinn can't obey the rules, then he still requires treatment. It's as simple as that." He hesitated. "I am more familiar with this than you can imagine, Detective," he continued confidently. "Tell me what you know."

Dewitt reviewed the case for him, including Collette's vivid description of his chess partner's past.

"He's right, you know? Quinn is *suspected* in half a dozen violent crimes. Missing persons cases. He's only been convicted of killing a few cats and dogs. Thus," he said, raising a finger, "his insidiousness.

"On the surface he had led a fairly normal life up until the departure of his common-law wife with their son. In fact, it wasn't normal. Quinn's father, a fisherman in New Bedford, Massachusetts, was a violent alcoholic, regularly beat his wife in front of his son. Quinn was a runaway at the age of fourteen. He fled clear across country to the Bay area. He was a radical in the sixties. Experimented with drugs. Dropped out of state college, where he was doing well in hotel administration. Odd jobs for a few years. Serious binges with alcohol. Then the child. It was his big moment. Temporary fulfillment. His wife deserted him, taking their son with her. Some people we see become violent, resentful, even aggressive after such a loss. Quinn became a recluse, remaining in a darkened room for weeks at a time, living on a combination of street drugs and alcohol. He experimented a good deal with hallucinogens during this period." He turned a page of a file. "This rejection shattered his self-worth. His criminal history begins some six months after the departure of his family. Mind you, all of this is sketchy, all of it related in third person—the psychopath's way of avoiding any self-implication—but it ties in surprisingly well with missing persons files during the same period.

"As you've mentioned, Quinn certainly qualifies as a trapper. I'm quite familiar with the trapper theory, and I accept it, although others in my profession remain skeptical. Is he beyond bloodletting? I wouldn't count on it. Michael Quinn is capable of anything." He glanced at Dewitt. "We try our best to categorize psychopaths, Detective, because it allows us a broad overview of those with whom we are dealing. As an *organized nonsocial*, Quinn's kills were always carefully planned, the body always moved a great distance. From what I've read, this behavior seems to fit your kills down there, as well. In all the cases, the victims' cars had been moved. Your cases share that, I believe.

"I should explain something, lest you think me irresponsible in my neglect to become involved. I have been following your investigation through the papers, Detective, all week. When I read about Detective Lumbrowski in the paper, I faced a very difficult decision . . . and herein lies the delicacy of my position. I didn't feel it was ethical to come forward and *offer* information about Quinn, when in fact that information might have nothing to do with the case, and could possibly lead 'hungry' authorities to an innocent man. This, despite my own personal suspicions. I'm no detective, after all. Dr. Shilstein approaching me on your behalf, however, I view in a completely different light. You coming to me, you see? No, I can see in your face that that doesn't make sense to you." He shrugged. "Perhaps I could have made an anonymous call to you, an overture of some sort, I don't know. I considered it. These are the demons I must live with, and I face them often. I can only be grateful that you reached me as soon as you did."

"I need one thing cleared up. You do believe Quinn *is* capable of the suicide murders?"

"He's capable of murder, certainly, though he's never been convicted of any, never directly confessed to any, and no bodies have ever been found."

"Would you testify to that fact—that he's capable of it—if necessary? Professionally?"

Christiansen considered this for a long time, a good deal of which was spent staring into Dewitt's eyes. "On a witness stand, I would have to be extremely careful. But if subpoenaed, I would certainly appear. That bothers you, I can see. And I can understand why." He cleared his throat. "As for copying another person's methods—Collette in this case—for a man of Quinn's intelligence, that's not difficult to imagine. By definition, Detective, the 'trappers' that we've seen don't give up. They return to reset the trap, or to change traps. You must realize there is both the snare and the pit; there is poisoning and there is the net . . ." Briefly, Dewitt believed Christiansen was enjoying this, like the person who tells the horror story around the camp fire, watching the other squirm. "The trapper is an extremely patient hunter. There are tribes in Africa that will spend weeks digging a single pit deep enough to trap a cat—walls so steep the cat can't jump out."

" 'Don't give up?' " Dewitt asked. "Give up on what? Are you saying there's a purpose behind these kills?"

"I am." Christiansen looked Dewitt in the eye. "I believe Quinn is merely using Collette's techniques to accomplish his own ends.

"Quinn can't walk away from his own personal demons. You must realize that the vast majority of the criminally insane either don't consider the repercussions of their crimes in the least or are totally convinced that they are smarter than the people out to stop them. I'm talking consciously, of course. Subconsciously, it's difficult—wrong—to generalize. We often hear that the patient understood the impropriety of his crimes but was *unable* to control himself. Not so with Michael Quinn. My guess is he understands exactly what he's doing."

Dewitt considered this in a heavy silence. Had he actually come from a few carpet fibers through reams of evidence and witnesses to arrive at the identity of the killer? He felt a dizzying elation at the thought. It was a much more potent feeling than he had ever experienced as a forensic investigator. This was the addictive nature of detective work, he decided. Like waving your baton in the 1812 and hearing those cannons go off.

"He killed my daughter," Dewitt said.

Christiansen said almost inaudibly, "I'm so sorry. His hate runs very deep. I have a theory I could share with you, but I should warn, it's nothing more than a professional hunch. More than a hunch, actually. You might call it professional extrapolation. I won't be held to it."

"Agreed."

He cleared his throat, toyed with his gray beard, and said, "First you need some facts you clearly don't have. I can extrapolate from there. Michael's wife, Patty, took their child when she left, as I've said. Patty was also a victim of substance abuse, and apparently felt little or no maternal responsibility toward the child. Not wanting her son to be with her inconsistent husband, she took the infant and delivered him to her sister's for safekeeping. Ironic, because the sister was in worse shape than she was. Robbing Peter to pay Paul, you might say. The sister abused the child sexually, physically, mentally. In the boy's early teens, she sold his services to homosexual men and fed her drug habit with the profits. It took Michael Quinn over ten years to eventually track down the whereabouts of his child. This 'trapper' mentality of his forbade any direct confrontation. He placed his son under surveillance, and in the process discovered what was going on. Enraged, and burdened with the guilt that he had not come to his son's rescue earlier, he decided to get even. He lured the young man out of the apartment by making him believe he had won a free double feature at a local theater. That night, having determined his sister-in-law was passed out asleep in the apartment, he set the building afire, killing her.

"Two things thing went wrong with Quinn's plan," the doctor continued. "Howard Lumbrowski and James Dewitt. His son was arrested for the arson murder of the 'mother.' The son carried the last name of this surrogate mother, not his own. His adopted name was Steven Miller."

Dewitt didn't move. He didn't speak.

"When I had him as a patient—Quinn that is—he was depressed and suicidal. This, following his son's death. After all, Detective, *he* was the one responsible for the crimes, not his son. The guilt proved too much for him to bear. He had lost the only thing dear to him—a result of his own failed plan. While institutionalized, he tried three times to kill himself. Then one day, his suicidal tendencies evaporated. I understand now that that timing coincides with the transfer of Harvey Collette. That I didn't know about at the time. As a professional, all that I saw was a remarkable change in the man. He wanted to live again. His suicidal tendencies vanished. I allowed myself to believe I had had some professional effect on him. I believed the medication had pulled him out of the depression.

"But there's another possibility. Hindsight is often a psychiatrist's best friend. Let's suppose that Michael Quinn was kept alive by one thought: avenging his son's death. Let's say Harvey Collette gave him an inspired thought. Revenge is powerful motivation, certainly capable of effecting his sudden reversal, diminishing his suicidal tendencies. He would be after two people: Howard Lumbrowski for his incompetence in arresting the wrong person, and you for shooting his son. Actually three people, for there's no doubt in my mind that he's after himself. He is still suicidal. All that this fantasy would do is delay his acceptance of his responsibility for his son's death."

"Are you telling me he killed the first two, Osbourne and McDuff, for no reason at all?"

"No reason? Those are your words. Michael Quinn is a complex individual, capable of intricate planning. Premeditation is an under-statement: A trapper must be prepared for any eventuality, especially catching the wrong animal. Who's to say? You see? You can't second-guess a Michael Quinn. If I'm right, if it is the thought of revenge that's keeping him alive; then there's no predicting him. He could change tactics—even change personalities—at any time. You under-stand that if I'm right, then you're next, Detective. You are the last step. And the closer he gets to that step, the more risks he can take. Mind you, all of this is only speculation on my part. Call it an educated guess."

Dewitt said nothing. He sat absolutely still. Fear built up in him like water behind a dam. Finally he nodded, stood, shook the man's hand, and left the office in silence.

4

Dewitt was in a commuter plane at the exact hour Michael Quinn was charged with the murder of Howard Lumbrowski. Clare O'Daly's laboratory findings, which linked the hair sample from Quinn's dog with hairs found at all three crime scenes, passed immediately from the desk of Karl Capp to that of District Attorney Bill Saffeleti. Saffeleti, citing these laboratory tests and the room key found *inside* Lumbrowski, bowed to considerable public pressure and delivered up a suspect. By California law, Quinn's preliminary hearing had to be held within his first fourteen days of incarceration. Although there were dozens of ways around such laws, Saffeleti felt it important to move quickly with Quinn—win the right to try him while the severity of his crimes was still fresh in the court's mind—and then spend months preparing a stronger case, one that didn't rely on dog hairs. He believed the key their best piece of evidence: Why would Lum-browski have swallowed the key unless it was meant as a clue? The trace evidence in the first two murders was supportive but far too circumstantial—too forensically technical—for Saffeleti to go after more than the one conviction. If they won Lumbrowski, they would be back for more, like kids after birthday cake.

Dewitt drank steadily from six o'clock until eleven, when both he and Clarence were forced to accept a ride out to the valley from Clare O'Daly, who had been talked into joining them late but drank lightly, unable to find a comfortable spot alongside two drunken best friends. She delivered Dewitt to his doorstep, helped him inside and into bed, but refused his invitations. He was asleep within minutes of his deposit, and Clare safely on her way home.

10

THE PREPARATION

1

On Thursday, January nineteenth, Dewitt awakened at nine o'clock and went immediately back to bed. By noon, he had showered and put away two cups of coffee. He spent the remainder of the afternoon and evening alone, working at the kitchen table on what seemed like endless paperwork. The system needed some way around all of this paperwork. Perhaps computers were the answer, or new legislation, or deeper pockets, but something had to be done. There were too few cops to have them spending a third of their time filling out triplicate forms.

Thursday evening, Saffeleti's deputy DA called to inform Dewitt that Quinn's preliminary hearing had been set for Thursday the twenty-sixth. At seven o'clock, Dewitt called Emmy at his mother's house in Shawnee Mission, Kansas, and told her to come home. He picked her up at the airport the following afternoon, and by that evening, the phone was ringing off the wall again. Life was back to normal. He felt good.

The next few days found him shuttling between his office, the Salinas lab, and the Monterey County Courthouse as the diligent DA quizzed him and Clare like high school students preparing for SATs. Saffeleti was clearly uncomfortable with the nature of the evidence and the relative inexperience of his two star witnesses in their present positions. As they drew closer to Tuesday, Dewitt realized Saffelti did not consider this an ironclad case, and Dewitt once again gained a keen appreciation for the difference in attitude concerning forensic evidence between those in the field and laymen. Ironically, it was easier to sell technical evidence to a naïve jury than to a seasoned judge—and the preliminary hearing would be heard by a judge—Judge Alberto Danieli, a stickler for procedure, and a man who kept a tight rein on his courtroom.

Sunday evening, Dewitt was asked to meet the DA on a street corner in Monterey, an improbable meeting place. The moist air smelled sweet with salt, and though chilly, Dewitt wore a sweater under his wool sports coat and was comfortable. Saffeleti surprised Dewitt with a knock on the driver's window of the idling Zephyr, a jerk of his coiffed head, and the blunt two-word statement, "Let's walk."

"What's up?" Dewitt asked after they had covered several blocks in silence.

"Didn't want to make this official. You got that? Far as I'm concerned, if anyone ever asks about this meeting—which they had better not—we ran into each other on the street. Got it?" he added rhetorically.

"Why the cloak and dagger?"

"Got it?" Saffeleti seemed an improbable public servant. With his Italian coloring and GQ wardrobe, he looked as if he had stepped off the set of a soap opera.

"Got it."

"I want to know what the fuck is going on."

"Meaning?"

"That's what I'm asking you."

"Speak English, Bill."

"Don't start with me, James. I'm in no mood."

"You want to talk about moods? Every time I bring your people some evidence, they make me write the whole thing out like a friggin' book report or something. It might help, Bill, if your people could read a forensic report; they come in handy in police investigations, in case no one in your department noticed."

"Some of my people are new."

"Tell me about it."

"I need to know what's going on," Saffeleti repeated in a more cordial tone.

"I caught that the first time around. Going on, as in?"

"In my line of work, as in yours, I'm sure you develop a certain feel for a case. Perhaps it's something a person tells you directly, perhaps something that comes to you indirectly, even something that *isn't* said, or an attitude in your opponent that *isn't* present. I don't mean to imply I run my cases based on feelings . . . certainly not. Call it a sixth sense, if you want. I have it, James. It's why I win five times as many cases as I lose. Sure, some of this job is picking the right cases, but what the hell governs that? A sixth sense for the ones you can win." They rounded a corner. Saffeleti was leading, though Dewitt recognized in the DA's hesitations at intersections that there was no destination to this walk. The District Attorney was merely buying time. Vamping. "The reason you've been asked to write out what all your forensic reports mean, James, is that I felt it important to see this case on paper . . . to allow my people to see it on paper. These damn prelims are rugged on a case like this: very little time to prepare and if we screw up, we have to refile and try again or abandon the case completely. That means everyone has to know what the hell is going on. Judges have seen hundreds of forensics reports. It doesn't mean they understand them any more than I do, or my clerks do. But it might help if we put together a brief, summarizing what those reports

211

tell us, connecting one piece of evidence to the next, showing the court how the hell you went from a dead body in a parking lot with a couple rug fibers to Room Twelve of that motel." They paused at a crossing and waited out the light. Saffeleti continued once they crossed the street.

"My biggest concern is that we've apparently lost any chance at connecting Quinn to Miller. What Christiansen told you will be considered hearsay. If a record of birth exists, my people can't find it. Ten to one, Quinn's wife gave birth to the kid in her own home. It was the sixties, don't forget. People weren't exactly eager to follow standard procedures like applying for a birth certificate. Hell, Quinn wasn't even filing taxes then. We can't even show he was claiming two dependents. We'll still try the Christiansen testimony—at least plant a seed in Danieli's car—but he's required to rule against such evidence. There's still a chance we may be able to track down a midwife or some other witness, but not by the prelim. That'll have to wait for the trial."

"But to make it to trial, we have to win the prelim," Dewitt spoke, regretting the comment. Of course the District Attorney was aware of this.

Saffeleti was silent for a moment. When he finally spoke, he seemed to be attempting to contain his anger. "So here we are less than a week before the hearing."

There was such a long pause, Dewitt added, "Here we are."

"And along comes a little birdie that whispers a few things into my ear and makes me crap fireballs."

"What kind of 'little birdie'?"

"Fucking Tweety-Pie, Dewitt! What the fuck does it matter?"

"It matters."

"It *doesn't* matter. What the little birdie says is what matters, and what I hear is that the defense has ordered DNA typing on those dog hairs. Even worse, I hear that Ramirez's computers kicked a name on that roll of masking tape found in Lumbrowski's car and that it has caused the convening of a special grand jury. That means secrecy, and I gotta wonder why."

"I don't see the problem with the DNA testing. You'll recall that both Clare and I thought it was the thing to do. But you were right

. . . it's expensive and dog hair has never been used in court. If they're lucky, they'll just end up doing our work for us, proving what they never wanted to find out. How did they afford it, if we couldn't?"

"No idea."

"Who's defense using?"

"Hart Laboratories."

"Well, there you go," Dewitt said. "Hart knows what he's doing. Next legislature, we may vote on a DNA base for felons, much as we have ALPS now. Can you imagine what the contract will be worth? Running DNA fingerprints on every convicted felon in the state? Jesus! He's probably offered this work for free. This is a high-profile case. He knows the value of publicity. If Hart Labs is associated with DNA fingerprinting, then they become a contender for at least part of that contract. One thing about Dr. Frederick Hart: He knows where the money is."

"I don't like the idea of an independent going over all our evidence. How good *are* our people, anyway?"

"I don't get it, Bill. Why so uptight? I thought you said Sibel was the perfect PD to go up against on this prelim. You implied he would basically give us the prelim and concentrate on the trial itself . . . try to beat us in the trial. How many PDs fight very hard at a prelim, anyway, especially when they're up against the District Attorney himself?"

"Sibel? Where the hell have you been, Dewitt? Sibel broke his jaw in a racquetball game yesterday afternoon . . . wired the trap shut for six weeks. Sibel's sucking dinner through a straw. It's not Sibel we're up against, it's that cunt Lay-ya Moaning. And she's *exactly* the kind of bitch to come after us hard at the prelim . . . knock us down before we get a full head of steam going. And the thing about Lay-ya is, she's one hell of an attorney. She's been blowing us out of the water lately. I don't like her, Dewitt. She's beaten both of my assistants in cases we should have won easily. Sibel would have been one thing; why he had to pick this week to go play fuckin' racquetball I'll never know."

"It's worse than you think," Dewitt said.

"How's that?"

"Mahoney and I don't exactly get along."

"Meaning?"

"She made a play for me during the Wood interview, and I passed. Worse than that. I called her on her whole act. I'm trying to get Wood to talk; she's trying to flash me cleavage. I was in no mood."

"Oh, perfect!" Saffeleti groaned.

"What about this grand jury thing? You want me to call Ramirez? We're friends."

"Okay, James, I owe you this. This is hearsay, but it's reliable hearsay." He hesitated. "Word is that a search warrant was issued for your place not two hours ago."

"My place? On what authority?"

"AG's office, from what I hear."

"The grand jury?"

"Rumors, James. The town's full of them."

"The Attorney General's office issues a search warrant for my place and you talk about *rumors*? What the hell's going on?"

"A rumor is all it is. Town's full of them on a case like this."

"No, people don't start rumors like that. The AG's office would have to have damn good justification to obtain a search warrant. You're the lawyer. Wouldn't they?"

"I'm assuming your relationship with Lumbrowski has come into question. They've called for an investigation. I doubt they have much. Election years are full of this shit."

Dewitt wanted to tell the man about his brawl in the front seat of the Mustang, but he was afraid to, was afraid it might panic Saffeleti into withdrawing the charges. No one had seen them fight outside; mention of it would only confuse matters. Dewitt had intentionally left it out of his report. Why? he would be asked. Because it would only confuse things, he would answer. He felt guilt at having manipulated the system in the same way people like Lumbrowski had. *Extenuating circumstances*: He knew all the terms. He had cut deals with Jessie Osbourne, had withheld information that he deemed unimportant. He withered with the thought. Was he just another Howard Lumbrowski, in khakis and a bow tie? He felt tempted to lie. He heard himself say, "Once Lumbrowski had the car fixed, I lost any evidentiary proof that I had reason to be there in the first place. It would have made my going after him look personal."

Saffeleti stopped. "What are you talking 'bout?"

"The night at The Horseshoe?" Dewitt said.

"We've been over that. You had words, so what?"

"We had words *in*side the bar. *Out*side, we had a fight. Lumbrowski found me taking an inventory in his car and he started swinging."

"Jesus Christ! You never reported this?"

"I would have had to charge him with assault and that seemed stupid at the time. It would have confused things."

Saffeleti searched Dewitt's eyes. He tugged on his crisp tie, stretching for air. He nodded.

Dewitt felt relief. Saffeleti believed him. He was obviously irritated that Dewitt hadn't told him of the fight, but he apparently understood.

"It *does* confuse things," Saffeleti said.

"They probably turned up some evidence in the car," the detective pointed out. "They're looking for more at my house." Dewitt could *hear* Saffeleti thinking; they were still eye-to-eye.

"Yeah. They'll use Hart—he's their expert witness—to try and get at you. But he writes textbooks. I can handle Hart. Believe it or not, James, this is good: This tells me how she's coming after us. What could they have against you?"

"A latent print maybe. Nothing to speak of. I was only inside the car a few seconds."

"No more surprises?" Saffeleti asked.

"I sure as hell hope not, Bill."

"I can handle this," the attorney assured him. "We're all right."

"Whatever you say."

"Dress up for your court appearance, James. The tenured professor look we don't need." He patted Dewitt on the arm, turned, and walked away.

When Dewitt returned home, he discovered a search warrant tacked to his front door. It had been conducted by the M.C.S.O. by authority of the Attorney General's office. He felt violated. He felt betrayed by his own people. He worried. *No more surprises?* What the hell were they after? His job? His reputation?

He and Emmy went out for a burger, though the conversation dwindled to nothing and they rode home in silence.

There was no counting sheep. No counting stars. He lay in his bed most of the night in a cold sweat, his imagination running wild.

11

THE HEARING

As Dewitt entered the Monterey County Courtroom in Salinas on the morning of Thursday, January twenty-sixth, Leala Mahoney was at the defense table, standing as she read from a folder. Green-eyed, long-legged, she had the learned, professional look—a tight-fitting gray suit, a sumptuous white linen blouse, sheer white stockings encompassing deliciously firm calves, and shiny black Italian pumps. She carried a yellow pencil behind her right ear—a nice schoolmarm touch. Her fingernails were painted bright red, as were her apparently wet lips. A judge killer.

He approached the two tables to leave off some last-minute paperwork for Saffeleti.

"Mr. Dewitt," she said, noticing him.

"Ms. Mahoney."

"You received proper notice of the search warrant?"

He studied her more carefully, irked by her controlled contempt. "Yes." He couldn't resist asking, "Your doing?"

She shrugged. "You'll find out soon enough, Dewitt. I thought you were known for your patience."

He deposited the folder on the prosecution's table and found a seat in the churchlike pews of the gallery. Nelson arrived after a few minutes, as did Clare, Dr. Frederick Hart, and a good many reporters.

Capp, Marvin Wood, Peter Tilly, Dr. Harold Christiansen, Hector Ramirez, Clare, and, in the very back, several uniforms.

The room resembled an advertisement for wall paneling and acoustical ceiling tile. The carpet was an indistinguishable brownish gray, the two flags on either side of the raised judge's podium, lifeless, the California state seal on the wall directly behind and above where the judge would sit. An easel with a huge sheet of blank paper stood next to the witness stand.

Quinn was led in and seated on Mahoney's left, wearing the shameful orange jump suit afforded all prisoners.

"All rise for the Honorable Alberto Danieli," cried the bailiff's deep male voice.

Danieli, in his early forties, had dark hair flecked with gray, a strong Roman nose, and drawn cheeks. He was a slight man even encumbered in the black robe.

Saffeleti looked smashing in a dark pin-stripe and a pinned collar. He wore a patriotic tie of red, white, and blue.

The drone of forced air poured from the ceiling vents. Dewitt looked up at the vent and pictured how Quinn had killed his victims. He banged his thumbs together nervously.

Clare wore a conservative navy blue suit, dark hose, and patent-leather heels. She had on oversized glasses with dark frames. She looked like an attorney herself. She carried a heavy briefcase, which rested at her feet. Her left hand was strangling a small handkerchief. No jewelry other than small gold studs in her ears.

Danieli said in a metallic voice that sounded overused, "The matter before the Court is a preliminary hearing in file thirteen-nine-seven-one, entitled *State of California* versus *Michael Quinn*. Is that your correct name?"

"Yes, sir," answered Quinn.

"The record should reflect the defendant is present with defense counsel. The state is represented by Bill Saffeleti, District Attorney for Monterey County. I am Judge Alberto Danieli. Is the state ready to proceed?"

"Yes, Your Honor."

"How about the defendant?"

Mahoney said, "Defense is ready, Your Honor."

"Do you wish the complaint read or the formal reading of it, or do you waive that?"

"We will waive that. I would, however, like to make a motion at this time to exclude witnesses."

"So ruled."

"Your Honor," Saffeleti said, "the state designates James Dewitt as investigating officer to assist."

"Fine," Danieli said confidently. "Detective Dewitt, you will join Mr. Saffeleti up front at the table, please. All other witnesses, you will be sequestered outside of the courtroom and will be called at the appropriate time. Thank you." There was some confusion and quite a bit of commotion for the next few minutes as names were read and witnesses, including Clare, left the courtroom. By the time the preliminary hearing was ready to resume, the gallery held only a handful of the curious, a half-dozen reporters, and two sketch artists.

"The state may call its first witness."

"Thank you, Your Honor. If I could have the clerk first mark some exhibits, I think it will speed things up." This took several minutes. "The state would call Detective Sergeant James Dewitt."

Dewitt stood, tucked in his shirt, and straightened his tie.

After being sworn in, Dewitt took the witness stand, a familiar seat to him from his days as a lab technician. Saffeleti approached.

DIRECT EXAMINATION

OF JAMES DEWITT

BY MR. SAFFELETI

SAFFELETI: For the record, please state your name.

DEWITT: James Dewitt.

Q. What is your occupation?

A. I'm an investigator with the Carmel Police Department.

Q. What are your duties as an investigator?

A. I investigate all cases above traffic citations that occur within the city of Carmel-by-the-Sea.

Q. All crimes?

A. I'm the only detective.

Q. How many years have you been involved in law enforcement?

A. Approximately fifteen.

Q. As a detective?

A. No. Years ago I was a patrolman briefly, then a forensic investigator, and later director of the Department of Justice's Criminalistics Laboratory in Salinas.

Q. Detective Dewitt, have you received any special training in law enforcement?

A. Yes, I have.

Q. Will you please describe for the Court the experience you have received, the training that you have received?

A. I have attended the FBI's National Academy in Quantico, Virginia. I've also attended training seminars with the California Department of Justice.

Q. How long was the FBI course that you attended?

A. A quarter . . . a college semester. I also hold a degree in forensic science.

Q. What were the subjects of that FBI course?

A. We covered all subjects from evidence collection to processing; chromatography to biochemistry.

Q. Detective Dewitt, I'd like to direct your attention to January tenth of this month, shortly after six in the morning. Were you on duty?

A. I was on-call, yes. I was summoned to a crime scene. A DBF— Dead Body Found.

Q. A homicide?

A. No. At that point it was believed to be a suicide.

Saffeleti led Dewitt through the evidence collection for both the Osbourne and McDuff crime scenes, the detective explaining how the sand missing from the bottom of Osbourne's shoes prompted an investigation that eventually led them to Marvin Wood's trailer.

Q. That was a day- or nighttime search warrant?

A. It was a daytime search warrant.

Q Who assisted in the search?

A. The main assistant in the search was Detective Peter Tilly of the Seaside Police Department.

Q. What were your duties during that search?

A. My main duties were the service of the search warrant, supervision of the search itself, and evidence custodian . . . taking charge of all evidence, processing it, packaging it, and documenting it.

Q. What premises were searched?

A. The residence of Marvin Wood.

Q. Did you discover or locate any stolen property or suspected stolen property?

A. Yes, we did. A car stereo matching the description of that stolen from Mr. McDuff's truck.

Q. Where did you locate this?

A. In a cardboard box adjacent to the water heater. There was other suspected stolen property, as well.

Q. Did you subsequently conduct an interrogation of Mr. Wood?

A. Yes.

Q. And did Mr. Wood indicate to you a general location where he may have stolen this tape deck?

A. He did.

Q. And what was this general location?

A. He indicated he had stolen the tape deck from a vehicle parked at a *motel*.

Saffeleti then steered Dewitt through the investigative process concerning the tracing of the hardware store that sold the Plexiglas, the bike track and stores, and discovery of Harvey Collette and the murder of Howard Lumbrowski.

Q. Did the medical examiner's report turn up any unusual evidence?

A. It did.

Q. And what was this evidence?

A. A key, a motel-room key.

Q. And did this key lead you to a particular location?

A. Not the key itself, no. The trace evidence combined with statements such as Mr. Wood's led us to a general search area. A task force was organized and a search conducted. It was during this search that the key was found to open Room Twelve of the Just Rest'Inn motel.

Q. And is the man who was managing this motel in this courtroom today?

A. He is. The defendant, Michael Quinn.

Q. In your opinion, was Howard Lumbrowski aware of the procedures of a homicide investigation?

A. Yes.

Q. He *knew* an autopsy would be performed on his body?

A. Absolutely.

MAHONEY: Objection, Your Honor. Speculation. Theatrical nonsense! I move counsel's question be stricken from the record.

THE COURT: Sustained.

MAHONEY: Your Honor, defense contends that this key is inadmissible on the grounds evidence was *removed* from the premises without warrant.

SAFFELETI: Removed?

MAHONEY: As to this key, we have yet to hear of its existence from the medical examiner. Furthermore, can it be proven where, how, or from whom Lumbrowski obtained that key? It could have been mailed to him. He could have found it on a sidewalk. His killer could have forced him to swallow it before killing him. The source of that key is entirely speculative.

THE COURT: Sustained.

Judge Danieli leaned forward onto his elbows, and directed his next comment to Saffeleti.

THE COURT: The Court will endeavor to keep an open mind concerning this key. Certainly additional testimony will be allowed concerning this evidence. But as to its relevance in this case . . . that decision will be reserved until all the testimony is heard. That's the very purpose of this hearing, is it not? Continue, Mr. Saffeleti.

SAFFELETI: Your Honor, may we approach?

Danieli nodded and switched off his microphone. Both attorneys approached the judge. From the witness seat, Dewitt could hear clearly, though he was certain the others in the courtroom could not.

In a hushed voice, Saffeleti said, "Your Honor, you'll pardon the pun, but this is the key to our case. I've shown this court the connective tissue that leads us to the motel, but it's the key that ties the body to the motel. I need a reversal here."

"Mr. Saffeleti," Danieli cautioned gravely, "this court will not be swayed by circumstantial evidence. You know that. The bleach on those fibers, dog hairs? Come on! You want me to bind him over," he said, referring to Quinn, "then give me something irrefutable. Miss Mahoney's being good to you. There have already been a half-dozen times she could have filled your ass with buckshot. And why hasn't she? Because, like me, she knows you have yet to submit a single piece of irrefutable evidence linking her client to the crime." Mahoney remained silent. "I'm not saying Dewitt hasn't done his job, I'm sure he has, but you had better have more than this," he said, dancing his eyebrows. "This hearing is about his rights," he said, gesturing toward Quinn. "Keep that in mind, Counselor."

Saffeleti and Mahoney stepped back. "I don't have any more questions. Thank you very much."

"Go ahead, Ms. Mahoney."

"Thank you, Your Honor."

223

She approached Dewitt slowly, her outrageous body attracting attention.

CROSS-EXAMINATION

OF JAMES DEWITT

BY MS. MAHONEY

MAHONEY: Detective Dewitt, would you tell the Court, please, how long you have actually been a detective?

DEWITT: Two months.

Q. Just two months?

A. That's correct.

Q. And you've investigated how many homicides?

A. Three, including Lumbrowski.

Q. Convictions?

A. None . . . but—

Q. Just answer the questions, please. So your *entire experience as a homicide detective* has been in the last week?

A. Two weeks. However, as a forensics investigator, I saw dozens of homicides.

THE COURT: The witness will just answer the questions, please.

Q. I have an affidavit here listing your qualifications. It seems to me—the way I read it—you're more of a forensic investigator than a detective. To put it bluntly, Mr. Dewitt, you have to satisfy this Court that you have the wherewithal to conduct an investigation of this magnitude. I, for one, am not satisfied. Was your experience ever questioned by your superiors?

A. It was discussed.

Q. Did you have the full support of your department?

A. No. Not at first.

Q. Is it true that you were personally involved with Howard Lumbrowski on a case that eventually concluded with your wife's tragic murder and your daughter's permanent hospitalization?

A. Professionally involved. Not personally.

Q. You knew Howard Lumbrowski, did you not? Personally knew the man?

A.   He was a police officer assigned to Seaside when I was director of the Salinas Criminalistics Laboratory. Of course I knew him.

Q.   You *worked* with him on several cases, didn't you? As a forensics investigator, I mean?

A.   I just said I did.

Q.   You worked with him on the Steven Miller case, did you not?

A.   I just answered that also. The answer is yes.

Q.   You lost that case, did you not?

A.   I did not try that case. I was only an expert witness, as I am here.

Q.   The *state* lost the case. In fact, Mr. Saffeleti lost that case, did he not?

A.   No. He elected to drop charges and refile at a later date. As an attorney, I'm sure you understand that's far from losing a case.

Q.   On what grounds were the charges dropped?

"Objection!" Saffeleti hollered, coming to his feet, his frustration apparent. "What possible bearing—"

"Overruled," the judge said immediately, waving his hand at Saffeleti. "I want to see where this is going, Mr. Saffeleti." Then to Mahoney, he added, "And it had better be going somewhere, Counselor."

Dewitt said reluctantly, "Insufficient evidence."

Q.   Evidence you collected?

A.   Some of it. Yes.

Q.   Some of it Mr. Lumbrowski collected?

A.   Yes.

"And you were arrested by the police subsequent to that," she said, reading a piece of paper. "Would you tell the court please on what charges."

Saffeleti was quick to his feet. "Objection! Improper impeachment, Your Honor."

Mahoney took long strides to her table, snapped up a blue soft-cover book, peeled it open, and read loudly:

225

*"For the purpose of attacking the credibility of a witness,
evidence that he has been convicted of a crime shall be admitted
if elicited from him or established by public record during cross-
examination, but only if the crime—one—was punishable by
death . . ."*

To Dewitt, she said, "Was the crime you were accused of, punishable
by death, Detective Dewitt?"

"I was acquitted. I was not *convicted* of any crime. But you *know*
that, Ms. Mahoney. So I can only assume—"

"This is grandstanding, Your Honor," Saffeleti complained. "Improper impeachment!"

THE COURT: Agreed. Ms. Mahoney, innuendo has no place in my
courtroom. I am striking this last little bit of high drama.

MAHONEY: Your Honor, I am attempting to show bias or prejudice,
which is my responsibility to my client. If Your Honor would like
an offer of proof, the defendant intends to show that Mr. Dewitt
had no respect for the decedent, in fact, disliked the decedent and
blamed him for his wife's murder. Defense intends to show that
Mr. Dewitt is not only inexperienced but is too emotionally
involved in this case to conduct himself in an unbiased manner,
and that, in fact, there remain unanswered questions as to Mr.
Dewitt's exact role in Mr. Lumbrowski's murder.

The courtroom buzzed and Danieli called for quiet. Mahoney was
staring Dewitt in the eye. The search warrant he had found on his
front door suddenly weighed heavily upon him. What the hell was she
after? She marched around the room, drawing everyone's attention.
"Have you ever threatened Mr. Lumbrowski with violence? I remind
you that you are under oath, sir."

Danieli complained: "Ms. Mahoney, does this look like a theater?
You want to discuss procedures? You are, I will assume, familiar with
the procedures of *my courtroom*, are you not? I'm calling a five-minute
recess. The witness will remain on the stand. Ms. Mahoney, Mr.
Saffeleti, you will join me in chambers."

*　　*　　*

Saffeleti followed Mahoney through the door behind the dais and into the back hallway that led to chambers. Danieli was a small man. He motioned for them both to sit, and he slid up onto the edge of his walnut desk, the robe hanging like a dress. "Where the hell are you going with this, Ms. Mahoney?"

"Your Honor, I have a direction. In present company, that's all I feel I should say."

"The implication is that Dewitt may have acted in a criminal way. Is that actually your intention?" He waited. "You'll answer that, Counselor."

"It is, Your Honor." She wouldn't look at Saffeleti.

"Shit," Danieli hissed. "You should have warned me of this development, Counselor. This is not the trial, I remind you. This is an evidentiary hearing."

"The evidence isn't there," she said, looking over at Saffeleti. "The evidence, in fact, points in an entirely different direction. I'm not going to see my client put through the humiliation of a trial based on *circumstantial* evidence. This is a probable-cause hearing, Your Honor. Does the evidence presented show probable cause that my client may have been responsible? I maintain it does not."

"Your Honor," Saffeleti retorted, "whether or not the evidence is circumstantial is the very purpose of this Court. It's not up to Ms. Mahoney to make that judgment."

"I'm well aware of that, Bill. Jesus, you two!" He looked them over silently. "I'm aware there is much more press at this hearing than we usually encounter. I am also aware it is an election year. But in case you weren't aware, my courtroom will not be used to garner votes, or to advance careers." He looked at Mahoney, "Nickel-and-dime sideshows won't help your cause, Counselor. If you stay on this same track, you better be damned sure of where you're going. I've heard you're an eager beaver, Ms. Mahoney. You and I have never had the privilege of sharing a courtroom. Perhaps other judges appreciate your antics, but I do not. You want to play Crusader Rabbit, do it in somebody else's courtroom.

"And Bill," he added, "let's skip the bullshit, shall we? You wasted an hour weeding through a pile of circumstantial evidence. Don't waste this court's time. Stick to the relevant evidence, and let's get on with it. I will not spend two days on this hearing. Either the accused goes on to a trial by jury, or he doesn't. We will not have a dress rehearsal here. That's all."

Dewitt sat there on the stand, the focus of attention. The five minutes drifted into seven. When they reentered the courtroom, Mahoney's neck was stained beet red, and Saffeleti flashed Dewitt an angry look.

"Detective Dewitt, I remind you that you are under oath . . ."

Mahoney's voice disappeared behind the sound of blood pulsating through his ears. How had he missed it? She was sitting near the rear of the courtroom, smiling at him. She waved. She must have come in during the brief recess. If he had noticed, he might have done something, but there was Emmy, dressed in her Sunday clothes, the makeup giving her the look of an eighteen-year-old, radiant, adorable. His daughter supporting him. Another little wave. And then, out of the corner of his eye, he saw a motion and he jerked his head, for he knew it was Quinn turning to chance a look at her. Quinn zeroed in on her and then looked back at Dewitt with absolute glee in his glassy eyes and smiled thinly. He nodded at Dewitt.

DIRECT CROSS-EXAMINATION

OF JAMES DEWITT

BY MS. MAHONEY—(CON'T)

MAHONEY: Mr. Dewitt?

DEWITT: Please repeat the question.

Q. I asked you if you ever threatened Mr. Lumbrowski with violence.

A. I may have.

Q. May have?

A. I did.

Q. Let's talk about the Lumbrowski crime scene itself, if we may. We've just heard you testify as to the similarities between this crime scene and other earlier crimes scenes you had investigated. Is that not so?

A. That's true. The Lumbrowski crime scene was, in some ways, very similar.

Q. From the standpoint of a top-notch, an *expert* forensic investigator turned detective?

A. In my opinion.

Q. Please allow me to get this right. I'm not an expert like yourself. Lumbrowski's body showed signs of violence, did it not?

A. Yes.

Q. And violence had been apparent on the other victims?

A. No.

Q. So that was not similar, it would seem.

A. No, but—

She waved a finger. "Just yes or no," she repeated condescendingly. "And what about luggage? You stated earlier that the first two victims were found with luggage in their vehicles. Did Howard Lumbrowski's Mustang have any luggage inside of it?"

A. No.

Q. No? I see. So that was not similar, either?

A. No.

Q. Not very similar are they? You mentioned bicycle tire tracks. Were bicycle tire tracks recorded at all the crime scenes, *Detective?*

A. No. But at those crime scenes the weather had—

MAHONEY: Your Honor?

Danieli reminded Dewitt to limit his answers to yes or no.

Q. In your expert opinion, in a simple yes or no, do you, does the state, have what you would normally call a good deal of hard evidence in this case?

A. That depends on how you define a "good deal."

Q. You have more hard evidence, or more circumstantial?

A. A forensic investigator's—this detective's—definition of circumstantial evidence differs with that of the Court.

Q. Using the Court's definition, please. We *are* in court.

A. More circumstantial. But that's the same with any case.

Q. You examined the Lumbrowski crime scene?

A. I studied it, yes. I did not conduct the investigation at that crime scene.

Q. You *studied* it. Did you take any precautions, or because it was someone else's crime scene were you careless?

A. I was *not* careless. I wore latex gloves and I was careful to avoid contact with the victim or the vehicle. I was only at the car a matter of minutes.

She grinned and nodded and Dewitt suddenly realized she had used his professional ego to trap him. Had he been thinking clearly, he might have used his presence at the Lumbrowski crime scene to explain away any possible evidence found connecting him to the vehicle. He felt tempted to alter his testimony now, but that might even dig the hole deeper, he realized.

He watched Mahoney smile shrewdly and wondered what kind of person enjoys tricking people for a living.

Q. You worked with a Ms. O'Daly from the Salinas lab on this case, did you not?

A. Ms. O'Daly was the FI on the case—the forensic investigator.

Q. And how many homicides had *she* worked on prior to the Osbourne fatality?

A. None.

Q. Have you personally, Mr. Dewitt, ever known, ever even heard of a homicide investigation where the forensic investigator had no experience as an FI on a homicide, and the detective had no experience as a homicide detective?"

A. No.

Q. A little louder, for the sake of the microphones, please.

A. No, I haven't.

Q. And these are our *expert* witnesses, Your Honor? These are the people we trust to give *opinion*? Do we rely on such *opinion* in this case, Your Honor? Is it worth the state's time and money to bring Mr. Quinn to trial? That is the sole purpose of this preliminary hearing, is it not, to determine if Mr. Quinn should be put through the humiliation and expense of a trial? To determine if it is worth the state's time and money? This based on the opinion of inexperienced investigators, one of whom, Mr. Dewitt here, has admitted to having a personal dislike of the victim?

THE COURT: Thank you, Ms. Mahoney, for your dissertation on why we are all gathered here. I wasn't sure why we were here, but I guess now I understand. Let's get on with it, shall we?

MAHONEY: No more questions.

Saffeleti dealt quickly with an affidavit from Dr. Emmanuel. Mahoney chose not to challenge it, although she did manage to get into the record her concern over his lack of experience as a medical examiner. The DA then called Clare O'Daly to the stand. Clare spent twenty minutes in corroborative testimony—a waterfall of words tumbling through microphones and tape machines and the stenographer's busy fingers. The chain of custody, the photography, dog hairs, Plexiglass, latent fingerprints, the bicycle-tire track, the paint chip. Dewitt listened absentmindedly, her words triggering images, his mind vividly recalling the events of the past weeks.

Mahoney, removing her suit jacket, her breasts heaving as she paced in a down-to-business stride, began her cross-examination in a strong voice.

CROSS-EXAMINATION

OF MS. O'DALY

BY MS. MAHONEY

MAHONEY: How long have you worked at the Salinas Criminalistics Lab, Ms. O'Daly?

O'DALY: A little over a year?

Q. "A little over"? Is that how lab technicians speak? I would think you might be more *precise* than that.

A. Thirteen months, two weeks, to be more precise.

Q. As a forensic investigator, you've been involved in how many homicide cases? Precisely.

A. Three.

Q. I didn't hear you, Ms. O'Daly.

A. Three!

Q. Only three? These three?

A. Three as a forensics investigator. Dozens as a lab technician. Several dozen, I would guess.

231

Q. You *guess*. Another one of those specific scientific terms. Let me ask you this, Ms. O'Daly, did you do a lot of *guessing* on this case?

A. No.

Q. But you did conduct nearly all the forensic fieldwork and much of the lab work, did you not?

A. Yes.

Q. That's a big job.

A. That's what I'm trained to do. That's what they pay me for.

Q. As with Mr. Dewitt, an affidavit of your qualifications has been submitted to this Court. You have all these qualifications listed and a lot of them deal with chemical analysis of controlled substances. Would you agree with that?

A. That's a great deal of lab work these days, yes.

Q. Very little experience with blood, fibers, and hairs listed on this affidavit. Had you, in fact, done *any* evidence collection on a homicide before the Osbourne case?

A. No.

Q. Lab work?

A. Some.

Q. And you are the state's *expert* on this case?

A. Detective Dewitt supervised me the whole way. He had thousands of hours in the field.

Q. But as a forensic investigator, not a detective. Isn't that so? No, it seems to me your credentials fall well short of the kind of foundation this Court looks for in its expert witnesses.

THE COURT: Mr. Saffeleti, you may respond.

SAFFELETI: Your Honor, I'm sure this Court has dealt with many preliminary hearings in which the Court accepts the testimony of a state criminalist. Most of the time, the criminalist's report will suffice. Would Ms. Mahoney like to conduct a blood analysis? I certainly defer to the expertise of Ms. O'Daly. Her reports are submitted as evidence. Does Ms. Mahoney question a specific in one of those reports? Or is she simply trying to impeach this witness, as well?

THE COURT: The Court is going to admit state's exhibits, Ms. Mahoney. Perhaps that will clear things up for you and allow you to *get on with it*.

Q. You determined an evidentiary connection between pieces of tape used to seal the windows of the cars of the first two victims . . . as we heard Mr. Dewitt testify earlier?

A. Detective Dewitt. Yes, I was the one.

Q. You must have discussed this behavioral aspect of the application of that tape with Mr. Dewitt. Is that so? Behavioral implying a specific pattern of behavior.

A. Yes, that's true.

Q. So Mr. Dewitt was aware of the specific order in which the tape had been applied, was he not?

A. Detective Dewitt was.

Q. Let me ask you this, Ms. O'Daly, and I remind you that you are under oath: If I was to hand you a roll of tape right now, and pointed to a car window, could you or could you not do a convincing job of applying that tape in the same manner as the tape found on the window of Howard Lumbrowski's car?

A. I could.

Q. So we can assume that someone with prior knowledge of the way in which the tape had been applied could, in fact, duplicate this application of the tape of Lumbrowski's car. Is that true?

A. Yes.

Q. Thank you, Ms. O'Daly.

Mahoney paced in front of the judge's bench.

Q. Mr. Dewitt was removed from the Lumbrowski case?

A. He was.

Q. And did he give you a reason he had been removed?

A. Yes, he did.

Q. And what was that reason?

A. He said his captain was worried about the implications.

Q. The implications? Why would his captain have said that?

A. You'd have to ask him.

Q. Detective Dewitt didn't mention Howard Lumbrowski by name?

A. He did.

Q. What reference was there to Howard Lumbrowski?

A. They apparently expressed some reservation over the fact that Detective Dewitt and Mr. Lumbrowski had a falling out over the trial of the accused's *son*.

MAHONEY: Your Honor, I ask that that response be stricken. Any such relation between Mr. Quinn and Steven Miller has yet to be proven in this court.

THE COURT: Am I to understand there *is* a blood relation between Mr. Quinn and Steven Miller?

Saffeleti patted Dewitt on the knee and whispered, "Mahoney dug herself in deep on this one. She should have stayed away from this. O'Daly gets the gold star of the day."

"But we *can't* prove the relation exists. At least not yet," Dewitt reminded.

"If I know Danieli, we won't have to."

Mahoney answered the judge, "No such relationship has been proven. It's irrelevant, Your Honor."

"Irrelevant? Mr. Quinn, are you, were you, related to Steven Miller?"

"Don't answer that!" Mahoney instructed her client. "Your Honor, my client has not been sworn in."

THE COURT: I asked the defendant a question. Motive behind a crime is central to the issue of probable cause, stated or not. I would like an answer.

Mahoney counseled Quinn privately.

QUINN: I wish to invoke my rights under the Fifth Amendment, Your Honor.

THE COURT: There's no need for that. As it has been pointed out, you're not under oath, sir. It's a simple-enough question. I expected a simple answer. In lieu of that response, Ms. O'Daly's statement stands. It will not be stricken from the record. Continue.

MAHONEY: Ms. O'Daly, you attended a fund-raising party at the Laughton residence in Pebble Beach, did you not?

O'DALY: You know I did, Ms. Mahoney. We were introduced at the party.

Q. Just answer the questions, please. If I want further editorial from you, I'll request it. You did attend the party?

A. I did.

Q. Were you later made aware of a private meeting Mr. Dewitt had with a notable state politician?

A. Yes, I was.

Q. And with whom had Mr. Dewitt met that night?

A. Jessie Osbourne, the mother of the first victim.

Q. Did Mr. Dewitt imply that as a result of that meeting, he might be asked back on the Lumbrowski investigation?

A. Yes, he thought there was a chance of that.

Q. In fact, he was asked back on to the case, was he not?

A. Yes.

Q. Thank you. Is it true that the evidence presented here represents only a small portion of the evidence collected at the Lumbrowski crime scene, Ms. O'Daly?

A. Yes, that is true.

Q. Can you explain why that is to the Court, please?

A. *Can* I explain, or *would* I explain?

Q. *Would* you explain, please?

A. I cannot. That is not my specialty. I suspect to submit everything found at a crime scene might takes days, even weeks. To explain to laymen such as *yourself*, might take even longer.

A few in the gallery chuckled. Danieli struggled with a grin.

Q. In your expert opinion as a lab technician, the remaining evidence is *irrelevant* to this case. Is that what you're saying?

A. I repeat: I am not prosecuting this case, Ms. Mahoney. Relevancy of evidence is not my specialty. Collection of evidence is my specialty.

Q. But you present evidence to the prosecution.

A. That's true.

Q. And did you present to Mr. Saffeleti all the evidence available to you?

235

A. I can't answer that "yes" or "no." As a forensic investigator, you sort through the evidence and present what you believe useful to the case. That's what I did.

Q. You are familiar with the dog hair in this case?

A. I am.

Q. How specific is a dog's hair . . . how individual?

A. There are a variety of identifying characteristics that qualify animal hairs to species and often to breeds within that species.

Q. But not to specific animals?

A. A specific combination of these identifying characteristics greatly increases the likelihood of individuality. An analogy might be Lumbrowski's Mustang. There are x number of blue and white Mustangs on the road; a lesser number of blue and white convertibles; fewer still of that particular year. And how many blue and white convertibles of that particular year with a bumper sticker on the left-hand side that reads, "I Brake for Nothing"? You see? The more identifying characteristics, the more individual.

Q. Any bumper stickers on the dog hair, Ms. O'Daly?

SAFFELETI: Your Honor—

Q. I withdraw the question. Can you tell the Court where you obtained the animal hairs for comparison to those found at the crime scenes?

A. I did not obtain the animal hairs.

Q. Where did they come from?

A. To the best of my knowledge, they were collected by the Seaside Police Department when Quinn was arrested. They arrived with his clothing.

Q. How were they collected?

A. I believe they were cut from the dog.

Q. You believe?

A. I know they were.

Q. Your Honor, I question with what legal authority these hairs were collected. Is there a search warrant that specifies the man's *dog* can be searched for evidence? Can the state produce such a warrant? I remind Your Honor of *People* vs. *Wainwright*. State Supreme Court overturned a lower-court conviction of an alleged precious-gems smuggling operation because the gems were allegedly brought into the country in the digestive tract of a thoroughbred mare. Customs officers operated on the horse without proper warrant. Is there a warrant in this case?

THE COURT: Mr. Saffeleti?

SAFFELETI: I know of no such warrant, Your Honor, but the animal was in the suspect's possession at the time of arrest. I will have to review *People* vs. *Wainwright* for similarities.

THE COURT: And so will I. I will, therefore, hold off on the admissibility of this evidence until further review.

MAHONEY: Defense may wish to recall this witness at a later time, Your Honor.

THE COURT: You may step down.

Saffeleti's witness parade continued to the lunch recess, but a sinking feeling of despair plunged James Dewitt into a mild depression. Mahoney had intelligently selected two basic cross-examination themes—the inexperience of the state's experts, and procedural elements involving the evidence itself.

As he returned from a desperately difficult lunch hour with his radiant and optimistic teenage daughter, Dewitt phoned a cab service and had her delivered back to school. He found Saffeleti in his walnut-toned office, pouting as he read up on *People* vs. *Wainwright*.

He looked up from the volume. "You know all these stories about Mahoney and her wild pussy? I'm beginning to doubt them. I have a strange feeling they were started by angry victims of her courtroom victories. And who cares? She's one sharp bitch, James. How she ever pulled out something this obscure . . ."

"She tore Clare and me apart."

"And she made Emmanuel look inexperienced. Dog hairs, James. The damn case hangs on some dog hairs and a swallowed key. Jesus Christ, I must be out of my mind!"

"If we could only prove Quinn's relationship to Miller, then, with the motive in mind, what he did makes much more sense: kill a couple people, making it look like the work of a serial killer, so that when you finally kill who you're after, he disappears into the bunch."

"Why did he go after Lumbrowski first?" Saffeleti asked. "Have you thought about that?"

"Of course I have."

"And?"

"Level of responsibility. That's the way I see it. Lumbrowski was there at the shooting: he had a role in it. But I actually shot the kid. We know Quinn's an intricate planner. That must be the way he had it planned: He saved me for last." Dewitt paused. "So what now?"

"What I gotta do now is do to her what she did to us. Technically, you're my assistant, James. You get any bright ideas, you let me hear them. One thing to keep in mind here . . . Danieli doesn't want to be the judge who lets this guy skate. You get that feeling? I do. It's a good sign. He's going to be fair; he's just going to be fair in our favor. Something else working for us . . . Mahoney's been winning cases left and right. Danieli himself called her a Crusader Rabbit. He's Italian; I'm Italian. Believe me, that helps." He checked his Rolex. "Let's go."

Mahoney knew the power of strong witnesses. Quinn's defense began with a woman psychiatrist, a delicate matron in her mid-fifties who spoke with a dignified British accent and wore a flower on her lapel. Miss Marple. To hear her speak of Quinn, one would think she was describing Bambi. Saffeleti lost hold of his cross, like an actor forgetting his lines, and finally stopped mid-sentence and sat down in defeat.

When she said, "Defense calls Dr. Frederick Hart, Your Honor," Mahoney was looking directly at James Dewitt, and smiling confidently.

As an expert witness, Dr. Frederick Hart had the prerequisite silver temples, the strong jaw, the crystal blue eyes, the white teeth, and wore a wool tweed jacket with leather-patch elbows! After he was sworn in, he took the witness stand and put on a pair of tortoiseshell reading glasses. Mahoney spent five minutes reviewing the man's credentials. One formed the opinion that this legend in the field had invented forensic sciences. He had written two textbooks presently in use, had narrated a number of police training films—which was where Dewitt remembered his voice from—had served with both the FBI's Quantico and Chicago DOJ's crime labs, and was a visiting professor at UCLA. As director of a private crime lab, modestly named after himself, his people had processed evidence in over seven *thousand* separate cases. Dewitt wondered aloud to Saffeleti; "You think she'll walk him across water just to drive home her point?"

DIRECT EXAMINATION
OF DR. HART
BY MS. MAHONEY

MAHONEY: We've heard testimony today concerning the forsenic evidence found at the crime scene in question, Dr. Hart. Have you had a chance to review this same evidence?

DR. HART: I have.

Q. For the purpose of?

A. I was retained on behalf of the defense to reexamine and evaluate all the evidence pertaining to this investigation.

Q. Evidence collected by the police?

A. Evidence collected by the police, as well as evidence collected by our own investigators.

Q. Is this a common practice?

A. It's been done before. It's our way to make sure nothing was overlooked, nothing missed. We wanted to double-check the trace evidence. It's a very specialized field.

Q. And in lay terms, can you explain your findings to this Court, please?

As he addressed the courtroom, Hart suddenly had the voice of a television preacher.

A. There is a great deal of evidence in any case and it is the job of the criminalistic laboratory and prosecutor to determine which evidence is of value and which is not. With this in mind, I think there are certain inconsistencies in the state's evidence.

Q. Such as?

A. First off, vegetable fibers, especially cotton, are found in such abundance at *any* crime scene that typically we discard them immediately.

Q. You say "typically." Can you be more specific?

A. Ninety-nine percent of the time. And dog hairs? Let me address the issue of dog hairs. Let's forget Mr. Quinn's dog altogether. Is the Court aware that *all* of the dog hairs found on Mr. Lumbrowski's clothing do *not* match?

Mahoney showed copies of papers to Saffeleti and then handed them to Hart, asking that he identify them, which he did.

Q. These are DNA typing charts—so-called DNA fingerprinting—comparing dog hairs found at the Lumbrowski crime scene. They clearly do not match. These are from different dogs.

Dewitt leaned to Saffeleti and whispered, "There's your opening. They *did* run the tests, which means, if we're right, some of the hairs did match Quinn's dog. It's testimony by omission. He's only showing you the cards he wants you to see."

The natty District Attorney nodded. On his pad, he wrote in bold letters, "FULL DISCLOSURE OF TESTS."

Mahoney produced another DNA chart and placed it on the easel alongside the others. A series of columns of small black boxes stacked, each box representing a specific gene.

Q. And this?
A. Ah, yes! You see, here we do have a match.
Q. And can you tell the Court, please, where this second chart is from? It *is* dog hair, I take it?
Q. Oh, yes, it is dog hair. But this dog hair was collected in a sheriff's search of the private residence of Detective James Dewitt.

The room went abuzz. Dewitt sat forward. Some reporters bolted for the door.

Q. You're saying that dog hairs found on the decedent are from Detective Dewitt's dog?
A. Yes. That's true.
Q. So If we are using dog hairs to try and imply guilt, then it is possible Detective Dewitt is guilty of the crime my client has been charged with?

SAFFELETI: Objection!

MAHONEY: I withdraw the question. Was there other evidence that your investigators found that was not in any of the state's reports but which you deem of significance to this case?

DR. HART: Yes, there was evidence of a struggle having taken place. Medical examiner reports confirm a contusion on Lumbrowski's skull. Trace evidence of blood and hairs in the front-seat area of the Mustang suggest Lumbrowski's head may have struck the framework of the convertible. Additionally, we found a third party's blood on the front lip of the driver's seat.

Q. Third party?

A. This blood sample was of a type that did not belong to either the accused or the decedent. It's all in my report.

Q. What type was this third party's blood?

A. Type A positive.

Q. Lumbrowski?

A. O positive.

Q. Mr. Quinn?

A. AB negative.

Q. What is this I'm handing you?

A. It appears to be a photocopy of an application form for a position with the Carmel Police Department?

Q. And whose name is at the top?

A. James Dewitt.

Q. And what blood type is listed?

A. A positive.

Q. Thank you.

The gallery rumbled with conversation. Two more reporters stood and left the courtroom in a hurry.

Mahoney waved the piece of paper for all to see. She placed copies in front of Saffeleti and the judge.

"Improper impeachment, Your Honor!" Saffeleti hollered.

"Impeachment, Your Honor?" she said innocently. "I'm attempting to set the facts of this case straight. As they have been presented by the state, they are anything but straight; they have been manipulated. I think that is quite obvious. In fact, I intend to prove they have been manipulated and why they were manipulated."

"Your Honor!" Saffeleti screamed, jumping up out of his chair. "I must protest against any of what Ms. Mahoney has just said going into the record. *She* is manipulating the Court, Your Honor. I beseech you to strike that last statement."

"Overruled," Danieli said. "The statement stands."

Mahoney practiced one of her ball of the foot pivots and said, "No further questions at this time." Hart looked at her with a pleading, confused expression.

Saffeleti saw this, leaned to Dewitt, and whispered, "Something's up."

William Saffeleti began his cross-examination of Dr. Frederick Hart in a surprisingly strong voice.

CROSS-EXAMINATION
OF DR. HART
BY MR. SAFFELETI

SAFFELETI: Dr. Hart, you have testified here today, that through DNA typing you were able to determine that animal hairs—dog hairs—found on Mr. Lumbrowski's clothing were not from the same dog as hairs that were found at the Osbourne and McDuff crime scenes, is that correct?"

DR. HART: Yes.

Q. *Some* of the animal hairs found on Mr. Lumbrowski, or *all* of the hairs?

A. Some.

Q. You are aware, are you not, that the Salinas lab found animals hairs on Mr. Lumbrowski that according to tests available to them *did*, in fact, match hairs found at the three other crime scenes?

A. I am.

Q. Did you, Doctor, or your people, find that the animal hairs taken from the defendant's dog in fact *matched* those from the crimes scenes?

A. Yes, we did.

Q. And yet you chose *not* to run genetic tests on these hairs. True or not true?

A. True.

Q. I see. So *you* were selective in *your* choice of evidence to test.

A. Yes.

Q. And yet, just a short time ago you condemned the Salinas lab for being selective with evidence. What compelled you to be so selective in your choice of evidence, Dr. Hart?

A. On advice of counsel.

Q. On the *advice of counsel?* You're referring to Ms. Mahoney, are you not?

A. Yes.

Q. So it was Ms. Mahoney's decision? Does Ms. Mahoney run your lab, Dr. Hart, or do you?

A. I do. But—

Q. *Just* answer the question, please. If I want editorial, I'll solicit it. Are these results—tests that directly link Mr. Quinn's dog to the crime scenes—present in this courtroom?

A. No.

MAHONEY: Your Honor, no such evidence has been admitted or even presented, and therefore testimony as to the existence of such evidence is hearsay. I request Mr. Saffeleti's question and the witness's response be stricken.

THE COURT: Sustained.

SAFFELETI: Your Honor, Miss O'Daly presented evidence similar. Dr. Hart's findings must be present in court. They are not!

THE COURT: Best-evidence rules apply. The objection is sustained. Saffeleti looked disapprovingly at Mahoney.

SAFFELETI: Were any animal hairs, any evidence whatsoever, found at the Osbourne or McDuff crime scenes that implicate Detective Dewitt in these crimes?

MAHONEY: Your Honor, objection. Irrelevant. This hearing does not directly concern either the Osbourne or McDuff murders, and Detective Dewitt is not the one charged with crimes against the state.

SAFFELETI: I'm glad to hear that, Your Honor.

THE COURT: Overruled. I'm interested in the response. The witness will answer the question.

DR. HART: No.

SAFFELETI: And having already determined that Mr. Lumbrowski and Detective Dewitt worked together on the same case for over a month, isn't it possible—just *possible*—that those dog hairs you recovered and linked to Detective Dewitt's dog had been there for months?

A. It's possible.

Q. Would you say *quite* possible? In your *expert* opinion.

A. Quite possible.

Q. Dr. Hart, you said earlier that in *any investigation* there is a great deal of fiber evidence you disregard. Is that true?

A. That's approximately what I said, yes.

Q. Now I understand that certain vegetable fibers are quite commonly found at any crime scene, but if you had to generalize, Dr. Hart, who is most commonly responsible for contaminating a crime scene, other than the perpetrator of the crime? I'm referring now to your own textbook, Doctor.

Saffeleti walked to the prosecutor's table, picked up the book and waved it in the air.

A. The investigating officer.

Q. Ah, the *investigator*. And let's see, initially who was the investigating officer?

A. Detective James Dewitt.

Q. Thank you, Doctor. No further questions.

MAHONEY: Your Honor.

THE COURT: Go ahead, Ms. Mahoney.

RE-DIRECT OF

DR. HART

BY MS. MAHONEY

MAHONEY: Would you identify this evidence for the sake of the Court, please?

DR. HART: Three evidence bags, two marked as from the Lumbrowski crime scene, one from the search of Detective Dewitt's residence.

SAFFELETI: Objection! The alleged search of Detective Dewitt's residence has no bearing on this case, Your Honor. That any such evidence should find its way into this courtroom—

MAHONEY: It has a direct bearing on this case. The search was authorized by the Attorney's General's office because of evidence discovered at the Lumbrowski crime scene.

THE COURT: Overruled. Continue, Ms. Mahoney, at your own risk. If this is improper impeachment, not only will this testimony be stricken from the record but your performance as a fair and proper representative of the defendant will come under question.

MAHONEY: Understood, Your Honor. And what is contained in each of these three evidence bags, Dr. Hart?

A. From the Lumbrowski crime scene, a roll of masking tape and a length of hose. From Dewitt's residence, a single length of hose.

Q. Upon visual inspection, as a forensic expert, is there any similarity between the two lengths of hose?

A. By color, diameter, this discoloring here that is on both hoses, they appear to be two different lengths of the same hose.

SAFFELETI: Objection. Speculation, Your Honor. Have tests been run?

THE COURT: Have they, Dr. Hart?

DR. HART: Not by my lab. No, sir.

MAHONEY: Your Honor, as an expert witness, this man may certainly give his opinion to this Court. That is all I asked of him. He merely said they *appear* to be the same hose.

THE COURT: Objection overruled.

MAHONEY: Defense would call Hector Ramirez.

DIRECT EXAMINATION

OF HECTOR RAMIREZ

BY MS. MAHONEY

MAHONEY: Your credentials were established earlier by the state, so we'll forgo that.

RAMIREZ: Fine with me.

Q. Are you familiar with this roll of masking tape?

A. Yes, I am.

Q. Have you examined it professionally? And if so, in what regard?

A. I have. Detective Rick Morn of the Seaside Police Department requested our fingerprint laboratory attempt to establish the identity of the individual belonging to a single thumbprint developed on the inside hub of the tape by technicians at the Salinas lab.

Q. And did your laboratory establish said identity?

A. We did.

Q. And how was this accomplished?

A. Our Automated Latent Print System. It is a computerized scanning system that digitizes a fingerprint's characteristics, whorls and loops, and compares these characteristics to prints in the data base.

Q. And the data base consists of?

A. At this time the ALPS data base has prints on file of all convicted felons in the state of California over the past fifteen years, all public servants, doctors, nurses, day-care-center workers, lab technicians, judges, elected officials . . . you name it. It's a considerable data base.

Q. So a policeman's prints would be on file?

A. Absolutely.

Q. Mr. Ramirez, would you please tell the Court the identity of the individual whose thumbprint was found on this roll of masking tape used to seal Lumbroswki's car?

A. First, I would have to ask how you obtained this roll of masking tape, Ms. Mahoney. That roll of tape was—

Q. Just answer the question, please.

Dewitt leaned across Saffeleti, stole the man's pen from his hand, and wrote in bold letters, "CHAIN OF CUSTODY. SOMETHING WRONG!"

A. The print belongs to Detective James Dewitt.

"What?" Dewitt barked from his place alongside Saffeleti. "Sam?"

Q. Your Honor, we heard testimony from Detective Dewitt that he did not touch in any way, any evidence inside Lumbrowski's

Mustang, and that even if he did, he was wearing latex gloves at the time. Should I have the court recorder reread this for the Court?

THE COURT: Mr. Saffeleti?

SAFFELETI: The state recalls this testimony, but objects to Ms. Mahoney's tactics. This reeks of offense, not defense. Is Detective Dewitt on trial here or Michael Quinn?

MAHONEY: As stated earlier, Your Honor, defense intends to show willful omission of evidence on the part of state's witnesses and manipulation of evidence. Hose found in Mr. Dewitt's back shed matches in appearance the hose on Lumbrowski's car. Mr. Dewitt's fingerprint is the only fingerprint on the roll of masking tape. Mr. Dewitt and Mr. Lumbrowski, by the detective's own admission, had an antagonistic relationship. Evidence offers one and only one story? Then what would that story be? No further questions.

THE COURT: Do you have questions for this witness, Mr. Saffeleti?

SAFFELETI: I do, Your Honor.

CROSS-EXAMINATION

OF HECTOR RAMIREZ

BY MR. SAFFELETI

SAFFELETI: Have you, in your years as a detective and later as director of the DOJ's fingerprint lab, ever known the investigating officer's fingerprints to contaminate a crime scene?

RAMIREZ: I have. It happens all the time.

Q. Even when the officer responsible claims he contaminated nothing?

A. It's so easy to accidentally leave a print here or there. Almost impossible not to. You would be surprised how few crime scenes *aren't* contaminated.

Q. Tell me about this roll of tape. It has been to your lab for examination?

A. Yes. In fact, the last thing I knew, we had passed it along to the Attorney General's office. I know nothing about them passing it on to Ms. Mahoney.

Q. But you seemed surprised just now at seeing it. Why was that?

A. We returned the evidence to the Attorney General's office yesterday afternoon. In order to maintain the chain of custody, when Ms. Mahoney first presented the evidence, she would typically show the sealed container it had been shipped in.

Q. Would you explain the chain of custody?

A. We follow strict rules in moving evidence, to ensure it is not tampered with; those rules ensure the proper *chain of custody*.

MAHONEY: Your Honor, I did not submit this evidence, I merely asked for opinion or recollection of services rendered.

SAFFELETI: My point is, Your Honor, if the evidence is not admitted, then the witness's testimony is hearsay. If the chain of custody has been broken, then the evidence should not be admitted.

THE COURT: Ms. Mahoney, can you demonstrate the chain of custody has been maintained?

MAHONEY: I can, Your Honor.

THE COURT: Right now? Let us see it please.

MAHONEY: The Federal Express container is in my offices—

THE COURT: So you *cannot* produce it?

SAFFELETI: Objection. Again, if that's the case, it's hearsay, Your Honor!

MAHONEY: If the Court will indulge . . .

THE COURT: The Court has *already* indulged. All testimony by Dr. Hart and Mr. Ramirez concerning this roll of tape, and the hose, will be stricken.

SAFFELETI: Thank you, Your Honor.

MAHONEY: I object!

THE COURT: You will *sit down*, Ms. Mahoney. Overruled.

SAFFELETTI: No more questions, Your Honor.

THE COURT: *Anything more*, Ms. Mahoney?

MAHONEY: Defense will rest.

SAFFELETI: In lieu of recently presented evidence, the state would like to recall Ms. Clare O'Daly at this time, Your Honor.

RE-DIRECT OF

CLARE O'DALY

BY MR. SAFFELETI

SAFFELETI: Ms. O'Daly, who examined the Lumbrowski crime scene?

O'DALY: Detective Dewitt handled the collection of some of the evidence, as did Detective Morn. I handled some. The Salinas lab was responsible for most of the analysis.

Q. So Detective Dewitt didn't handle this evidence alone?

A. Heavens no.

Q. Would you say Detective Dewitt followed proper procedures?

A. Absolutely. He's a stickler for procedure.

Q. In your opinion, did Detective Dewitt at any time *attempt* to take control of this investigation away from you or anyone at the Salinas lab, or in any way to suppress evidence?

A. No. That's absurd. He followed standard procedure the whole way. Nothing unusual at all.

Q. And were you aware of difference in dog hairs, and the presence of wool fibers?

A. Yes, I was.

Q. Didn't you, in fact, mention those differences to me?

A. I did.

Q. And how did I respond?

A. You weren't interested.

Those in the courtroom laughed.

O'DALY: We had plenty of circumstantial evidence in this case. We didn't need any more.

SAFFELETI: To what did you attribute the presence of the other dog hairs?

O'DALY: To Detective Dewitt, of course. He owned a dog. It went with him everywhere.

Q. And that didn't alarm you?

A. Alarm me?

Q. That he might somehow be involved. That's what counsel for defense has implied.

MAHONEY: I made no such *implication*, Your Honor. I have merely questioned evidence.

SAFFELETI: I'm glad to hear that. I certainly hope *that* will go on the record.

Q. Ms. O'Daly, where is Detective Dewitt's dog at this time?

A.   The dog is dead. It was found hanged in Detective Dewitt's garden shed.

Q.   In your expert opinion, Ms. O'Daly, would it be possible for a person—let's say Mr. Quinn—to remove a length of garden hose and some masking tape—

MAHONEY: Objection!

Q.   —from that shed and to use that hose and tape in Howard Lumbrowski's murder?

MAHONEY: Your Honor, I object!!

Q.   Wouldn't that, in fact, explain why Mr. Quinn didn't run from the burning motel? I submit he *knew* whose fingerprints would be found on either the hose or the tape.

MAHONEY: The question is leading and—

SAFFELETI: I withdraw the question, Your Honor.

Saffeleti paced the room. He stopped and studied Quinn thoughtfully. He shook his head.

Q.   Did the presence of other dog hairs alarm you, Ms. O'Daly?"

He turned and faced her.

A.   No, it is quite common for police officers to contaminate a crime scene. Even one so experienced as Detective Dewitt. It's almost impossible not to. It is so common, in fact, that investigators are schooled on ways to lessen the risk. I admit that when I first discovered new fiber evidence I was quite excited. When I later realized they were from the detective . . . well, this kind of thing happens all the time.

Q.   One other question. Did you and Detective Dewitt approach me about the use of DNA typing in this hearing?

A.   We did. I suggested to you that we run such tests at outside labs, and you turned us down.

Laughter from the gallery.

Q.   I did, did I?

A. You said that DNA typing on anything but humans had never been used in court. You were skeptical of the Court's acceptance of this evidence and worried by the substantial fees involved.

Q. Thank you, Ms. O'Daly. No more questions.

"Your Honor," barked Mahoney. "If I could have just a minute please? I have a few more questions."

She didn't wait for a reply. She fished around in her briefcase and then leafed through the file quickly. She located something from the file, straightened her spine with confidence, and approached Clare on the stand.

Mahoney's confidence troubled Dewitt.

CROSS-EXAMINATION

OF CLARE O'DALY

BY MS. MAHONEY

MAHONEY: Do you recognize these photographs?

O'DALY: I do. They're photographs of the Lumbrowski crime scene.

Q. And would you read for the Court what is written on the back of the first photograph, please?

A. There's a case number, H-four—homicide, I assume; the date— Lumbrowski Crime Scene it says.

Q. Are they all labeled in approximately the same way?

A. They are.

Q. Ms. O'Daly, are hairs and fibers more likely to be carried by a sport coat or by a rain slicker?

A. A sport coat.

Q. Not a rain slicker?

A. The smooth rubberized surface of a rain slicker wouldn't be as likely to hold hairs and fibers . . . perhaps a few by static electricity, but not many.

Q. And will you tell the Court what is depicted in these photographs, please?

A. It appears to be Detective Dewitt.

Q. Appears?

251

A. It is Detective Dewitt.

Q. And is Detective Dewitt wearing a sport jacket? One that is capable of carrying hairs and fibers?

A. I'm not sure.

Q. And why is that?

A. Because he's wearing a rain jacket.

Q. Thank you.

Again the courtroom buzzed. Danieli called for quiet.

Q. I have one last question for you, Ms. O'Daly. I promised the Court I would get to motivation. Have you at any time in the last month been romantically intimate with Detective James Dewitt? By romantically intimate, I mean, in the embrace of, or perhaps—

A. I *know* what you mean. I refuse to answer. It's a private matter.

Clare looked over at James, concern and anger on her face.

Mahoney strutted in front of the defense table. "I submit, Your Honor, that the relationship of this witness to Detective Dewitt in the collection and analysis of evidence at the Lumbrowski crime scene, and by also having an intimate personal relationship with the detective assigned the case, constitutes a conflict of interest that could possibly prejudice the collection of evidence and therefore the state's case against my client."

"That's not true!" Clare objected.

Mahoney said strongly, "Based on this prejudice, I request an immediate dismissal of charges and the subsequent discharge of my client!"

"Objection!" thundered Saffeleti, leaping to his feet. "Your Honor, this is nothing more than petty jealousy. I request the Court ask the exact question of Ms. Mahoney. Is her attack of Detective Dewitt purely professional, or was there, in the recent past, a personal conflict between the two? Specifically, I'm referring to the morning of Saturday, January fourteenth, at the Seaside Police Department."

"What?!" shrieked Mahoney.

"Order, order," shouted Danieli, searching for a gavel. "Where the hell's the gavel," he roared at the bailiff, who turned to the court recorder.

Saffeleti continued over the clamor: "Ms. Mahoney made advances on Detective Dewitt, Your Honor. Shall we discuss prejudice? A person's social life is not being heard here this afternoon. This is hearsay and should be stricken from the record."

"You fucking bastard!" shouted Mahoney, arms stiff at her sides, fists clenched.

Danieli located the gavel and nearly broke the handle pounding it onto his desk. "Silence!" he hollered. "There will be no profanity in my courtroom! I'll hold you in contempt!"

"Bastard!" she repeated. Mahoney wasn't yelling at Saffeleti; she was looking into the amused, laughing eyes of James Dewitt.

Danieli gained control of his courtroom and then sat reading notes for nearly ten minutes. He looked up, removed his glasses, and recited the case information for the sake of the court recorder. Then he said, "This courtroom has been a circus today, something which I regret and find inexcusable. Certainly all parties involved, including myself, failed in their appointed tasks. Defense has raised some grave allegations concerning Detective Dewitt, and then, Ms. Mahoney, you had the gall to suggest you were not implicating him in the crime. Frankly, Counselor, that was one of the most appalling displays of theatrics I've seen in my years on the bench. I find the approach insidious, unethical, and unfair to Detective Dewitt. It's unacceptable behavior in my courtroom.

"As for the state's case, it appears weak, based predominantly on circumstantial evidence and hearsay." He continued: "Yet it would be an irresponsible act to release the accused at this time, given the gravity of the charges and the probative weight of much of the evidence.

"Therefore, the Court finds insufficient evidence in support of the charge of first-degree murder. The testimony of Detective Dewitt, Ms.

O'Daly, and others do not sufficiently indicate to the Court that there is probable cause to believe the truth of the charge.

"However, Mr. Quinn, I will, at the prior request of the District Attorney, order that you be held in custody in county jail pending arraignment on arson charges and until such time as a preliminary hearing can be scheduled.

"The exhibits will be kept in the court file.

"The defendant will be remanded to the custody of the Monterey County Sheriff's Office. Bail will be continued at one million dollars.

"Court is adjourned."

Dewitt looked over at Saffeleti in disbelief. "We lost?"

Saffeleti packed his briefcase.

"You planned on losing? Is that why he was ready with the arson charges?"

"I made contingencies. You plan ahead in this business, James. We didn't want him walking out of here."

"He's a murderer, Bill."

"Not until we prove it," reminded Saffeleti. "The rumors I heard were obviously true, James: You're the subject of a grand jury hearing. How do you think that makes Danieli feel? I'll refile in the morning. We'll subpoena Hart's records and we'll order DNA tests of our own. We'll get him, James. It's merely red tape now. You know it, I know it, and Mahoney knows it. Look at her. Does that look like the face of victory? She should have plea-bargained with me. I won't give her an inch now . . . it's too late. By trying to win it all here, she's backed her client into a corner."

"Can we hold him on the arson charges?" Dewitt asked.

Saffeleti shrugged. "We'll see," he replied. "For your sake, I sure as hell hope we do."

12

TRAPPER JOHN

1

In the soft resonant peace of morning, James Dewitt finally fell asleep. He had been awake all night, drinking. Drinking in anger, drinking in solitude, drinking in the hell of accusal. That the system could be perversely misused seemed to him the greatest crime. His frustration had moved him through the better half of a bottle of Scotch, and though his head throbbed as he sank into the depths of sleep, the real pain was in his heart, the pain of broken pride. He had *never* been so humiliated in a courtroom before. Even the fiasco of Lumbrowski's perjury at the Miller trial paled in comparison. That his professional abilities should be challenged and contradicted, indeed, turned against him, was a degradation he could not face. He seethed with anger. He understood much more clearly why Quinn had pointed at him the night of the motel fire: Quinn had planned to frame him from very early on; Rusty's murder had been required to silence the dog as Quinn gained access to the shed and its damning contents. Dewitt and the entire system he represented had been manipulated to Quinn's advantage. Dewitt felt used, soiled, like a prostitute must feel after opening her hand and accepting money for the first time. And yet, in his drunkenness, he allowed himself to see there was something beautiful about his situation as well: He had been pushed over the edge, and the hopelessness of his position inspired him. He would talk to Quinn—as the investigating officer he had the right; he could interrogate him a dozen times if he so desired. He would make Quinn slip up; he would seek out the crack in the veneer and drive a spike through it. He would prevail. His resolve, his determination, had never been greater.

He took Friday off, picnicking with Emmy on Point Lobos that evening when the air and the weather breathed change across the coast, announcing the arrival of spring. He didn't talk to lawyers, excluding Bill Saffeleti, with whom he spoke several times; he didn't relive the preliminary hearing a dozen times; he disconnected for two long days, dedicated to his daughter and to his own unwinding. Relaxation came to him with great difficulty. He found himself in battle with himself—half of him determined and dedicated to over-coming Quinn's challenge, the other half wanting out and away. He made Emmy agree to leave the phones unplugged for these two days. He wouldn't be drawn back into it by reporters and talk-show producers and the curious. By Monday, his home number was changed and unpublished: Emmy was free to plug in the phone again, with only her close friends and the station house being given the number. Life was not back to normal—he doubted it would ever be—but it was tolerable, and you accepted graciously what gifts you were given.

Monday night, Clare knocked on the door with a cold dinner for three. They ate around the living room coffee table while watching a made-for-TV movie that Emmy was determined to see. They said nothing of the hearing. Near the end of the movie, Dewitt caught himself not watching the television set but looking between the two, wondering whether any such arrangement would ever work on a permanent basis. Clare, or a woman like her, could never take the place of Julia, but could she find a place? Would Emmy ever be able to make such an adjustment? Would he?

He saw Clare to the car that night, feeling Emmy's eyes boring down on him from behind a parted blind. Clare must have sensed this, he thought, for she made no movement to kiss him or hold him. Instead, she looked at him confidently and said, " 'Don't worry. Be happy.' " She was quoting a popular song. She added, "Things tend to work themselves out." But it wasn't her words or even her comforting smile that drew them closer that night; it was something in her eyes, a genuine concern, a reassurance, a selflessness that flattered him, touched him, and provided him with something missing from his life for the past six months.

James Dewitt had fallen in love.

Tuesday, January thirty-first, James Dewitt hurried to the county jail, where Bill Saffeleti awaited him. "Are you sure about this?" Dewitt asked.

Saffeleti and James Dewitt stood outside Interrogation Room C in the Monterey division headquarters of the Monterey County Sheriff's Office, both with their arms crossed. Dewitt wore a blue bow tie and a worried expression. "I owe you for this, Bill," he added.

"Damn right you do. I still don't know what you hope to get from this."

"Christiansen thinks Quinn will open up if I can get him talking."

"I wouldn't count on it. You're not going to get anything close to a confession, James. That's dreaming."

"I don't expect a confession."

"Are you sure? That's what it sounds like to me."

"He's framed me for Lumbrowski's murder, Bill, I have to do something."

"I understand that."

"I'm being investigated by a grand jury, for Christ's sake!"

"I understand that also. I'm just trying to warn you not to expect too much."

"This guy killed my dog, stole stuff from my shed, and then used it all against me. He killed my daughter. He pulled my life apart piece by piece. He obviously had it planned from the very beginning. What else did he have planned? What else don't we know about? Am I right about any of this? That's important information to this investigation—to me—even to my testifying at the grand jury hearing."

"Agreed. But he's not going to admit anything. Forget that. Give it up."

"There are still questions that have to be answered. Too many. These guys like Quinn will often open up if you steer them into third person, keep them away from first person. Like Ted Bundy." Dewitt added, "How much leeway will Mahoney give me? I can't see her letting me get a word in."

Saffeleti said, "Mahoney's butt is on the line. She screwed up by taking that evidence away from the grand jury. The AG is plenty pissed off at her. Even so, she's going to have to defend Quinn again, and she knows that. Don't expect her to let her client box himself in."

"I wish we could have gotten the meeting one-on-one."

"No way. You can talk to Quinn as many times as you like, but not without Mahoney hanging on your every word. She's been dying for something high profile; now she has it and wishes she didn't. She can either lose, or lose big. Her victory in the courtroom was an unpopular one; Danieli will make sure of that. She's *very* good, James. She just picked the wrong fight."

They entered the clean, plain interrogation room. Dewitt found it disconcerting that Quinn was attractive, even in an orange jump suit and manacles. Mass murderers were supposed to look like Harvey Collette—act like Harvey Collette. Quinn looked and acted like a well-behaved college graduate. Mahoney looked plain and overtired, a middle-aged woman without her makeup. She cast Dewitt a spiteful glance and then finger-combed her hair in an insecure move he had not expected. He sensed in her a fiery restlessness tempered by reluctance, the child condemned to sit in the corner and watch.

"Ms. Mahoney," he said.

She nodded.

"I've got nothing to say to you," Quinn told the detective before Dewitt had sat down. Saffeleti took a chair alongside Dewitt. He didn't look at Mahoney; his attention was fixed on the man in the jump suit.

Saffeleti said, "Yes, you do."

"No," Quinn snapped.

"You explained it to him?" Saffeleti asked Mahoney. He asked without taking his eyes off the suspect.

"Yes. My client has no interest in negotiating out of the death sentence—"

"He's the killer," said Quinn, staring at Dewitt, then gesturing with an unflattering stretch of his neck.

Dewitt glared at Saffeleti. No one had told him there had been an offer of dropping pursuit of the death penalty. Lawyers played games Dewitt would never condone. This particular moment was no time to argue with Saffeleti. "The killer?" Dewitt asked Quinn. "Which killer?"

"You killed the boy."

"Yes," Dewitt rammed back. "The 'boy' who killed my wife. Right before my eyes. And the eyes of one of my daughters."

"Right before *my* eyes, you mean. I was locked up at the time, Dewitt—also a mistake—and then it was on television. In color. They showed it in slow motion. They showed it for days. You know what that was like? You cornered him. What did you expect him to do?"

Dewitt started to roar, then stopped. It was madness to argue with a madman. To the business at hand. "What about the suicide killer? What about him?"

"I told you: I have nothing to say."

"Why would this man kill two people before killing Lumbrowski? Why not just kill Lumbrowski? He's not stupid is he, this killer?"

Quinn remained silent, eyes boring into Dewitt. Then he said,

"You'll pay, Dewitt. Sooner or later, you'll pay. You know why I wanted this meeting?"

"No. Why? We were just talking about that."

"Because I wanted to see you. Simple, isn't it?"

"Was it to test the trap?" the detective asked. Christiansen had informed Dewitt over the phone that Quinn's past suggested he always tested his traps carefully before going after his quarry. He had theorized that both Osbourne and McDuff might have been nothing more than dry runs before attempting to cage Lumbrowski. A way to test the motel room's effectiveness against flight. "Or was it because he needed bait?"

"You're not listening. Your type never listens."

"What is my type?"

"Ignorant. Self-serving in the name of public service. Ironic, isn't it? You say that I'm a killer. With no proof. You're an admitted killer and yet you're walking free. I'm the innocent one, and I'm in handcuffs. How is that right, Dewitt? How can that be? You killed my boy; you just admitted it."

Mahoney interrupted, "Mr. Quinn! I beg you to—"

"Quiet!" Quinn snapped. "I know what I'm doing."

"I don't think so," she protested.

Quinn stared her down. Mahoney sat back glancing at Dewitt in frightened disbelief. "Very well," she said.

"Why would someone like this have bothered with Osbourne and McDuff?" Dewitt asked.

"Bothered? It's no bother," Quinn said with a faint smile. "You don't appreciate some things that Hawkeye and I might. That's all. Believe me, it's no bother. It's very satisfying to some people."

"A guy like Hawkeye would enjoy it then, that's what you're saying?"

"Enjoy it very much. Yes. It's no bother."

"And would Osbourne and McDuff have been useful to him?"

"Let's say for instance that Hawkeye intended for the first one to appear to be a suicide. Let's say he also intended for the first one to be useful to him later, a means to lure Lumbrowski to a meeting. Would you consider that useful?"

"Is that how it worked . . . would have worked, for him?"

"You're missing the bigger picture, Dewitt."

"Motivation," Saffeleti said.

Quinn tried to point, but his handcuffs were interlaced and as his bound hands stopped abruptly, frustrated anger colored his face. "Exactly," he said. "Because the point is that there was only one of you to kill, and one to be left alive. Any plan is governed by its limiting factors, its restraints. This was no different.

"Death is the easy way out," he continued, now facing Saffeleti. "*I know* suffering. Suffering is a far greater punishment than death could ever be. Death is peace. This person had no intention of giving Dewitt peace, nor any intention of going on once the job was completed. This person also knows the darkness of emptiness, the unfathomable pit of isolation that is a father without his child. It is an endless, unforgiving cold, a frigid stinging cold. It must be passed on to be fully understood. This person found warmth in the idea of inflicting justice, but should the deed be done, there would be no reason for him to live on; he, too, would seek the solace of eternal peace."

"Justice is not something that's inflicted," quipped Saffeleti. "That's an absurd notion."

Dewitt frowned at the attorney. For the first time, Quinn had relaxed, had begun to open up, and Saffeleti's comment clearly rattled the man.

Dewitt said, "So Osbourne was supposed to appear a suicide."

"The trouble with you, Dewitt, is that you stick your nose where it doesn't belong. Did you have evidence against Steven? Absurd! Steven was innocent, and yet you and Lumbrowski had *evidence*. Absurd, isn't it? And then the first one . . . you said it was a *homicide*. This person we're discussing heard you quoted on television. It's not that he didn't have contingencies available, certainly he did; but it would have been so much easier . . . So much simpler—"

"I think that's enough, Michael," Mahoney interrupted.

"You interrupted," said an angry Dewitt.

"I've said enough," answered Quinn, checking with Mahoney.

"Quite enough," Mahoney said.

"I just hope you understand, Dewitt, that it isn't over until it's over. There are forces at work here you haven't even begun to grasp." He looked *through* the detective then, as if Dewitt was not there. "Are you familiar with the work of John Dryden? With *Absalom and Achitophel?*" He quoted:

> *"How ill my fear they by my mercy scan!*
> *Beware the fury of a patient man.*
> *Law they require, let Law then show her face."*

"You want *law?* I'll give you *law.* Not from books. Not from a courthouse. These are the *laws of nature* I'm talking about. These are things bigger than all of us. This person we're talking about . . . he's a *patient* man, Dewitt. Very patient. Beware the *fury.* Surprisingly patient. And he's able to adapt. Quickly. The right plan is the one that works. That's the only *law* he obeys. Beware the fury, Dewitt. You've *never known* such fury, such determination. The darkness will find you, Dewitt. The darkness will steal *everything* away. The darkness is intolerable. For you, it is inescapable. You won't sleep; you won't eat. It steals everything. Drains your soul of all purpose. Steals *absolutely* everything."

After ten more minutes of trying to get Quinn to continue, Saffeleti and Dewitt abandoned their efforts and stepped outside the interrogation room. Dewitt carried the tape in hand. "He thinks Mahoney is going to get him off," Dewitt said. "He thinks there's still a chance to get me. He's wrong, I take it?"

"The arson is worth a couple years at least. Fire Marshal says there's a good case. The rest depends on our refile. I feel good about that. As far as your involvement . . . that may need to be heard first in order to clear the air. We'll have to wait and see."

"He won't help my case any, that's for sure. It's his frame. He intends to hold me in it."

"No, but we knew that going in." Saffeleti stuck out his hand. "We'll get our proverbial shit together, refile, and put him on death

262

row. Michael Quinn may think he knows what darkness is, but he's got a lot to learn."

"Maybe," said James Dewitt. He walked away with an altogether different feeling turning his gut. There had been a glint in Michael Quinn's eye. A disturbing glint. One that frightened James Dewitt.

That night he found himself awake in the darkness.

2

Quinn wondered whether Dewitt had understood his message. He thought himself so brilliant. Yes, a brilliant stroke that "confession." The icing on the cake. *Foreshadowing* indeed. He had reached his decision once he saw the inside of the county jail and came to realize that at night only two guards were posted. One had to thank his lucky stars that the public was so tight with their money; people would rather have good garbage service than three guards doing nothing in their county jail at night.

He was no longer Michael Quinn; he thought of himself as Trapper John.

Trapper John peeled the only sheet from the hard mattress and bit into the edge of the fabric, carefully tearing it into long strips. On his fourth effort, he chipped his front tooth and nearly screamed out in pain, able at the last second to contain himself. When he breathed now, teeth clenched, he whistled. *Whistle while you work.* He remembered the Disney films from when Steven was young.

Thirty minutes later, he had the sheet completely shredded into three-inch strips, and he began knotting these pieces together, end to end, fashioning several long "ropes." It had been a week and three days since speaking with Dewitt, just the right amount of time for the fear to subside. He had been a model prisoner, putting the guards at ease. The thing about a trap—it had to be carefully set. You could trap anything if you used the right bait.

The mistake the county made was training their young rookies in the jails. It was the blond kid tonight, and he was perfect. For a multitude of reasons, it had to be tonight.

He guessed it was around six o'clock. The shifts had changed like clockwork—another of their mistakes: predictability. The blond kid would make his check in another half hour, come for the dinner tray. Perfect.

Quinn slipped out of the orange jump suit and tied a length of sheet around his thigh. Another around his other thigh. He continued until he had created a harness that joined a third piece, which he ran up his crack and slung over his shoulder. He got back into the jump suit and snapped it shut. Making the neck noose was easy: He had made plenty of nooses in his time. He slipped the noose around his neck and braided the line from the harness with it. Illusion, the key to any trap. Now it was a matter of climbing the bunk and getting the single line secured around the porcelain light fixture in the center of the ceiling. He tied a quick release slipknot and leaned his full weight against it and it held. Perfect. He puckered his mouth then and pretended he was trying to take a shit, pushed all the blood he could into his face. He did this for several minutes, and by the time he heard the blond kid open the bars at the end of the hall, he knew his face was damn near purple. Still leaning out away from the bunk, he let the entwined sheets take his full weight. He felt the sheets tighten on his thighs, cutting his blood supply but carrying his weight well. The noose proved the perfect length: just tight enough to strain his neck and add to the effect of his crimson face. He canted his head to one side and, as a final touch, eyes open, allowed his tongue to slip from his lips. The eyes open was the good part—what a touch!—he could watch everything as it unfolded.

The kid reached his cell, looked in, saw him, and went straight for the key. The beauty of inexperience. He called out then: "Harry!" A complication but nothing Trapper John couldn't handle. He was inside the cell, the door wide open. He came straight for the body. "Holy shit," he said under his breath, seeing that face and tongue.

Trapper John kicked him in the groin as hard as he could. The kid gasped and went down white, unable to utter a sound. Trapper John one-handed himself up, loosened the slipknot from around the light fixture, and fell to the cell floor, delivering another kick into the boy's face and then crushing his ribs and sternum with the full weight of a knee drop. He took the head by the hair and slammed it once strongly against the floor, then slid the body under the bunk, fetching the keys in the process. The only thing they did smart was leave the guards unarmed.

The element of surprise was his strongest weapon. He waited until he heard Harry approaching at a run and jumped into the hall to confront him. Harry stopped abruptly, startled. Trapper John thought of himself as placekicker, the man's nuts as a football. Harry went down. Trapper John crushed his chest, as well.

Adaptation was the key to survival.

Officer Harry's head made a crunching sound when Trapper pounded it into the floor. He dragged him into the cell. Harry's uniform fit, and that was a good start. The thing to do now was to find this kid Billy Talbot and work through the final act. *Foreshadowing* indeed.

Show time!

They proved smarter than he had imagined. The only weapons he could find were shotguns; he had been counting on a pistol to help him in his escape—though he had no intention of actually using it. His heart beat heavily with the excitement. Finally, he would pay Dewitt back. Nothing would stop him now. His time was limited, his choices narrowed. If it ended up a show, it would have to be a pistol for Emmy Dewitt, despite his own reaction to the sight of blood. At this late point, his reaction didn't matter—this was indeed the final act, for him there would be no more. Certainly, no more jail cells; he had had enough of that. And to run? To hide? Out of the question. He knew how the thought of paying back Dewitt had kept him alive these past few months, how he had fed on it; he had no desire to give Dewitt the luxury of anticipated revenge. Let Dewitt steep in the darkness for the rest of his life. Let him suffer as only a childless father can suffer.

He wasn't about to walk around with a shotgun in hand, even if in uniform. No, he would have to improvise. Again. Tonight was one of Dewitt's aquarium nights, father and daughter would be in the same place at the same time. There would be a crowd. A show. Hopefully, the conditions would be much the same as when Dewitt killed Steven. There was poetic justice in that thought for Michael Quinn. What he needed was a way to control the situation from the start, to gain the upper hand.

Billy Talbot was the key to his plans. He would know for certain where Emmy Dewitt was; he could be used to lure her if necessary. The proper bait. Aquarium nights, the kids spent smoking on the third-floor-balcony overlook. The girls smoked cigarettes; Talbot smoked pot.

They had left him a police car out back. Considerate of them. He could use it briefly, radio on, but not for too long—they might come looking for the car. Only two sets of keys to try. Second one slipped into the ignition and started the car. He was off. Talbot offered a solution to his transportation, as well. He had a hot little red car that blended in well with every other car. Simple solutions for simple problems.

3

James Dewitt enjoyed being back at the aquarium, enjoyed having his life back to normal. He answered the questions of the pale tourists with enthusiasm and verve, embellishing as he had seldom embellished, reveling in his knowledge of the Kelp Forest and its inhabitants. Wax the turtle pedaled by, steering her ample housing through the shiny swirl of King Salmon, ignoring the cat shark, jawing her way as if she were talking. Dewitt pressed his face to the thick glass and jawed back at her. Uninterested, she waved her way past and maneuvered herself to disappear into the towering kelp.

He wasn't thinking about his upcoming grand jury testimony, wasn't worried by the backlog of work with which he had to contend. In point of fact, at Emmy's insistence, he had left his pager behind tonight, as he had for the past several nights when he left the house. He had no desire to be dragged into some petty investigation as he so often was at all hours of day and night. If there was a professional down side to the Quinn investigation—he no longer thought of it as the suicide murders—it was his discovery of the insignificance of so much of his work for the department. After dealing with three murders, a stolen wallet or missing bike seemed trivial matters. He had this attitude problem to overcome if he was ever to get his heart back into his job. He no longer believed in the system. He had watched it fail. He would have to overcome that if he was to continue as a detective.

No one had bothered him for the last few minutes. Thin crowd tonight. He checked his watch: Emmy and Briar were just finishing up with Tae Kwon Do. They were due here any minute. That would liven things up around here.

4

Quinn left the radio car parked amid the hundreds of cars at the Monterey Mall and headed to the Soundings Music Emporium, feeling dapper in Harry's uniform. People looked upon him with respect. No wonder uniformed cops were so cocky: This went to your head quickly. He was wearing Harry's mirror sunglasses and hat, worried his picture had been plastered on every front page for a few days. One nice thing about news, it grows old quickly. Yesterday's murderer is replaced by today's airplane. It was the other nice thing about a uniform: It was the last place a person looked for the face of a convicted murderer.

With Emmy Dewitt as a central target from the beginning, he had followed her a great deal, knew all there was to know. The one person who controlled her—aside from her father—was Billy Talbot. Talbot would make the perfect bait. Talbot would lure Emmy away from the aquarium.

Predictability was such a fine thing. As expected, there were Talbot and his hoodlums huddled around a long-legged young tart, trying to impress her with their intimate knowledge of hard-rock recordings. As best Quinn had been able to determine over the past few months, one of Talbot's gang worked here most nights. He wasn't absolutely certain, but he believed they dealt in items other than musical recordings when the manager wasn't around. That's what accounted for the popularity of the place and the constant loitering. "William Talbot?"

When Talbot saw the uniform, his face twitched as if he had just been hit.

"Monterey County Sheriff's Office."

"I can see that."

"We'd like to have a few words with you downtown. Would you come with me, please?"

"What's this all about?"

"You own a red Ford Escort, right?"

"Yes."

"Police business. I'm not at liberty to discuss it."

"*I'm not at liberty to discuss it,*" Talbot repeated in a mocking tone. "You had better discuss it."

"We can do this one of two ways, kid. With or without you wearing a pair of bracelets, okay? Your choice."

"Chill out, okay? The charges?"

"No charges, William. I told you, at this time we only want to have a few words with you concerning the operation of your vehicle. You want to keep your license or not, William? You're making this difficult and I don't appreciate it one bit. You think I like playing baby-sitter?"

A friend encouraged Talbot to go.

"So let's go," he told Quinn.

When they were outside, Quinn said to him, "Show me to the vehicle, please."

"Why?"

"William, if you're a law-abiding citizen and have been operating you motor vehicle in a manner appropriate to city and state motor-vehicle codes, then you have nothing to worry about."

"This about my insurance or something? My dad *did* renew the insurance, didn't he?"

Quinn didn't answer. It was everything he could do to suppress his grin. Hook, line, and sinker. Believability was the key to a verbal trap: acting a role and staying with it. He felt wonderful.

They stitched their way through the parking lot and reached Talbot's Escort.

"So what now?"

"Open it, please."

As Talbot worked the key into the lock, Quinn made a quick assessment of his surroundings. Clear. The door came open.

Quinn took Talbot by the hair and leveled the boy's head into the door frame, which smacked him in a straight line across the forehead. With Talbot dazed, nearly unconscious, he folded the boy up and propelled him into the front seat, stuffing him over to the far side as he followed him inside. He seized Talbot by the windpipe and squeezed. A little harder and he could kill the kid. But he didn't want to, yet.

"We're going for a little drive. Are we feeling like cooperating?" Another nod. "No hassles?" A nice firm shake of the head. "Okay," he said, fishing out the handcuffs from Harry's belt, "onto the floor, hands out on the seat." He released Talbot's throat. Like an obedient little kid, Talbot scrambled into the tight space in front of his seat.

Talbot lunged forward, arm stretching beneath the seat. Quinn reacted instinctively, sensing trouble. He reared his foot back. The handgun came out from under the seat, aimed into his eyes. Quinn's foot caught the barrel of the gun and swung it around so quickly that Talbot shot himself in the chest. The kid's body quivered violently and went still. The smell of excrement filled the car. Blood! Quinn sat transfixed by the sight of it. Nauseated. Small beads of blood dripped from the end of Talbot's little finger. It dripped for nearly a minute and then stopped. The dead don't bleed.

Finally, Quinn took his eyes from the corpse. He knew death well

269

enough. He kept his foot pinned against the body just the same. He switched on the headlights and placed the car in reverse, finally lifted his foot off the boy, and leaned to get hold of the gun.

Win a few, lose a few. Adapt. Maintain your cool. Stupid kid had gone and screwed up his plans. Everyone kept screwing up his plans. Then again, he had a pistol now. Maybe it was fate talking to him. Emmy would be heading over to the aquarium at any minute. Maybe he didn't need Talbot, after all. He could use the gun to his advantage.

Maybe he could do this alone.

5

At the same moment Michael Quinn pulled the Ford Escort into an outlying parking lot near the Monterey Aquarium, James Dewitt's pager was sounding on his dresser bureau. The plaintive electronic beeps rang out unheard in the empty room.

Board member Cynthia Chatterman's shrill voice caught Dewitt by surprise from behind, actually causing him to jump. "Phone call for you, James. Man says it's an emergency. I had it transferred—"

"Tell him I'll be right there, Cynthia. And don't transfer it anywhere. I'll take it at Information in a minute."

"He said it's an emergency."

"I'll bet he did."

"James?"

"It's not an emergency, Cynthia. Don't worry," he said, walking in long quick strides alongside of her. He gave her a nudge toward Information and nearly ran to the bank of pay phones at the member's entrance, expecting any second to intercept Billy Talbot coming his way. When he reached the pay phones, however, none was off the hook and only one in use, this by an overweight man in a loud Hawaiian shirt and jogging pants. Christ, he'd been fooled again; no doubt Talbot, using a different phone this time—the gift shop perhaps or even one outside.

He knew damn well that there wouldn't be anyone on the other end of the phone Cynthia Chatterman was holding for him. As he attempted to pass her by, she called out to him, "He's pretty upset, James. Says he's with the Sheriff's office. Insists it is an emergency."

Mention of the MCSO stopped Dewitt. *An emergency* . . . The last time he had heard those words, Anna had been left to die. Emmy and Briar had arrived only minutes before. They were in the upper levels somewhere. It *couldn't* have to do with Emmy. And that left . . .

He walked to the Information booth slowly, wearily, looking upon the waiting receiver as a messenger of bad news. He accepted it from Cynthia and pressed it to his ear. "Dewitt," he said.

The husky voice on the other end introduced itself as Desk Sergeant Hack. "We got a problem here, Dewitt. Quinn has escaped. Injured two guards, stole one of our radio cars. We got out a BOL and APB, but my lieutenant says to track you down and let you know. When you didn't answer the page, one of your people figured you might be there at the aquarium."

"Escaped?" Dewitt gasped. The incongruous peacefulness of the aquarium didn't fit. "I'll be right in."

He dropped the phone, jumped the counter, and sprinted for the stairs, the only thought in his mind, the only image before his eyes, the innocent face of his daughter.

His feet slapped the stairs as he bounded up toward the third level, and he was momentarily relieved to see the back of a uniform just cresting the stairs. However, the brief flirtation with relief was squashed by his distrust of coincidence, and his voice failed him as the man reacted to the approaching footfalls by glancing over his shoulder. Dewitt found himself fact-to-face with Michael Quinn. There was a gun in his hand. A police issue .38. Dewitt fished under his coat for his.

As Dewitt reached the third level, Quinn had Emmy's neck in the crook of his elbow, the gun waving in the air carelessly. "*Always* fucking up the schedule, Dewitt. What is it about you?" He motioned for Emmy's friends to get back.

Dewitt could envision his wife in the grasp of Steven Miller—this man's son—standing not ten feet away; could feel the warm grip of Lumbrowski's gun in hand, the crisp coolness of the trigger. He could summon no words.

Where his wife had hesitated, however, his daughter did not. She had practiced the move a hundred times, and she executed it swiftly and professionally, as if showing off for her teacher. Her leg rocked forward and shot back, connecting squarely with Quinn's knee, while in the same seamless motion, her right elbow found his ribs and her left hand swiped the gun out of her way. She ducked, rolled, and dove to the floor.

At the same moment, Dewitt squeezed the trigger. Quinn staggered with the blow to his knee, and Dewitt's shot missed. But Quinn had fled out through the fire doors to his right. The door alarm sounded. DeWitt looked out to see Quinn running between the open mouths of the huge display tanks.

Dewitt dove to cover his daughter, convinced he would feel Quinn's shots pepper his back.

"I got him!" Emmy proclaimed in an uncharacteristically enthusiastic voice.

He pulled her to her feet, holding her face-to-face. "You okay?"
She nodded.

"Straight to Security. I'll meet you there." He slapped her on the bottom. "You did good."

She took off down the stairs at a run. "Call in Monterey," he added. The cop's daughter acknowledged by waving overhead.

The door alarm still sounding, Dewitt hurried out onto the rooftop. Before him was the open top of the Kelp Forest and, across the flat roof, the huge piston that drove the wave motion.

He was only seconds behind the uniformed Quinn, who was checking the various available doors in search of escape, unaware that this rooftop area only offered access to the research and workshop laboratories. None of these doors was left unlocked. By the time Dewitt spotted him, and he Dewitt, Quinn had exhausted his possibilities. In panic, Quinn stuffed away the gun and leaped up onto the slick gray slate of the rooftop, wet from the continuing drizzle. He slipped, regained his footing, and ascended to the peak. The ridge lines of the enormous structure interconnected one to the other. Quinn straddled the peak and ran.

Dewitt clambered up from behind, gun returned to his holster. His feet went out from underneath him. He slid, planted his heels, and braked himself, clawing his way quickly back up. Quinn's attention, like a teenager at his first night of ballroom dancing, was fixed firmly on his feet. Although the slant of the roof to his left led down to the third-story research area from which he had come, to slip to his right would leave him a fall of forty feet to cement.

Dewitt proved fast on his feet, agile and well-balanced. In deft footfalls, he quickly closed the distance between himself and the fleeing Quinn, who glanced over his shoulder repeatedly.

Quinn turned sharply left and, with bent knees, dropped into an intentional slide, like a person playing on ice, skiing down the slick slate before leaping catlike to the adjoining roof and scrambling up the side to the peak.

Dewitt followed closely, also balling himself into a tuck and springing to the connecting roof. Midway into the ascent of this next section, he managed to reach out and bat Quinn's ankle from below, sending the man into a spin, during which both men lost purchase and scraped sideways down the slant, groping for control. Quinn caught hold of a vent stack, braking his fall, and Dewitt caught hold of Quinn's left foot. The escapee delivered his right shoe onto the bridge of Dewitt's nose, breaking the glasses off his face, the shattered lens slicing the skin below his eye. Dewitt let go and slid away, stopped only when his toes caught in the rain gutter, which bent and tore from the roofline as it assumed more of his weight. He pressed his cheek flat against the cold slate and spread his arms, lowering his center of gravity and distributing himself as evenly as possible.

Quinn collected himself and continued toward the peak.

Handhold by handhold, Dewitt drew himself up the roof and

reached the stack vent. Quinn danced his way along the ridge, more surefooted now, increasing his lead. Dewitt reached the peak, pressed himself to standing, and hurried quickly behind. He looked up in time to see Quinn make a spectacular leap to the oceanside rooftop of the second level, the third-level balcony immediately to his right. As the man landed, he lost his footing, came down hard on his face, and then rolled down the pitch, able at the last possible moment to check his roll by briefly catching his fingers on the gutter. He dropped to the balcony feetfirst.

Dewitt pushed harder with each stride, the upcoming gap growing ever closer and seemingly wider. The gap was created by an EMPLOYEES ONLY passageway from the third-level balcony to the back side of the research areas. Dewitt flew across it, pulled his feet beneath himself, and smacked into the shale, tumbling down the pitch in a ball and crashing painfully to the balcony's cement. "Don't!" he shouted as he looked up. Quinn, perched and poised on the balcony's retaining wall, sprang into the drizzle and disappeared. Dewitt expected the thud of flesh on rock. He painfully came to his feet and raced to the edge of the balcony in time to witness Quinn's slow descent. The escapee had leapt straight out and had taken hold of the very top of a planted tree and was now riding it as it bent with him past the second-story balcony, down, down, down, to the outdoor Great Tide Pool. Dewitt watched on as Quinn released his grip and dropped to the rocky edge of the pool as gently as if he had ridden an elevator. His ride damaged the tree. It did not return but, instead, remained bent in a long curve. Quinn sprinted toward the end of the building and disappeared around the corner.

Dewitt ran down the two flights of stairs and hurried to the phone at Information, his disheveled wet appearance drawing the attention of the tourists. He phoned the Monterey department and issued an update to the BOL, providing Quinn's last location, hoping, miracle of miracles, they might pick him up yet.

He caught up with Emmy in Security, pulled her out of her chair, and threw his arms around her, holding her tightly to himself, congratulating her, refusing to let go despite her complaints that he was wet. At last, she gave in and returned his hug, her words muffled. Dewitt thought he heard her say, "Now I know how Mom felt." He couldn't be sure. When she looked up at him, she said, "I was lucky."

13

LAST CALL

1

The early-morning phone call caused Dewitt to sit straight up in bed, and before he had even fully opened his eyes, the Smith and Wesson was in his hand. Despite the fact that he had posted uniform guards at both his front and back doors, he didn't trust the situation. He wouldn't feel right until Emmy was back on that plane again, and this time he would deliver her personally to his mother's, would guard her until Michael Quinn was taken into custody.

He answered the phone only after he heard the ringing stop and realized Emmy had beaten him to it. "I've got it," he said to his daughter, who hung up her extension.

"Dewitt?" It was Nelson's voice. *Sergeant* was the proper way for Nelson to address him. The familiarity annoyed him. You give these guys an inch . . .

"What is it?"

"A suicide, Dewitt. In the beach parking lot. It's him. I was going to call it in, but you're not on-call and I thought you would want to have it. You want me to call it in?"

"No. Wait for me," Dewitt said wearily, stumbling through his words, alarms sounding inside him. He dressed quickly, checked with both uniforms standing guard, and headed to the trunk of the Zephyr. He found it in the back, under a bunch of stuff that he had to move to get at it.

2

The sun was hinting at the sky, spreading a bluish wash into the blackness. Images—including the red Ford Escort with the garden hose running from its exhaust pipe—were hazy and dull, like looking through fogged glass. No other cars but Nelson's radio car. He appreciated being given the first look at the body. Dr. Christiansen had been right: suicidal.

The uniformed patrolman waved and approached from the far side of the lot, where he was establishing the crime scene with the familiar Day-Glo police tape.

Dewitt approached the Escort slowly, his full attention on the cloudy driver's window. He hesitated by the driver's door, exhaust seeping from the seams, slipped on a pair of the latex gloves, removed his gun, and pulled the door open, ready to shoot.

The head and body of patrolman Buford Nelson slumped out of the car, falling into his arms, his head badly cut where he had been clubbed.

Movement from behind him! As Dewitt spun around with the .38 in hand, the uniformed man, Michael Quinn, held the handgun trained on Dewitt's chest. "Sucker," he said, squeezing off his first shot.

The muzzle flash lit up in Dewitt's eyes—something every cop heard about, was warned about, and never wanted to witness. That peculiar brilliant color of sulfur yellow that warned of a bullet coming directly at you. A piece of Dewitt's left arm disconnected from his body and sprayed across the car. The next shot bore into his chest, as did the next and the next, sledgehammers at this distance. He felt the suffocating crush of his ribs breaking. Darkness threatened from the edges of his eyes, and he thought only of Emmy, that she was safe. Alive. He thought of God and he wondered how a man like Michael Quinn could be allowed to walk the earth while his girls had been taken from him. Justice, he thought, is something that doesn't exist in nature. It is a creation of mankind. Darkness willed him into unconsciousness, but he would not obey.

The loud barking of the handgun ceased, the smell of cordite overpowering the exhaust.

"Bastard," he heard Quinn say.

Michael Quinn turned toward Dewitt's police car. James Dewitt, peering out from squinting eyes, drew the hammer back on his weapon and struggled to his feet. His left arm screamed at him. He could barely breathe, but he managed to say to the man's back, "Sucker."

Quinn pivoted around, staring in complete disbelief at the gaping holes in Dewitt's police vest, where no blood ran.

Dewitt said, "We don't call them suicides, Quinn. We call them DBFs. We don't call it the beach parking lot. It's Del Mar. No uniform would ever call me first. They would call dispatch. Nelson gave you away."

Quinn stood there in a daze, staring at the empty holes in the police vest. "I shot you," he mumbled. "It's over."

Dewitt told him to drop the weapon.

Quinn raised his arm slowly, the gun aimed well away from Dewitt.

"Drop it!" Dewitt demanded, bringing the bead of his barrel level with the man's chest.

In a graceful arc, Quinn brought the barrel level to his own ear. "You think I'd give you the pleasure?"

Michael Quinn pulled the trigger.

3

Dewitt wouldn't leave Emmy for the remainder of the day. He arranged for the two of them to go whale watching: He needed to wash his mind of the image of Quinn's head exploding. They rode the determined chop ten miles offshore for two hours. A weather front threatened from the horizon but thankfully left them alone. They sat in silence, father and daughter, while a group of Japanese and a couple from Iowa cackled nervously, awaiting the anticipated show. The Japanese took pictures of the empty horizon. At 3:30 a pod of seven gray whales streamed by the boat, so close that for the first time in her life, Emmy touched one. She remained ecstatic throughout the chilly afternoon ride back to shore, beaming, looking to her father with a permanent grin. To pet the whales had always been one of Anna's dreams. They sat huddled together like lovers, she cradled inside him, his face in her hair. She fell asleep in this pose. Somewhere close to shore, James Dewitt began to cry.

That evening, he and Clarence Hindeman were drinking beers in front of a Lakers game.

"I couldn't call it in," Dewitt explained as Magic Johnson took the free-throw line. "Quinn was too savvy for that. Any other action—any cars, any anything—and he would have left Nelson and tried again another time. My mistake was thinking he would be the one inside the car. He fooled me there. I didn't expect him in Nelson's uniform, and even though I wore the vest, I didn't think he would shoot me. I thought he might try to scare me with the gun, scare me into getting Emmy for him so he could return the favor. I misjudged him every step of the way."

"His confession was a warning?"

"According to Christiansen it was." Dewitt tugged on his bow tie.

"He already had his escape planned. He wanted a chance to taunt me, show me how brilliant he was, to lull me into a false confidence that we had him . . . to explain it all to me. His shot at superiority."

"You should have called it in."

"I know."

"I might have lost a detective."

"You might have."

"And a friend."

"You would have." Dewitt gulped down another sip of beer. "Just glad he didn't kill Nelson. Probably wanted a hostage if his trap failed to interest me. A guy like Quinn, we'll probably never know what he was thinking."

"Emmy?"

"Fine. Better than fine. She accepted the whole Talbot thing without a problem. Accepted Anna. Youth adds elasticity, Clarence. I envy her her youth."

"Point Lobos?"

"Soon," Dewitt nodded. "Before my testimony, I think. We both want to move on. We both want this behind us."

14

POINT LOBOS

The fine green needles of the Monterey pine dripped with the remains of the passing storm. After weeks of rain, the sky's present state of clarity, the crisp vibrant blue, seemed significant to James Dewitt. He took the carryall from her with his one good arm. Emmy wrapped hers around his waist. A team, he thought.

He had been reassured by his attorney that his twice-delayed grand jury appearance was a formality, something that had to be carried out because the paperwork had been begun and couldn't be stopped—another quirk in the system. He wasn't so sure. His preparations continued. He didn't trust lawyers. He didn't trust the system.

The preserve had officially closed a few minutes before; they had special permission to be here. "What about her," Emmy asked, looking up at her dad. "How come you haven't even called her?"

"Because of the grand jury, Em. Everyone thought it better that we don't communicate."

"But you like her?" she asked.

He glanced down at her, but she was no longer looking at him; she was eyeing the woods. "Do you?"

"Does it matter?"

"Yes, of course it does."

"I like her, Dad."

"I thought so."

"Is she transferring to the city, too?" she asked.

He laughed. "No. We're not even sure *we* are, right? Clarence has been trying to talk me out of that. He says the forensic work won't be as fulfilling now that I've been a cop. There's pressure on Capp to step down. That job may open up."

They walked without speaking for the next few minutes, the only sounds the distant pounding surf, the birds, and the wind. The more he thought about the urn in the carryall, the tighter his throat became. A family cut in half *in a little less than a year*. He forced it out of his mind temporarily and thought instead of how grateful he was to have Emmy and all that was around him.

They climbed up the narrow dirt trail, beneath the twisting limbs of arthritic trees, shadows flickering across their faces, and came to rest on a point of rocks overlooking the Pacific. The turbulent turquoise water churned white with foam. The wind was pleasantly warm, announcing the impending arrival of spring.

Emmy took the bag from him, removed the urn, and handed it to her father.

"I'll do this, Em, but I thought you wanted to," he offered.

She reached into the handbag and came up with a second urn.

"Mom," Emmy whispered, turning the ceramic vase slowly in her small hands, studying it. "She belongs here with Anna and Rusty, Dad. This was her place," she said hoarsely.

Dewitt attempted to speak but found himself only able to nod. He watched through a blur as his daughter popped the lid off of his wife's ashes; he did the same for Anna.

"Are you going to say something?" she asked, hair blowing off her face. She looked more like Julia each day.

He shook his head no.

"It's all right, Dad," she said, suddenly the strong one.

Emmy raised her mother's urn toward him. They bumped the two urns together in a toastlike fashion, the dull click of pottery lost on the wind.

She counted to three. They threw them in unison, and then tangled in an embrace, watching as the ashes spread in the wind, as the urns tumbled end over end, growing inexorably smaller, finally swallowed by the waiting sea.

15

GRAND JURY

Dewitt had borrowed a suit from Saffeleti and he looked good. His attorney's assistant, Howard Carstien, sat next to him in the hallway of the Sacramento courthouse. His appearance before the grand jury was pro forma. There were questions to answer, but the likelihood of any charges being brought against him was insignificant. Carstien, a tall man with black curly hair and bright eyes, asked somewhat nervously, "Did you hear about Mahoney?"

He was trying to pass the time and it bothered Dewitt. "No."

"Turns out she obtained the grand jury evidence improperly. Had no right to it. Word is she's likely to be disbarred. Even if she isn't, she'll end up a PD in East LA or something."

Dewitt said nothing, although he smiled.

The door opened. It was Clare. She was smiling. "James, they're ready for you now." Dewitt stood.

They passed in the doorway, nearly touching. She looked incredibly good today. Beautiful as always. They stopped, eye-to-eye. He missed her and he told her so, then turned and walked through the door held open by a uniformed court guard. "See you tonight," she said. He heard the door close shut behind him. The table on the dais was enormous; the jurors were staring at him.

A moment later, he stood by the witness chair.

Jessie Osbourne was in the gallery. The withdrawal of her candidacy had been announced the night before in a dramatic televised press conference where she had called Dewitt a hero. Her presence in this courtroom was a very good sign indeed. She caught his eye and nodded reassuringly.

"State your name please," said the bailiff.

He didn't trust a system that could let Quinn be released, that could retire a man like Capp with honors, that could turn Marvin Wood back into society with nothing more than a slap on the hand. However, at the moment, he couldn't think of anything to take its place.

He tugged the handkerchief from his pocket first, then removed the glasses and let his other hand do the polishing. He squinted at the bailiff, who was holding the Bible.

"James Dewitt," said the man in the chair.

16
EPILOGUE

James Dewitt was sworn in as Captain of the Carmel-by-the-Sea Police Department on the same day Buford Nelson took over as detective sergeant. There was a minor celebration in a local bar, with beer and drinks bought by Clarence Hindeman. Retired Commander Karl Capp showed for the ceremony but not the drinks. He and his wife had scheduled a nine-month RV tour of the southwest.

District Attorney Bill Saffeleti missed the swearing in but not the drinks. He showed up with Leala Mahoney on his arm. There were plenty of rumors but no confirmation on exactly how Saffeleti had salvaged Mahoney's career. She was now a deputy district attorney.

There were other rumors going around about Mahoney and Saffeleti, but there were rumors about O'Daly and Dewitt, as well, and he knew there was no substance to these, so he didn't trust any of the rumors.

Clarence Hindeman became so intoxicated at his party for Dewitt that while he and Dewitt stood side by side at the urinals, he announced his engagement to Tona.

"Have you told this to Tona?" Dewitt asked.

"No," Hindeman replied, "but she'll be the next to know."

Clare was nowhere to be seen, and it began first to irritate and then to concern Dewitt. There was supposed to be a dinner party following the drinks, although by the look of those involved, the condition of the party was quickly degenerating. At any moment, someone would order a burger and there would go the dinner party.

The door opened promptly at seven o'clock. Hindeman held the group's attention with a hair-raising yarn about a rafting adventure. With Dewitt's back to the door, he missed the entrance of Clare and his daughter; but when Clarence spotted them, he stopped mid-sentence. Dewitt turned slowly around in his chair as he heard Clare say, "Nothing, no one, can ever take the place of anyone else, James. This is intended as a gift, a new beginning. Congratulations."

Emmy stretched out her arms, her eyes bubbling joyfully with tears. The gathering applauded. Dewitt accepted the puppy into his arms and engulfed its soft fur into the crook of his neck. The blue bow around its head got caught in his bow tie and was the source of great amusement.

"It wasn't easy finding a shepherd/collie mix," Clare added. "It was Em's idea."

"What are you going to call him?" Emmy asked anxiously.

Dewitt considered this a minute. "Lobos," he said to his daughter.

The job of captain came to Dewitt with great effort. Although it provided him endless excuse to spend his mornings talking to Clarence over coffee, he envied Nelson the fieldwork. He settled into the job uncomfortably, eventually amending his job description to include more case work. Ever so slowly, his paperwork began to pile up and he was missing from his office more and more, out on a case with Nelson. Hindeman discussed the backlog of paperwork with him and made some suggestions on job balance, but it became clear to both men that Dewitt belonged in the field. Without telling Dewitt, Hindeman wrote a few letters.

Lobos sat curled by the filing cabinet, chewing on a rawhide bone, trying to break in his puppy teeth. Dewitt, reading through one of Nelson's stolen property reports, made some corrections that included involving him more directly in the case next time.

Clarence Hindeman knocked on the open door, a grave expression on his face.

"Hindy?" Dewitt asked. "Why the glum look? Paperwork again?"

"I've just had a request to loan you out," he said. "The state task force."

"Loan me out?"

"There's an investigation. They need you. You remain captain here, but your duties are suspended until the investigation is through."

"*The* state task force?"

"It's quite an honor, James."

"What investigation? What are you talking about? They don't just *ask* for you."

"I wrote a few letters. I didn't want to lose you. I thought it worth submitting your name for the task force. Give you something to sink your teeth into every now and then."

"What investigation?"

"Harvey Collette electrocuted a guard while the guy attempted to repair his VCR. He stunned two others with the guard's stun stick and escaped Atascadero an hour ago. The AG wants you to head up the task force. He's a trapper; you're viewed as the resident expert. What do you want me to tell him?"

Lobos gave up on the bone, rolled over, and sighed. After a long and heavy silence, James Dewitt said, "Tell him I'm on my way."

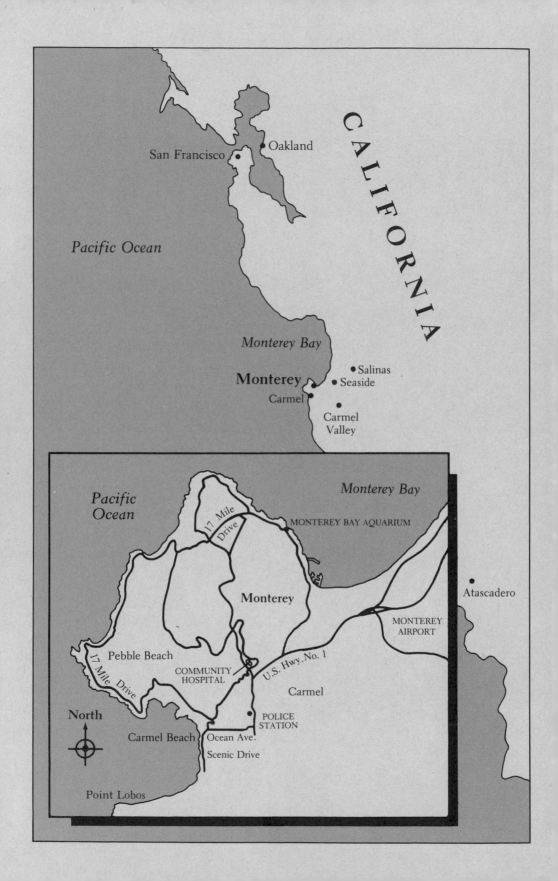